# HIGH COUNTRY MURDER

# HIGH COUNTRY
# MURDER

▼▼▼▼▼▼▼▼▼▼▼▼▼▼▼▼▼▼▼▼

## An Angela Biwaban Mystery

# BY J. F. TRAINOR

KENSINGTON BOOKS

KENSINGTON BOOKS are published by

Kensington Publishing Corp.
850 Third Avenue
New York, NY 10022

Library of Congress Card Catalog Number: 95-078006
ISBN 0-8217-5124-7

First Printing: November, 1995

Printed in the United States of America

This one is for
Karl S. Drown
Krista I. Paynton
Carolyn Rzepecki
Peter E. Crook
Paul A. Crook
Who were there at the beginning.
October 19, 1965
I.N.S.E.C.T. Lives!

*"If you sow too many wild oats, you may not like the harvest."*

WANDA G. CUNNINGHAM

▼▼▼▼▼▼ **ONE** ▼▼▼▼▼▼

"So why didn't you show for the holidays?" Aunt Della asked.

Clutching the telephone receiver, I turned in my swivel chair. The window showed me a stream of noonday traffic shooting down Sioux Avenue, heading for Griffin Park and the hospital.

"Previous engagement, *Ninoshe*," I replied, using our people's affectionate word for *aunt*. "I was in the Northland."

"So I've heard." Tart tone. "Denise tells me you danced at the Lac Courtes Oreilles powwow."

I winced. Sometimes I wished my parents' sisters weren't such good friends.

"I do enjoy seeing you once in a while, *Nishimiss*. And I don't mean looking at the wanted posters in the Heber City post office!"

"Well, that's the reason I can't come to Utah, *Ninoshe*." I stared glumly at the computer's blue screen. "There's still a warrant out on that grand larceny rap."

We were speaking our people's language, my aunt and I. Which is why I had no qualms about discussing my legal problems over the telephone. Only a handful of people here in

Pierre, South Dakota, understood Anishinabemowin, and they were highly unlikely to be tapping the telephones at the distinguished law firm of Hipple, Tanner, Page, and Sutton.

Aunt Della cleared her throat. "You know, I've been meaning to talk to you about that—"

Uh-oh! Incoming lecture! I cut right in. "Say, how did Uncle Matt like that mackinaw shirt?"

"He liked it just fine, *Nishimiss*, and don't change the subject." I heard a soft sigh at the other end. "I've been thinking. That lawyer friend of yours—"

"Mickey Grantz," I added.

"Well, now that he's back in Salt Lake, perhaps he could approach the authorities and arrange your surrender."

I sat bolt upright. "My *surrender?*"

"You heard me. It's high time you put an end to this nonsense. *Pocahontas*, indeed!"

"I didn't come up with the code name, *Ninoshe*. It was the FBI."

"It'd go a whole lot easier on you if you surrendered," she advised. "There's only that one charge. Mickey could get it reduced to simple larceny. Of course, you'd have to spend a year or two at Draper—"

The thought of doing time at the Utah women's prison sent a cold surge rocketing up my spine. "Listen, *Ninoshe*, Draper isn't exactly finishing school!"

"When you do something wrong, Angela, there's a price to be paid. Your mother and I *both* taught you that."

"It's not that simple, *Ninoshe*. I'm wanted in other states as well. Michigan and Washington. Not to mention that federal warrant for bank robbery. If the Bureau ever finds out that Angela Biwaban is *Pocahontas*, they'll throw away the key!"

"So you plan to stay on the dodge indefinitely?"

"Until I think of something better . . . yes!"

Aunt Della let out a bleak sigh. "I'm afraid I don't approve of your decision, Angela. But I will respect it."

*"Miigwetch, Ninoshe,"* I said, thanking her.

"And will you *please* think seriously about putting your life in order?" she added. "You're a grown-up, you know. You can't go through life as . . . as America's avenging debutante!"

*"Eyan, Ninoshe,"* I agreed. Humble Angie. Good thing she couldn't see my wall-to-wall grin. Being a latter-day Lone Ranger is really quite exhilarating.

"So when am I going to see you again, *Nishimiss?"*

"I don't know." My gaze landed on the desk calendar. Bold black letters and numerals heralded Monday, January 19. "Say, don't you have a winter vacation week coming up?"

Aunt Della answered in the affirmative. *"Eyan, Nishimiss.* What do you have in mind?"

"Well, I thought we might get together for the Birkebeiner next month. All three of us—you, me and *Nimishoo.*"

"That's a wonderful idea." Aunt Della's voice brightened. "But will you be able to get away? You just started your new job."

"Don't remind me!"

I grimaced at the computer screen. An expression my one-time prison mom, Becky Reardon, had called a fussbudget face. Narrowed obsidian eyes. Two vertical ridges above the bridge of my nose. Tightly compressed lips.

"What's the matter?" Aunt Della inquired. "I thought you enjoyed secretarial work."

"Not at Hipple, Tanner, Page, and Sutton!"

"Why not? It's the most prestigious law firm in South Dakota. What seems to be the problem, Angela?"

Before I could reply, the *problem* reared its shiny blond head. Across my cluttered desktop fell a slender feminine shadow. A smoky contralto voice snapped, "Angela!"

I looked up at once. Standing beside my computer printer was an elegant and lissome blonde in a stylish peach-colored woolen suit. Jewel-neck cardigan jacket, hip-hugging slim skirt, lacy white blouse and soft, silken wing tie. She was a couple of inches over my petite five-foot-four, a regal lady with a pert nose, a delicate chin, and eyes like irridescent emeralds. Impeccably coiffed hair glistened like ripe cornsilk, curling inward at the jacket collar. Styled sheepdog bangs, parted in the center, concealed her high, intelligent forehead.

Her mouth tensed in irritation. "Angela . . . what have I told you about personal calls?"

My expression turned apologetic. "Uhm . . . don't make them."

Emerald eyes glittered. "Well?"

"And I didn't," I added, covering the speaker with my palm. "Aunt Della phoned me."

Sharp exhalation. "Will you kindly tell your aunt not to call the office during business hours?"

Aunt Della's voice sounded in the receiver. *"Nishimiss, awenen da naa awedi?"*

"My boss, *Ninoshe*. Sarah Sutton." Junior partner in the law firm and the main reason I wasn't enjoying this new Work Experience position. "Listen, I'd better hang up."

"Put that woman on," Aunt Della said coolly. "I'd like to talk to her."

*"Gawiin, Ninoshe!"* Frantic shake of the head. The last thing I wanted to do was referee a debate between those two tigresses. "Don't worry. I'll handle it." Offering an apologetic smile, I switched back to English for La Sutton's benefit. "Aunt Della's calling from Utah."

"For the last time, I hope," Sarah planted her hands on her hips. "Wrap it up, dear."

Back to our ancient language. "I'll call you tonight, *Ninoshe*. Take care."

Under Sarah's watchful eye, I tenderly placed the receiver in its cradle. Her smile held no warmth. "Do you enjoy chatting on the phone, Miss Biwaban?"

"Sometimes . . ." I wondered where she was going with this.

"Good! Then I'll trouble you to relieve Ginny at the reception desk." Dainty knuckles came to rest on my blotter. "You do remember the reception desk, don't you?" Her blond head tilted toward the lobby. "You were supposed to be there *five minutes ago!*"

Wincing, I glanced at the wall clock. "Sorry . . ."

"Sorry doesn't cut it around here, Angela."

While Sarah's dainty high-heeled pump tapped impatiently, I grabbed my purse, a notebook, a clean cardboard coffee cup, and a sizable paperback romance novel, then darted down the carpeted corridor. Anishinabe princess in her ruffled white blouse, lengthy tapestry vest, and black velvet slim skirt. My tall heels made no sound on the plush bronze carpet.

It took me about two minutes to reach the lobby. Hipple, Tanner, Page, and Sutton owned the entire top floor of that brick office building at the corner of Sioux and Highland avenues. It's one of the oldest law firms in Pierre (pronounced *Peer*), founded in 1880 by a New Hampshire attorney named Josiah Hipple. His first client was one Alexander McDonald Putello—better known as Arkansaw Al—who was arrested for discharging a firearm within the city limits. Unfortunately for Mr. Hipple, the case never came to trial. That November, the defendant was gunned down at the foot of Pierre Street by the vigilantes.

From these humble and embarrassing beginnings, the Hipple firm grew and prospered. Many a South Dakota judge began his career poring through the law books in that oak-trimmed library. Today, fifteen years into the firm's second century, the staff consists of four partners, fifteen lawyers, six legal assistants, an office manager, a computer manager, an accountant, and a large covey of secretaries. Including yours truly, Angela Biwaban, recently paroled ex-convict and Work Experience participant.

Ginny Montoya and I spent a few delightful moments chatting at the coffeemaker. Then, after she left, I carried my steaming cup to the desk, took my seat, studied the switchboard, flipped open the telephone log, set my brand-new Alicia Scott novel on the typing stand, got out my nail file, and waited for the phone to ring. It did!

"Hipple, Tanner, Page, and Sutton!" I sang, running the file upside my lacquered thumbnail. The receiver nestled between my left ear and my left shoulder.

"I'd like to speak to Mr. Page, please."

"Just a moment, sir." Tapping the intercom button, I thought, Sure hope you're comfortable, pal. Once he gets going, Baldy Page spews more sound than a compact disk.

Hey, don't look at me like that. I'm not being fresh. His name really is Baldy. Short for Baldwin Page Jr. Although, to be perfectly frank, the shingles are getting a little sparse on the roof.

Then there's the senior partner—Clark Darius Hipple. Nice old gent. We rarely see him in the office. Mostly he hangs around the statehouse, playing draw poker with the speaker of the house. And occasionally writing petroleum-related legislation for some very grateful lobbyists.

Baldy's intercom light began blinking, so I hung up. My gaze circled the lobby, taking in the pale green walls and varnished cherrywood trimming, the small decorative fireplace, the white maple coffee table, and the low-slung Naugahyde love seats. Might as well get comfortable, folks, while our attorneys take your money.

You know, I could almost come to like it here . . . if not for Sarah Sutton!

Just then the elevator doors zipped open, and a tall, curly-haired man stepped into the lobby. My smile widened in welcome. "Hey! *Kemo Sabe!*"

That, of course, is my nickname for my parole officer, Paul Holbrook, the man responsible for sticking me in all these Work Experience jobs. Paul thinks it means *trusted friend.* Actually, it's Paiute for *horse's ass.*

Paul used to be a Marine sergeant. And it shows in his ram-rod spine, broad, squared shoulders, and well-shined shoes. I figure he's about two inches over the six-foot mark, with curly wheat-colored hair, a lantern jaw, low, thick eyebrows, and a pair of warm, bright, chestnut-brown eyes.

"Angie!" Beaming, he removed his topcoat and draped it over his good arm. "How goes it, princess?"

"Could be better." Smile widening, I playfully tweaked the fabric of his blazer sleeve. "Herringbone again? Paul, don't you have anything else in your closet?"

"What are you talking about? It's brand new. My parents gave it to me for Christmas." Paul's head tilted inquisitively. "What do you mean ... *could be better?*"

"Well, let me put it this way . . ." My hand hovered at my chin. "I have had it up to here with Queen Sarah!"

"Uh, I take it you have a little problem with Mrs. Sutton's management style."

"Paul, her management style consists of planting her dainty shoeprint on everybody's ass. Law students run whenever they see her coming. She really is the Office Witch!" I complained. "And I'm Cinderella!"

Paul tried hard not to smile. "Take it from me, Angela. A little discipline never killed anybody."

"No, it just makes them wish they were dead!"

Shaking his head, he chuckled. "Princess, you never would have made it through day one at Parris Island."

"I have no desire to go, thank you." Twirling a pencil with my fingertips, I added, "I'm telling you, Paul. That woman's turned this place into the Ministry of Fear. Take out your compact at your desk, and ziiiiip—off to the woodshed!"

"Woodshed?" he echoed.

"Queen Sarah's office," I explained. "That's where she reads you the riot act. She keeps a big box of tissues on the corner of her desk. Just in case anybody feels like crying."

"Are you speaking from personal experience, Angie?"

"You bet!" I glared at him. "The day I started here—she let me have it!"

"What happened?" he asked.

"Well, I knew I'd be starting work, so I bought a two-toned jacket dress over the holidays. White top and long sleeves, navy-blue pinstripe from the bodice down. Even had a black hat and black gloves to go with it. I mean, I was looking good when I walked into that staff meeting!" Frown of reminiscence. "Then Mr. Hipple came in with the Little Queen tagging along right behind. He gave us all a little pep talk. 'Here we practice law—' And I piped up, 'And sometimes we get it right!' Everybody laughed—except *her!* When the meeting ended, she called me into her office."

"And then?" Paul prodded.

"She tore right into me!" I quoted from memory. " 'This is a law office, Miss Biwaban, not a fashion show!' She accused me of deliberately making fun of Mr. Hipple. Said my comment was 'inappropriate' for the staff meeting."

"Well, maybe she has a point."

"Really, Paul, it was only a little joke."

Suppressing a smile, he replied, "Not everybody appreciates your sense of humor, Angie."

"That's for damned sure!" Still seething about La Sutton, I added, "Then she dictated some goofy office dress code she made up on the spur of the moment. She made me retype it *seven* times! And then I had to make photocopies and circulate them around the office."

"You know, Angie, dress codes are part and parcel of many private sector firms."

"Paul! You're missing the point. It had nothing to do with my outfit," I added, trying to be patient with him. "Sarah Sutton is a tart-tongued little martinet, and her chief pleasure is tormenting me!"

His voice held a touch of reproof. "That's awful strong language for the lady who got you this job."

"Oh, really?"

"Yes, really." Mild bureaucratic scowl. "The Elderkins wanted to keep you on, but there isn't that much work during the winter. I was trying to figure out what to do with you, and Sarah suggested this place."

"So I'm supposed to curtsy whenever Slinky-dink passes by, is that it?"

"You know, it wouldn't exactly kill you to show the woman a little respect." Brown eyes zeroed in on mine. "Why don't you start by dropping the juvenile nicknames? From now on, make it *Sarah* or *Mrs. Sutton*, all right?"

My mouth dropped open. Paul had never used that stern tone on me before.

"I mean it, Angela. I don't mind a little kidding around now and then, but, with you, it's getting out of hand. Sarah was good enough to offer you this job. So you're going to treat her with the respect she or any other employer deserves. Am I coming in loud and clear, Miss Biwaban?"

"Perfectly!"

Avoiding Paul's gaze, I clenched my teeth. I knew full well why Sarah Sutton had offered me this secretarial job, and it had nothing to do with the lady's supposed generosity.

Sometime in the past, Sarah had had a relationship with Paul. I still wasn't clear about the details. Holbrook was notoriously closemouthed when it came to La Sutton. But I'd seen her reaction the day we ran into Paul at the courthouse in Mitchell. Take it from me, gang. Divorce decree in hand, Slinky-dink was definitely stalking Husband Number Two.

With Angie in the steno pool, Paul would be stopping by once a week to do some counseling. Which gives the lady lawyer numerous opportunities to vamp my parole officer.

I felt Paul's fingertips beneath my chin. Lifting my face a quarter-inch, he flashed his warm East River country-boy smile. As always, that smile sent a gentle tremor through my heart.

"No sulking, princess."

I refused to let Paul realize the effect he was having on me. "It's like that, is it?"

"That it is." His smile turned wry. "It's for your own good, Angie. Your parole still has another year to run. You can't keep jumping from job to job. If you want to impress those employers, you've got to pick one and stick with it."

"Paul, why don't we discuss this over lunch?" I glanced at the wall clock. "I'm off at one. We could head down to Country King and—"

Paul's face showed sincere regret. "Ah, that won't be possible, Angie. I've already made—"

Before he could finish, I heard the drumroll of high heels punctuated by a familiar contralto voice. "Hello, Paul. All set for lunch?"

Turning, I saw Sarah striding into the lobby, toting a truly lovely lambskin coat. Her eyes sparkled in anticipation.

"Yes, Paul." Masking my anger behind a sugary-sweet smile, I folded my hands. "Where are we going for lunch?"

"You're not going anywhere, dear," Sarah snapped. "At least not until two o'clock."

While I sat there with my mouth open, she offered Paul her coat. "Would you do the honors?"

Obedient as a British butler, Paul held open the coat. Sarah slid her arms down each satin-lined sleeve. She lingered momentarily in his casual embrace, then buttoned up and offered him an over-the-shoulder smile.

Somehow I managed to hold my Anishinabe temper in check.

"Mrs. Sutton," I said, my voice sugary. "My lunch hour begins at one o'clock."

"Not today, I'm afraid. Ginny's taking an extra hour. Dentist appointment." Her cool-eyed stare pinned me to the seat. "Don't you read the bulletin board, Miss Biwaban?"

My fists thumped the blotter. Ooooooh! I thought, my gaze

livid. She's making me look like a total ditz. And right in front of *Paul!*

"I'll be sure to check it," I snapped.

"Do that." Serene as the prairie at dusk, La Sutton hastily surveyed the contents of her patent-leather purse. "And while you're at it, make a list of all the materials I'll need at the BuRec conference. Photocopy a list for yourself, too."

"What for?" Surprised Angie blink. "I'm not going to Denver."

Sarah let out an exasperated sigh. She cast Paul a look that said *See what I have to put up with?* Then, turning to me, she added, "You really ought to start reading the bulletin board, Angela. You're coming with me to Colorado." A lovely smile for Paul. "I'm bringing her along as secretarial support. You don't mind, do you?"

"Of course not, Sarah."

"Uh, *Kemo Sabe . . .*" I waggled my hand. "I thought parolees aren't supposed to leave South Dakota."

"No problem, princess. This is a work-related trip. I'll clear it with Mr. Langston."

Squeezing my eyes shut, I thought, I don't *be-leeeeeve* this! I have to beg for furloughs on my knees. Slinky-dink snaps her fingers, and he gives her anything she wants!

"Thank you, Paul." Smiling coyly, Sarah patted his forearm. As an afterthought, she glanced at me. "Make sure we have *everything* for the conference, Angela. If anything gets left behind, the cost of faxing is coming out of your salary. So let's see a little diligence, eh? Oh, and be sure to hold Mr. Tanner's calls. He'll be in Aberdeen through tomorrow. That's everything, I think." She offered Paul her arm. "Shall we?"

Paul hesitated. He cast me a small apologetic grimace. "I'll, uhm, give you a call tomorrow, Angie. Take care."

As he escorted her into the elevator, Sarah remarked, "You know, I've been giving some idea to that retraining-center idea of yours. State funding is kind of tight right now, but we could send a query to the Fairmont Foundation . . ."

Sliding doors concealed them from view.

My chin came to rest on the heel of my hand. I aimed a torrid glance at the humming elevator. *"Kemo Sabe!"*

An hour later, I was still at Ginny's desk, sorting pink message slips and thinking nasty thoughts about Mrs. Sarah Sutton, attorney-at-law.

It's just not fair! I thought, tapping my fingernails on the blotter. There can't be more than three or four years between us. Yet she always makes me feel like a little kid.

Queen Sarah! Boy, you got that right, Biwaban. The way she stands there like Marie Antoinette, so poised, so regal. And the way she looks down her pert nose. Ooooooooohhh, do I *hate* that!

A light winked repeatedly on the console. I plucked the receiver out of its cradle. Naughty Angie smile. "Hipple, Tanner, Page, and Starch Girdle!"

"Starch Girdle?" The woman's voice was a braying contralto, as strong and resonant as a canyon echo. Sudden gust of laughter. "That's a good one, gal." Curiosity altered her voice. "You wouldn't be talkin' 'bout Sarah Sutton, would you?"

"The one and only!" As my surge of resentment receded, I realized to my horror that Sarah's new nickname was about to make the rounds. "Uh, you're not a friend of hers, are you?"

More braying laughter. "Oh, no, I'm not a friend . . ."

My shoulders sagged in relief.

". . . I'm her *mother!*"

"M-mother?" Aghast, I gaped at my reflection in Ginny's glass urn. Long, straight raven-black hair, high cheekbones, slim aquiline nose, and soft, lush lips. Bright obsidian eyes glazed over in alarm.

Feigning a chuckle, I added, "Uh, just kidding, ma'am."

"Oh, that's okay, gal. Sally always was the bossy one. Shoulda seen her orderin' Becky 'n' the others around. Reckon that's natural, seein' she was the oldest," she replied. "Patch me through, would you?"

"I'm sorry, ma'am. Mrs. Sutton is out to lunch right now." I reached for the message pad. "If you'll give me your number, I'll have her call you as soon as she gets in."

"Well, ain't that a kick in the ass!" The lady's casual vulgarity gave me a jolt. "And just when I need to reach her, too. Okay! You tell her to get on the horn, and . . . say, what's your name, gal?"

"Angie Biwaban."

"Oh, yeah! You're that Indian gal just went to work there. Paul Holbrook's client."

Wry glance at the receiver. My, my, Sarah's mother was certainly up on our local gossip.

"Sally said you were in the can. Where?"

"South Dakota Correctional Facility for Women," I replied. She had a tone of command that was hard to resist. "That's in—"

"Springfield!" Bark of laughter. "No shit! Say, is Kathy Sue Holmgren still one o' the guards?"

"Yeah." Puzzled Angie blink. "She's deputy chief now."

"Still totin' that big ol' shotgun?"

I had a sudden mental image of the scowling sandy-haired correctional officer and her Mossberg twelve-gauge riot gun. "That's right." My eyes narrowed curiously. "How did you know that?"

Blithely ignoring me, she added, "Did she tell you that piece was loaded up with double-ought?"

"You bet."

"She's a damned liar, honey. State won't let them screws use double-ought. Kathy Sue loads it with birdshot and rock salt. And I oughta know." Sarah's mother chuckled ruefully. "Reckon I'm the only woman in Colorado who's ever been shotgunned in the ass. Happened while I was tryin' to bust out of Springfield."

Slowly the unbelievable truth sank in. "*You* were in Springfield?"

"Damned right! Spent four years as a guest of the state of South Dakota. Took the fall for armed robbery. 'Course, that was a while back. Sally was in high school then. You probably never heard of me. Say, how old are you, Angie gal?"

"Twenty-eight."

"Ever heard of Madge Rooley?"

Shaking my head, I replied, "Afraid not, ma'am."

" 'Course not. You're too young. You were only nine when we hit that casino. Newspapers called me the Border Bandit Queen. On account of we hit all over the tri-state area. Custer, Spearfish, Belle Fourche. Gillette and Newcastle over in Wyoming. Alzada up there in Montana." Mild sigh of regret. "Hell of a mess in Deadwood, though. There was an off-duty cop at the roulette table, and he pulled a snubby on Homer. Jeff nailed him. Then the bartender popped up with a sawed-off. All that shootin' brought them Deadwood laws on the run. Next thing you know, there's bullets whizzin' all over the damned place. So I just tossed my piece, flattened out on the floor 'n' yelled, 'I'm out! I'm out!' I had four young'uns back home, and I wanted to see 'em again. Good thing too, 'cause I was the sole survivor on our side. Laws got Homer 'n' Jeff 'n' Rimfire. One o' them laws—he used to be a paratrooper in the Hundred 'n' First, and he said he hadn't seen a firefight like that since Quang Tri!" Her tone softened in reminiscence. "Soon's they finished questionin' me, I got hustled out in handcuffs. More damned TV cameras than I'd ever seen in my life. You'd've thought I was Raquel Welch or somethin'! It was some circus. Paramedics cartin' out the boys. Deadwood laws posin' for pictures. All them pissant Feebees runnin' 'round. I tell ya, there was rejoicin' aplenty at the Bureau when they found out Homer's toes were pointin' at the Milky Way."

"Homer?" I echoed.

"Homer Stirewalt. The deadliest man in Arkansas. I was his woman for a spell. He's daddy to my son Troy," she said matter-of-factly. "Came from Eutaw Springs. Told me he'd killed eight men in stand-up shootin', includin' two deputies and a state trooper. He was on the dodge in Durango when I met up with him. I never saw a man with such an appetite for poke greens. There'd still be snow along the creek, and he'd be out there gatherin' poke. Real finicky 'bout the way he wanted it cooked, too. I'd have to sauté them poke shoots in bacon drippings, toss in some scrambled egg, sprinkle in some white flour and cornmeal, fry the whole batch till it's good 'n' brown. Then Homer—he'd clean that plate like a starvin' coyote. What an appetite!"

I still couldn't quite believe it. "You did time for armed robbery, Mrs. Rooley?"

"That's *Miss* Rooley, gal. Or Miz Rooley for a woman my age. Never did get around to tyin' the knot. Better yet, make it Madge. Everybody calls me that." Her carefree attitude made me grin. "Yeah, I put my time in at the Springfield laundry. Ain't no Club Med, that's for damned sure, but I've seen worse. Like that lockup in Grants, New Mexico. That's a shithole and a half, Angie—take my word for it."

"You did time in New Mexico!?"

"Bet your ass! I've toted laundry baskets all over." She seemed to take a perverse pride in the fact. "Springfield, South Dakota. Draper, Utah. Grants, New Mexico. And Canon City right here in Colorado. If I knew how to put two words together, I could write a book."

"I don't understand, Madge," I said, leaning back in the receptionist chair. "How could you serve four whole prison sentences in just twenty years?"

"Thirty years," she corrected me. "I was nineteen the first

time I went up. Bad-check charge." Warming to my questions, she explained, "I did it by playin' the system, Angie. I was always careful to behave myself on the inside. I knew I was goin' to be there a spell, so there was no use cryin' and carryin' on. I always made parole. Got hit for three in Utah and was out in one. Only time I got in trouble was at Springfield. Then again, I had a mighty compellin' reason for wantin' to bust out."

I waited for the reason, but Sarah's mother suddenly changed the subject. "Warden gave me a choice. One more year tacked onto my sentence or six months with Miss Carlotta. I was eager to get home to the kids, so I chose Billsburg. Thinkin' back on it, though, I wish I'd taken the extra year. That Carlotta is just plain crazy!"

I smiled in sympathy. "Tell me about it, Madge."

Tone of surprise. "You were a *Bobbi Jo?*"

"Uh-huh. I spent sixteen months at Miss Carlotta's School for Girls."

"Is that what they call it now? In my day it was known as Petticoat Junction."

"It still is," I told her. In fact, that particular nickname for the Disciplinary Unit is the reason why an inmate is called a Bobbi Jo.

"Well, that's a good place to stay out of, gal. Sixteen months—ouch! You sure must've pissed off ol' Carlotta."

Sour Angie grimace. "Mrs. Calder said I was *difficult.*"

"Stiff-necked little gal, eh?" Madge let out a pleasant laugh. "Doesn't that sound like somebody I know! Matter of fact, it sounds like *two* people I know."

"One of them wouldn't happen to be named *Sarah,* would it?"

"Got that right, Angie! You couldn't find a more stubborn child on the Western Slope than Sally Anne Rooley."

My grin widened. "Sarah had a mind of her own, did she?"

"From the time she learned to walk!" Chuckle of recollection. "Oh, I wore out more'n one willow switch on Sally's ass. She turned out just fine, though. Mighty big help to me with Becky and the others." Madge's voice turned mysterious. "I like to think I've returned the compliment. Which reminds me, gal. When you see Sally, you tell her I've got the same ol' problem. And it's her problem, too. Understand?"

Scribbling on the message pad, I muttered, "Same old problem . . . Sally's problem. Got it!"

"She'll know what I'm talkin' 'bout, Angie. Don't you bother your head none."

Tearing off the top sheet, I added, "I guess you're all pretty proud of Sarah down there in—"

"Crested Butte," she interjected. "Oh, Sally's made quite a name for herself." Tinkle of laughter. "Joke around here is Sally became a lawyer just so's she could spring *me* out of the can!"

I didn't know how to ask. But it would drive me crazy if I didn't find out. Clearing my throat, I added, "Uhm, Madge, you've retired from your . . . *profession* . . . haven't you?"

"Bet your ass! I'm gettin' too damned old to be totin' them laundry baskets. That's a young woman's game. No more stickups for me, gal. Soon as I get everythin' squared away, I'm goin' to mosey on down to Alamosa and find me some ol' cowpoke who's sick 'n' tired o' bunkhouse cookin'. High time I had another man in my life."

Fond Angie smile. "Do you really think it'll be that easy?"

She laughed. "I never had any trouble catchin' a man, Angie. Just holdin' on to him, that's all."

"I wish you luck."

"Thank you." Madge wanted the dream so badly, I could sense her longing over the telephone. "Yeah, that's what I'll do. Marry some ol' bachelor cowpoke, move into a line cabin up there in the high country, spend the rest o' my life enjoyin' my grandchildren."

"Got a place picked out?" I asked.

"Well, there's a mighty nice cabin on the south slope of Blanca Peak. Owner might let it go for a hundred grand, I hear."

I uttered a hushed whistle. "That's a little steep."

"No problem at all, Angie." A tone of breathless excitement charged her husky voice. "Matter of fact, I expect to be comin' into some money soon. Real soon." Knowledgeable chuckle. "Why, you might even call it my inheritance."

I wanted to ask Madge what she meant by that intriguing remark. But before I could speak, the elevator doors snapped open, and her legal-eagle daughter stepped into the lobby. Believe me, that was not the moment to be lounging in the chair, with my slender legs demurely crossed, happily chatting on the telephone. One look at me, and Sarah's lovely green eyes glistened in annoyance.

*"Angela!"* Tall heels pummeled the floor as she approached my desk. *"What* did I tell you about personal calls?"

I'm afraid I just couldn't resist the impulse. Lips curving upward in a sassy smile, I held out the receiver. "It's for *you,* Mrs. Sutton."

Surprised blink from the lawyer lady.

"Your mother," I murmured. Schoolgirl Angie. Innocence personified. "She's calling from Colorado."

Sarah's look of embarrassment vanished, replaced by her usual cool demeanor. Peeling off her beige gloves, she turned sharply away from my desk. "I'll take it in my office."

"Yes, ma'am!" Secretarial Angie. "She'll pick up in a moment, Miz Rooley. Please stay on the line."

After punching Sarah's intercom button, I sat back and let out a schoolgirl giggle. Oh, I would have loved to have seen La Sutton's face when she learned the gist of our conversation.

I was sorely tempted to eavesdrop, but I decided against it. I was already in enough trouble with Sarah. And besides, Madge Rooley had provided enough hilarity for one afternoon.

I decided then and there that I liked the old girl. Indeed, I liked Madge a whole lot better than I did her daughter. I looked forward to chatting with the lady again.

I didn't know it then, of course, but I still had quite a bit to learn about Sarah Sutton's mother.

And the lessons would be deadly, indeed!

# TWO

I wasn't the first person in my family to visit Colorado, you know. A drought ravaged the Midwest back in 1783, destroying the wild rice in Minnesota's lakes. Our Anishinabe people were forced onto the prairie to hunt buffalo. My family spent that summer in the land of a people calling themselves the Awishi—you newcomers know them as the Arapaho—a place noted for its swift-running creeks and fruit-bearing trees. My five-times-great-grandfather, Odugamis, called it *Okwaymin-zibi*—Cherry River.

My grandfather, Charlie Blackbear, passed through a hundred and sixty years later on his way to Camp Pendleton. He was a Marine Raider in the war he calls "the Big One." By then, however, the new people had reared a huge city on the site and had dubbed it Denver. In honor of James W. Denver, the territorial governor of Kansas.

And, of course, Aunt Della was stationed there thirty years ago, back when she was known as Lieutenant Blackbear, USAF.

Thursday, January 22, found me about two miles from my people's old campground, in that magnificent Convention

Center at the corner of Fourteenth and California, shaking my numb right hand and dutifully trailing Sarah Sutton through the high-ceilinged lobby.

My hand felt as if I'd been playing squash without gloves. For the past five hours I'd been taking voluminous shorthand notes at the Bureau of Reclamation bidders' conference. My purse-size notebook was already three-quarters full, and there was one more seminar scheduled for three-thirty P.M., right after this midafternoon break.

Seeing me flex my fingers, Sarah suggested, "You'd better soak that hand when we return to the hotel."

"We could invest in a tape recorder," I suggested. "That way, I'd be certain to get everything."

"Unh-unh!" Teasing sidelong glance. "You need the practice, kiddo. Your Gregg is terrible."

"This may come as a real surprise to you, Mrs. Sutton ma'am," I replied. "But being a secretary is *not* my idea of the perfect job!"

"Well, you'd better forget about the perfect job, young lady, and start concentrating on *this* one." Sarah's mouth curved in a knowledgeable smile. "You're not ditching this job the way you did all those others."

Fussbudget face. "I suppose you wouldn't be interested in my side of it."

"Not particularly." Her free hand brushed a wing of shiny blond hair away from her jacket collar. "The way I see it, Angela, you're making a fresh start. I really don't care what happened at those other Work Experience sites. You're going to work hard, rehabilitate yourself, and become a productive member of society. Just like your friend Jill Stormcloud." Sidelong glance of amusement. "Your ass is mine, Angela, and I'm not turning it loose until you've met my standards for competent secretarial performance."

Fuming, I bit back my initial retort. "And if I don't like the arrangement?"

She gave me a no-nonsense stare. "You know very well what happens to you if you break parole. It's straight back to the prison laundry for you, dear. Paul tells me your sentence still has a year or two to run."

I don't know what bothered me more, Sarah's veiled threat or that casual reference to my parole officer. Sudden disturbing memories of the recent Christmas holidays. How much time had she spent with Paul, anyway?

"So if I were you, Angela, I'd straighten up and fly right," she added, lifting a delicate forefinger. "We're going to be working together for a while, so let's make it as pleasant as possible, hmmmm?" Sudden superior smile. "I'm putting you back on the straight and narrow, dear. After that, I'll see about finding you a suitable husband."

"Don't do me any favors!" I snapped, clutching the strap of my black leather shoulder bag.

"I'm not doing it for you." She showed me her daintily chiseled profile. "I'm doing it for Jill. She thinks very highly of you."

"And vice versa," I replied. "She's a good friend."

Having put me in my place, Sarah turned to one of the computer displays. The BuRec conference had drawn every manufacturer from Boulder to Estes Park, and their sales booths jammed the lobby. All the latest in hardware—desktops, notebooks, and personal digital assistants. Truly a sellers' marketplace.

Sarah stopped in front of the colorful DataComp display. Folding her arms, she studied the array of desktop computers. I studied her. She wore a tailored cranberry suit, shawl-collar jacket with a single knotted gold-tone button, and a slender hip-hugging skirt. Her silken black camisole highlighted a strand of elegant pearls.

Like the boss lady, I, too, was smartly turned out in corporate style. Two-piece dress in forest green—double-breasted jacket with a faux pocket hankie and flattering slim skirt. I must've lacked the executive touch, though. When the salesman appeared, he hurried right over to Sarah.

"This, ladies, is the latest thing in subnotebooks," he said, gesturing at a black laptop computer. The salesman was a wiry guy in his middle twenties. Unruly hair and gold-rimmed glasses. What we incorrigible Park Point teens used to call a nerd. Couldn't get a date in high school—now he's pulling down the big bucks from Colorado's leading computer company. I glanced at his left hand. Smiled at the sight of that wedding ring. I bet his wife looks like Kim Basinger.

"The Wizard 3000." Scrawny fingers touched the top of the active-matrix display screen. "It includes the new cradle-mounted Omniscan 75MHz chip—"

"Cradle-mounted?" I echoed, standing at Sarah's elbow.

"You bet! Now you can upgrade your CPU by replacing the old chip with new ones as they become available on the market." Blue eyes shone with affection. "We're talking top-of-the-line here, ladies. Advanced color display, 64-megabyte RAM, onboard CD-ROM drive, 360-megabyte hard disk, full-function keyboard and trackball—"

"We're a law firm." Sarah cut short his sales pitch. "We're really not interested in subnotebooks."

"How about a complete law library on CD-ROM?" he suggested.

Sarah gave her head a skeptical tilt. "You have the annotated laws of South Dakota on a compact disk?"

"Ma'am, we have the statutes of all fifty states on compact disk, plus the entire U.S. Code. A complete law library on ten CDs." He pantomimed a bookshelf with both hands. "Not only that, our CD package has a built-in cross-reference feature that allows you to search for and display the relevant statutes for any combination of states." Briskly he rubbed his sinewy hands. "I'd be happy to have our regional sales representative set up a demonstration at your home office."

"That'll make our law students' lives a lot easier," I remarked, eyeing the compact disks.

"You just might have something there, Angela."

After pawing through her plush Tignanello handbag, Sarah produced a business card. The salesman grinned as she handed it over. "No need for me to keep it, ma'am. Watch this!"

Stepping up to the table, he tucked Sarah's card into an electronic gizmo the size of a matchbox. The tiny machine swallowed the card, made a faint humming noise, and then spat it out again.

"This is something no law firm should be without," he said, returning Sarah's card. "DataComp calls it the Meet & Greet. The scanner reads the information on your card, then instantly files it away on the hard disk. It's like having a permanent record of everyone who comes to the office."

Flashing a lovely smile, Sarah shook hands with him. "Very impressive!"

As we reached the escalator, a male voice rang out behind us. "Sarah!"

Weaving his way through the crowd was a heavyset man in his late thirties. Swarthy moon face, a protruding underlip, high bushy eyebrows, gimlet brown eyes, and unruly auburn hair parted in the middle. A hefty black leather briefcase nestled beneath his right arm. Dour expression of worry.

Sarah smiled a greeting. "Hello, Malcolm. What's up?"

I'm afraid Malcolm never would have made the cover of *Gentleman's Quarterly*. Not in that rumpled heather-brown suit, pale blue shirt and paisley tie. The sort of tie frat brothers wear on Halloween.

"We've got trouble, Sarah." His stubby thumb pointed at the white ceiling. "They're having a meeting in Conference Room B. Congressman Bissell just walked in." His tone turned ominous. "And so did G. P. Hayes!"

Sarah stiffened at once, becoming as alert as a cougar. "Are you sure it was Hayes?"

Vigorous nod. "I've seen him often enough in Cheyenne." Malcolm flashed her an anxious look. "Sarah, are you thinking what I'm thinking?"

"A caucus." Instantly she shouldered her bag. "We'd better get up there before our Wyoming friends walk off with the entire appropriation." Those emerald eyes turned my way. "Angela, you're going to have to attend the seminar on your own."

"Yes, ma'am."

"They'll be distributing project proposals for the coming fiscal year. Make sure you get a copy of every proposal slated for South Dakota. And be sure to ask the chairman for a copy of the bidders' list. As soon as the meeting breaks up, send that copy to Mr. Hipple." Clutching her handbag, she darted toward the escalator. "There's a fax machine right here at the center."

"Yes, ma'am."

"I'll see you back at the hotel."

With that, she hurried away, flanked by the anxious Malcolm. Long, shapely legs scissored briskly beneath her narrow skirt. South Dakota's blond paladin, off to do battle on behalf of the Coyote State.

I wonder what that's all about, I mused, making my way to the snack bar. Quick glance at the wall clock. I had ten minutes until the next seminar. Plenty of time to grab a hot cup of coffee.

No doubt Sarah would be telling me all about it when she returned to the Brown Palace Hotel.

As things turned out, I really didn't need Sarah's explanation. The Bureau of Reclamation's final seminar of the day provided all the necessary answers.

The issue was money. Lots of it. Congress had made available $92 billion for new dam construction in our arid western states. BuRec would be able to fund about three hundred irrigation projects. Naturally, Wyoming wanted the lion's share of those projects, with new dams dotting the high desert from Evanston to the Rattlesnake Hills. Which is why good ol' George P. Hayes, Cheyenne's notorious glad-handing lobbyist, was here in Denver, slapping congressional backs and distributing tickets to the Super Bowl. All seats on the fifty-yard line, natch!

One look at the BuRec proposals list, and I suddenly realized why Sarah Sutton was so eager to crash that caucus. High up on the RFP list was a proposal for the construction of a $165 million rolled-earth dam in South Dakota. The proposed dam would create a seventy-square-mile reservoir in the canyons behind Buffalo Pass, with the prime beneficiary being Merritt County's largest employer—the Bar-F-Bar ranch. That's F as in *Fairmont*. Fairmont Foods, to be exact, one of the largest food distribution chains in the West.

By some strange coincidence, Sarah just happened to be the corporate counsel for Fairmont Foods. And, rumor has it, a close personal friend of the owner, Frederick Fairmont IV, a man whose annual income exceeds the aggregate wealth of Chile, Chad, and Romania.

By five-thirty, I was back at the Brown Palace Hotel, gratefully slipping off my ouch shoes. BuRec handouts formed a stack eight inches high atop the oaken chest of drawers. The plush carpet felt good beneath my nyloned feet. I took off my blazer and hung it on a sweet-smelling cedar hanger. Then, reaching behind me, I unzipped my skirt, slid it down over my hips, folded it very neatly, and draped it over the hanger's horizontal crosstie.

My clothes hung on the left side of the walk-in closet. Sarah's, on the right. I had asked for separate rooms. Believe me, the *last* woman I wanted for a roommate was Slinky-dink.

But La Sutton had overruled me, and so we shared this elegant double-size suite on the sixth floor.

The suite boasted queen-size beds with hand-sewn quilted comforters, an Art Deco bathroom, twenty-four-hour room service, and a large oak-rimmed window offering a panoramic view of downtown Denver. Early evening shadows cloaked the century-old office buildings of Seventeenth Street. Falling snowflakes twinkled in the glow of the streetlights. Smoothing my satin slip, I crossed the room and drew the gauzy drapery.

Flopping down on my bouncy comforter, I crossed my legs at the ankles, uttered a weary sigh, and grimaced at the strange fate that had made me that woman's assistant.

Oh, I knew all about the proposed Buffalo Pass dam. We environmentalists had been fighting that irrigation project for years. With the help of many small ranchers out there in Merritt County. Their cattle are thriving just fine without BuRec irrigation, thank you very much. And they realize that the proposed reservoir would destroy just as many ranches as it irrigates.

To say nothing of the wildlife on that dessicated prairie. The pronghorns, the badgers, and the blacktail prairie dogs. Plus numerous species of *Rodentia*. Western harvest mice, deer mice, pinyon mice, whitefoot mice. No useful purpose, you say? Well, what do you think keeps those canyons from being overrun by insects?

Perhaps when Freddie Fairmont is up to his knees in grasshoppers, he'll be willing to rethink the wisdom of the Buffalo Pass dam.

Frowning, I reached for the complimentary newspaper on the night table.

I opened the *Denver Post*, looking for something to cheer me up, and smiled at the sight of those full-page clothing ads. Well, well! Look at all the sales at the Cherry Creek Mall.

Just then, the bedside telephone rang. Putting down the

newspaper, I sat upright and scooped the receiver out of its cradle. "Hello?"

"Hi, this is the front desk." Vibrant Colorado baritone. "Got a long distance call here for Mrs. Sutton."

"I'll take it."

"Sarah?" Clark D. Hipple had the deep resonant voice of an itinerant Methodist preacher.

I dropped back onto the pillow. "Nope. Just me. She isn't back yet, Mr. H."

"Angie!" His tone warmed. I think he likes me. "How did you enjoy the conference?"

Crossing my fingers, I replied, "Oh, it was great, Mr. H. I really learned a lot."

"Good." He cleared his throat. "Listen, have Sarah call me the minute she comes in. Tell her I've seen the list, and I've already talked to potential contractors. Clear on that, girl?"

"Uh-huh." I grabbed my pen, then jotted some quick notes on the top sheet of my BuRec pile. "Uhm, Mr. Hipple . . . ?"

"Yes, Angie?"

"Now that the conference is over, the workday is officially over. Right?"

He chuckled. "That's how it usually goes."

"Then you don't mind if I head out to the mall this evening, do you?"

The chuckle became a laugh. "Not at all! Just don't charge anything to our corporate account, eh?"

"I won't, Mr. H. No problem!"

Another resonant laugh. "Have a good time, Angie."

The phone clicked in my ear. I replaced the receiver, hopped off the bed, and trotted into the bathroom. Make it quick, princess. Shampoo, shower, hasty session with the blow dryer. And then it's off to Cherry Creek Mall!

After doffing my blouse, I leaned over and twisted the gold-plated faucet. No sooner did I have the water at just the right temperature than the telephone jangled again.

Uh-oh! I thought, darting back into the bedroom. I sure hope Mr. Hipple isn't having second thoughts!

As I lifted the receiver, I heard a hushed, unfamiliar masculine voice murmur, "Sarah?"

My obsidian eyes blossomed in surprise. Don't tell me Starch Girdle has a boyfriend salted away in Denver!

"Sally? You there?" He had a low-pitched bass voice, one that came straight from the diaphragm.

Hoping to learn more, I swallowed hard and came up with a passable imitation of Sarah's contralto. "Who is this?"

*Click!* I winced as he hung up.

"What happened, pal? Did your wife suddenly walk in?" I slammed down the receiver. "Pervert!"

Sitting down on the bed, I began peeling off my pantyhose. And wondered if La Sutton really did have a little action going here in the Mile-High City.

Possible. I didn't see Sarah as the slap-and-tickle type, but you never can tell. She had quite the reputation in the steno pool. According to Ginny, the boss lady had been an overnight guest on many occasions at the Fairmont ranch. And they say Freddie the Fourth is mighty partial to blondes.

Boy, would I like to find out more about Sarah's Colorado heartthrob! I knew just who to share the information with, too.

*Oh, Paauulll! Did you know that Slinky-dink is doing the deed with a telephone pervert?*

With that cheery thought in mind, I left my No-Nonsense hose in a diaphanous pile on the carpet and returned to the bathroom.

By seven o'clock I was all set to go. Anishinabe princess in her pleat-front faille blouse, dark blue Shaker-knit cardigan, lengthy mixed-print plaid skirt, and polished black spike-heeled boots. No sooner had I finished buttoning my cardigan than the telephone rang. I reached for it, then hesitated. Suppose it was *him* again?

Take a gamble, princess. "Hello."

"Hello, Angela." Cool and pleasant contralto. "Listen, the meeting just broke up. We're taking Congressman Bissell out to the Wellshire for dinner. I don't know what time I'll be back." Sarah sounded really beat. "Any calls?"

"Just Mr. Hipple." I decided not to tweak her about the boyfriend. Save that tidbit for another time. "He needs to talk to you about Buffalo Pass."

"All right." Contralto sigh. "I'll give him a buzz. If he calls again within the next fifteen minutes, Angela, tell him I'll be at the Wellshire Inn. Don't worry—he knows the number." Take-charge Sarah. "What about you? Have you eaten yet?"

"Not yet. I thought I'd grab a bite at Cherry Creek Mall."

Sedate query. "You're going to the mall?"

"In about two minutes, Mrs. Sutton ma'am."

"Angela—"

"Mr. Hipple said it was all right," I cut in.

Sarah made a humming sound. "I suppose you have a good reason for this little jaunt."

"Three good reasons," I replied. "Neiman-Marcus, Lord & Taylor, and Saks Fifth Avenue."

Expecting a reproof, I was surprised to hear her laugh. "Can't argue with those reasons! Saks, eh? I just might drop in myself before we head back home."

What's this? I asked myself, La Sutton making a genuine stab at friendship?

"I'll go scout out the place," I promised.

"Do that. I'll talk to you later tonight." She paused for a moment. Her silence simmered with unasked questions.

"Sarah?" I prompted.

"Angela . . ." I caught the undertone of concern in her voice. "Did you check for messages at the front desk?"

"Sure," I replied. "Just as soon as I got here. Nobody called while we were at the conference." Then I thought of the unknown man who had phoned. "Were you expecting a call?"

"Yes. Mother knows I'm here in Denver. I thought she might have . . . ohh, skip it! It's not important." Her tone turned cheerful. "Have fun, Angie. I'll see you tonight."

"Take care, Sarah."

*Angie* instead of *Angela*, eh? I thought, putting down the receiver. And she didn't threaten to ground me if I came in after midnight. No doubt about it. The fearsome Mrs. Sutton has a soft side, after all.

All at once my smile diminished. Maybe I should have told her about her telephone admirer. . . .

Shrugging, I headed for the window. No problem! I can always tell her later.

As I pushed one of the lime-colored drapes aside, I let out a soft murmur of dismay. Thick snowflakes pummeled the window. I mean, it was really coming down. I couldn't even see the high risers on Colorado Boulevard.

Doing a swift about-face, I hastened to the closet. Another dismayed groan. All I had with me were my black and brown leather topcoats. Well, that was Sarah's fault. She had insisted that we travel light.

All at once my gaze fell upon Sarah's full-length camel-hair coat. Sudden Angie grin. That would certainly keep me snug and dry in the midst of a Rocky Mountain snowstorm. Obsidian eyes sparkling, I lifted it off the hanger.

After all, what's the sense of having a roommate if you can't occasionally help yourself to her clothes?

Slipping on the coat, I studied my reflection in the dresser mirror. The coat's tawny hem easily reached my boots. Hmmmm—a little bulky in the shoulders, though. But nothing I couldn't manage.

After putting my suitcase on the bed, I did some hasty rummaging for accessories. Settled on a pair of black kid gloves and a matching hoodwrap. Facing the mirror once more, I donned the hoodwrap, tucked away my glossy raven tresses, buttoned the coat, and smiled in satisfaction.

Neither rain nor snow nor Colorado blizzard will keep Angie Biwaban from getting to the mall!

As I rode the hotel's antique elevator down to the lobby, I reminisced about my adolescence back home in Duluth. Mother and I lived in a second-story apartment on Lake Avenue South, about two miles down the sandspit peninsula called Park Point. Of course, we get a lot of snow up there in the Northland, but that never kept Angie home on a Friday night.

No, like a complete idiot, I used to stand in front of the Bay Side Market, snowflakes pelting my toboggan cap, waiting for the DTA bus to come along. In no time at all I'd be at the Holiday Center on Superior Street, watching the snowfall from Mickey Dee's. Me, Tanya Lahtinen, and Mary Beth McCann. We'd gab with the girls we knew from Central, East, and Denfeld, teasing one another into striking up a conversation with a good-looking UMD college boy.

Colorado's silver barons had spared no expense to make the Brown Palace Hotel the epitome of Victorian elegance. Stepping into the lobby was like entering a cathedral. Before the hand-carved oaken desk lay a spacious rotunda soaring six stories to a vaulted stained-glass ceiling. Ornate wrought-iron balconies circled the lobby at each hotel floor. Antique lion-footed chairs and plush red leather sofas clustered together in small groups throughout the room.

Pulling on my gloves, I strode briskly toward the front entrance. My boot heels raised a clatter on the highly polished floor. All at once, the fine hairs rose at the nape of my neck. A chilly tickle rippled through me. An old familiar sensation. That instinctive awareness of hostile intent.

I reacted instantly, stopping in my tracks, shooting quick glances over each shoulder. On my second glance I thought I saw a fern quiver beside the lobby's side door. Eyes narrowing in suspicion, I took a step in that direction.

The fern remained motionless. Fussbudget frown. Surely I didn't imagine it . . .

But there was no one there now.

I stood motionless, trying to decide what to do. I could be merely jumping at shadows. On the other hand, that instinct had saved my behind on more than one occasion at the Big Dollhouse.

I ran down the names in my personal rogues' gallery, wondering if some enemy might have followed me to Colorado.

That's the trouble with being America's avenging debutante. You pick up enemies the way velvet attracts lint.

Ice congealed in my bloodstream. Oh, shit! I thought. What if it's the FBI? They were itching to lay their hands on the elusive Pocahontas. Some fed might have recognized me from the artist's sketch.

Hands trembling, I resumed my journey. If it was the FBI, he'd be sure to follow. I had to lead him away from this hotel. Make it look as if I were simply visiting. I couldn't afford to let him come across the name Angela Biwaban on the register.

Descending the front steps, I flashed the doorman an amiable smile and paused beside the *USA Today* dispenser. Sure, that's what I'd do. Shop a couple of hours at the mall, take a cab back downtown, check in at another hotel as Joanne Larue. Good thing I still had my, ah, *Joanne's* SunWest credit card tucked away at the bottom of my bag.

Just one problem, though. There was a distinct lack of taxicabs out in front of the hotel. Turning up my coat collar, I ambled impatiently down the snowy sidewalk.

Turning my gaze skyward, I blinked as the snowflakes gently dampened my face. The hotel's ornate façade was a skillful blend of dressed stone blocks. My amateur geologist's eye picked out the red granite and the Entrada sandstone. Gargoyles in the form of deer, elk, and bobcats lurked just above the arched seventh-floor windows.

My gaze zipped back to the taxi stand. Still empty. Tucking my bag under my arm, I headed for the corner. Perhaps I could flag down a passing cab.

Just ahead of me, the traffic light turned red.

Had I never experienced that apprehensive shiver in the lobby, I never would have heard it. I would have been walking down the sidewalk. The perfect target!

But I had sensed that instinctive warning, and so I was expecting trouble. My ears scanned the backdrop of city noises—the rush of passing cars and the *whicker-whisk* of windshield wipers—alert for the slightest discordant sound.

And then I heard it—the sudden laboring acceleration of a car engine. Alarm bells jangled in my mind. No one steps on the gas pedal when approaching a red light!

Instantly I glanced over my shoulder. Obsidian eyes widened in terror. A snow-covered Mazda, its high beams blazing, hurtled down Seventeenth Street, veering toward the sidewalk. Heading straight for me! The front tire bounced as it jumped the curb.

I reacted like a spooked jackrabbit, leaping into the slush-filled gutter, then darting across the street. Tires squealed as the driver brought the Mazda around. Mindful of the engine roar close behind me, I lowered my head and ran.

Ahead of me stretched a line of parked cars. The Mazda's engine roar grew louder.

Leaving my feet, I hurled myself across the snow-covered hood of a Pontiac. The Mazda's brakes screeched like a wounded wolverine. The Pontiac bucked beneath my legs, sending me cartwheeling into the snow.

When I was three years old, the kids at the Park Point playground dared me to go face-first down the slide. I did, and the sensation was not unlike skimming across the hood of that Pontiac. Halfway down the chute, however, I changed my mind and tried to turn over. And fell off the slide! I landed the same way as in Denver, hitting the slush in a loose-limbed tumble. Rolling, rolling, rolling . . .

Facedown in the snow, I listened to the cacophony of collision sounds. Explosive impact of Mazda grille against Pontiac

door. Tinkling of shattering headlight glass. Hissing of a rup-
tured radiator.

Thoroughly stunned, I crawled across the sidewalk, then
rose to all fours. The hoodwrap blanketed half my face. I
heard a man yelling "Stop!" and the Mazda's laboring engine.
Groping for the nearest parking meter, I struggled to reach
my feet.

Pulling off the wrap, I peered over the Pontiac's crumpled
hood just in time to see the lightless Mazda heading for Colfax
Avenue. The hotel doorman ran into the street, waving and
yelling for the driver to stop. But the Mazda kept right on
going. I swore. Crusted snow covered its rear license plate.

So there I was, hugging the meter, my knees as wobbly as a
newborn fawn's. The doorman hurried over. Portly man with
a gold-braided cap and a concerned Irish face. His uniform
was fancier than Muammar Qadhafi's. Getting a grip on my
upper arm, he helped me stand. "Miss, are you all right?"

I nodded. My mouth was too dry to speak.

Glaring up the street, he barked, "That guy nearly hit you!"

"Uh . . . yeah, right." Closing my eyes, I counted to ten.
When I opened them again, Seventeenth Street had stopped
its kaleidoscopic whirling.

"Are you a guest at the hotel?" he asked, helping me across
the street.

Another feeble Angie nod. My legs seemed to be moving of
their own volition.

"Come on." He shepherded me up the steps. "I'll have the
desk clerk phone the police."

"Ah, no need for that." I showed him a gracious Angie smile.
The last thing I wanted was a cozy chat with the Denver P.D.
"I—I'm sure he didn't mean any harm."

Grizzled eyebrows rose sharply. "You know him?"

"Oh, sure." Hastily I groped for an alias. "That's my
brother-in-law Randy." Somehow I always end up using the
name of Paul Holbrook's boss. "Randy Langston! It's Thurs-

day night . . . you know, payday. He always gets liquored up. He was just kidding around." Touching the doorman's sleeve, I added, "Don't worry. He won't get far with the front end bashed in." My head shook sadly. "Poor Susan! Guess she's going to have to go bail him out again."

The doorman's features hardened in disgust. "Maybe this time they'll yank his license."

Looking down, I noticed my hoodwrap dangling from my left hand. My black bag lay half buried in the snow.

Licking dry lips, I murmured, "My purse. Could you—?"

"Go on in and sit down, miss." He gave my shoulder blades a gentle push. "I'll be right there."

My knees still quaking, I trudged into the lobby. That's the price of playing Outlaw Angie, gang. When trouble rears its ugly head, you can't pick up the phone and dial the local police department. Not when you're wanted for assorted felonies in three states.

If I talked to the Denver police, they would naturally want to know why the Mazda driver had gone gunning for me. And if I gave them the honest answer—*"I don't know!"*—they would next poke about in my background.

If I was going to retain my freedom, I had to keep my real name out of law enforcement computers.

With a weary sigh, I seated myself on a plush red leather sofa. My gaze flitted toward the side exit.

No doubt about it, I thought. He saw me enter the lobby, ducked out the side door, and hopped into his Mazda. Meaning it wasn't the FBI I saw earlier.

My lips compressed thoughtfully. Then who—?

Just then the doorman returned with my bag. The desk clerk swiftly joined us, heard my story, and voiced sentiments of dismay. He went running to the coffee machine.

Gratefully accepting the coffee, I let the gentlemen fuss over me. The desk clerk was extremely solicitous. Gesturing at the grayish splotches on my camel-hair coat, he said, "If you'd like, miss, I can send that right out to the cleaners."

"Would you?" Setting down my paper cup, I stood and doffed Sarah's expensive tawny coat. Gave it a quick but thorough examination. No popped seams or missing buttons. Nothing worse than caked slush. Mild shudder of relief. "How soon can you get it back?"

"Eight-thirty?"

"Great!" Displaying a grateful smile, I handed it over. Believe me, I did not want to explain those stains to Sarah.

Sipping hot coffee, I rose from the sofa and slowly walked across the lobby. I found the potted fern I'd seen earlier. Touched the leaf that had been moving. Glanced at the well-polished floor.

Oh-ho! What's this, princess? Two wet footprints to the right of the big clay pot. Male feet. Size ten or eleven, maybe, with a sharply defined starburst on the arch. Water rimmed the edge of each print, the remnants of melted snow.

I glanced at the paneled door. No, I hadn't imagined it. He'd come in through the side entrance sometime after six. That's when it began snowing in earnest. Hmmm, better make it seven, Angie. The meltwater hasn't even begun to dry.

Standing behind the wet footprints, I glanced in the direction of the elevator.

Isn't *that* interesting, Angela? Our friend couldn't have possibly seen my face. From this vantage point, all he saw was a woman in a camel-hair coat and black hoodwrap departing the lobby. How had he known it was Angie Biwaban?

My frown deepened. Same story out in front of the hotel too. The Mazda came at me from behind. The driver never really got a good look at me.

I had a queasy feeling about all this. I was no longer quite so certain I was the intended target.

Had our friend seen the camel-hair coat and mistaken me for *Sarah?*

My mind leapt back to that mysterious phone call earlier that evening. A male voice had whispered, "Sarah?" And when I did respond, he'd immediately hung up.

Question—had the caller seen through the gag? Had he realized he was talking to an impostor?

Or did I inadvertently convince him that Sarah was upstairs?

And was he waiting there in the lobby for her to come down?

Taking another sip, I headed for the elevator.

Mrs. Sutton, you and I need to have a long talk!

# THREE

"Angela . . . wake up."

The familiar contralto voice drifted somewhere overhead.

"Come on, Angie. Go to bed."

Cool night air caressed my bare legs. I felt pages beneath my fingertips—the paperback I'd been reading. A thick dry taste enveloped my mouth. "Mmmm?"

"You fell asleep," Sarah whispered. "Go to bed."

My eyes fluttered open. I found myself propped against a trio of pillows, clad in my royal blue camisole, my legs stirring on the comforter. "S-Sarah?" I brushed the wild hair away from my forehead. "Wh-wha' time izzit?"

"Twelve-thirty." The lamp's circle of light underscored the lady's weary features. Picking up my paperback, she gave the cover a glance. "*Scandal's Lady.*" Green eyes blinked in surprise. "I didn't know you were a Regency fan."

"I'm partial to Mary Kingsley and Jo Ann Ferguson."

Frown of severity. "We have to do something about your taste in books, dear."

Swinging my legs over the edge, I sat up. "Sarah, we need to talk—"

"Tomorrow, kiddo. I've had it!" With a pert about-face, she stalked off to the bathroom. "I hereby declare today over!"

"But this is important."

"Angie, I just spent five hours helping to rewrite BuRec's priority list. I don't want to hear *anything* until my wake-up call tomorrow morning."

"Wake-up call?"

"Uh-huh." She turned on the bathroom light. "I've got a busy morning on tap. I'm having breakfast with George Hayes at seven-thirty. Then we're meeting with Congressman Bissell. You're going to have to cover for me at the conference. I'll join you as soon as I can." Closing the bathroom door, she added, "By the way, did my mother call?"

"No, but there was this—"

"Angela! There's no time for chitchat. Get some sleep." Her muffled voice sounded through the wood. "That phone's going to be ringing at six A.M."

Standing up, I turned back the blankets. Oh, well, it could probably keep until tomorrow. . . .

Friday morning found me back in the Convention Center, occupying a foldout chair seven rows back from the orchestra pit, notebook on my lap and pencil in hand, listening to the BuRec people argue with some very angry delegates from Oregon.

Hasty glance at the wall clock. Nine forty-five. Still no sign of Sarah. I wished I could have talked to her earlier that morning, but she ducked out while I was still in the shower.

The chair to my immediate right was vacant. Reserved for Sarah. My copy of the *Denver Post* covered the seat. I'd picked it up at the center's snack bar that morning, along with a small can of tomato juice. Found this intriguing item in the police blotter:

CAR STOLEN—A car belonging to a Sheridan woman was stolen from the McNichols Arena lot sometime during the Nuggets game last night. Cynthia van den Bergh told police there was no sign of her year-old Mazda when she returned to the lot at 11:15 P.M. The car was described as a blue two-door Mazda 323 bearing Colorado license plates.

Of course, the killer would have abandoned the Mazda by now, I thought.

And so, looking very secretarial in my double-breasted burgundy jacket and matching slim skirt, I opened my notebook on and dutifully took shorthand notes. Tried to think of a way to question Sarah without hurling her into a panic.

Twenty minutes later, my sidelong glance found Sarah hastily traversing the row. High-powered lawyer in her tailored gabardine suit, elegant lace-trimmed blouse, and trademark silken wing tie. She picked her steps carefully, offering gracious smiles to the seated delegates.

Offering a welcome smile, I whisked the newspaper off her chair. Smoothing the back of her skirt, she sat down. "This has been some morning," she whispered, slipping off her shoulder bag. "Fill me in."

"Well, they presented the revised priority list first thing this morning," I murmured, reviewing my notes. "Now Oregon is up in arms. They were counting on an appropriation to repair a dam, but that project's not even on the list."

Frowning, Sarah pinned a plastic nametag to her lapel. "I thought Dick Miller was going to handle that."

"He tried his best, Sarah, but it's no go." I aimed my pencil at the BuRec project director up onstage. "Those Oregon people are pretty upset. The Toscobuk Dam dates back to World War One. It's in serious need of repair."

"So are a lot of dams in the West." Scowling, Sarah watched the tumult up front. "I don't see the point."

"Toscobuk's in the northeast corner of the state. Those are high dry plains, Sarah, right on the edge of the Owyhee Desert. Farmers really need that irrigation water."

Sarah's pretty face reflected sudden comprehension. "How much longer will the present dam last?"

"Not more than a year. That's what Mr. Crutcher said. Collapse is imminent." I kept my voice low. "If that dam goes, Mintonville has had it. Those farms will be without irrigation for two or three years. The Oregonians think Toscobuk ought to have top priority. Can't say I blame them."

"Did Crutcher offer a cost estimate for the repair job?"

I nodded. "Bottom line, sixty-two million."

"Lord, we can't possibly fit them *all* on the priority list." Soft groan of dismay. "I may *never* get back to South Dakota." Wry smile. "I'm spending so much time with George Hayes, people think we're married." Seeing my expression, she added, "I'm not kidding! I walked up to the cashier's stand this morning, and the woman said, 'Did you enjoy your breakfast, Mrs. Hayes?'"

Just then an usher appeared at the end of the row. I saw him signaling, and nudged Sarah. Pointing at the exit, he said, "Mrs. Sutton? There's someone here to see you."

My gaze followed Sarah's to the rear, and I did an instant double take. Two grim-faced troopers of the Colorado State Patrol loitered in the entryway, looking around in a nonchalant fashion.

Giving the usher an inquisitive look, Sarah inquired, "Do you know what this is about?"

"No, ma'am."

Lips pursing in concern, Sarah shouldered her bag. "Keep an eye on things, Angie. I'll be right back."

Nodding, I watched her hurry up the center aisle. A sudden chill tickled my stomach. Had they come for *me?*

Easy, princess! Rein in the paranoia, eh? If this was a Pocahontas bust, they wouldn't be standing around up back. They would have come right down here. And a squad of Feebees would've been with them.

Frowning, I peered over my shoulder. On the other hand, this could be about the Mazda. The state patrol might have traced me from the hotel.

I watched as Sarah chatted with the two troopers. All at once she flinched as if she'd suddenly been punched. Then an invisible weight seemed to press upon her shoulders.

Rising from my seat, I thought, *Uh-oh! Trouble . . .*

As I started up the aisle, Sarah bolted from the auditorium. Her shoulders trembled uncontrollably. The troopers looked at each other, then turned to leave.

"Officer!" I called.

One trooper turned my way. He was tall and broad and stalwart, a ginger-haired fella with small sapphire eyes and a rancher's tan. He held his campaign hat under his right arm. The silver badge gleamed on his dark uniform jacket.

"Yes, miss?" He had a voice like thunder in a back canyon, low-pitched and vibrant.

"Why did Mrs. Sutton leave?"

Exchanging a quick glance with his partner, he responded, "What's it to you?"

Daintily I touched my nametag. "I'm Mrs. Sutton's administrative assistant." Lacing my fingers together, I asked, "Is anything wrong?"

The trooper exhaled heavily. "Mrs. Sutton's mother was killed last night."

*"Killed!"* All at once I thought of the Mazda. "Where? How?"

"Monarch Pass," he replied. "She was headed east on 50. Her pickup skidded off the road. Tumbled six hundred feet into Agate Creek. We got the call this morning from the barracks in Salida."

"What time did it happen?" I asked.

"We're not sure, miss," he replied, shaking his head. "A Chaffee County deputy found the wreck just past dawn this morning. Coroner's pretty sure Ms. Rooley was killed in the crash. Family said she left the Crested Butte area around four in the afternoon. Apparently, she was on her way to Denver." He gave me an inquisitive look. "Was Mrs. Sutton expecting her mother's arrival?"

Swift nod. "I—I think so. She asked me twice yesterday if her mother had called." I took the initiative once more. "Was there anyone else in the truck?"

He shook his head. "Near as the boys in Salida can tell, Ms. Rooley was alone when her truck slid over the edge."

"What was the condition of the road?" I asked.

The trooper glanced at his partner. "I don't know. Did you see that highway advisory, Ted?"

He nodded. Ted was the truly grim one. Thirtyish, short brown hair, and Polaroid sunglasses. "They had some snow up there yesterday mornin'. Got plowed out by midafternoon. Still quite a few icy spots, though. And there's no guardrail till you get to Barrel Springs. Once that wind starts blowin' over the ridge, drivin's sorta like ice skatin' in a wind tunnel."

"How high up is the pass?" I inquired.

"Eleven thousand feet." The ginger-haired trooper held his right hand level with his forehead. "It's a four-star nightmare up there in January. Most drivers get white-knuckle fever long before they reach the Springs. Hell, we get reports on spinouts two or three times a week. Lot of 'em tend to roll, too."

I had many more questions to ask, but I let them pass. After all, I couldn't afford to have the troopers wondering why a secretary was so interested. Flashing a polite smile, I added, "I'd better see to Sarah. Excuse me."

"That's okay, miss." The ginger-haired trooper lifted his

hand in farewell. "When she's feeling up to it, have Mrs. Sutton give us a call."

"Will do, Officer. Thanks again."

I hurried into the spacious lobby, my purse slapping my hip. A handful of people loitered beside the tall windows. No sign of Sarah in the waiting area. Then my gaze picked out the ladies' room farther down the hall.

As I pushed open the door, I caught a glimpse of Sarah in the wall-size mirror. The reflection showed a distraught blond lawyer seated on the vinyl settee, sobbing silently, twisting a handkerchief in her quivering hands. I hesitated for a moment, uncertain whether or not to intrude upon her grief. Then I remembered my own mother's death—how my friend Jill Stormcloud had comforted me.

Do it, Angie. Right now she needs a sympathetic shoulder to cry on. And no mention of the Mazda. That can wait.

With a long swallow, I let the door slam. "Sarah?"

Sniffling, she looked up at me. Gone was Take-Charge Sutton. In her place sat a stranger, a desolate blond woman afflicted by silent racking sobs. Tears streamed from her emerald eyes, and her soft mouth twisted in anguish.

"An-An-Angieeeee!" Oh, she was taking it hard. Never had I seen a woman so shattered. "My-my . . . m-my m-mother . . . she's—"

Her words gave way to a sudden keening wail. She couldn't quite make herself say it. Head bowed, she began weeping again like a lost little girl.

"It's all right," I murmured, sitting down beside her. "Go ahead and cry. Everything's going to be all right."

Sarah huddled against me, her tear-stained face burrowing into my shoulder, accepting my offer of solace. And wept.

Me, I did a lot of thinking. About a blue Mazda and a hit-and-run attempt and a snowy Rocky Mountain pass.

No, I didn't like the pattern. I didn't like it at all.

Shortly after two P.M. I stepped up to the public telephone in our hotel lobby and, one by one, popped a handful of quarters into the coin slot. The phone's musical *tinkle-ding* failed to erase my fussbudget frown.

We had just returned to the hotel from the state patrol headquarters in Lakewood. I advised Sarah to get some rest, but she would have none of it. Instead, she picked up the telephone and put through a long distance call to her younger sister, Rebecca, who ran the family ranch.

I had a call of my own to make, so I slipped out of our room and made a cat-footed dash to the elevator.

Lifting the receiver, I glanced at the lobby's oakwood grandfather clock. Two-twelve Mountain Time. Or three-twelve Central Time at Fond du Lac. With luck, my quarry would still be at the senior center.

My forefinger tapped out the area code. Two-one-eight . . .

The phone at the other end rang four times, and then an elderly woman's voice came on line. "Dave Savage Memorial Library. Good afternoon."

*"Watchiya, Ninga Kishkadina."* As always, I had no trouble making the switch to my people's language. I've been speaking Anishinabemowin since the days when I was known as *Awasiskwe*—Baby Girl. *"Nimishoo imaa ingoji ayaasin?"*

"Angie Biwaban! Is that you?" The librarian let out a delighted laugh. *"Eyan,* your grandfather's here. I spoke to him at lunch. *Hishi!* I hear you danced at Lac Courtes Oreilles last month."

"True enough, Mother Kishkadina."

"So you've finally come to your senses and moved back home."

"Ah . . . not quite." I grinned, lounging against the podium. "Unfortunately, I was home only for the holidays. Listen, could you put my grandfather on? I'm on a pay phone here, and it's kind of important."

"Oh, I've already sent one of the children after Charlie.

He'll be here in a minute." Madeleine Kishkadina took a deep breath, readying herself for some heavy-duty conversation. "How's your aunt Denise? And your grandmother? You know, I haven't seen Juliette since Ni-Mi-Win."

"She's doing fine, Mother Kishkadina. But I don't think she's getting off the top of Goat Hill till after ice-out."

"Your aunt Della was at Ni-Mi-Win too. *Tayaa!* I haven't seen Della in years. Her boys are all grown-up now. Why didn't you come with her, *gijikwe?*"

"Urgent business, Mother Kishkadina," I replied. Namely, finding the murderer of my cousin Billy, Aunt Della's oldest son.

"Your cousin Laura was up here last weekend. She and her husband just renovated their house. Did she mention that at *Niba-anamiaygijigad?* Oh, and I ran into the Attikamegs at Wal-Mart. They came all the way from Bad River. . . ."

And so it went. Mrs. Kishkadina spent a good four minutes updating me on the doings of all my Northland relatives. Then the operator broke in and asked me to contribute some more coinage. I wound up charging the call to my AT&T card. When I got back on line, I heard the gravelly voice of my grandfather, Charlie Blackbear.

*"Noozis! Aandi gaa-ki?"*

I smiled. In Anishinabemowin, we're no longer Chief and Angie. We become *Nimishoo* and *Noozis.* Grandfather and Granddaughter.

"Right here, *Nimishoo.* I had to talk to the operator for a minute. How's everything at Fond du Lac?"

Irascible sound. "Okay, I guess."

"Have you been up to Tettegouche at all?"

*"Eyan, Noozis.* I was up there on Sunday. Had to get some of that snow off the roof."

I had a horrifying vision of my seventy-five-year-old grandfather balancing himself on a high ladder, knocking snow from the roof with his trusty broom.

"By yourself?" I snapped.

*"Gawiin!* Of course not! Jim McLaren was with me."

Oh, lovely! Two senior citizens dancing around on a snowy roof in sub-zero weather!

*"Nimishoo . . ."*

"No need to fret, *Noozis.* It'll take more than a few snowflakes to kill a couple of old wolverines like me and Jim." Chief hastily changed the subject. "I hear a lot of voices in the background. Where are you calling from? The bus station?"

"A hotel, *Nimishoo.*"

"A hotel?" he echoed. "Where?"

"Denver, Colorado."

*"Banaydjiiwewin!"* he exclaimed. "What are *you* doing in *Denver?"*

"It's a long story, *Nimishoo,* and it's taken a decidedly nasty turn. Listen well . . ."

So I laid it all out for him, telling Chief about my initial telephone conversation with Madge Rooley, my trip to Denver as her daughter's Girl Friday, the mysterious phone call, and my narrow escape in front of the hotel. He listened in silence, offering a grunt of affirmation here and there. And when I was finished, he made a thoughtful sound.

*"Nin nissitaywendain.* That's too many coincidences for one afternoon, *Noozis.* Sure sounds like attempted murder." He kept his voice low, not wanting to be overheard at that end. "So what do you have in mind?"

*"Nandobani,"* I replied. An old word among our Anishinabe people, fraught with spiritual meaning. Going *nandobani* means giving up your normal life. You become a hunter of men. You melt into the forest, trailing your hidden foe, and then you take him out with a single well-aimed arrow.

Chief sighed. "Got another quarter on you?"

*"Eyan, Nimishoo."*

"Then why don't you drop it on the Colorado State Patrol?"

he suggested. "I'm sure they can do a much better job of protecting Sarah Sutton."

Grimacing, I switched the receiver to my other ear. "I can't do that, *Nimishoo*."

"Why not?"

"Because if I tell them I believe someone's trying to kill Sarah, they're going to invite me to Lakewood for a chat."

"I see! And some sharp-eyed detective's liable to notice the resemblance between you and that Pocahontas character on the FBI wanted poster." Bass chuckle. "Maybe you ought to start wearin' glasses like Clark Kent."

"It's no joke, *Nimishoo*. I don't have a choice. I have to help Sarah."

"I'm not sure I follow, missy."

Taking a quick breath, I added, "Sarah isn't going back to Pierre. Not for a while anyway. She's headed down to"—it took me a moment to remember the name—"Crested Butte for her mother's funeral."

Grunt of understanding. "If those Mazda guys tried once, they just might try again."

*"Eyan!"* I added with a sharp nod. "If Sarah gets killed, I could wind up a suspect. The Colorado police would begin stalking my back trail—"

"You really think they'd blame you!?" Chief interrupted.

*"Gawiin, Nimishoo."* Lightly I shook my head. "That's not what I'm worried about. I'm sure an investigation would clear me. But it just might turn up a few recent events I'd rather not talk about."

"Like that scam you pulled back in Mitchell," Chief added. "I see your point. Looks as if Mrs. Sutton's got herself an Anishinabe guardian angel." Thoughtful growl. "Aren't you biting off kind of a big chunk, girl? Just how do you plan to hunt the killers *and* keep an eye on Sarah?"

Mischievous smile. "I thought I might call in a little help."

His tone turned suspicious. *"Whose* help?"

"*Nimishoo*," I murmured sweetly.

"*Gawiin!*" he shouted, emphasizing both syllables of the Anishinabe negative. *Gah-ween.* "I've got better things to do than run off to Colorado."

"Come on, *Nimishoo!* I really need your help."

"Who do you think I am—Captain America? I'm supposed to go tear-assing around the countryside righting wrongs?"

"I think that was Don Quixote, *Nimishoo.*"

"It's still a dumb idea, young lady." Chief's tone softened. "There's no other way out of this jam, eh?"

I shifted the receiver again. "I can't stand by and let Sarah be killed, *Nimishoo.* And I'm pretty certain it was the same bunch who killed her mother."

"Bunch?" he echoed.

"I figure there's two to start. The lookout who made the call to our hotel room. And whoever was behind the wheel of the blue Mazda."

Prolonged sigh. "All right. I'll come and baby-sit your boss for you."

"Clunky's parked at the Dunning House in Pierre," I said, my spirits lifting. "I'll call Mrs. Sadowski tonight. She'll give you the key."

"Don't bother, *Noozis.* I'll rent a four-wheel-drive pickup when I get to Denver."

"Great! I'll meet you in Crested Butte. That's—"

"I know where it is," he interrupted. "One thing more, missy. We're not going to do any grandstanding out there. This is a fact-gathering mission, pure and simple. We dig up enough evidence to put these boys away. Then we hand off to the sheriff and do a quick and quiet fade."

"Quick and quiet! Nothing would please me more, *Nimishoo.*"

A curious tone filtered into my grandfather's voice. "You seem pretty damned sure Miz Rooley's death and the attempt on her daughter are connected."

*"Eyan, Nimishoo."*

"What makes you so sure?" he asked.

"That phone call," I explained. "When I picked up, our mystery caller said, 'Sarah?' I was startled to hear a man's voice. When I didn't respond right away, he got kind of antsy. He said, 'Sally? You there?' "

"He called her *Sally*. So what?"

*"Nimishoo,* no one calls her that. Back in Pierre, she's either *Sarah* or *Mrs. Sutton,*" I replied. "I spoke to Madge Rooley earlier this week, when she called the office. She referred to her daughter as *Sally.*"

"Anyone in Denver call her by that name?"

"No one uses that nickname. Not even Paul Holbrook." And I had reason to believe those two had been quite intimate at one time.

"That means it's somebody who knew Sarah when she was a kid. Somebody from Crested Butte." Timbre of warning. "Watch yourself out there, *Noozis.*"

"I will," I promised. "Listen, I've got one more call to make, *Nimishoo.* We'll talk again when you get there. Bye!"

"Take care, *Noozis.*"

After hanging up, I ran my plastic card down the AT&T slot. Computer beeps echoed in my ear. A robot voice invited me to tap out my number.

This particular number I knew by heart!

One short ring, followed by a familiar baritone voice. "Department of Corrections. Holbrook speaking."

"Hi, *Kemo Sabe.*" Somber Angela.

"Angie!" He instinctively reacted to the sadness in my voice. "What happened? Where are you calling from?"

"Denver." Leaning against the lobby wall, I sighed. "We've got some trouble here, Paul. Sarah's mother was killed yesterday. A car crash up in the mountains."

"Oh, no!" Tone of sincere regret. "How did it happen, Angie?"

I repeated everything the troopers had told me at the Convention Center. Then I described Sarah's reaction. Naturally, I made no mention of the mysterious evening phone call or the blue Mazda.

"How's Sarah taking it?" he asked.

"Very hard." Mild sigh. "She's headed home tomorrow for the funeral. Paul, I—I really don't think she should go alone."

"What do you mean, princess?"

"I mean she's wrapped a little too tight." And, believe me, I was not exaggerating. "She hasn't gotten off the phone since we got back to the hotel. She's calling her sister, talking with lobbyists, trying to take charge of everything at once. It's a wacky form of denial. If she plunges into enough tasks, then she won't have to deal with her mother's death."

Paul hummed thoughtfully. "Internalizing it, you mean."

"Exactly! She's trying to be Superwoman, Paul. And she can't be. Nobody can. Not at a time like this."

For a lengthy moment he said nothing. And then . . .

"What do you have in mind, Angie?"

"I thought I'd tag along. Sarah needs time to cope. I can buy her that time. I can field any calls from the firm."

"Angie, you're no lawyer—"

"True, but I can cover for her. It'll be one less hassle."

Another hum. "I forgot. You've been through the mill on this, haven't you?"

"I know what she's going through, Paul. I lost my mother last year." My voice wavered. "If not for Jill, I never would've made it."

"Angie, I don't know if I can ask you to do this." The sympathy in Paul's voice put a gentle squeeze on my heart. "After all, you've had losses of your own. Your cousin Billy, for one."

"That's why I'm best qualified to help, Paul. And you don't have to ask—I'm volunteering." Crossing my fingers hopefully, I murmured, "What do you say?"

"All right." I heard Paul's pen scribbling on paper. "I'll tell

R.T. you're going to be in Colorado for a while. Have you discussed this with Sarah?"

"Unh-unh! I thought it might be better if it came from you."

"Good thinking. She's less likely to decline if I ask."

Mouth open, I glared at the receiver. And what do you
mean by *that*, Mr. Holbrook?

Blithely unaware of my warpath scowl, Paul added, "Good
luck, princess. Give me a call when you get to the RJ Bar."

I blinked. "Where?"

"The Rooley ranch. It's on Roaring Judy Creek."

Unable to resist the impulse, I went fishing for leads. Innocent tone. "Have you ever been there?"

"Unh-unh," Paul responded casually. "Sarah's told me all
about it, though."

Under what particular circumstances? I wondered.

He spoke softly. "Angela . . ."

"Yeah?"

"None of this is going to be easy for Sarah." Paul seemed to
be groping for the right words to say. "I mean, she had it hard
growing up. There were times she had to live with kinfolk
while—"

"While her mother was in prison?" I offered.

Shocked tone. "How did you hear about that?"

"I had a long talk with Madge. She enjoyed chatting with a
fellow Bobbi Jo."

"Yes . . . well . . ." The topic made Paul highly uneasy.
"Sarah's early life was anything but pleasant. Her mother
was constantly in and out of prison. And when she hit her
teens . . ." All at once, he let the subject drop. "What I'm trying to say is, it isn't going to go the way you expect, Angie."

That sounds ominous, I mused.

Just then I heard a female voice in the background. Stepha-
nie Poulsen, the department's topkick secretary. "Paul, Mr.
Langston's on line four. He wants to talk to you about the
Etheridge case."

"Sorry, princess, I've got to cut this short," Paul said, "Duke Etheridge jumped parole. He's supposed to be heading for Bismarck. Listen, I'll talk to you Monday. Okay?"

"Good enough, Holbrook. Talk to you then."

Shortly after nine A.M. on Saturday, January 24, our commuter Bonanza landed at the Pitkin County Airport, just west of Aspen. While I lassoed a brawny male to help with the luggage, Sarah went straight to the Hertz desk to rent a set of wheels.

I was a little surprised by her choice. Instead of a ladylike Subaru or Datsun, Sarah selected a rugged Isuzu Trooper, a mountain-hopping model with four-wheel drive, a heavy-duty V6 engine, and a power winch able to haul five thousand pounds.

The rationale for her choice became apparent when we left Colorado 133 in Marble. A car wouldn't have made it to Crystal. Not on that rutted, unpaved Forest Service road. Indeed, a mountain goat would have had trouble picking its way up that steep and treacherous slope. But somehow the Trooper made it, bouncing in and out of snow ruts, fishtailing on the ice, its 175-horsepower engine roaring in the thin alpine air.

Soon we were tooling along at ten thousand feet, past windswept mountaintop snow fields. "Through the attic," Sarah called it. Down the winding Jeep trail numbered 317, past frozen Emerald Lake and its snow-smothered subalpine firs, and out into a broad, high valley. Thrusting more than twelve thousand feet into the frigid blue sky was Avery Peak, with light snow blowing from its glistening spire. Thick forests of Engelmann spruce littered the lower slopes. I nearly missed the buildings of the Alpine Research Station as we drove past the old mining town of Gothic. From the road they resembled so many matchboxes. Across the valley, burly Gothic Mountain—Avery's twin—loomed like a persistent salesman.

I sneaked a glance at Sarah. Gone was the elegant lady lawyer in her haute couture gabardine suit. Twin bags of flesh, looking a bit like poached eggs, nestled beneath her eyes. She looked like a rancher's wife in her grape-colored poplin ski jacket, oak-brown corduroy slacks, and toboggan hat. A tension crease marred the corner of her mouth.

I frowned. Sarah was under a lot of stress, and this mountain driving was certainly no help. "Would you like me to spot you for a while?"

Sarah shook her head. "Thanks, Angie, but you don't know the road. Let me get us down on the flat. Then you can take the wheel."

"We're coming up on a toboggan slide, eh?"

"That's for sure!"

Peering out the side window, I watched snowy Snodgrass Mountain slide by. My breath left a damp spot on the chilled glass. I wiped it clean with my mitten. "You really know these back trails, don't you?"

"Absolutely." Bittersweet smile. "We Rooleys are an old mountain family."

"Where from?" I asked.

"Clinch Mountain, Tennessee, originally." Sarah's smile warmed a bit. "My great-great-grandpap liked country where it was uphill both ways."

"He was the first Rooley out here?"

"Uh-huh! Byron Lee Rooley."

"One of Crested Butte's founding fathers?" I asked.

"Ah, no . . ." All at once, Sarah seemed reluctant to talk about him. "He, uh, got his start in Telluride."

I began another question, but she beat me to the punch. "One of these days I'll take you into town, Angie. You can talk to a few people at Kochevar's. They'll tell you all about the *unruly Rooleys.*"

I wanted to hear more, but Sarah's tone forbade further discussion. So I let it drop.

We veered to the right, away from the river, passing beneath the rugged north face of Crested Butte. The mountain was a true alpine *massif,* a rising accumulation of snow-laden ridges, glacial cirques, steep-walled arretes, and precipitous avalanche slides, all leading up to a slightly lopsided Matterhorn peak. Fir and spruce forests struggled in vain to reach the summit.

We stopped for a refill at an Amoco station on Gothic Road, and I got my first look at the town of Crested Butte. A unique blend of architectural styles. Ultramodern condominiums, aging stores from the Age of Ike, and the original false-front buildings.

After paying for the gas, Sarah let me take the wheel. Heeding her advice, I hung a left at the Ore Bucket Building, scooted past the Oh, Be Joyful Baptist Church, and headed south on Seventh. The street merged with Colorado 135 just beyond the Stepping Stones Children's Center. In no time at all, we were back in cow country again.

The road darted down a broad, snow-covered valley bracketed on either side by sizable mountains. Sarah identified them for me. Whetstone on the right, Point Lookout on the left. Five miles past the airport, just behind Point Lookout's forested flank, we came upon a snow-plowed road angling off into the high country. Sarah told me to stop, and we changed seats again.

That was Forest Service Road 740, and it carried us high above eleven thousand feet. The flight ceiling of the Sopwith Camel during my great-grandfather's war. Twin jets of snow gushed from the Trooper's rear tires as it slip-slided down a winding private road past the hot springs.

Glancing out the window, I noticed that Engelmann spruce had crowded out the firs. Ten-inch clots of snow weighed down their dark boughs. Twin peaks loomed on either side of the road—Cement Mountain and its sister, East Cement.

Then, as we rounded a steep granite bluff, I sighted the ranch entrance fifty yards ahead. A whitewashed Old West wooden arch flanked by iron-rimmed wagon wheels. Simple black lettering identified it as the RJ Bar Ranch.

The Rooley house was a two-story bungalow cottage, light blue with white wood trim and coffee-brown storm shutters. There were two porches—an open one with a fieldstone railing at the front of the house, and an enclosed porch facing south. The cottage dated from the twenties. Sometime in the past half century, the family had added on upstairs, putting a pair of bedrooms just above the enclosed porch. A good twelve inches of snow smothered the cottage's steep overhanging roof.

A dozen yards behind the house stood the venerable gambrel-roofed barn, a brand-new stable, two rusting silos, a well-built smokehouse, and a dilapidated woodshed. Nearby stood the original homestead cabin, now surrounded by a tall wire fence. A goat's head appeared in the doorway, followed by two others. They seemed most interested in our arrival.

A pair of toddlers, snug in their hooded suits, cavorted with a hyperkinetic Border collie in the deep snow. Nearby their teenage sister hacked away at the drifts with a broad-bladed shovel. Her long blond hair was the same shade as Sarah's. It spilled out from under her knitted cap, slapping the shoulders of her navy-blue stadium jacket.

Oh, she was a Rooley all right. Same emerald eyes, pert, tip-tilted nose, and firm lips. The cold painted her lovely cheekbones a rosy hue. She smiled prettily as our Trooper rolled to a stop. But when Sarah stepped down from the cab, her welcoming smile vanished.

Scowling, she jammed her shovel into a waist-high pile of snow. I could feel the girl's hostility all the way across the yard.

La Sutton, as usual, was poise personified. "Hello, Karen."

"Well"—the girl's mouth turned ugly—"if it ain't the rich city lawyer lady."

Sarah flinched as if she'd been slapped. Green eyes blinked

rapidly. She drew a quick, calming breath. "How have you been?"

"What do *you* care?" Emotion clotted the girl's lovely contralto voice. "Rich city lawyer lady!"

I marveled at Sarah's self-control.

"Where's Becky?"

"Inside!" With that, the girl did a quick about-face and flounced up the shoveled walkway.

Shouldering my bag, I followed suit. Karen was fourteen or fifteen. Same age I was when Mother had her first operation and I spent the year living in Utah with Aunt Della.

You don't know how lucky you are, girl, I thought, as Karen removed her snowboots. If I'd ever called Aunt Della a rich Utah teacher lady, it would've been straight to the woodshed, double-quick time!

I truly felt sorry for Sarah. Now she had to deal with a resentful kid sister on top of everything else.

The Rooley kitchen was modern colonial, with tall cupboards, walnut paneling, a burly green two-door refrigerator, a gas range, and a Formica-topped counter. Childish drawings hung haphazardly on the refrigerator doors. Bracing the wall nearby were four walnut shelves stocked with home preserves.

Busily working at the counter was a slender ponytailed blonde in a bulky white sweatshirt and taut indigo jeans. If she heard our footsteps, she gave no sign. Her boning knife sawed away at a chunk of baked ham.

"Becky . . ." Karen hooked her thumb over her shoulder. "That rich city lawyer lady's here."

"Karen Lynn Rooley, what did I tell you about that?" Becky turned at once, wiping her hands on a moist dishrag. Lovely features tensed in disapproval. She was a decade older than the girl, another Rooley beauty with the trademark emerald eyes, high forehead, and soft chin.

Between Sarah, Becky, and Karen, I had a feeling that over

the years, the RJ Bar had been a popular destination for the boys of Gunnison High.

Karen's chin rose stubbornly. "Name fits."

Ignoring the girl, Becky crossed the kitchen, her arms outspread in welcome. "Sally!"

So I stood by the counter and watched the Rooley women hug tightly and peck one another's cheeks. Hushed murmurs of greeting.

Then Sarah formally introduced me to sister Rebecca, who, incidentally, was the mother of the twins I'd seen playing in the snow. As she turned to Karen, the girl avoided her gaze, speaking directly to Becky. "I'd better go hunt up Merry and Troy."

She vanished before Sarah could even speak.

Stunned by Karen's rudeness, I watched her flee through the dining room. I couldn't help myself. Sarcasm seemed most appropriate. "Your sister has such lovely manners."

Becky laughed. "Karen's not my sister!"

Surprised Angie blink. "Well, she's certainly not your *daughter*."

"No," Sarah intruded, showing me a bleak expression. "She's *mine!*"

# FOUR ▾▾▾▾▾▾▾

I should have seen it coming. Goodness knows, Paul had given me a broad enough hint over the phone.

Then there was Jill Stormcloud. She'd once told me about Sarah's volunteer work. Five years ago, La Sutton had helped to found the Verendrye House in Fort Pierre, a shelter and support program for adolescent single mothers. Many times I'd wondered about Sarah's interest in the plight of unwed teenage mothers. Now I understood. Sarah herself had been one. She must have been seventeen when she gave birth to Karen.

Displaying a tepid smile, I glanced at the lawyer lady. Tried to think of some charming thing to say. Mortification must have dimmed my wits, however, for the best I could do was . . .

"Y-y-your daughter!?"

"My daughter." Thin smile of satisfaction. Sarah really enjoyed catching me off base. "Believe me, Karen was taught manners. She seems to have misplaced them, though."

"Sarah . . . I'm sorry . . ."

"No need to apologize, Angela. This has nothing to do with

you." Her simmering gaze drifted toward the parlor. "I've been butting heads with that kid for years." Sidelong glance at Becky. "Which reminds me. Did you call the courthouse?"

"Sure, Sally. Clerk postponed the hearing until after the funeral. No problem."

"I wouldn't say that." Unzipping her winter jacket, Sarah nodded in my direction. "Angie, you must be famished. Feel free to help yourself. I—I have a few calls to make."

No sooner was Sarah out of earshot than I heard her sister's chuckle right behind me. Turning slowly, I watched Becky fold her slender arms and grin.

"First off, I guess you'll be wantin' a crowbar." Feminine chuckle. "So you can remove that foot before we eat."

I winced. "It was kind of a boneheaded thing to say."

Becky's green eyes danced. "You really thought Karen was my sister?"

Anishinabe nod. "There's a definite family resemblance."

"You ain't the only one to comment on it. Hungry?"

"Thanks, Becky, but I think I can hold out till supper." I tilted my chin toward the window. "How long has Karen been living here?"

"Four years. Ever since Sally's divorce."

"From Mr. Sutton?"

"Gal, I wouldn't dignify Pete Sutton with the title *Mister*." Remembered resentment tightened her voice. "Until I met that man, I never knew shit piled that high."

"Rotten husband, eh?"

Brisk nod from Becky. "Somebody forgot to tell Pete when you put the ring on, it means you're out of circulation." She carried a platter of fresh ham slices to the refrigerator. "Sally put up with him for seven years. Don't ask me how. Son of a bitch chased every skirt in Pierre."

"How old was Karen when your sister married?"

She thought a moment, then answered, "Four. Pete's the

only daddy Karen ever knew. Kind of hard on the kid, ya know?"

Nod of comprehension. I'd lost my own father at age twelve, to a fatal accident on the taconite docks.

"She had no idea why her family was breaking up," Becky continued. "And Sally was too damned proud to tell her. Sally wanted a clean break. Turned out it was anything but! Karen blamed Sally for the divorce. Those two used to scrap like a pair of bobcats. Then Momma got out of prison and offered to take Karen for a spell." Rueful smile. "Y'know, it was supposed to be a *temporary* arrangement."

I frowned. "Sarah never mentioned a daughter."

"No surprise." Balancing the platter on one hand, she opened the refrigerator. Her smile turned cagey. "We Rooleys ain't ones to let folks know our business."

As Becky put the ham away, I heard the front door slam and then a flurry of voices. Grinning, Becky led me into the parlor and introduced me to the siblings.

The baritone belonged to Troy, a broad-shouldered nineteen-year-old with the chiseled back-country good looks of Randy Travis. Strong chin, long nose, deepset brown eyes, low, bristly eyebrows, and a shock of wiry brownish-blond hair. At six feet two inches, he towered over his sisters. Stepping forward, he offered me a tanned, knuckly hand and an aw-shucks smile that showed the upper tier of white teeth.

We shook hands. I tried hard not to grimace. Troy had a grip like a forged-steel clamp.

Then there was Meredith—*Merry* for short. Another Rooley blonde but with a natural wave to her hair. Like her sisters, she shared the Rooley cheekbones and high, intelligent forehead. But her lovely chin ended in a dainty cleft, and her eyes were a startling shade of Bimini blue. Like her brother, she wore ranch denims and a sheepskin jacket.

"You here for a visit?" asked Troy.

Before I could open my mouth, Merry announced, "Nope.

Sally says she's stayin' for a spell." She had a musical contralto voice. Turning my way, she added, "We're gonna put you in Momma's room. Hope you don't mind."

"Not at all," I replied.

Curiosity gleamed in Merry's blue eyes. "Where are you from, Angie?"

"Minnesota."

Troy's smile widened. "Well, I reckon you're no stranger to milkin' cows."

"Milkin' goats is little trickier, though." Merry's sinewy hand closed around an invisible teat. "You've got to give it a little pull when you squeeze."

"You'll pick it up fast enough," her brother predicted.

"Rein up, you two." Becky stepped between us. "Angie ain't workin' for us. She's workin' for Sally." Warning glance at me. "Don't you let them two talk you into anything."

"Can't blame us for tryin', Becky." Troy shed his winter jacket and draped it across the washing machine. "We've got sixty-three Angora goats, Angie, and there's only the three of us. We do it all by hand, too."

Merry waggled her fingers. "Twenty goats twice a day."

"And it's more work than it sounds like." Becky smoothed the sides of her tight-fitting jeans. "Takes three hundred pulls on the nipple just to come up with a gallon of milk."

Lounging against the counter, Troy cast a somber look around. "Hey! Where'd Sally run off to?"

Becky's thumb jabbed ceilingward. "Making some calls."

Nudging her brother, Merry said, "Let's go say hi."

After the younger Rooleys left, Becky grabbed her brother's sheepskin jacket and hung it on an old-fashioned coatrack. She paused suddenly, her face swiveling toward the dining room. Then she strode purposefully to the doorway.

"If you're going to stand and sulk in the parlor, girl, I'll sew up a lamp shade so you can blend right in."

Cry of adolescent indignation. "I am *not* sulking!"

Doing a brisk about-face, Becky headed back to the counter. "Well, any time you're feelin' sociable, I've got company in here."

Karen joined us sixty seconds later, her coat unzipped, unruly bangs littering her forehead. And that pout! Give that girl an award for this year's fussbudget face.

She tossed a sullen gaze at the ceiling. "Is *she* up there?"

"If that's your momma you're talkin' about . . . yes, she is." Becky swung open the cupboard doors. Reaching for canned vegetables, she added, "Good time to head upstairs if you want to say hi."

"Well . . . maybe." Karen's lips compressed tightly. At least she was giving the decision some thought.

Becky set two cans on the counter. "You might try an apology on for size while you're at it."

Karen's lower lip jutted in defiance. "No way!"

Becky's eyes narrowed, giving her an uncanny resemblance to her older sister. "Sure about that, girl?"

Too late! By now Karen's mind was made up. She felt she had to put on a show. Expression of teen martyrdom. "Look, I never asked her to come back here."

Becky's tone tensed. "You about done with that shoveling?"

Adolescent nod. "Uh-huh."

"Fine!" Becky's emerald eyes flashed fire. "Go out to the stable and put on your mucking boots. I've got some more shoveling for you."

"*What?*"

"You heard me." Becky's chin jutted toward the kitchen window. "Fetch yourself a wheelbarrow and a long-handled shovel and start cleaning them stalls."

"Beck-*eeeee!*"

"Go on! You know you've got it comin'." Stern glance. "Rich city lawyer lady! You couldn't *wait* to throw that at your momma."

"People have a right to say what they think—"

"And it helps if they *think* before they say it!" Becky aimed her forefinger upward. "Did you ever give a thought to how she feels about Nana dyin'?" Slight shake of the head. "No, I didn't think so. Well, Miss Karen Lynn Rooley, why don't you go shovel horseshit for a couple of hours and think on it some?"

Karen's mouth dropped open. For a moment she looked as if she were going to snap right back. But she didn't. Instead, she turned her pert nose upward—just like her mother, I might add—and flounced out of the kitchen.

A few minutes later I peered out the window and saw Karen, shovel in hand, on her way to the stable. Suppressing a smile, I glanced at Becky. "You handled that well."

Dumping sliced carrots in a stewpot, she showed me a dispirited look. "I've had plenty of practice."

"Cheer up. She'll be eighteen before you know it."

"Yeah, I know. I try to think of it as on-the-job training." Puckish smile. "Reckon I'll be saddlebroken by the time Luke and Laura are that age." She cast a quick glance out the window. "You know, between the two of us, Momma and I could ride herd on that girl. But now that Momma's gone . . ."

Becky left the rest unsaid. But I could feel her apprehension. "Getting to be a handful, is she?"

"I'm afraid one of these days Karen's gonna up and go. Just hop on some boy's motorcycle and ride off into the sunset. Get herself in one hell of a mess!" Sympathy flooded Becky's pretty face. "Worst of it is . . . I know what she's going through, Angie. I've *been* there."

I remembered my telephone conversation with Becky's mother. Madge's words echoed in my mind. *When you see Sally, you tell her I've got the same ol' problem. And it's her problem, too.* Madge must have been talking about Karen.

Just then, frenetic canine barking permeated the glass pane. Leaving the pot on the stove, Becky rushed to the window.

"Damn! Can't leave those kids alone for a minute." Her knuckles rapped the frosted glass. "Hey!" Maternal bellow. "Keep that dog out of the snowdrift! He's gonna sink over his damned head!" Quick apologetic glance. "I've got to get out there."

"Go ahead," I said, folding my arms casually. "I'll keep an eye on the carrots."

Becky fled the kitchen. Harried and ponytailed young mother in her ranch-cut jeans. Listening to those toddler shouts and that canine fortissimo, I wondered what it is about snowdrifts that turns the average dog into an ersatz badger.

We buried Madge Rooley on Monday morning, January 26. I was surprised by the number of people who turned up at the Oh, Be Joyful Baptist Church. The crowd filled the little corner church to overflowing. Somber men in dark suits and gray Stetsons lined the aisles on either side.

In the front row stood Sarah, Becky, Meredith, and Karen, clad alike in unadorned black dresses and matching veiled pillbox hats. Troy stood by the casket with the other ushers. I was three rows back, wearing the black dress I'd picked up Saturday evening at Le Chat Boutique, holding my well-worn prayer book, standing beside Sarah's aunt and uncle, Mr. and Mrs. McCannell.

I'd met the McCannells Sunday afternoon at the RJ Bar. They owned a horse ranch on the far side of the valley, just below Gunsight Pass. Sarah and Becky had lived with them while Madge was sorting laundry in prison.

One unusual mourner drew my attention. An elderly man, wiping his red-rimmed and rheumy eyes. Shoulder-length ash-gray hair and a beard as wild as a tumbleweed. He looked as if he'd stepped right out of a Tim Holt movie. Copper-riveted Levis held up by a pair of striped suspenders. Mackinaw shirt and patched denim sherpa-lined jacket. Pulling out a long red bandana, he gave his nose a lusty blow.

When the minister finished his eulogy, Troy and the others lifted the casket and carried it down the center aisle. The Rooleys followed them out. I watched in mild amazement as the crowded rows emptied in perfect precision.

Later on, Mrs. McCannell told me it was an old Highland custom. That silent, solemn march from the kirk to the cemetery. Mourners moved along in a column of twos, their eyes downcast, their stride at once deliberately formal and hurriedly anxious. Their Scotch-Irish forebears had brought the custom with them to the mountains of Tennessee, and their grandchildren had carried it farther west to Colorado.

Soon we were standing in a windswept cemetery, beneath an icy cerulean sky. When the graveside service concluded, Becky dabbed at her tear-stained cheeks and invited everyone to the ranch for lunch.

Yes, southern hospitality still exists. It's just moved to the Rockies, that's all.

As the funeral crowd broke up, I watched the grave digger climb aboard his idling yellow backhoe. It'd take some digging to punch a hole in that frigid ground. Then Mr. Red Bandana crossed my field of vision, wearing a ragged felt sombrero. The front brim had been pushed up, making him look like a Rough Rider. He buttonholed the minister, rubbed his whiskered jaw, licked his chapped lips, and put out a hand.

Now, the minister looked like one of those bespectacled, stern-lipped clerics, but, believe me, he was a soft touch. Clutching a five-dollar bill, Mr. Bandana bustled down the snow-covered road and clambered into a black, rattletrap 1956 Ford pickup, headed no doubt for the nearest bar.

Giving Mrs. McCannell a nudge, I asked, "Who's that?"

"Hmmm?" The lady's green eyes shifted my way. Bump Sarah's age up to fifty-five, add forty pounds to her figure, and you had a reasonable facsimile of Alice McCannell. Glancing past me, she said, "Oh, that's Pop Hannan. He worked for Madge off and on."

"Doing what?" I asked.

"Stringin' fence. Cuttin' timber," she replied. "Odd jobs around the ranch. He's worked for me and Brett, too."

"If that's what you want to call it." In his sugarloaf Stetson, Brett McCannell looked as tall as a Ponderosa. He had a lean, bony face as brown as old saddle leather. Hawklike nose, deepset, squinting gimlet eyes, and the fearsome, stiff-spined dignity you find in most back-country ranchers. "We don't see too much of Pop in the summer, Angie. Mostly he comes down on the flat at first snow."

"What does he do in the summer?" I asked, peeling wind-blown raven hair out of my face.

"Prospects." Alice gestured at the forested mountain slope. "The silver played out back in the 1880s. But Pop—he thinks they missed the mother lode. He's spent *years* up there in the Collegiate range. Knows every deer trail from here to Twin Lakes."

"Personally, I think he's after the gold," Brett said.

"Gold?" I echoed.

"You heard right, gal." Flashing a sudden grin, Brett gave his wife a hearty one-armed hug. "The gold her great-granddaddy stole."

Alice flushed in irritation. "Brett—!"

I did some quick mental math. One generation separated Sarah from her aunt. Add that generation to Alice's great-granddad, and you get . . .

"Byron Lee Rooley?"

Brett's gimlet eyes blinked. "You've heard of him?"

"Sarah mentioned him in passing."

The rancher's grin broadened. "Bet she didn't mention he rode with the Wild Bunch."

My turn to blink. "He rode with Butch Cassidy and the Sundance Kid?"

"He surely did! He and ol' Butch met in Telluride. Butch spent a month there in 1895. Story ain't too clear on how they met. Come autumn, though, B. L. Rooley turned up at Hole-in-the-Wall. Butch and Matt Warner had just formed the Bunch. Papers gave 'em that name, y'know. They called themselves the Train Robbers' Syndicate. They needed riders, and Byron . . . well, he was a two-fisted Tennessee boy mighty handy with a loop and a runnin' iron."

Alice's features tensed in annoyance. "No shame in that. There's a whole lot of cowpokes who rode with the Bunch."

"Yeah, but they didn't all hold up the Mountain Zephyr."

"Great-granddaddy had nothing to do with that!"

"Come on, Ali. A dozen passengers saw him holdin' the horses. Blond man on a raindrop Appaloosa." Brett's eyes held a teasing gleam. "If that wasn't Byron Lee Rooley, I'll go to Eye-rack and kiss ol' Saddam Hussein."

"What's the Mountain Zephyr?" Curious Angela.

"Express train, Angie," he explained. "Used to make the run from Denver to Santa Fe. Service ended back in the early fifties, when I was a kid." Warming to the subject, he added, "The train got robbed back in 1897. That was a busy year for the Wild Bunch. That April, Butch Cassidy, Bob Meeks, and Elza Lay walked into the payroll office at Castle Gate, Utah, and held it up. They got away with eighty-seven hundred dollars. Then, about a month later, three riders hit the Zephyr at Price Creek. Tom McCarty, Dutch Bohle, and *you-know-who*." Chuckle of admiration. "Slickest job the Bunch ever pulled. Them boys chopped down some cottonwoods and had their mounts drag the logs across the tracks. When the train stopped, Tom and Dutch boarded the baggage car and dynamited the big Adams Express safe. The boys rode off with fifteen grand. Biggest raise ever here in Gunnison County."

"Fifteen thousand," I commented. "It doesn't sound like much."

"Gal, we're talking fifteen thousand in *gold!* That train was carryin' approximately one thousand five hundred U.S. ten-dollar gold pieces fresh from the Denver mint." Brett's voice tingled with awe. "Lord only knows what it'd be worth today. Have to ask some coin collector, I expect."

I glanced at the mountains. "And Pop Hannan thinks the money's up there?"

"Damned right." The rancher nodded vigorously. "Tom McCarty turned up in Butte, Montana, a year later. That's when he helped Matt Warner rob the faro parlor. Folks think Tom took his cut and lit out after the Zephyr job. Now, Dutch Bohle—he got shot in Carbondale a couple of months after the holdup. Trouble was, ol' Dutch's saddlebags were mighty light when the law caught up with him." Eyeing the wintry ridge-line, he added, "Assumin' Tom McCarty's cut was one-third, there's still one thousand gold pieces unaccounted for. Dutch's share and By—the *third man's* share. Folks figure it's tucked away in either the West Elks or the Collegiates. Pop says it's got to be the Collegiates."

"Why?" I asked.

Doing a slow burn, Alice snapped, "Because Cement Mountain's in the Collegiates, and that's where the RJ Bar is!" Green eyes sizzling, she confronted her husband. "Are you all done runnin' down my family?"

"Ali, a whole lot o' folks saw ol' Dutch in Crested Butte that summer—"

"That doesn't mean he was holed up at the RJ Bar!"

"Honey, I heard it from ol' Harry Tiggs hisself. He was five years old. Happened right in front of Kochevar's, it did. Dutch paid him a quarter to lead his mount to the livery stable. Few years later, he saw Dutch's picture in the *Police Gazette.*"

"Harry Tiggs was a hopeless alcoholic. Before he died, he told that story in every saloon between here and Omaha."

"He swore it was Dutch."

"Ohhhhh! He'd have sworn it was *Elvis* if you'd bought him a drink." Exasperated, Alice turned to me. "You see what my family has to put up with?"

"Well, they sure have kept the Colorado law hoppin'!"

"Ohhhhh! Keep it up, Brett McCannell, and I'll—"

"Don't get riled, sugar."

"Great-granddaddy had nothing to do with that robbery," she said heatedly. "He was buying cattle in Salida. Folks saw him drive the herd right through Gunnison. He had the bill of sale to prove it, too."

Giving his wife another one-armed hug, Brett chuckled. "'Course, some folks think Byron took some o' them gold coins and bought hisself a four-footed alibi."

"That does it!" Features livid, Alice knocked his arm away. "I am *not* going to listen to this. You know where you're sleeping tonight."

"Come on, honey. I was only funnin'."

"At my sister's *funeral!*"

"You know I didn't mean any harm by it. Anyway, Madge would have laughed—"

"Not when you throw dirt at us Rooleys!"

"Ali, there were outlaws in my family, too." Tenderly he squeezed her shoulders. "No shame in havin' a great-granddaddy who was lonely on the mountain."

"Well, I'm glad you think so, Brett McCannell, because you're going to be lonely on the *couch!* For the next two or three weeks, I'd say!"

"Honey!"

At that point I took my leave. Sarah's aunt and her dismayed husband carried their spat down the street. Alice's tart voice carried far in the frigid air.

"... unruly Rooleys, are we? Just wait till I get you home. You're going to find out firsthand just how *unruly* I can be!"

Trying not to grin, I strolled over to Sarah's Isuzu. Felt a twinge of sympathy for Uncle Brett. That's the problem with fun, guy. Sooner or later it has to be paid for.

By early afternoon we were all back at the ranch. Between them, Sarah and Becky put out quite a buffet for the visitors.

Two sizable tables piled high with munchies stood before the frost-rimmed windows. Merry's chicken salad. Becky's maple corn bread and fluffy potato biscuits. And Sarah's beef and onion stew. Apparently, Rooley women did not believe in caterers.

It had been a very strange experience that morning, coming downstairs at six A.M. and finding the imperious Mrs. Sutton hard at work in the kitchen. An unusual sight—Sarah in her flannel blouse and ranch jeans, dicing onions at the kitchen counter. No doubt she did this all the time back in Pierre.

Still, it didn't quite match my original impression of a take-charge lady lawyer. Guess I thought she dined out every night with bigshots like Freddie Fairmont.

While Sarah accepted the well-wishers' condolences, I made the rounds of the dining room, smiling and shaking hands and aiming visitors at the food. Then I caught Becky's four-year-old twins, Luke and Laura, smuggling roast beef cold cuts to a very excited Border collie.

"Hey, now," I murmured, genuflecting at the kids' side. "That's for the guests."

"Nobody fed Ralph this morning," Luke complained.

"He's hungry," Laura chimed in.

Two pleading canine eyes peered up at me. There was a brief burst of tail-wagging, followed by a heartbreaking diminuendo.

"We'll feed him," I said, taking custody of the purloined meat. "Where does Mommy keep the dog food?"

The twins pointed out the proper shelf. I grabbed a can of Alpo, let it spin beneath the automatic opener, then spooned the contents into Ralph's plastic dish.

While Ralph feasted, Becky's kids tried to get better acquainted.

"Mommy said you're an Indian," Laura observed.

"That's right." Kneeling beside the counter, I gave Ralph's furry spine an affectionate rub.

"Are you a Ute?" Luke asked, slightly awed.

"No, but my uncle Matt is." Cheery Angie smile. "He's a *Nuche* of the Taviwach clan. He owns a small horse ranch in Heber City, Utah."

Luke's small mouth tasted the word. "Noo-chay."

Eyes wide with wonder, Laura asked, "Are you a princess?"

"You bet! Daughter of the Sun House of the *Nokaig*—the Bear clan. Genuine Anishinabe royalty."

Finishing lunch, Ralph began slurping at the water dish. An excited Laura told me he was supposed to take a pill. I found the plastic bottle of heartworm pills on the cabinet's bottom shelf, shook one out, and, sitting on the floor, engaged in a brief tussle with the collie.

Keep the pill well hidden in your fist. Move the fist in front of his snout as if you're hiding a treat from him. When the canine jaws part, pop it in. Then, before he can spit it out, tilt his nose skyward and gently run your palm down his throat.

Hearing him swallow, I let him go. Then the twins galloped off to the rumpus room with a tongue-lolling Ralph right behind. Standing up, I smoothed my dress, then grimaced at the sight of all those Border collie hairs. Made a mental note to ask Becky for a lint brush.

Just then Karen walked into the kitchen toting a pair of empty serving trays. She gave me an icily polite nod. I was an adult and an employee of the rich city lawyer lady's and therefore not to be trusted.

Hoping to break the ice, I remarked, "Aunt Becky's got you playing waitress, eh?"

Karen opened the refrigerator door. "You might say that."

Try again, Angie. "How's the food holding out?"

"Goin' fast." She did a bit of rummaging. "Looks like we're gonna need those deviled eggs."

I closed the cabinet door. "You did a good job on those oatmeal cookies."

For the first time, Karen faced me. "Thank you."

"Did your mother teach you?"

She let out a derisive snort.

"Becky?"

Blond tresses shook briskly. "Nana." Gingerly she set the tray of deviled eggs on the counter. A fluid motion of her knee snapped the refrigerator door shut. "She had this favorite saying. 'Kissin' don't last—cookin' do!' Said she'd turned all three of her girls into competent cooks, and I sure wasn't goin' to be the exception."

At least I had her talking. That was definitely a promising start. Quickly my gaze circled the kitchen, seeking another topic of conversation. And found one.

Sitting beside the toaster was an antique ceramic rolling pin, its white cylinder littered with upraised blue designs. It lay in a varnished cedar cradle beside the bread box.

"Was this your grandmother's?" I asked, standing beside the counter.

Karen gave it a quick look. "Uh-huh." And reached for a pile of paper napkins.

"It's a Meissen, isn't it?"

Instant teenage double take. "How'd you know that?"

"My aunt Della collects these things," I replied, running my fingertips along the bumpy ceramic cylinder. "She owns over a hundred antique rolling pins. Everything from hand-carved pioneer rolling pins to 1950 Munisings."

"Munisings?" Uncomprehending blink.

"A company in Michigan's upper peninsula. Before they went under, they specialized in white maple kitchenware." Hefting Madge's showpiece, I grunted. "Mmmmm—heavy!"

"It's solid all the way through." Piling the napkins on her tray, Karen flashed me a curious look. "Do you know how much it's worth?"

"A genuine Meissen? One or two hundred, I guess." I set it

back in its cradle. "If it's from Germany, you ought to get it appraised."

Karen gave me a pensive look. "Nana told me it came from Gothic."

"Gothic?" Echo of mild surprise. "You mean that ghost town up north?"

"It wasn't always a ghost town, Angie." For the first time since I'd met her, Karen Rooley smiled. A very nice smile, warm and vivacious, highly reminiscent of her mother's. "A lot of folks lived up there a century ago."

"One of them owned a kiln?"

Perky nod. "Farm family. They were . . . what do you call 'em? Those folks who ride around in buggies."

"Amish?"

"I think so." Her forehead crinkled as she tried to remember. "Sure wish I'd listened better when Nana told that story. Her daddy left her that rollin' pin. Nana said it's been in this kitchen for as long as she can remember."

Just then, Merry's impatient voice drifted in from the dining room. "Karen, where are those hors d'oeuvres?"

The girl's smile turned apologetic. "Lord, I'd better get out there. I'll tell Becky what you said about Nana's rollin' pin."

"Just don't let it go at a yard sale," I advised.

"I won't." She breezed out of the kitchen. "Talk to you later, Angie."

Casting a glance at Madge's prize antique, I remembered what Aunt Della had told me about Meissen ceramics. That pattern had been very popular with Amish families in the latter half of the nineteenth century. Had Madge's trophy come from a local farm kiln, it might be worth a whole lot more than two hundred dollars.

Standing in the doorway, I watched Karen tote her heavily laden platter to the buffet table. Her mother stood in the middle of the room, chatting with two men. Sarah's gaze followed the girl as she strode past. Womanly lips compressed in mild anxiety.

I found myself making little coaxing motions with my hands. Go on, Sarah. Say something. It's only your daughter. She's not going to bite.

The moment passed. Oblivious to her mother's indecision, Karen left with Merry. An odd expression filled Sarah's face, a curious blend of regret and frustration.

Then she gave her full attention to one of the men. A tall mountaineer in his early forties with wiry chestnut hair parted in the center. Twin curls arched toward his wrinkled brow. He had a square, boyish face, large ears pressed flat, sparse eyebrows, and a lantern jaw. That prominent De Gaulle nose made his close-set dark brown eyes seem smaller than they were. A bristly outlaw mustache perched above his broad smile. It was the kind of smile you see on the very best salesmen, the ones who greet you like a long-lost relative the minute you turn up on the used car lot.

Judging from his outfit, he was doing very well at his chosen trade. He wore a white broadcloth western shirt with a black string tie, a suede-look yoke blazer in heather gray, and dark gray dress slacks with a crease sharp enough to cut birch bark. One look at his thick-heeled boots, and I cut an inch off his height. Those polished Dan Post cowboy boots were responsible for boosting him up to six feet one.

Just then Troy came through the front door. He stamped twice on the mat, stooped, and unlaced his snowboots. He spent a few minutes talking to Merry and Karen. All at once he spotted Sarah's companion, and his country-boy smile vanished.

Emerald eyes ablaze, Troy closed in on the guest. "What are you doing here, you son of a bitch!"

"Hello, Troy." The salesman's smile wilted a bit. He stood his ground, however, as masterful as the maître d' in a four-star restaurant. "Just paying my respects, that's all."

"You've got your nerve showin' up around here!" Troy grabbed the man's lapel. "You thievin' son of a bitch!"

All eyes zeroed in. Troy looked ready to uncork a hard overhand right. The man struggled but couldn't quite free himself of that youthful grip.

"Troy!" Sarah grabbed her brother's wrist. "For goodness' sake, Matt's our *guest!*"

"What the hell is he doin' here, sis!?"

"It's all right, Sally." Although startled by the sudden assault, Matt managed to keep his composure. "Son . . . believe me, I—I can understand what you're going through."

"I ain't your damned son!" Troy shouted.

At last Sarah pried her brother's fingers loose. Matt took a shaky step backward, tugging sharply at both lapels. His smile alternately dimmed and brightened.

Troy's mouth turned ugly. "I asked you a damned question, Stockdale!"

"Like I told you, Troy. Paying my respects." For a man so recently involved in a violent assault, he made a surprisingly easy transition to a tone of reverence. "Madge was always more than just a client to me. I thought the world of your mother. We all did." Dignity stiffened his spine. "Maybe I'd better go, Sally."

"You'll do nothing of the kind, Matt." The return of Take-Charge Sutton. She swiveled to face her brother. "And *you*, young man, you're going to apologize!"

"Yeah, I'll apologize!" Troy's forefinger stabbed at the gentleman's nose. "I'll apologize when that flatland son of a bitch gives back the money he stole from Momma!"

"Will you *please* calm down?" Sarah urged, blocking her brother's path. "This is neither the time nor the place for—"

Stockdale made a soothing gesture. "Troy, I know what you're thinking. A lot of ranchers feel the same way. You've just got to have some faith, boy. Things will work out. You'll see." Seemed to me Mr. Stockdale was playing to the crowd. "I'm good for it. Everyone in Gunnison County knows that."

"Oh, I'll have faith, Mr. Stockdale sir." Troy's teeth clenched. "I'll have some faith when I see Momma's twelve thousand dollars laid out there on the table. Same way it was when you put it in that fancy attaché case o' yours."

Striking a pose of wounded dignity, Stockdale turned again to Sarah. "I'd better go." He gave her hand a tender squeeze. "Sorry about your mother, Sally."

Matt paused at the entryway—well beyond Troy's immediate reach, I might add—and gave him a stern look. "This time I'm letting it go, boy. But the next time you call me names, you're going to answer for it. You hear me?"

Lunging at him, Troy shouted, "You want to settle this right now, Stockdale?" His fists doubled. "I'm ready!"

*"Troy!"* Gripping his shoulders, Sarah held him back.

I watched Stockdale lift his cream-colored Stetson from the coatrack. His tanned hand shook noticeably. I think he realized what a narrow escape he'd had. The front door slammed loudly in his wake.

Sarah relinquished her grip. "Are you ready to simmer down?"

"I guess." Anger had turned Troy's face the color of a Colorado sunset. "Sally, I can't believe you let that man in our house!"

"He only stopped by to offer condolences. You had no call to take a swing at him."

Outraged shout. "He stole Momma's money!"

"Troy . . . it's not as cut and dried as that."

"Isn't it?" he challenged.

"What do you know about it, Lawyer Lady?" Karen stepped forward. "Were *you* here?"

Sarah flinched suddenly. In a voice edged with steel, she snapped, "Don't . . . you . . . *start!*"

We were about sixty seconds away from an old-fashioned

Rooley brawl when Merry suddenly cut in. Placing a hand on each teen shoulder, she said, "Come on, you two. Let's get some air."

Of course, Karen had to have the last word. "Used to be Rooleys always sided with kin."

Merry swatted the girl's shoulder. "Enough!"

Indeed, it was more than enough for Sarah Sutton. She went straight to the buffet table and busied herself sorting napkins. Deliberately ignored the youngsters' departure. Becky joined her sister. Her gentle hand came to rest on Sarah's forearm.

The door's slam seemed to reverberate like a sharp echo in a vast canyon. I wasn't at all certain I could close the rift between Sarah and her daughter.

But I was going to give it one hell of a try!

# ▼▼▼▼▼▼▼ FIVE ▼▼▼▼▼▼▼

Tuesday morning, January 27, found me wedged between Meredith Rooley and the passenger door of the family's venerable Ford pickup. Brother Troy had the wheel. Behind me, two dozen milk cans noisily jostled each other on the truck's flatbed.

We were hurtling down Cement Mountain, bouncing and sliding on 740's rutted snowpack. The frozen Colorado sky was a startling shade of porcelain blue. Despite the best efforts of the cab's heater, a plume escaped my lips every time I exhaled. As we neared the creek, I caught a glimpse of the West Elks beyond the spruce-covered flank of Point Lookout. Their snowy peaks splintered the cerulean sky.

Once I peered out the side window. *Once!* The sight of the Ford's snow tires spinning a whopping six inches from the ice-rimmed brink hurled my stomach into a somersault. Troy kept right on going, however, pushing the pedal to the metal, absentmindedly whistling a Garth Brooks tune.

Earlier that morning Troy and Merry had introduced me to the fine art of goat milking. Which is a little different from the bovine version. For one thing, when a cow doesn't wish to be milked, she doesn't hook her forelegs over your shoulder and start nibbling your hat.

It took me twenty minutes to get the nanny to mount the milking stand, then another forty minutes of hectic nipple squeezing before I extracted the first jolt of warm milk.

Another entry for your résumé, princess. Accounts receivable clerk, prison inmate, reluctant waitress, carnival daredevil, apprentice farmer, legal secretary, and now . . . *goat milker.*

Angela Biwaban, truly a woman for all seasons!

At the breakfast table I tossed my bright idea at Sarah. Since we were staying at the ranch for a week or so, I pointed out, it might be a good idea if we rented a laptop computer and a pocket modem. That way we could stay in touch with the home office in Pierre.

Of course, I had another use in mind for that computer, but I couldn't very well tell Sarah. She might disapprove of my using the computer to concoct false identification.

La Sutton gave me a whole lot of static. In the end, though, she came around, especially when I pointed out that we could rent by the week. So she told me to accompany Troy and Merry on their daily milk run and drew up a list of office supplies to be purchased down in Gunnison.

Gradually the spruce gave way to fir and aspen. On our left, Roaring Judy Creek, swollen with glacial meltwater, foamed and gushed and splashed against its ice-rimmed banks, adding bulk to the fearsome icicles. The cascade's roar drowned out the Ford's grinding engine.

"You sure we don't need to call the clinic?" Troy frowned, downshifting with his right hand.

Merry shook her head. Like me, she was wearing a heavy stadium jacket and a woolen cap. "No, Capitan's okay. That rash on his belly—it's an allergy, that's all. Change his feed and he'll be all right."

"You're the family vet."

Mild sadness flavored Merry's smile. "I wish!"

The girl's expertise impressed me. "Are you studying to be a veterinarian, Merry?"

Self-conscious shrug. "Been taking a few courses at Western State. Nothing serious."

Troy grinned. "Don't let her shit you, Angie. She knows as much as any D.V.M. on the Western Slope." He downshifted once again, and the truck's plunge visibly slowed. "She used to drive Momma and Aunt Alice crazy, bringin' all those sick animals home. Pretty near every ailin' horse in this end of the county's had his nose in a Rooley feed bag."

Grimacing in embarrassment, Merry thumped her brother's ribs. Letting out a sharp laugh, Troy swerved the Ford's front end to the left—away from the brink.

"Do you like it?" I asked, wondering if my heartbeat would ever slow down.

"More than anything else, Angie."

"Then why aren't you majoring in veterinary medicine?"

Dispirited sigh. "Costs money to go to school full-time. And money's about as scarce as ripe pineapples on the RJ Bar."

Troy's mouth tightened. "Guess we can thank Mr. Stockdale for that."

Seeing an opportunity to learn more about Madge's finances, I echoed, "Stockdale?"

"He was at the house yesterday, Angie." Animosity deepened Merry's soft voice. "Friend of Momma's."

"Some friend!" Troy's knuckles whitened as he gripped the wheel. "That son of a bitch took Momma for twelve thousand dollars!"

Inquisitive Angie. "How?"

"He sold her this mortgage that was no damned good!" Troy added explosively. "And she ain't the only one he cheated. There's a whole lot of ranchers down in the valley who—"

"Troy!" Merry interrupted, slapping his forearm. "If you

don't keep your eyes on that road, we're going to fly right off this here mountain!" Anxious glance. "Let me tell it, okay?"

Troy's shoulders shrugged. "Be my guest."

"Great-granddaddy commenced to raising goats a long time back," she began. "They don't eat nearly as much as sheep, and the high altitude doesn't seem to bother them."

"The Swiss discovered that long ago."

Merry's grin exceeded mine. "Used to be, a family could make a little money at it. Especially during the fifties. See, the Army got caught short when the Korean War broke out. They needed wool for winter uniforms, and by that time most of America's wool was coming from imports. In 1954, Congress set up a little subsidy program for American goat ranchers. The U.S. Department of Agriculture pays a $2.41 subsidy for every dollar of wool sold. 'Course, we Rooleys never got rich at it. But between the subsidy and an occasional wool sale and selling goat milk to the creamery down in Gunnison, we managed to get by."

"What do they do with the milk?" I asked.

"Lot of things," she replied. "Some they sell to this old boy up in Aspen. He turns it into yogurt. It's real popular with the skiers—you know, low fat and everything. Mostly they pasteurize it and sell it to folks who are allergic to cow's milk."

Troy let out a knowledgeable chuckle. " 'Course, Momma 'n' Becky have done some pasteurizin' of their own."

Scowling at her brother, Merry snapped, "You hush!"

"Come on, sis. That still's practically a historical landmark here in Gunnison County."

"Don't you go giving Angie the wrong idea, Troy." She flashed me a flustered smile. "These days we're out of the white mule business."

"All the way out?" her brother teased.

The reference threw me for a second. Then I remembered that the Rooleys hailed from Tennessee. "Genuine mountain dew, eh?"

"One hundred and eighty proof," Troy said, steering us around a sharp mountain bend. "Becky brews up a batch once a year. Just to keep her hand in, I reckon. But we don't have to sell it anymore like in the old days."

"Time was when Great-Granddaddy's home brew was the only thing bringing cash money to the ranch," Merry commented.

"Are you still getting that USDA subsidy?" I asked.

"Right now, yeah, but it ain't nearly enough. Congress has been cutting back gradually," she explained. "Wool prices are still in the cellar. We need another cash crop—and fast! That's why Momma come up with her idea."

"What idea?"

Merry nodded. " 'Way Momma figured it, it boiled down to three choices. One, sell the ranch and go live in town—"

"Become *flatlanders!*" A choice not at all popular with Troy.

"Two, fire up the still and go whole hog into the white mule business." She aimed her thumb at her brother. "I don't know about this wild man, but I don't relish spendin' the rest of my life totin' a twelve-gauge and blastin' BATF asses out of the chokecherry patch."

Masculine grin. "You can tell she's the peaceable Rooley!"

"Three . . ." Merry added, "Momma figured maybe we could cash in on some of those city folks coming into the valley."

"City folks," I repeated.

Graceful feminine nod. "Skiers, Angie, mostly from Denver. They swarm all over Crested Butte every weekend. There's new ski condos going in every summer. And there wasn't even a *snack bar* up on Mount Crested Butte when I was born!" Look of mild amazement. "First those city folks started coming to ski. Next thing you know, they're here in the warm weather too, complete with backpacks and mountain bikes. So Momma took a good look at our place and all those old mining trails leading up East Cement. Said maybe we ought to build ourselves a stable. Board city folks' horses. Offer trail rides to tourists. Lead overnight trips up into the high country." Her expression turned somber. "Trouble was, we needed money to build. Momma went to the bank, and they turned her down. Poor credit risk, they said."

"Did either of you apply?" I asked.

Merry shook her head. "No sense in that. We didn't have much in the way of collateral. The ranch belongs to Momma." Glum frown. "Leastways, it used to!"

I noticed the T intersection with Colorado 135 a mile downslope. "What about Becky?"

"Same problem as Momma," she added.

Troy sent the pickup bouncing down the centerline. "Bigassed bankers in Gucci shoes don't fall all over themselves offerin' money to the unruly Rooleys."

"How did your mother get the money to build the stable?" I asked.

"Mr. Stockdale got it for her. He owns this company—Gunnison Guaranty Corp. It's a finance outfit." Indignation flared in Merry's eyes. "Momma didn't have much luck with those damned bankers. Her bein' an ex-convict really worked against her. Oh, they offered her a loan, all right! Payable in ten years at twenty percent interest! No way we could handle that. Momma was feelin' pretty low. Then she saw Mr. Stockdale's ad on the cable TV. 'Get your money now. It's as easy as 1-2-3.' Mr. Stockdale called it the Quick Start program."

"Quick Start?" I echoed.

Merry nodded. "Special program for ranchers needin' help with construction loans. Mr. Stockdale came out to the house and explained it. See, you pay Gunnison Guaranty some cash money up front, then Mr. Stockdale goes to the bank and gets you a special kind of loan." Turned to her brother. "What'd he call it, Troy?"

He scowled, trying to remember. "A-a *buy*-something . . ."

"*Buydown?*" I offered.

Masculine features brightened. "Yeah! That's it, Angie. A buydown. Said if we could come up with a little cash, he'd get us a construction loan from the Tomichi State Bank."

Nod of understanding. I'd run into buydown deals before. Six years ago, as a student intern at Lodgepole Realty up in Bozeman, Montana, I'd worked nights and weekends for old Ben Scoggins while pursuing my master's at Montana State University.

Usually, in a buydown deal, you give the money directly to the lender. In return, the lender significantly reduces the interest for the first few years of the loan.

Mr. Stockdale appeared to have thought up a new angle on the deal. He approached the bank on behalf of the ranchers. No doubt he deducted his commission from the cash they contributed to Gunnison Guaranty.

"The bank offered to cut your interest rate," I commented. "So much the first year, so much the second year, and so on."

"That's right," Merry replied. "The bank loaned Momma $250,000 to build the stable. Mr. Stockdale got us an interest rate of twelve percent. But that didn't kick in until the fourth year. For the first three years, all we had to pay was nine percent."

Troy scowled. "Like the TV lady said, 'It's as easy as 1-2-3!' "

Seeing their troubled expressions, I added, "But . . . ?"

Defeated sigh from Merry. "Tomichi went under, Angie. It happened back in October. Fifteen months after we finished the stable. Momma got a letter in the mail from Grand Junction."

"Some damned bank we never even heard of!" Troy muttered.

"United Mountain Bancorp," his sister added. "They said they'd purchased all of Tomichi's assets, and our loan was one of them. They invited us in to renegotiate."

I took a deep breath. "At a higher rate of interest, I take it."

"*Sixteen* percent!" Merry's mouth tensed angrily. "There's no way we could afford monthly payments that high. So me, Momma, Becky, and Troy—we all went in to see Mr. Stockdale. He was real sympathetic. He even offered to go to Grand Junction in person. But it was no damned good. His hands were tied, he said. United Mountain held the loan, and we were obliged to renegotiate."

"Did you talk this over with Sarah?" I asked.

"Before Momma even signed the loan, we mailed a copy to Sally up in Pierre. She read it over, talked to Mr. Stockdale over the phone, made a few changes in it, and told Momma it was okay to sign." Misery flooded the girl's features. "Poor Sally! She was just sick over the whole thing. She blames *herself* for lettin' Momma sign." Forlorn glance. "Who ever expected Tomichi to fail? That bank's been in Gunnison since before Momma was born."

"What was Sarah's advice?"

"She said we didn't have much choice. We could renegotiate at the higher rate of interest. Or we could find another lender and borrow the money to pay off the Tomichi loan. Bank's been calling every couple of weeks. Momma's been stallin' them till we can figure out what to do."

"I'm with Pete Ritter," Troy declared. "He says Matt Stockdale stole our cash money same as if he'd rustled a dozen head. He promised us low interest for three years if we paid our money. So we paid our money, and now the deal's off? Well, fine! Now that son of a bitch can give us Momma's twelve thousand back!"

Merry shot her brother a warning look. "Troy . . ."

"Ol' Pete don't hold with them big money boys, and neither do I!" Fierce glance at his sister. "That twelve grand was all the money Momma had in this world. Stockdale didn't deliver, and now he gets to hold on to it?" His mouth twisted in fury. "Next time I see that slick-talkin' bastard, so help me, I'm gonna—"

"You're not going to do *anything*, Troy Seth Rooley!" Merry interrupted, her voice like steel. "Unless you want to end up down there in Canon City, grinding out license plates!"

"In the old days, they'd have been shakin' out a loop for that thievin' son of a bitch!"

"Well, these ain't the old days, brother of mine. And you'd better toss a loop around that temper. You ain't in high school anymore. You're getting too damned old to be taking a poke at people." Tone of warning. "Sheriff Quinn's already busted one Rooley. He wouldn't mind at all making it *two.*"

Fussbudget face. During our telephone chat, Madge had made a fleeting reference to her "inheritance." Yet, according to Troy, that twelve grand was the only money she had.

Backtrack a bit, princess.

"Troy, who's this Pete Ritter you mentioned?"

"Rancher. Friend of Momma's. Owns the Rockin' R over by Willow Creek," he explained, glancing at me. "Another one o' the folks who got stung by that Quick Start program. The Crenshaws, the Pucketts—there's a whole bunch of us, Angie."

"What happens now that your mother is no longer alive?"

Merry's lips puckered thoughtfully. " 'Way Sally explained it, the ranch's title becomes part of Momma's estate. Because of that loan, she says United Mountain now has a claim against the estate."

"Is there a will?"

"Oh, sure!" Fond smile. "Week after she got her law degree, Sally hauled us all down to Mr. Spitzer's office and had him draw up a will for Momma. We all witnessed it."

Troy chuckled. "That sure was a new experience for Mr. Spitzer—gettin' talked down to by Sally Anne Rooley!"

"Who inherits the RJ Bar?" I asked.

"We all do," he replied. "Share and share alike. That's how Momma wanted it. Sally had him write it up just that way."

"Was anything else mentioned in the will?"

Curious blink from Merry. "Like what?"

"Stocks, bonds, annuities . . . any kind of inheritance from your grandfather."

Troy's forehead creased in confusion. "What the hell's an *annuity?*"

"An investment contract with an insurance company that eventually provides you with an income," I explained. Angie the business major.

His sister looked at me askance. "Momma never had a steady job. Except for when she was in the pen. And she got paid only fifteen cents an hour for doin' laundry."

Oboy! Does that sound familiar, I thought.

"And all Grandpa ever left her was the ranch, the herd, and a wily old mule named Big Red." Troy slowed the pickup as we approached the city limits. "Momma had money after a score, sure! But she never spent it on stocks and bonds."

"Certain about that?"

"Angie, other than the RJ Bar, the only thing my momma had was a ten-thousand-dollar insurance policy she got off of Becky's American Express card," Merry added. "Good thing too, 'cause that's how we buried her."

My frown deepened. None of this dovetailed with what I'd learned from my telephone conversation with Madge. The woman had been talking about buying a cabin near Alamosa. A hundred-thousand-dollar cabin. She'd talked confidently of her supposed *inheritance.*

Now Madge's children were telling me that there was no inheritance.

Or at least none they were aware of.

Key question, princess—was there an inheritance? And, if so, what had happened to it?

Or had Madge merely been bragging over the phone?

I quickly discarded the second option. Madge Rooley was a hardheaded woman who'd been in and out of jail. She'd raised her brood on a household budget consisting mainly of milk and wool money, USDA subsidies, AFDC benefits, hardscrabble dollars, and an occasional armed robbery bonanza.

Would such a woman have gambled her last twelve thousand on a Quick Start construction loan?

I didn't think so.

On the other hand, if Madge did have a bundle salted away, she might be willing to part with twelve grand in cash to build that new stable for the RJ Bar.

Time for some research, Angela . . .

Ten minutes later, Troy and Merry dropped me off at the corner of Georgia Avenue and North Main Street. We agreed to meet that afternoon at Mike's Mobil. An unpleasant task still awaited the Rooleys. Namely, the disposal of their mother's wrecked pickup truck.

Gracefully aging storefronts greeted me as I sauntered down North Main. Frosted plate glass windows, cement scrollwork, and neatly shoveled sidewalks. A handful of cars and trucks had their front grilles pressed against the snow piles at curbside. A colorful poster invited me to the Winter Carnival in Jorgensen Park.

Three doors down, I turned left and entered a well-stocked computer store called Mainframes Plus. Had a pleasant conversation with the helpful and personable Chicano gentleman who owned the store. Yes, indeed, he had the Wizard 3000 subnotebook in stock, along with a Panasonic pocket modem. And, yes, he was willing to negotiate with the lovely, raven-haired representative of the distinguished South Dakota law firm, Hipple, Tanner, Page, and Sutton.

After reading the rental agreement, I thought of a way to expedite payment, asked to use Mr. Echevarria's phone, and put through a call to the ranch. Sarah was most agreeable, and I gave her the store's fax number. Then she asked to speak to the owner.

Ten minutes later, Ramon Echevarria and I heard the

printer whine and then watched as a Bank of South Dakota money order creeped out of the fax slot. I recognized the elegant signature of Clark Darius Hipple.

His smile doubling in diameter, Ramon asked if there was anything else he could do for me.

"You bet!" Showing a mischievous smile, I snapped open my shoulder bag. "As a matter of fact, I'm in the market for some peripherals. You see, my cousins have birthdays coming up. Troy and Merry. They were both born in February. They're really into computers."

"*Claro!* What did you have in mind, señorita?"

So I told him. One Mustek hand-held color scanner with 800 dpi resolution. One Focus 300-watt DC/AC power converter. One Caviar backup hard drive. One Hamilton Beach electric laminator kit. Four boxes of diskettes. Plus the latest generation software for Windows, Quicken, and OS.2.

Expensive? Sure! But I could afford it. I still had quite a few bucks squirreled away back home in the Northland. Leftover war funds from my U.P. *nandobani* on behalf of Mary Beth Tolliver. I pulled out one of my many SunWest credit cards, charged it to my Judy Lear account, and arranged to have Sarah's Wizard subnotebook delivered to the Rooley ranch.

By the way, my fantasy selves—Joanne Larue, Judy Lear, and Jane Larkin—are all excellent credit risks. Indeed, American Express is still after Joanne to apply for a gold card.

With my peripherals tucked away in a plastic shopping bag, I wished Ramon a pleasant day, exited the store, and headed back to Georgia Avenue. I hung a right at the corner, walked a block, took another right onto North Wisconsin, and then sauntered up the front walk of the Ann Zugelder Public Library.

The librarian, Mrs. Gainey, made me welcome. She was an amiable woman in her middle thirties. Pert nose, aviator glasses, stylishly cropped chestnut hair, and flawlessly varnished fingernails. The slim woolen skirt fit snugly around her meaty hips. When I asked if the library had a CD-ROM version of the Reader's Periodical Guide, she flashed a proud smile and pointed out the array of computer stations at the resource desk.

Seating myself, I set the heading for Newspapers and tapped out R-o-o-l-e-y. A surprisingly large listing of news stories appeared onscreen. I zapped the information to the printer, plucked a dollar from my wallet, paid Mrs. Gainey for the copy, and asked to use the microfilm reader.

While Mrs. Gainey set up the tape for me, I studied the notices on the library's bulletin board. Found out all about the Jolly Bunch Pinochle Club's annual luncheon and gift exchange. And wondered if the bunch had ever invited Madge.

Judging from the number of news stories starring Sarah's mother . . . probably not!

The local newspaper was called the *Gunnison Country Times*, and they had devoted a considerable amount of ink to the doings of the Rooley family over the years. Seated at the desk, I watched the highlights of Madge Rooley's criminal career pass before my eyes.

## LOCAL WOMAN SENTENCED TO 90 DAYS

District Court Judge William G. Boyle sentenced a Crested Butte woman to three months in the county jail for forging her name on stolen checks.

Madge Rooley, 19, was found guilty in the theft of ten blank checks from the office of her employer, Apex Office Supplies, in Crested Butte.

Town Marshal Chester B. Hurtig arrested Miss Rooley in September after the store management reported the checks missing.

## ROOLEY GUILTY IN UTAH HOLDUP

*OGDEN, UTAH* (AP)—Madge Rooley was sentenced to three years at the state women's prison in Draper for her part in last April's robbery at Newgate Mall.

Ms. Rooley, 23, formerly of Crested Butte, and Cecil Brownlow, 34, of Belgrade, Mont., were both found guilty of multiple robbery charges in Superior Court last week.

Rooley and Brownlow robbed the Fatted Calf Restaurant of $12,500 in a daring daylight robbery.

## MADGE ROOLEY JAILED IN NEW MEXICO

*PORTALES, N.M.* (AP)—A former Colorado woman was sentenced to five years at the state women's prison in Grants yesterday.

Madge Rooley, 27, most recently employed as a truck-stop waitress, drew the five-year prison term for her part in the holdup of the Fred Meyer store last July.

According to the county sheriff's office, Ms. Rooley obtained employment at the store three weeks before the robbery. She reportedly persuaded assistant manager Mordecai LaGrange to let her remain in the office during the delivery of the daily cash shipment.

According to Sheriff Gene Zinnecker, Ms. Rooley "played that ol' boy like a violin. She told Mordecai he had a real nice butt and she liked to watch her men take their pants off. So he did this real slow strip-tease with his back to Madge. And when he turned around, she had a .357 Magnum pointed at him. Then she called her buddies on the phone and told 'em to come on up."

Ms. Rooley and her companions fled the store with

$30,000 in cash, which the store management had ordered to cover the Fourth of July sale.

## THREE SLAIN IN DAKOTA SHOOTOUT

*DEADWOOD, S.D.* (AP)—Three men were killed in a gun battle with local police when they allegedly attempted to rob the Lucky Horseshoe Casino yesterday.

Killed by police gunfire were Homer Stirewalt, 34, of Eutaw Springs, Ark., Jeffery Blanchard, 20, of Hill City, S.D., and Clarence "Rimfire" Davis, 35, of Hulett, Wyo.

According to the FBI, there were many outstanding federal and state warrants on Stirewalt and Davis.

Stirewalt was wanted in Arkansas for the murders of two deputies and a state trooper.

Surviving the shootout was Madge Rooley, 30, of Durango, Colo. Following the battle, she was arrested and charged with armed robbery.

Trooper Michael Ralston estimated that "at least 400 shots were fired" during the confrontation.

There was much, much more. Nineteen years ago, the newspapers had had a field day with the saga of the "Border Bandit Queen."

I wondered if Madge's family had visited her during the Springfield years. Must have been a long drive for Aunt Alice. She would have brought Sarah and Becky, of course. How had they reacted, I mused, seeing their mother penned up in that place?

Merry and Troy probably didn't even remember. They were both too young.

Newspaper tales of the unruly Rooleys reached back nearly fifty years. I found this 1949 gem about Madge's father.

## CB MAN NABBED IN BANK ROBBERY

*PONCHA SPRINGS, COLO.* (AP)—Deputies arrested a Crested Butte man in connection with the holdup last week of the Cattleman's Bank.

Thomas J. Rooley, 34, was charged with bank robbery and held on $40,000 bond.

A lone robber walked into the bank last Tuesday at 9 A.M., leveled a Browning automatic rifle (B.A.R.), and demanded that tellers fill his gym bag. He fled with $11,000 in cash and negotiable bonds.

And then there was this more recent news story!

## COUNTY GIRL SENTENCED IN
## LIQUOR HIJACK

Rebecca A. Rooley, 18, was sentenced to three years at the Colorado Women's Correctional Institution in Canon City yesterday for hijacking a liquor shipment.

Miss Rooley, who lives at the family ranch on Roaring Judy Creek, was escorted from the courthouse by Sheriff Chester B. Hurtig and remanded to the custody of the Colorado State Patrol.

Two weeks ago, Superior Court found Rooley guilty of stealing a delivery truck loaded with 400 cases of Johnnie Walker whiskey. The missing truck and shipment were later found hidden on East Cement Mountain.

Switching off the microfilm reader, I leaned back in my chair and sighed. *Becky!* I made a pronounced fussbudget face. Why, I could hardly believe it. If anything, she was even more levelheaded than Sarah.

I returned the tape to the front desk and thanked Mrs.

Gainey for her help. My scowl persisted as I left the library. I'd gone there looking for names from Madge Rooley's past. People I could question concerning a possible motive. But instead of coming up with a lead, I'd been overwhelmed by the sheer weight of information.

So many names! Madge must have been chummy with half the armed robbers in the West. And she'd developed a consistent M.O. over the years. No ladylike embezzlement schemes for our Madge. Just rush in with the boys and grab the cash.

One name had come up twice, however. Chester B. Hurtig, the one-time town marshal turned county sheriff. He'd arrested both Becky and her mother. If Hurtig still lived in Crested Butte, he might be worth talking to.

As I trotted down the library steps, I glanced idly at the snow-covered lawn, then stopped short. A curious symbol had been drawn in the snow. A huge semicircle with three feathers dangling from the ring.

An arch smile erased my thoughtful scowl.

Just then, I heard a muffled sound. *Churrr-churrr.* The soft, low-pitched warble of the mountain bluebird. Hands on my hips, I said, "Don't bother, Chief. I know it's you."

Footsteps broke through crusted snow. I spotted my grandfather at the building's corner. White-haired Anishinabe senior citizen in his dark green mountain parka and a khaki Stetson. He's a heavyset man in his middle seventies, a good four inches taller than me, with small, flat ears and deepset obsidian eyes bracketed by noticeable crow's-feet. He also bears a striking resemblance to old Chief Rain-in-the-Face, which is why I gave him that irreverent nickname.

"I thought I had that one down pat," he said.

"Not quite," I replied. "The bluebird's a member of the thrush family. They're not so loud."

"I forgot you spent a summer up in the North Cascades."

I gave him a welcoming bear hug. "So how long have you been in Gunnison?"

"Got in yesterday afternoon. I'm staying at the Water Wheel Inn." He tilted his head westward. "Couple of miles outside of town."

"How'd you find me?"

"Dumb luck, Angie," he replied, holding me at arm's length. "I was on my way to breakfast when I saw you hurrying down the street." His obsidian eyes twinkled. "Thought I'd cook up a little surprise for you when you came out. How do you like it?"

I glanced at the snow drawing. "Our people's symbol for *chief*? Mmmm—it has a certain class." Twinge of curiosity. "How did you draw it?"

By way of reply, Chief pointed out a long-handled shovel standing upright in the piled snow at the walkway's edge. A snow stripe ran vertically down the wood.

Shaking his head, he commented, "You've got to start being a little more observant, missy."

"I'm just bleary-eyed from staring at a viewscreen all morning."

"Excuses, excuses."

"Been up to the ranch yet?"

He shook his head. "Not yet, Angie. Not until I get myself a good pair of bearpaw snowshoes."

"Pick up a pair for me too, okay? Those drifts are pretty deep."

"Ain't no surprise. Folks in town say Gunnison's had close to three hundred inches of snowfall this winter." My grandfather flanked me as we headed down the street. "Learn anything in the library?"

"Plenty!" I replied, and, as we walked to the gas station, I discussed Madge's outlaw career in detail.

Mike's Mobil sat at the corner of Teller Street and East Tomichi Avenue, about seven blocks from the library. It was a stylish, pitched-roof beige sandstone service station of a style quite popular during the Age of Elvis. I almost expected to see carhops on roller skates offering to check the oil. Mammoth glass windows offered a glimpse of the station's busy convenience store. The other half of the building was devoted to three well-equipped repair bays, each of them sporting a hydraulic lift.

". . . leaving us with no shortage of motives, Chief," I concluded as we crossed Teller Street.

"Why do you think it's one of Madge's old buddy boys?" he asked.

"The blue Mazda. Whoever clouted it off the stadium lot knew what he was doing. He's no novice to auto theft." Entering the lot, I watched the attendant scurry around the full serve island, hitching and unhitching nozzles. "If he is a career criminal, then he probably worked with Madge in the old days. Maybe he's got some kind of grudge against her."

"Such as?"

"I don't know." Puzzled shrug. "It could be anything. Maybe he holds Madge responsible for a botched job. Maybe he thinks she stiffed him on the take."

"Maybe." My grandfather lifted the brim of his Stetson. "There's just one question, Angie. Where does the daughter come into it?"

I shot him a quizzical look. "Which daughter?"

"Sarah. One of those guys called your hotel, looking for Sarah. How come?"

Mammoth fussbudget face. I couldn't even begin to answer that one. And, looking into the central repair bay, I thought, Maybe I don't have to!

Nudging my grandfather, I murmured, "Look."

Parked in the bay was a badly battered 1979 Ford Ranger, dull red with heavy-duty Goodrich snow tires. The cab looked as if Godzilla had used it for an easy chair. The demolished roof nearly touched the windshield wipers. One flabby tire swerved inward. Numerous deep dents festooned the doors. A noticeable gasoline stench lingered around the wreck.

Soft Angie whistle. That truck had sustained a lot of damage during its six-hundred-foot tumble into the creekbed.

My grandfather switched to our langauge. "Is that her car, *Noozis?*"

My gaze found the bent Colorado vanity plate bolted to the truck's rear gate—*UNRULY.* "It is." Glancing toward the gas island, I watched the manager collect payment. "We can't afford to be seen together, *Nimishoo.* Not for a while yet. So here's what I want you to do . . ."

After giving Chief his instructions, I rounded the corner and took up position beside the compressed-air pump. Leaning against the cinder-block wall, I stayed out of the winter wind and close enough to eavesdrop.

Minutes later I heard the crunching sound of rubber soles on fresh snow. And then a hearty neighborly baritone. "Howdy!"

"Howdy!" my grandfather replied. "That bell just keeps on ringin', don't it? Busy day?"

Sudden guffaw. "Busy week! Peak season for the skiers. Them hot dogs just keep on comin'." His voice betrayed a touch of curiosity. "Ain't seen you around here before."

"Oh, I'm just visitin' my granddaughter up at the college."

I had to smile. Chief's getting much, much better at casual intrigue.

More footsteps, followed by Chief's voice. "That's some wreck, ain't it?"

"You can say that again. Lady spun off the road up in Monarch Pass and got killed. Madge Rooley."

"Sorry to hear it."

"Yeah, we're all gonna miss ol' Madge. Hell on wheels, that gal." Warm tone. "Name's Cutler. Wade Cutler."

"Lester Blue Lake." I guessed that they were shaking hands. "What are you plannin' to do with the wreck?"

"Just holdin' it till Troy shows up. He's supposed to be here any minute now."

"Troy?" Chief's echo was most convincing.

"Madge's son." The pneumatic bell dinged in the background. "You interested in that truck, Lester?"

"Might be. Got me a scrap metal place up in Keota. Always could use a few spare auto parts."

"Well, you'll probably want to talk to Troy, then. Make him an offer. Not much I can do with it. Drive train's shot to shit, and that radius arm looks like somethin' the dog chewed on."

"Do me a favor, Wade." My grandfather's voice diminished as they entered the bay. "Raise that Ford up on the lift and let me have a look at the chassis."

"Sure, Lester."

Suddenly, I heard a metallic *dreeeee-ump*, punctuated by the steady thrumming noise of hydraulic pumps. Then a locking *clank* and a final compressed-air hiss. Inching closer to the corner, I listened for their voices. Background garage sounds reduced their conversation to an unintelligible murmur.

I peered around the corner. Maybe if I could get a bit closer to that open bay door . . .

Casually I walked in front of the garage. Cast a fleeting glance at the farm wife pumping gas at the self serve island, then at the quartet buying munchies at the convenience counter. Satisfied that no one was watching me, I backpedaled my way to the closed bay door, turned my head, and peered through the grimy glass.

The battered red pickup perched on the lift's X-frame. Wade Cutler and my grandfather hunched beneath the bent wheel, chatting and examining the driveshaft. Wade's blackened finger pointed out the double cardan and the slip yoke.

Slowly I inched my way closer to the open door.

And then a cold, brutish hand snagged my parka collar, yanking me fully upright. A merciless baritone caressed my ear.

"What are *you* up to, sugar?"

## SIX

A relentless grip spun me around. My shoulder blades smacked the garage door. I had a dizzying impression of a wide, solid masculine torso tightly packed into a quilted ski jacket. Then a callused and knuckly hand, instantly reminiscent of an orangutan's, rocketed across my field of vision, catching my upraised wrist.

Gravelly voice. "What's it all about, sweetheart?"

He punctuated the question with a brutal lobster pinch. Wrist bones ground together, sending a spurt of agony leaping up my arm. Instant soprano squeal. "Owwwww! Let go!"

"Glad to, sis. Soon as you give me a straight answer." His merciless smile displayed uneven, tobacco-stained teeth. "What were you doin' spyin' on that truck?"

I swallowed hard. He was a granite-faced bruiser of indeterminate age—somewhere between forty and fifty was my best guess—with a shelf of jaw that clearly identified Neanderthal man as his great-grandpa. Leathery skin with a spray of ancient acne scars beneath his high cheekbones. Hard Dutch-chocolate eyes set far apart. His high forehead, bisected by two parallel creases, ended in a scraggly widow's peak. The eyebrows were high, too, resembling a pair of well-groomed caterpillars. Large, flat ears and noticeable hound-dog jowls. His mouth didn't quite match the overall simian appearance, however. He had a poet's sensitive mouth, vaguely reminiscent of the old-time movie actor Cornel Wilde.

My captor topped five feet ten inches in his Tony Lama heels, and I'd say he reached that span in the shoulders as well. Definitely a big boy! Strapping shoulders, wrestler's chest, a loose, tubby midriff, and the kind of thighs you see on Russian weightlifters.

Feeling my hand go numb, I let out a supersonic hiss. Think fast, princess!

"Who's spying?" I parlayed my sudden fear into a reasonable facsimile of indignation. "I—I'm just waiting for the manager."

His eyes remained unreadable. As emotionless as a gila monster. "What for?"

I tilted my head toward the corner. "I need the key. I've got to use the can."

A sliver of tongue ran across his sensitive lips. He couldn't quite make up his mind about me.

"Why didn't you ask the cashier?" he challenged.

"With *that* line?" Faking an exasperated expression, I glanced at the convenience store. Even as we spoke, I was subtly changing my personality. Turning myself into a hard-boiled prison princess. "You kiddin', man? By the time he got around to me, I'd be carryin' a fresh load in the seat of my jeans."

Clutching my upper arm, he rumbled, "C'mere!"

Rounding the corner, we halted in front of the ladies' room. Shooting a suspicious glance at me, he grabbed the dull brass doorknob. Moment of sheer panic! But I relaxed when I heard the bolt rattle loudly.

With a grunt of satisfaction, the bruiser released my arm.

Returning circulation sent a stinging sensation from wrist to elbow. Grimacing, I palpated my sore wrist.

"Satisfied?" I asked.

The bruiser didn't know what to do. Finding the door locked added credence to my impromptu story. His hard-knuckled fist walloped the wood just above the knob.

"Gonna break it down for me?" Sassily I canted my slender hip to one side. Penitentiary Angela.

"Shut up!" Stepping away, he shot me a sudden menacing glare. "You know who owns that truck?"

*"Truck?"* By now I had my role down pat. Perfect imitation of my old prison nemesis, Elena Varo. "Hey, like I could give a shit, you know? I'm just passin' through this jerkwater town." Insolent shrug. *"Ay!* What's it to you, anyway? You the federal can inspector or something?"

Sudden fury glimmered in those dark brown eyes. "Watch it, dolly!"

He ambled down the driveway, his stride pigeon-toed. I waited until he was well out of reach, then gave him one last retort. "Hey, stick around, *pachaco!* I'll let you unwind the toilet paper."

His right hand chopped downward in a gesture of irritation and dismissal. Muttering to himself, he hurried across the vacant street.

I took a mental snapshot of his car. A maroon year-old Chevrolet Cavalier. Packed snow obscured the license plate. I wondered if he'd done that on purpose.

Frowning, I glanced at Madge's damaged Ford. Why should Magilla Gorilla care if I'd been eyeballing the wreck? And why had he been so disturbed by my presence here—disturbed enough to cross-examine me?

I watched the Cavalier scoot up the street. Who was he? I wondered. And why was he so interested in Madge's truck?

Just then, the pneumatic bell chimed twice. Wade Cutler came running out of the repair bay, pasting on his best servile smile. Slipping into the building, I found my grandfather wiping his oily hands on a chamois rag.

"How'd you make out?" I murmured.

Chief answered in our language. "*Ondass, Noozis.* See for yourself."

"What am I looking for, *Nimishoo?*"

"The master cylinder. Right up there."

Peering upward, I spotted the master cylinder, a greasy metallic object shaped like a squat sewer pipe. Many, many hours of repair work on Clunky had taught me the function of a master cylinder. Namely, to pump pressurized fluid into the vehicle's brake drums.

Eyebrows rising, I glanced at my grandfather. "Cutler found something wrong with the brakes?"

He shook his head. "I asked him point-blank about the brakes, *Noozis.* He said they were just fine. So I asked if I could have a look for myself." Curious frown. "Who's that guy you were talking to out front?"

"Tell you later." Craning my neck, I peered into the wheel well again. "What did you find?"

"Look closely at the tubing," he suggested.

I did. Beads of iridescent liquid gave the hydraulic lines a mild sheen. I fired a quizzical glance at Chief.

"Gasoline?" I asked.

"Give it a taste, *Noozis.*"

I swept my fingertips along the slender piping. The substance felt as oily as peanut butter. Gingerly I touched the tip of my tongue. An invisible fire sizzled my taste buds. I grimaced and spat. "Ugh! Tastes like gin!"

"Close," my grandfather replied. "It's denatured alcohol."

"What's it doing in the master cylinder?"

"Somebody had a little fun with Miz Rooley's brakes," Chief explained, pointing upward. "Wade told me he brought the wreck up from Salida yesterday morning. Gave it a complete inspection. When he checked the brake system, he found the master cylinder working—the drums in good shape—the plastic reservoirs containing the brake fluid sealed and watertight. Everything in order, he thought. But he missed that."

"You still haven't answered my question, *Nimishoo.*"

Grim Anishinabe smile. "You're right. It's very simple, *Noozis.* Garages use alcohol baths to clean all the internal parts of the master cylinder. Snap ring, main piston, spring retainer, piston cup, you name it. Someone's taken this apart very recently. Not more than five or six days ago, I'd say."

"Local garage?"

Vigorous head shake. "Not likely, *Noozis.* When he reassembled this thing, he put the original brake fluid back in. You're not supposed to do that."

"Why not?" I asked.

"Once exposed to the air, the fluid begins to break down. It loses its consistency. Doesn't put the same hydraulic pressure on the brakes. A repairman's supposed to put fresh fluid in the reservoirs after each brake job." His blunt fingers touched the greasy line. "Also, he's supposed to push the piston a few times and force the remaining air out of the lines. Our friend didn't bother with that, either."

Mischievous Angie grin. "You learned a lot working at Blazer's Auto."

"A bit." His grin matched mine. "Anyway, it paid for your mother's summer camp."

"Bottom line, *Nimishoo?*"

Stepping out from under the lift, he said, "Every time Madge Rooley stepped on the brake pedal, the pressure forced a mixture of trapped air and alcohol through the O ring. The alcohol traveled up the tubing. It would've dried soon enough, but, as I said, it happened only a few days ago."

"Deliberate sabotage," I murmured.

Solemn nod. *"Eyan, Noozis.* He didn't wreck the brakes completely. Just fixed them so they wouldn't respond right away."

I shuddered. "Kind of a major handicap on an icy mountain road, don't you think?"

Another nod. "Especially up there on Monarch Pass."

"How long would it have taken to do the job?" I asked.

"Depends." Chief draped his chamois cloth over the steel tire balancer. "He would have needed . . . let's see . . . a line wrench, a screwdriver, a couple of plastic jars. One for the alcohol. One to hold the brake fluid." Thoughtful hum. "If he had a garage lift handy, he could've done it in thirty minutes. On the other hand, he could have laid a tarp on the snow, slid beneath the truck, and worked on it for a couple of hours."

Fussbudget frown. A couple of hours. Well, that ruled out the RJ Bar. No way could he have spent a couple of hours tinkering at the ranch. Ralph the Border collie and the other animals would have smelled him out and raised a ruckus.

I made a mental note to ask Becky and Merry about their mother's trusty pickup.

"What do you plan to do, *Noozis?*" he asked.

"For now, I'm going to let the truck sit right here," I replied, leading him toward the open door. "I'll talk to the Rooleys. Have them convince Mr. Cutler to stable it here for a while." Thoughtful sidelong glance. "Later on we can have Sarah show it to the sheriff."

"That's red-hot evidence you're sitting on, girl." Chief's features turned grimmer. "If that fella sent Madge Rooley up to Monarch Pass with a defective master cylinder, then he killed her just as surely as if he'd put a gun to her head."

"I know that, *Nimishoo.*" Grimace of frustration. "But I mustn't be the one to report this. I can't afford to end up on the witness stand."

"Why not?"

"Because some eagle-eyed cop's liable to tag me as *Pocahontas!*"

"Good point." Chief sent an anxious glance toward the gas islands. "Listen, I'd best take off before Wade gets back."

*"Miigwetch, Nimishoo,"* I said, thanking him.

Casual farewell wave. "I'll be in touch."

So now I had more questions for Sarah's siblings. Had their mother taken the truck in for repairs? If so, where? And did she complain about those brakes before her final trip?

Questions, questions!

Wade returned a few minutes later. When he found the bay empty, his expression shifted from anticipation to disappointment. Turning to me, he said, "Excuse me, young lady. What happened to that Indian fella who was just in here?"

Pointing down East Tomichi, I responded, "Oh, he had to go. His granddaughter dropped by. He said he'd be in touch."

Neighborly Colorado smile. "Can I help you?"

"Just waiting for a ride, thanks." I stepped away from the bay door. "Troy Rooley told me to meet him here."

"Yeah?" Judging from the mirthful expression on his face, I suspect Mr. Cutler thought I was Troy's latest girlfriend. The bell went *ding.* Wade's head swiveled toward the pumps. Sudden pleased grin. "There's Troy now."

Into the gas station lot rumbled Troy's pickup. Merry waved to me from the passenger seat. Quickly I strolled across the salt-strewn asphalt.

"Sorry we're late, Angie," she said, opening the pickup's door.

"No problem." I glanced back at the garage. "Listen, you two, about your mother's truck . . ."

Four o'clock found me back at the RJ Bar. Seated in the old-fashioned study, to be exact, at the Rooleys' antique desk, inserting a modular cord into the telephone jack. A similar cord ran from the pocket modem into our new Wizard 3000 sub-notebook computer.

Beside me stood Karen's nemesis, the rich city lawyer lady, who, at the ripe old age of thirty-two, looked more like the girl's big sister. Sarah was still in her country-casual mode.

Turquoise work shirt with button-down yoked pockets and a pair of black form-fitting jeans. Touching her lower lip, she watched me adjust the pop-up screen.

Blue screen gave way to Ramon Echevarria's preloaded Windows program. Tap some keys. Twiddle the trackball. So far, so good, Angie. *Terminal* came front and center. I did some more frantic typing, added our law firm's phone number, hit the Enter button, and sat back with my fingers crossed.

Sudden series of beeps. I grinned at my employer. "Success!"

"I'll take over now, Angie," she said, gently tapping my right shoulder. "I'll download my own files."

"Diskettes are right here," I added, gesturing at the supplies I'd purchased in town.

Flashing a grateful smile, Sarah seated herself and entered her personal access codes. I played Angie the Secretary for a few minutes, straightening piles of paper, stacking pencils, opening the diskette box. When I looked her way again, Sarah was staring intently at a list of names onscreen. Her lips set in a troubled moue.

"Problem?" I asked.

"A couple. My correspondence is piling up. I've got to get some letters out." Her fingers danced up and down the keyboard. "We should have rented a printer, too."

Fortunately, Sarah couldn't see my devilish grin. "That's a good idea." Ohhhh, the fun I could have with a printer! "Why don't I head back to Gunnison tomorrow and pick one up?"

"All right." Onscreen, Sarah's ghostly reflection showed a sudden surge of frustration. "You can ride with me."

She said it as if Gunnison were the last place on earth she wanted to go. Unable to contain my curiosity, I asked, "Why are you heading for town?"

Through gritted teeth, she snapped, "My daughter has an appointment in juvenile court."

Instant retreat. Sarah looked to be in an ass-chewing mood,

and I wanted my Anishinabe rear well out of range. Any talk about her offspring was likely to set her off, so I sauntered into the kitchen. Said hello to Becky.

"Where are the twins?" I asked.

"Catchin' up on Tiny Toons." She tucked a stray lock of blond hair behind her ear. "Say, Angie, are you really thinkin' about buyin' Momma's truck?"

Leaning against the counter, I crossed my moccasin boots at the ankle. "I'm considering it." My imagination conjured up a believable cover story. "I'm in the market for a new car. My old green bomber's just about had it."

Toting the teakettle to the sink, Becky flashed me a curious look. "Yeah? How old is that car of yours?"

"It's, uhm, a 1969 Mercury Montego," I replied, hoping that Clunky, my faithful mechanical steed, would forgive the subterfuge.

Crooked grin. "That *is* kind of old!"

Ah, but he's served me well, Becky, since the day I found him in that farmer's barn. Most recently in South Dakota, where he saved me from a madman named Dietz.

"That truck's going to need a lot of work," Becky warned.

I shrugged. "Cab and front wheels, mostly. Mr. Cutler said it needs a new drive train." Smoothly I slid into interrogation. "How did your mother like it?"

"Just fine." Smile of happy reminiscence. "Momma put on a lot of miles, zippin' around this end of the state."

"How did it drive?" I asked.

"Okay, I guess. Momma put a new muffler on it, oh, 'bout a year ago December. Brake pedal was kind of mushy, too."

Fine hairs prickled on the nape of my neck. "Mushy?"

Becky nodded. "Took about a second for the brakes to grab hold."

I remembered what Chief had told me about the trapped air in the master cylinder. "When did your mother notice that?"

"She didn't. *I did!*" Becky's features saddened as she

opened the cupboard. "The morning Momma died. We had a real bad freeze the night before. Sixty below with the wind chill. Just after dawn I took the battery out of the house and hitched it up. Managed to get the engine runnin'." A solitary tear sparkled beneath her lower eyelash. "When I backed it up, I noticed it was a little mushy at first. But then it held. I—I didn't think anything of it, Angie. I—I put it down to the cold weather. It's h-happened before. T-truck always did act a little funny when it gets real cold like that." The tear meandered down the curve of her cheek. "I should've said something, Angie. I—I never should've let her go to D-Denver!"

Crossing the kitchen at once, I murmured, "Don't." My hands came to rest on her drooping shoulders. "Don't do this to yourself, Becky. It's not your fault."

"B-but if I—I'd said something . . ."

"Maybe she still would have gone to Denver. Maybe not. Who knows?" Lifting her chin, I experienced a jolt of sympathy for this vivacious woman, who, suppressing her own grief, had assumed the role of matriarch in the Rooley household. "It wasn't your fault, okay? Nobody knows what happened up there." Although I did have my suspicions. "The state patrol thinks it might have been a wind shear. I'll tell you one thing, though. It *wasn't* the brakes. Talk to Wade Cutler. He found nothing wrong with them."

True enough, that part. But the rest left me with a queasy feeling at the bottom of my stomach. I do believe that was the most difficult lie I've ever told.

Chief and I knew full well that Madge's pickup had been sabotaged. That the job had been done by someone who knew about Madge's planned trip to Denver. Still, I couldn't let Becky know that. She'd blame herself for not warning her mother, and I wanted to spare her the burden of guilt.

I turned away as she reached for the tissue box. My lips compressed in a sour smile. Moment of self-reproach.

Angela Biwaban, I mused. Anishinabe princess and avenging debutante. Vigilante heroine telling an endless series of lies in the pursuit of justice.

Is it glamorous? Is it fun? Yeah, sometimes. But you don't spend all day in the saddle, waving your hat and coaxing the big white stallion onto his hind legs. There are times when you have to lie to the good ones. To people like Rebecca Rooley. And that's no fun at all.

A few minutes later I volunteered to help with supper. Becky put me to work chopping onions for her chicken and chili casserole. Then she wrestled a package of frozen hash brown potatoes out of the refrigerator. In no time at all we had chili, onion, and sour cream bubbling away on the stove.

I told Becky about tomorrow's trip down the mountain. She offered to draw up a grocery list. A very resilient lady, our Becky.

"Your sister said something about juvenile court," I remarked, greasing the baking dish.

"Yeah." Rueful smile. "Afraid my niece has been a bad little girl."

"What happened?"

Chicken grease sizzled as she lifted the pan lid. "Karen ditched school a couple of weeks ago. Went wanderin' around Gunnison with her friends. They all decided to get drunk, so they commenced to teasin' each other, seein' who had nerve enough to walk into the liquor store with a phony ID." Then she looked over the newly chopped green chilis. "Naturally, that niece of mine just had to prove that a Rooley ain't afraid of nothin'. So she walks in there, bold as you please, and the clerk says, 'You're awful young-lookin' for eighteen, gal.' And instead of walkin' out, she starts arguin' with the fella. There they were, yellin' at each other, when the deputy walked in." Weary sigh. "So now Karen's makin' her debut in court."

"What's the charge?" I asked.

"They call it 'bein' delinquent in the act of unlawful purchase of alcoholic beverages.' "

I handed her the baking pan. "You quoted that one by heart."

"I've been there, Angie. That's what I got charged with the first time I went up before Judge Brouillard." Emerald eyes twinkled as she glanced at the study. "Sally, too! But that's not for publication."

Instant Angie double take. "Sarah was a *defendant* in juvenile court?"

"Uh-huh." She put the baking pan on the stove. "Sally got busted for delinquency when she was fourteen. Happened only that one time and never again. She sure learned her lesson." Her expression turned wistful. "Sure wish I had."

"I gather you were trying to live up to the legend of the unruly Rooleys."

Features showing embarrassment, Becky nodded vigorously. "Oh, I had a wild five years, gal. Getting drunk. Racing junk cars. Sassing deputies. I could've given that Tonya Harding lessons on how to misbehave." Mild chuckle. "Then my boyfriend and I heard about this ol' boy who was payin' cash money for wholesale booze. I had this half-assed idea we could keep the good stuff for ourselves and fill the bottles with white mule. So one day I saw this liquor truck sittin' by the side of the road, and . . ." Her pretty face reddened in mortification. "I was nineteen. Old enough to be tried as an adult. And to know better! Hijacking's a class two felony. The judge sent me to Canon City. I did a year and a day, and I was never so happy to get out of that place." Rueful grin. " 'Course, Momma was there at the same time, too. The day I arrived, she looked mad enough to chew nails! That was one rough three-hundred-and-sixty-six days, believe you me! I had screws tellin' me what to do . . . and *Momma* tellin' me what to do!"

Just then Ralph trotted into the kitchen, tongue lolling, and let out a crisp bark. He circled Becky's denim-clad legs, then went over and sniffed his supper dish. Another impatient bark.

"Hey! Does this look like a doggie restaurant?" Becky snapped, brandishing a wooden spoon. "You wait for your supper, boy, just like everybody else."

Ralph cast a mendicant glance at me.

"You heard her, Ralph." Sarah's voice sounded right behind me. "Back to the den." Head bowed, the collie made his retreat, and she joined us at the stove. "What's on the menu, Becky?"

"Chicken and chili." She dangled a potholder in front of her sister. "You're in charge of the chicken."

Chuckling, Sarah turned away. Black denim fit snugly across her curvy derriere. "Far be it for me to interfere."

*Whap!* Becky's palm planted a crisp wallop. "Grab an apron, Lawyer Lady!"

Sarah's wide-eyed expression was a blend of indignation and embarrassment. But she did as she was told.

I let out a peal of surprised laughter. Wall-to-wall Angie grin. A Kodak moment, and me without my camera!

You know, I was really beginning to enjoy the unruly Rooleys and their impulsive ways. I mean, where else could you see the high-and-mighty Mrs. Sutton catch one on the behind?

In no time at all we had the baking dish in the oven. The sisters had a lively discussion over how long to set the timer. I washed my hands at the sink. And then, patting them dry, I heard the front door slam.

"Hi, Angie!" Karen beamed as she strode into the kitchen. "How was your trip to Gunni—?" The second she spotted Sarah, she tensed right up. The cheery smile evaporated.

Sarah's features hardened in displeasure.

"All finished feedin' the goats?" Becky inquired.

"Uh-huh." Karen inched her way toward the door. "I'd better go give Troy a hand. Talk to you later, Angie."

"Not so fast." Putting down the saucepan, Sarah turned to her daughter. "I want to talk to you, girl."

Folding her arms tightly, Karen muttered, "What about?"

"The envelope that came in the mail today."

Crimson flooded Karen's face. "That wasn't for you."

"I beg your pardon!" Sarah replied. "The address read *To the parents of Karen L. Rooley.* If you'd care to dispute that, I'll dig up your birth certificate."

I bit my lower lip. Ohhhh, Sarah, go easy. This isn't a court of law.

Scowling mightily, Karen looked away.

"Well?" Sarah snapped.

"Well what?"

"One C, one D, and three F's. That is a piss-poor report card, young lady!"

"Nobody asked you to *read* it, Mrs. Sutton."

Sarah's shoulders went rigid. "I'd like an explanation, Karen."

Dead silence overwhelmed the kitchen. Becky shot me a here-we-go look.

"And while you're at it, I'd like an explanation for those fourteen absences! What are you doing? Taking a day off every week?" Anger sharpened Sarah's lovely voice as she turned to her sister. "Don't they take attendance at that school?"

"Depends on the teachers' contract," I chimed in.

"And *you!*" Whirling, Sarah pointed at me. "You stay out of this! Understand?"

"Yes, ma'am." I had something very witty to say, but I thought it best not to tweak Sarah in front of her daughter.

Deep calming breath. "I'm still waiting for that explanation, Karen Lynn Rooley."

Resentment reddened her features. "That report card wasn't for *you!* It was for Nana, not *you!* You had no business reading it—"

"I had every business reading it. I'm your *mother!*"

"Don't remind me!"

"Karen!"

"You didn't want to be part of my life. You wanted out— fine! *You're out!*" Tears gleamed in Karen's green eyes. "Don't you get it, Lawyer Lady? I don't want you back in!" She sobbed. "Why don't you just go back to Pierre where you belong?"

"I've got news for you, Karen. When I return to Pierre, *you're* coming with me!" Sarah's index finger zeroed right in. "I'm your mother *and* your legal guardian. And I'll be damned if I'm going to stand here and take a load of crap from a fifteen-year-old! There are going to be a few changes in your life, and they're going to start with those grades. One more F this year, and you're spending the summer in a classroom."

"*If* I'm still around!" Karen shouted.

"Oh?" Sarcasm glazed the older woman's tone. "Are you going somewhere?"

"You bet!" Lifting her chin in determination, Karen bolted from the kitchen. "As far away from you as I can get!"

"I'm not finished, Karen!"

"Well, I am!"

Sarah followed her daughter into the living room. "Karen, don't you *dare* walk out on me!"

Halting at the foot of the stairs, she whirled to face us. "Why not? You did it to me . . ." Her face crinkled in misery. "*Bitch!*"

Footsteps pounded the stairway carpet. Seconds later, a bedroom door slammed shut. Standing in the kitchen doorway, I caught a glimpse of Sarah's reaction. Her spine stiffened, and her arms rose in a gesture of hapless wrath. Rigid fingers curled inward. And then, her head bowed, she let out a muted sob.

Easing past me, Becky murmured, "Better go check on that casserole, Angie."

I took the hint, puttering around the kitchen while Becky took her sister aside for a quiet chat. Tuck the baking pan into the stove. Check the temperature. Set the timer. From time to time my gaze turned ceilingward, and I gave some thought to the self-exiled fifteen-year-old. Then I untied my apron, draped it over a kitchen chair, and headed for the stairs.

The year I lived in Utah, Uncle Matt's mother was a frequent guest in our home. Mother Shavano. A rather large, white-haired Nuche lady who steadfastly held to the old ways. I'm afraid I didn't exactly impress her the first time we met. She told my aunt, "Teach this girl the loom, Della. That'll take her mind off those Mormon boys."

Still, whenever Aunt Della and I had a bruising battle—and those occasions were frequent, believe me!—Mother Shavano was always there to listen to Adolescent Angie's complaints. I can still see her sitting on the deacon's bench, her gnarled hands deftly stringing beads, nodding and listening.

Right now, I decided, Karen Lynn Rooley could use a Mother Shavano in her life.

I gave the bedroom door a tentative knock. From within, a suspicious voice answered, "Who is it?"

"It's me, Karen. Can I come in?"

"Suit yourself."

Pushing the door open, I found Karen sitting cross-legged on the narrow canopied bed. Textbooks lay scattered about the quilted coverlet. Nearby stood an antique cedar chest of drawers and a matching vanity table. A Princess phone nestled on the windowsill.

"I knew it wasn't the Lawyer Lady." Mammoth pout. "She *never* knocks."

Closing the door behind me, I flashed a gentle smile. *"Lawyer Lady*—that's kind of a mouthful, isn't it? How about something shorter? Like . . . say, *Mom?"*

Scowling, Karen avoided my gaze.

"Okay, okay. So you're not that close," I added, crossing the room. "Why don't you make it *Mother?*"

"I know who she is. I don't need a reminder."

"Karen . . ." I took a deep breath. "You've been on her case since we arrived. You go out of your way to hurt her. Why?"

"Lawyer Lady's got it coming!"

"Nobody else around here seems to think so."

"They didn't have to live with her."

"You know, there are usually two sides to every divorce. Have you ever even *bothered* to discuss it?"

Lowering her chin, Karen fumed. "You can't talk to her! All she does is snap out orders." Indignant eyes met mine. "Who the hell does she think she is? That envelope was addressed to Nana—"

"No," I interrupted. "It was addressed to *her*. And you know something? She's absolutely right. That is a shitty report card. There's no reason why a girl with your brains shouldn't be getting A's and B's."

*Tayaa!* I thought. Listen to me! I'm starting to sound like Aunt Della.

"How am I supposed to do that?" Karen shot me a defiant look. "By going to summer school?"

"If need be."

"No way! I've got things to do this summer."

"Fourteen absences." Clucking my tongue, I wandered over to the chest of drawers. "Seems to me, Karen, that you've already had your vacation."

"So you're taking her side, huh?"

"No, I'm taking *your* side," I snapped. "Keep those F's coming, girl. The college admissions board is going to have a great big laugh when they see your transcript."

Clenching her teeth, she muttered, "I don't want to talk about it."

"Anything you say, dear."

I let her simmer in silence. My wandering gaze found the

framed photos atop the chest of drawers. Nostalgic color shots of Madge and her family. There was ten-year-old Sarah with a sisterly arm around beaming five-year-old Becky. Pint-sized cowgirls in yoke shirts and ranch denims. Another one from a few years later, featuring four-year-old Merry and two-year-old Troy sitting in a little red wagon. Hmmm—what are you going to do with that paintbrush, Troy? Plus a decade-old photo of a laughing Karen riding a tire swing, with her slim, trim grandma frozen in mid-push.

It was my first glimpse of Madge Rooley, and it left me with a distinct sense of unease. She looked like Sarah would nine or ten years from now, a strikingly lovely woman in her early forties, with the same cornsilk hair, delicately hewn features, and striking emerald eyes. But the body language was all wrong. She seemed to lack her daughter's poise and reserve. Her stance was aggressive. Legs apart, buttocks provocatively outthrust, ample breasts crowding the V of her tank top. Wild hair and damn-you-all-to-hell eyes. Her snug-fitting camp shorts showed a lot of leg. She might have been a carhop at Bubba's Big Beef Bar-B-Q or a barmaid at a Wyoming roadhouse.

From a distance, seeing her push Karen's swing, it would've been hard to think of Madge Rooley as the Border Bandit Queen. Ahhhh, but seeing this photo close up—seeing the tension in her emerald eyes and the wanton set of that mouth—you could easily envision this woman shooting it out with the Deadwood P.D.

"Doesn't matter," Karen said with a sigh.

I faced her once more. "Pardon?"

"I said, it doesn't matter." Karen slid her denim-clad legs over the edge of the bed. "Soon as I'm sixteen, I'm out of here!"

"Eighteen," I corrected her.

"*Sixteen!*" she snapped. "And maybe sooner if she doesn't lay off. Maybe the day after we get back to Pierre."

"Given any thought to where you'd like to go?" I asked, crossing the room.

Karen blinked. The question caught her by surprise. "I don't know . . . L.A., I guess."

My eyelids shut. I had a horrifying vision of homeless Karen, canvas bag slung over her shoulder, roaming the streets of Los Angeles. Moderate sigh. "I'd think long and hard if I were you, girl. I hear those California juvenile detention centers are no picnic."

"Well, it's no picnic living with *her!*" Karen gestured at the floor. "I'm supposed to respond every time I hear her voice. And if I'm two seconds slow—boy, do I hear about it! She criticizes all my friends—the clothes I wear. Once she even yelled at me because my knees were dirty. I was playing soccer, for Pete's sake! And what business is it of *hers* what my knees look like?" Her fist walloped the pillow. Perfect imitation of Sarah. "Sorry doesn't cut it around here, young lady! Brush your teeth! Do your homework! Lower your voice! Ha! Did *she* lower *her* voice when she was spatting with Pete? I don't think so!" Tone of desperation. "I—I just can't please her, Angie. No matter what I do or what I say, I just don't measure up." Her tone became shrill. "Maybe it's no picnic out in L.A., but it's a lot better than trying to please the world's most perfect woman!"

Listening to the daughterly lament, I guessed at the reason behind Karen's reluctance to go to Pierre, and living with Sarah was only a part of it. Most of all, Karen missed her grandmother and their life together. In her own way, she was still trying to come to grips with the loss.

Comforting Angie smile. "When did you go to live with your grandmother?"

"Four years ago. Sixth grade." Karen shrugged haplessly. "I was eleven when Moth—*she* divorced Pete."

"I guess it was a big change for you, moving here to the ranch."

She shook her head lightly. "We didn't live here at the ranch. Not at first. Nana had an apartment on Elk Avenue."

Surge of curiosity. "Really?"

"Uh-huh. Nana used to work at the Little Sew 'n' Sew." Her expression turned glum. "She lost the job a couple of years ago. So I moved in with Becky, while Nana went up north huntin' for work."

"No luck in Crested Butte, eh?"

"Not much." Karen left the rest unsaid. After you've done time for armed robbery, folks are mighty shy about letting you near the cash register.

"Where did she go?"

"Malta. She rented a room there."

Puzzled frown. "Where?"

"Near Leadville," Karen explained. "Nana had a job at the Silver Kings Mall."

"Doing what?"

"Saleslady, I think." Teenage shoulders shrugged. "She never talked much about it, Angie. I asked her once, and she changed the subject. Guess she didn't like it much."

"Why do you say that?"

" 'Cause it didn't last." Karen's lower lip began to quiver. "She came home last summer. Home to stay."

"I'm surprised you didn't go with her."

"Landlady didn't want any kids around. That's what Nana told me. I—I wish she could've found something closer. A job in Gunnison or Lake City, maybe. I—I w-wish . . ." Grief overwhelmed her at once, shattering her composure, triggering a surge of tears. "I—I wish everything could be the way it was! I—I miss Nana. I miss her so damned much. Why did it have to happen, Angie? Why did she have to die?"

There were no glib answers, of course, so I offered Karen my shoulder and told her to go ahead and cry.

Feeling the warmth of Karen's face against my shoulder, the dampness of her grieving tears, I felt a twinge of guilt.

This was Sarah's rightful place, and I couldn't help feeling as if I'd somehow usurped it.

Twice Karen had had her home life yanked out from under her. The first time came when Sarah divorced her husband. Then the girl had managed to build a new life with her grandmother, only to have Madge shuttle her off to the RJ Bar.

My gaze zipped back to the framed photograph. At last I'd found something about Madge Rooley I didn't like. That tendency to put her own selfish needs ahead of the people most dependent upon her.

And I couldn't help wondering if Sarah and Becky had felt the same way when their mother had packed them off to Gunsight Pass to live with the McCannells.

All at once I'd discovered a new bend in the road. Why would Madge Rooley suddenly abandon her granddaughter and head for Leadville? Surely she could have found another job somewhere in the Gunnison area.

What had been going on in Madge's life two years ago? What *hadn't* she told granddaughter Karen?

I thought of Madge's old drinking buddy, Pop Hannan. Grizzled veteran of those Crested Butte bars. If anyone could fill in the gaps in Madge's biography, perhaps he could.

Definitely it was worth a try.

# SEVEN ▼▼▼▼▼▼

"What have you got there, missy?" Chief asked.

We were passing through Almont, my grandfather and I, heading north on Colorado 135 in a rented GMC Sierra. Steep Ponderosa-clad hills seemed to reach down and choke the narrow highway. The community bulletin board whizzed by on my left.

"False identification, Chief." I flipped open the black plastic wallet. Pinned to the interior was a circular silver badge bearing the legend *Special Investigator*. "I picked it up at Ed's Trading Post."

Chief's expression soured. "Angie, that badge won't fool anybody."

"Well . . . maybe not like *this*," I replied, plucking the badge from the plastic. My cavalier toss sent the black wallet cartwheeling over my shoulder. "But when we pin it to this nice leather army surplus M.P. wallet—"

Sudden Anishinabe double take. "Wh-where'd you get that?"

"The army-navy store." I fitted the badge to the leather wallet's interior, then dug a small laminated card out of my purse. "Some professional-looking ID in the plastic window—and *voilà!* We're in business."

"Let me see that!" Aged fingers snatched the card away.

It was a five-by-three-inch identification card showing your Angie's smiling face in the upper left corner and the seal of the Department of Labor in the upper right. Between the two was a neatly printed legend reading . . .

U.S. DEPARTMENT OF LABOR
*Mine Safety and Health Administration*
*Special Investigator*
Name: Janice Kanoshe
Employee Status: GS-5

Chief's obsidian eyes blossomed in amazement. Shaking his head, he handed it back. "I'm almost afraid to ask."

"It's the latest thing in *flash*, Chief." That's what we Springfield grads call false identification. I slipped the card into the wallet's plastic window. "Looks pretty official, eh?"

"All right. I'll bite. How did you do it?"

"Sarah's Wizard subnotebook," I explained, tucking the M.P. wallet into my purse. "I sneaked downstairs after midnight and did a little computing. Copied the Department of Labor seal out of the encyclopedia. Then used my scanner to lift the ID photo off my South Dakota driver's license. After that it was just a matter of merging both images, sharpening the resolution, and dreaming up an alias."

Incredulous glance. "You can do all that with a computer?"

"If it's loaded with an OS\2 program. That lets you drop-and-drag everything."

"I'll take your word for it, Angie." His gnarled hand patted the Okidata printer. "Did your pal Ramon let you use this at the store?"

"Uh-huh! I told him I wanted to run a test program before

we rented." My grin widened. "Thirty varieties of typeface to choose from!"

"Where'd you get it laminated?"

"At a print shop." I zipped my shoulder bag shut. "Thanks again for the lift."

"Don't mention it." Chief's hands kept a firm grip on the wheel. "What time do I have to have you back in Gunnison?"

"Two o'clock. Sarah said she'd meet me in front of the library."

Whetstone Mountain loomed on our left. My grandfather's lips tensed worriedly. "Hope we can find this fella right away. We ain't got a hell of a lot of time to play with."

Fifteen minutes later, an ornate wooden sign appeared in our windshield.

WELCOME TO
## CRESTED BUTTE
A NATIONAL HISTORIC DISTRICT

Deep snow enveloped the sign's fieldstone base. A spindly fir stood sentry on its left. Just beyond loomed the snow-covered rooftop of the Old Town Inn.

We left the Sierra in the parking lot behind the town tennis courts, now padlocked for the winter, and strolled down Elk Avenue. Our first stop was the C.B. Drug Store. While Chief admired the various pipe tobaccos, I had a quick peek at the Gunnison County phone book.

Since it was highly unlikely that a high-country hermit like Pop Hannan owned property of his own, I figured he must be staying at a cut-rate motel. My forefinger drifted through the Yellow Pages.

Hmmmm—Crested Butte Club . . . conference room? Jacuzzis? Nope! Definitely not for transient prospectors.

The Elk Mountain Lodge . . . historic inn . . . Diner's Club? Unh-unh! Pop didn't strike me as the credit-card type.

Ah, this looks promising. The Teocalli Hotel. No ads, no swimming pools, just the address—2785 Teocalli Avenue.

We found the hotel four blocks to the north. Like its counterparts on Elk Avenue, the Teocalli had gone up during the fabled silver boom. But no one had bothered to replace the weatherworn boards of its ornate façade or to scrape the grime from its red sandstone foundation. Cheap shades discreetly covered most of the windows. A rusting sign reading HOTEL FOR MEN leaned haphazardly from the building's front corner.

Just as we approached, our quarry descended the front stairs. Pop's hands scratched the seat of his faded jeans. Frosty breath tickled his hedgerow beard. Lowering his battered felt sombrero, he sauntered across the street.

Turning to my grandfather, I murmured, "Follow us at a distance, *Nimishoo*."

"*Eyan, Noozis*."

I set off in quick pursuit, unzipping my shoulder bag, charting an intercept course. Hastily I composed a plausible cover story.

As my prison mentor, Toni Gee, would say, a successful con game is about ten percent flash and ninety percent presentation. My phony ID would never fool a legitimate employee of Uncle Sam's, but, with the proper tone and expression, I just might be able to flimflam Madge's old buddy.

When I was in college, I worked summers as a rangerette for the Student Conservation Association. The Park Service gave us superb training in how to handle visitors. I knew just the approach to take.

"Excuse me." Rangerette Angie.

"Huh?" Turning, Pop gave me a searching squint. Bravely I ignored the whiff of gin-flavored halitosis. "Whatcha want, sis?"

"Are you Pop Hannan?"

Suspicion colored his squint. Dirty-nailed fingers stroked the wild gray beard. "Mebbe. Who's askin'?"

Flashing a bright rangerette smile, I whipped out my M.P. wallet and gave him a lengthy glimpse. "Mr. Hannan, my name is Janice Kanoshe, and I'm with the Department of Labor. Could I have a moment of your time, please?"

The badge made him nervous. "Well, I dunno, sis . . ."

Unable to resist playing girl bureaucrat, I interjected, "You are Pop Hannan, aren't you?"

"Hell, sure!"

"The same Pop Hannan who prospects up in the Collegiates?"

"That's right. Say, what's this all—?"

"And you do have a valid permit from the Bureau of Mines allowing you to prospect on federal land?"

Shuffling from one foot to the other, Pop cast an anxious glance back at the hotel. "Well, not on me, no! But—but I'm good for it, sis. It's up in my room. You want to see it?"

With a smile of reassurance, I put away my phony ID "That won't be necessary, Pop. I'm not interested in your claim." Alpine cold congealed my breath into a fine mist. "Are you familiar with the proposed changes to the 1872 Mining Act?"

He wasn't, but he couldn't resist the opportunity to impress a pretty woman. Slowly he tucked his ample tummy in. "Reckon I've read up on it some."

"Then you know the Mine Safety and Health Administration has been charged with examining every abandoned mining claim here in Colorado. I'm responsible for the mines up in the Gunnison National Forest. I'm told you know every deer trail in the Collegiate range."

His chest puffed a bit. "Heard right, gal."

"Then maybe we could sit down and you could help me pinpoint those abandoned mines on a map."

"Uhm, I dunno, sis." Leery expression. "I ain't much for talkin' first thing in the mornin'.'" He slid his tongue over chapped lips. "Throat gets kinda dry, y'know?"

"It is a bit chilly." Mischievous Angie smile. "Would you care for something to warm the inner man?"

Bristly whiskers parted, betraying a snaggletoothed smile. "Well, now that you bring it up, miss, the cold really sets my joints to achin'."

I said the magic word. "Kochevar's?"

Bloodshot eyes widened with glee. "Why, that'd be right fine, Miss Janice. That'd be fine, indeed!"

Kochevar's was one of the oldest bars in C.B., a century-old saloon featuring original Victorian woodwork, wall-mounted dartboards, and a shuffleboard table. Antique one-armed bandits occupied unobtrusive positions between the potted plants and the saloon's original cuspidors. Pop selected a cedar booth with a fine view of the town's bus stop. When the waiter arrived, I put in an order for Jack Daniel's. And advised him to leave the bottle.

Seeing the pleasure on Pop's face, I added, "Courtesy of the United States government."

"Thank you kindly, Miss Janice." Pop rubbed an eager hand over his whiskered mouth. "Hot damn! This has got to be the first time Uncle Sam's ever done anythin' for me."

While waiting for our drinks to arrive, I spread my U.S. Geological Survey topo map across the tabletop and began my questions. Thirty minutes—and several shots later—Pop's patience began to fray.

"No, no, no!" He emptied his shot glass. Rasping sigh of satisfaction. "Not there! Ain't no mines on the north face o' Cathedral Peak. And what's that lake doin' there? Belongs up by Electric Pass. Who the hell drew this thing?"

"The Bureau of Land Management," I replied. "What about this area—Cataract Creek?"

Whiskey tinkled into the glass. "Hmmmm—there's one I

know of. Seventy yards in off'n the trail. Bill Sawyer told me about it. It's up toward the rim. Ain't never been there, though." He paused for a swallow. "How long we gonna be at this, gal?"

"Just a few more, Mr. Hannan."

He found map work very tedious. "Seems like a consarned waste o' time to me! Are you tellin' me you've gotta go up in the high country and mark ever' one o' them damned mines?"

"That's what they pay me for," I said, reaching for my own drink. A very tepid Bloody Mary.

"How come the gov'mint wants 'em all tagged?"

"Abandoned mineshafts are a hazard to hikers."

"Hazard?" he echoed, reaching for the bottle again.

I nodded. "Some of those pits are right in the middle of a trail. People have fallen in. There've been lawsuits. The bureau's handling it on a district-by-district basis."

Swearing mightily, Pop refilled his glass. "Goddamned waste o' the taxpayers' money—that's what it is! Damn squir- relheaded hikers! If they kept their eyes on the trail like they're *supposed* to, they wouldn't be fallin' down some shaft! Hikers . . . backpackers . . . *city folk!* Damned nuisance— that's what they are! Lookin' every which way 'ceptin' where to put their feet!" Up came the glass. "Only thing worse'n backpackers is them fools on the mountain bikes. Crazy bun- cha . . . I was pannin' for gold up on December Creek last sum- mer, and a whole passel of 'em come tearin' down the trail, whoopin' and hollerin'! Hell, I've seen chipmunks with more sense! There was this one dolly in a halter top and skintight elastic pants. Smilin' and laughin', pumpin' and jigglin'." Dreamy sigh. "I can still see that gorgeous ass bouncin' up 'n' down on the bicycle seat. Up 'n' down . . . up 'n' down! *Shit!* I musta run forty yards tryin' to keep her in view. Forty yards! At my age! Lucky I didn't keel over from a heart attack!" Querulous frown. "I ask you, Miss Janice. How's a man sup- posed to pan for color with distractions like *that!*"

"I can't imagine, Pop."

Downing his glassful, he asked, "When do you figure on goin' up there, gal?"

"Sometime after the melt."

Nodding in approval, he added, "Good thinkin'. You'd better plan on July, sis. High country's had a lot o' snow this winter. First chinook that blows through is gonna cause one hell of an avalanche."

Now that I had his confidence, I did a sidestep into interrogation. "I'm going to need a guide, Pop."

"Well . . ." He scratched his belly. "Sure wish I could help you, Miss Janice, but I sorta got my own business interests, if you catch my meanin'."

"I hear there's a local woman who really knows her way around the high country. Madge Rooley. Think she'd be willing to guide me?"

His features saddened. "Gonna have to find somebody else, sis. Madge is dead."

"Sorry to hear that." Putting down my glass, I prodded, "Was she a friend of yours?"

"Yeah. Me 'n' Madge go back a long way." He lifted the bottle and poured once more. "Knowed Madge Rooley since she was a kid. Her daddy was a barroom buddy o' mine. I've stayed at the RJ Bar more'n one winter."

"Ranch hand?"

"Ranch hand, huntin' guide, truckdriver, welder—you name it, Miss Janice, I've done it. Anything to pay for groceries while I'm waitin' for the melt."

"Where are you originally from?" I asked.

"Kansas." Loud sniffle. "Got mighty used to cold weather over there in Korea. I headed up to Gunnison just as soon as I got out of the army. Yeah, I've known them Rooleys a long, long time."

"You know, Pop . . ." Folding my arms, I leaned forward on

the polished table. "I've been hearing some stories myself about that family."

With a hoarse chuckle, he upended the shot glass. "Then you know all about ol' Tom's granddaddy."

"I heard he rode with Butch and Sundance."

"Heard right, Miss Janice." Squinting one eye, he pointed out a glass case near the bar. "You see that?"

I glanced in the direction indicated. Behind the glass nestled an antique Colt .45 revolver. "Uh-huh."

"That piece belonged to ol' Butch hisself." Sitting back, Pop scratched his ample belly. "Byron Lee Rooley saved his ass. Sundance's, too. Happened right here, sis. Right here at Kochevar's." His chin jabbed at the ceiling. "Used to be a bordello upstairs. The Bunch used to come around all the time. Well, anyways, to make a long story short, the Pinkertons got word that Butch and Sundance were in town. They put together a posse. Butch was playin' poker"—Pop's red-rimmed eyes scanned the near-empty room—"right over *there*. And Sundance . . . well, I reckon you've heard all about him and the ladies. Happened back in August of 1897. Rooley came ridin' into town on his raindrop Appaloosa. Rushed in here and told Butch the Pinkertons were five miles behind him and closin' fast." Hearty chuckle. "Well, ol' Butch didn't wait around for no engraved invitation. He swept his winnin's into his hat, and Rooley ran upstairs to fetch Sundance. Then all three of 'em lit out. 'Course, in all the excitement, Butch clean forgot his gun. Left it sittin' on a green-felt tabletop." Sudden rasping laugh. "And there it sits today, Miss Janice. Proof positive that Butch Cassidy once patronized Kochevar's. Just like you 'n' me."

Although enchanted by Pop's story, I managed to stay on track. "Did Butch and Sundance ever stay at the RJ Bar?"

"Might have. Probably did." He gave his nose a scratch. "The Bunch hid out on a lot of ranches up and down the divide."

"Did your friend Madge ever go hunting for the treasure?"

"Gal, *everybody* in town's gone lookin' for that cache at one time or another. I've been huntin' it off and on for forty years."

My chin tilted toward the window. "And you really think it's up there?"

All at once, Pop's gaze turned dead serious. "I *know* it's up there, Miss Janice. Listen . . ." Refolding the map, he slapped it against the tabletop. "Them boys hit the Zephyr at Price Creek. There's no way they could've gone straight up to Storm Pass. Terrain's too damned rough. They'd have killed their mounts, totin' all that gold." His grimy fingernail drew a line to the right. *"East!* That's where they went, Miss Janice. Up around the back of Flat Top, then straight down Alkali Creek. From there, it's a hop, skip, and jump to the Rooley ranch."

"That's assuming B. L. Rooley was one of the gang."

"Oh, he was one of 'em! Don't you bother your pretty little head about that. Folks on the train all made mention of that raindrop Appaloosa." Grim nod of satisfaction. "Only one horse in the valley fittin' that description, and he was wearin' an RJ Bar brand!"

"So what do you think happened, Pop?"

"I think McCarty took his cut and vamoosed," he said, a far-away look in his eyes. "That was McCarty's style. Byron Lee Rooley played it cute, though. He rode on down to Salida and bought himself an alibi. Which means ol' Dutch must've hidden the gold *before* he ran into the posse."

"Posse?" I echoed.

Slow nod from Pop. "Couple of towns got up a posse. That bunch from Irwin—by pure dumb luck they ran into Dutch up on Brush Creek. Sheriff's men got off a few shots, but Dutch lit a shuck right quick." Hasty whiskey cough. "That boy was movin' mighty fast for a man weighed down with gold."

"You think he cached it right after the robbery?"

"Damned right, gal. And if he was hidin' up by Roaring Judy like I think he was, then that gold has got to be within a day's ride of the RJ Bar."

Dainty sip from my Bloody Mary. "Interesting theory, Pop."

"It's more'n a theory, Miss Janice." Fervent belief hardened his dullish eyes. "The posse winged ol' Dutch. That's a known fact. Them deputies found blood on the trail. From my own personal experience, I know an injured man could never make it over the divide in May. Snow's too deep." Another swift drink, punctuated by a satisfied sigh. "So where was Dutch Bohle from May twenty-fourth until mid-August? That's the question."

"And your answer?"

"The Rooley ranch. He had to be. He was holed up there, recuperatin' from that gunshot wound. Once he was strong enough, he came into town."

I remembered my own conversation with Sarah's uncle. "A little boy's supposed to have seen him."

"Harry Tiggs." Pop let out an affectionate chuckle. "Lord, I miss that ol' cuss. I've lost count of how many times I've heard that story o' his. But I'll tell you somethin', Miss Janice. All the times I heard it, he never changed it so much as once. Told it the same damned way *every single time.*"

"Dutch was killed in Carbondale, wasn't he?"

"Indeed he was! Tuesday, September 7, 1897. Dutch had just tied his horse in front of the saloon when Marshal Stewart Palmer stepped out of the sheriff's office. Palmer recognized Dutch from the Pinkerton flyer and called on him to drop his gun. Dutch slapped leather instead."

Pop lapsed into sullen silence. Soiled fingers toyed with the empty shot glass. His hard-eyed gaze turned to the window, scanning the snow-clad mountains that had consumed so much of his life. And I wondered if the Mountain Zephyr legend had drawn him here in the first place.

"They know more than they're tellin'," he muttered.

"Who?" I kept my voice soft, watching the Jack Daniel's take effect.

"Them Rooleys." Did I detect a note of resentment in the prospector's voice? "Ol' Tom . . . Madge . . . all cut from the same tarp, them Rooleys. They're holdin' back somethin'."

"Like what, Pop?"

"I wish to hell I knew." His mouth turned surly. "I've been all over the Collegiates with Madge. She said she has no idea where it is." Drunken sigh. "Oh, I wish I could believe you, Madge Rooley. I surely wish I could. But you know damn well your great-granddaddy patched up Dutch Bohle. And if Dutch told anybody, it woulda been him."

I said nothing. Pop's bleary-eyed gaze drifted back toward the snowcapped mountains.

"He was a wanted man, f'chrissake!" Whiskey splattered his wrist as he refilled the glass. "Dutch'd gotten word to the RJ Bar somehow. Had plenty o' time to set it up. Gold's still up there. All that *bee-yoo-tiful* gold . . ."

I caught the bottle as it slipped from his grasp. Set it upright beside the ashtray. "You okay, Pop?"

"Never better," he slurred. "Ohhhh, I never could tell with Madge. Never could tell when she was havin' me on. Those green eyes'd glisten, and she'd give me this big sassy smile. I'd have this feelin' she was lyin', but I never really knew for sure . . ."

All at once he sat upright, his own eyes losing their dazzle, fearful that he'd said too much. His hand quivered slightly as he reached for the glass. "Don't get me wrong. I liked Madge Rooley. I surely did."

I thought he seemed a little too eager to convince me. "Sure, Pop."

"Y'know, there wasn't a decent woman in this town who'd even *speak* to Madge when she came home from the pen. Not me! First thing I did was buy her a drink. Welcome home,

gal!" Taut grimace. "Straight up. That's the way Madge always drank it." Surly mumble. "Knowed that gal since she
was nine years old."

"You two were pretty close, eh?"

"You bet! I got on better with Madge than her own sister."
Sudden smile of reminiscence. "Hell, even better'n Sally.
'Course, most people got on with Madge better than Sally."

"Mother versus daughter?"

"More like the other way around." Pop shook his head sadly.
"Y'know, Madge was crazy about that gal. Sally was her favorite. She'd do anything for that kid. Hell, she even got her
ass shot off for her."

I sat up straight. *"What?"*

"Lord's truth, Miss Janice." He drew a shaky cross on his
shirtfront. "Happened when Sally was, oh, sixteen, seventeen.
Madge was doin' time up in South Dakota when she got word
Sally was in trouble. So she tried to bust out and caught some
birdshot in the ass. Madge told me that was the worst time of
her life, knowin' Sally in trouble and not bein' able help."

I'd heard this story before, of course. From Madge's own
lips. And I was more than a little curious about the role Sarah
had played in her mother's attempted breakout.

"Trouble?" I remarked. "What kind of trouble?"

Embarrassment altered Pop's expression. "The usual kind
seventeen-year-old gals get into."

I nearly gave myself away. The name *Karen* hovered at the
tip of my tongue.

"Madge's daughter became pregnant?"

Silent nod. "Yeah, I'm afraid Alice wasn't havin' much luck
keepin' a rein on Sally. Never know it to look at her now—she
sure puts on the airs—but that gal was a wild one as a filly."

"Really?" I suppressed a feline smile. Do tell me more, Mr.
Hannan.

"Oh, yeah, Sally had her share of boyfriends at Gunnison
High," he said, smoothing his beard. "Then she got serious

about this young fella. He was nineteen or twenty, as I recollect. Sally wanted to get married, but that boyfriend o' hers— he sure wasn't ready for the harness. Lit out for Nevada the day after she broke the news. And it sure didn't get much easier when the school committee found out."

Puzzled Angie glance. "I don't understand, Pop."

"That's 'cause you ain't from around here, sis." He had difficulty keeping his eyelids open. "That ol' biddy, Mrs. Longworth, was ramroddin' the committee back then, and she just couldn't wait to tie a can to Madge Rooley's daughter."

"What are you getting at, Pop?"

"Ol' lady Longworth had Sally expelled," he muttered. "If it'd been anyone else, they'd have let her come back to school after the baby got born. But not Sally. That old dragon was determined to run her off." He frowned in recollection. "Madge was frantic. There she was, up in that South Dakota prison, and she thought sure Mrs. Longworth was gonna run Sally clean out of the state. But I reckon things worked out okay. 'Tween us, me 'n' Alice McCannell looked after Sally. She gave birth to little Karen. Damn if that gal ain't the spittin' image o' Sally in her teens!"

Curious, I asked, "Why did Mrs. Longworth have it in for Sally?"

Showing me an awkward glance, Pop reached for the bottle. "Ancient history, Miss Janice. 'Sides, if I tell you about that, Madge's ghost'll haunt me for sure! No thank you!"

Checkmated, I tried another avenue of inquiry. "You said Madge returned to Crested Butte a few years ago."

"Uh-huh." He began pouring. "Right after she made parole."

"Any idea why she was living in Malta?"

*Tink-tink!* Glass chimed as the bottle tapped the rim. Pop's hand trembled noticeably at the word *Malta.*

I could sense him pulling away from me. That was one question too many, princess. Should've quit while you were ahead.

Avoiding my gaze, Pop went off on a different tack. "Yeah, we go back a long way, me 'n' Sally." Feeble smile. "Spent many a summer weekend up there on Grizzly Peak. Me 'n' Madge 'n' Sally 'n' Becky. I'm the one taught 'em how to pan for color. Don't believe me? Shit, you go and ask 'em. They'll tell you. Ask 'em 'bout ol' Pop Hannan . . ."

Three times I dropped Madge's name, and each time Pop sidestepped, treating me to a chatty tale of weekend prospecting. I gave up. I would have had better luck digging a mine shaft with a teaspoon.

Wishing him well, I left the booth and went to pay the cashier.

Behind Kochevar's stood a cozy country-style restaurant called Karolina's Kitchen. A short corridor connected the two establishments, complete with a hole-in-the-wall museum. There I found my grandfather. Chief busily studied a photo montage.

"What are you looking at?" I asked.

Standing to one side, he gestured at a blown-up 1882 photograph of nine Nuche men. Seated in the front row was a heavyset fellow with a black felt hat on his knee. I recognized him at once—Chief Colorow of the Taviwach Nuche.

My grandfather pointed to a young brave standing directly behind Colorow. "Look familiar?"

I gasped. There was no mistaking those deepset eyes, high cheekbones, and Roman nose. "Billy!"

"Or your uncle Matt as a young man."

Chief's eyes were sad. Like me, he was thinking of my forest ranger cousin, Bill Shavano, dead these past six months.

"That must be Uncle Matt's . . . what? Great-grandfather?"

"Most likely." Doleful smile. "I've got to ask Tinker if he has a postcard of this. Della and Matt would love to have it."

"Who's Tinker?" I asked.

"Tinker Eilebrecht," he replied. "The curator. He's taking a leak. He'll be right back."

I moved the photo montage on its swivel mount, bringing a second one into view. "Quite a collection here."

"You bet! They've even got some of the Wild Bunch."

So I spent a pleasant three minutes looking over the pictorial history of Crested Butte. One poster highlighted the career of C.B.'s most notorious summer resident, the colorful California secessionist, Miguel Antonio Loveless. There was the diminutive doctor in a brougham, accompanied by his lovely dark-haired mistress, Antoinette Beauchamp, and his disciples, Voltaire Rappaport and Joshua Norton. Yellowed clippings from the *San Francisco Call* described his many battles with federal agents.

Someone had pinned a column of century-old headlines to the right side of the poster, inadvertently charting the doctor's rise from outlawry to prominence.

## THE LITTLE MONSTER THROWS HIS HAT IN THE RING

## THE DWARF SLANDERS GOVERNOR STANFORD!

## MIGUELITO WOOS MUGWUMP SUPPORT

## LOVELESS WINS IN PRIMARY UPSET

## DR. LOVELESS ADDRESSES LEGISLATURE, DENOUNCES "RAILROAD REPUBLICANS"

Well, I just had to laugh! And then a languid baritone spoke up behind me. "Yeah, he used to come here every summer."

Turning, I came face-to-face with the curator. Tinker Eilebrecht was a short, wiry guy in his late sixties. Snub nose, small mouth, slightly recessed chin, intelligent blue eyes, and a few tufts of white hair strewn carelessly across his bald top. He wore a red mackinaw shirt buttoned at the throat and a pair of stonewashed ranch jeans.

Gesturing at the brougham, he added, "Back then, folks thought ol' Doc Loveless was the most dangerous man in America. 'Course, that was *before* they found out about the scandals of the Grant administration."

"Like the Indian Ring?" I remarked.

"Yeah!" He let out a chuckle. "Doc Loveless doesn't seem like such a villain by comparison, does he?"

Amiable Angie smile. "I always got a kick out of George Robeson, Grant's secretary of the navy. Congressional investigators found $320,000 in Mr. Robeson's bank account, and he had absolutely no recollection of how it had gotten there."

"You must be the granddaughter." Tinker smiled, smoothing the strands on top of his head. "First time in C.B.?"

"That's right, Mr. Eilebrecht."

"Call me Tinker. All the folks do hereabouts." Swinging the montages to one side, he said, "Your granddad's been telling me you're interested in the Wild Bunch."

"You bet."

Chief and I stood by while Tinker displayed the poster devoted to the outlaw gang. There was Ben Kilpatrick, the "Tall Texan," standing head and shoulders above his buddies. And Harry Longbaugh, a.k.a. the Sundance Kid, one boot on the wooden sidewalk in front of Kochevar's, lighting a cheroot.

Just then I spied a photo of two cowpokes lounging against the hitching rail in front of the old Town Hall. One was tall, blond, and clean-shaven, trying very hard to look like a gunman. Tied-down Colt .45 and a gambler's flat-crowned black hat. He bore a spooky resemblance to Sarah's baby brother, Troy Rooley.

My gaze shifted to the other cowpoke. Lean and hard-eyed man in his early thirties. Bristling eyebrows and pistolero mustache. Crisp Stetson, work shirt, black leather vest, and a pair of worn striped trousers. The look he gave the photographer would have had most sheriffs seriously considering retirement.

"Who's that?" I asked.

"Dutch Bohle," Tinker replied. "He was with the Bunch in the early years. Got killed about five years before Butch and Sundance lit out for South America."

"Colorado boy?"

The curator shook his head. "He was from back east somewhere. Indiana, I think. First turned up in Telluride in 1885. He was a friend of Matt Warner's. Damned good with a gun, too. Right up there with Mesquite Jenkins and Nolan Sackett."

"Gunfighter?" Chief remarked.

"When necessary." Tinker folded his arms. "Dutch killed six men in stand-up shootin'. Two of 'em in a saloon fight over in Creede. Fast on the draw, all right. But there's a curious legend about him."

"Legend?" I echoed.

"Dutch refused to draw a gun on a Mennonite."

Seeing my expression of disbelief, Tinker added, "No, it's true, gal. It actually happened. There were witnesses."

"What'd they see?" asked Chief.

"Happened back in 1896. Down in Lake City," Tinker replied. "Dutch was walkin' down Silver Street, and he saw this family of Mennonites in front of the general store. He gave 'em a wide berth, but that Mennonite elder—you know the kind . . . old farmer with the black hat and the overalls and the long gray beard—he commenced to glarin' at Dutch. As Dutch walked by, the old coot said, clear as a bell, 'You're a disgrace.' Dutch stopped, one hand on his gun. And that stiff-necked ol' Mennonite—he just puffed out his chest and kept right on glarin'. By then Silver Street's emptied right out, and folks are wonderin' if they ought to grab some cover." His hands moved in a spirited pantomime. "Dutch turned to the farmer and said, 'What'd you call me, mister?' And that dumb ol' farmer—he ain't even got brains enough to smile and act like it was a joke. He says it again. 'You're a disgrace, boy.' And everybody's thinkin', *Well, here comes number seven!* It's as quiet as a saloon on Sunday morning. Then, all of a sudden, Dutch took his hand off his pistol and walked away." Ragged sigh. "Folks couldn't believe it. They couldn't believe it was the same Dutch Bohle who'd shot Shorty Farrell and Gopher Montague at that bar in Creede."

"Or the same Dutch who robbed the Zephyr," I added.

Tinker's blue eyes shone. "You've heard about that, eh? You know, it happened the other side of Flat Top, over on Price Creek. See, the Zephyr used to leave Denver at . . ."

My grandfather and I listened politely as Tinker repeated the tale of the area's most celebrated train robbery. When he reached the part about the raindrop Appaloosa, he gestured at the blond cowpoke in the photograph.

". . . the one who held the horses. Byron Lee Rooley. 'Course, he was never charged. Family still lives in the area. Owns a ranch up on Roaring Judy Creek."

Leaning against the brick wall, I inquired, "What do you think, Mr. Eilebrecht?"

"About what, gal?"

"The loot from the Mountain Zephyr. Do you think Dutch buried it somewhere in the Collegiate range?"

"Horseshit!" Tinker let out a hearty laugh. "Oh, there's some that think that. I ain't one of 'em, though." He shook his head. "No, that gold's long gone, miss. If there was a treasure, do you think the Rooleys'd still be living on some hardscrabble ranch?"

Couldn't deny the logic in that. "A fella in the bar told me Madge Rooley's been hunting for it off and on."

Rueful smile. "That's true, but . . . well, no disrespect to the dead and all, but that Madge chased them dollar signs for years. Always dreamin' about hittin' it big. She was nothing like her sister Alice."

"You know the family?"

"Well enough. They're a fine bunch, them Rooleys." Tinker's bony knuckle rapped the photo. "They may be descended from ol' Great-Grandpa here, but they're fine, upstandin' folks. Family always did tend to run to girls. There's lots of folks at this end of the valley with some Rooley blood in 'em. And, I'll tell you, for every hell-raiser like Madge, there's five or six who are good, solid, hardworkin' ranchers."

"Madge had something of a reputation, eh?"

"Totally deserved, too. And if you don't believe me, then ask Chet Hurtig."

"Hurtig?" I echoed. The name rang a small bell.

"Used to be sheriff hereabouts. He busted Madge Rooley many a time." Chuckling, Tinker glanced at the photo. "That Madge! There's always one who feels they have to live up to the family's outlaw image. The unruly Rooleys!" Shaking his head, he added, "Prison usually straightens them right out, though. Take Becky, for example. She did her time, settled right down, and now she's runnin' the ranch."

Tinker's words warmed my heart. How nice to see that the Rooleys had friends in Crested Butte. They weren't quite the pariahs Pop Hannan would have had me believe.

"How long have the Rooleys lived in the county?"

"Oh, little over a hundred years, I reckon."

I tossed out the name Pop had mentioned. "Like the Longworths?"

Tinker showed me a wry expression. "Now you're talkin' about a whole other corral, miss. The Longworths . . . hell, they're one of the county's first families. They run a mighty big herd on the Rafter L."

"How big?" I asked.

"Say about three thousand head." All at once his tone turned respectful. "Their money ain't all in cattle, either. They own big-assed chunks of some local banks. Plus a truckin' outfit or two. And you've probably seen the Big L Hardware store here in C.B. They've got 'em in Gunnison, Lake City,

and Poncha Springs. 'Course, that's chickenshit money compared to what Mineral Mountain brings in."

Chief's turn to play echo. "Mineral Mountain?"

"Mineral Mountain Natural Gas Corporation. It's a wholly
owned subsidiary of Longworth Enterprises. Biggest damned
employer in the south county."

"What do they think of Mrs. Longworth?" I asked.

Tinker did a double take. He was surprised I knew the
name. Smoothing his sparse hair, he sighed. "Let me put it
this way. Every time Cordelia Longworth takes a drive to
Lake City, them town councilmen fall all over themselves rollin' out the red carpet."

"What did Mrs. Longworth think of Madge Rooley?"

Shifting from one foot to the other, Tinker cast a worried
glance into the corridor. "Lord, woman, you *do* know how to
put a fella on the hot seat!"

"I take it the ladies weren't friends."

"Not even close, gal." Tinker's chin wobbled nervously.
"Dee Longworth's got a short temper and a long memory.
And when Madge took up with Arthur . . ." He let the rest trail
off.

Instant comprehension. *"Mister* Longworth."

Tinker nodded vigorously. "Uh-huh! It was a long, long
time ago, miss. I reckon Becky was still in diapers. Dee and
Arthur had one hell of a scrap. She sent him packin' with her
shoeprint on his ass. Then she changed all the locks on the
house and waited for him to come crawlin' back. Three weeks
later, she was still waitin'." Muted chuckle. " 'Course, Artie
liked it just fine livin' in town. Once Madge found out he and
Dee were on the outs, she moved right in. That gal never did
have much trouble snaggin' a fella. Once she started wavin'
that fancy tail at Artie, he went down like a gun-shot deer. Oh,
it was quite a scandal. Mrs. Longworth's bridge buddies made
sure she got every juicy detail." Sighing, he rubbed the back
of his neck. "Madge was kind of hopin' Dee would get mad

enough to file for divorce. But she didn't. She acted as if it didn't bother her at all. Clenched her teeth and waited it out. Sure enough, seven, eight months later, Madge got bored with Artie, and the poor fella came back to the Rafter L. That took some courage, I reckon. I'd sooner jump off the Headwall than face Cordelia Longworth!" Sympathetic expression. "Well, you can be sure Dee exacted some heavy penalties. Wasn't much she could do about Madge, though. She was out of Dee's jurisdiction, sorta. But if ever you wanted to make that woman scowl, just mention the name *Madge Rooley.*"

Now I understood Mrs. Longworth's eagerness to humiliate Sarah. She'd been striking at the hated Madge through her teenage daughter. Nasty lady!

Just then I felt Chief's elbow on my arm. As I glanced his way, he tilted his chin toward the wall clock. It was twelve-fifteen.

"Listen, we have to be going." Courteous Angie smile. "We're meeting someone for lunch. Thanks for your help, Mr. Eilebrecht."

"Don't mention it, miss." He had a warm, tenative handshake. "And don't you waste any good cash money on some worthless treasure map. I ain't mentionin' names, mind, but there's some in C.B. who's got up a little cottage industry, drawin' them maps for the tourists!"

Rush of Angie laughter. "We'll keep that in mind, Mr. E. Thanks again."

# ▼▼▼▼▼ EIGHT ▼▼▼▼▼

Promptly at twelve-thirty, Chief and I parted company. He returned to the parking lot to retrieve our truck, and I trotted over to the chamber of commerce building to pick up a street map, hoping to find Madge Rooley's old workplace.

I slid my forefinger down the row of names. Ahhhh, here we are—the charmingly named Little Sew 'n' Sew. It turned out to be one of the many shops located in the Ore Bucket Building, which I vaguely remembered from my first drive through Crested Butte. I asked the receptionist, and she pointed out a venerable pioneer bonbon a few yards up Gothic Road.

No fewer than ten businesses made their home in the Ore Bucket. Office supplies, sports medicine, real estate, lawyers, and chiropractors. Aging radiators pinged as I stepped into the foyer. A pastel blue corridor led into the house, with shops on either side. Stamping my snowboots on the thick rubber mat, I unbuttoned my coat and strolled down the hall. My feet made no sound on the plush navy carpet.

All at once, I halted before a frosted glass door. Black stenciled letters read

GUNNISON GUARANTY CORP.

How about that? I thought. Our friend Matt Stockdale has a branch office here in Crested Butte.

I wondered if Madge had applied for her Quick Start loan in there.

First things first, princess. The sewing shop awaits.

A century ago, the room housing the Little Sew 'n' Sew had been a spacious Victorian sitting parlor. Hand-carved juniper molding circled the high ceiling, and the floor beneath was genuine mountain oak. However, some demented architect far too fond of Colonial New England had ruined it by filling the square cedar archway with a mock vinyl storefront that resembled red brick. An antique cowbell jangled as I pushed open the door.

"Just a minute!" a womanly voice sang.

Approaching the counter, I glanced at the wide array of knitwear. Two-toned caps and mittens for toddlers. Scarfs, mufflers and Peruvian-style sweaters in alternating shades of white, lipstick pink, and surf blue. My gaze found a stack of business cards at rest in a clear plastic holder. I memorized the fine print. ADRIENNE BOUSQUET-OWNER.

Seconds later, the lady who shared my initials breezed out of the storeroom. Adrienne was a tall woman in her middle thirties with a diamond-shaped face, flawless teeth, deepset gray-green eyes, and a long, slim, tip-tilted nose. Glossy brick-red hair swirled about her collar, offering a momentary glimpse of a large, circular Chinese earring. Her smile engendered noticeable lines around the mouth, accentuating her lovely cheekbones and firm chin. Give the lady ten points for high fashion. Tartan bouclé jacket, midnight-blue campshirt, and tailored black stirrup pants.

"Hi!" Without thinking, she gave her fine hair a girlish toss. "Welcome to the Little Sew 'n' Sew. Taking a day off from skiing?"

Thank you, Adrienne, for saving me the trouble of dreaming up a cover story. "Uh-huh! I've been telemarking up on Keystone Ridge."

"Where are you from, dear?"

"Cable, Wisconsin," I replied. Telemark capital of the Northland.

"First time in C.B.?"

"Not exactly." Looking around the shop, I launched my tale. "I stopped by a couple of years ago. Purchased a quilt for my aunt Della. Your saleslady was *soooo* helpful." Gracious smile. "So, now that I'm back, I figured to drop in, have a look around, say hello."

Light chuckle. "I'll be sure to forward the message, dear. Who did you talk to?"

"Madge Rooley."

Adrienne's reaction came as a total surprise. The cheerful gleam vanished from her eyes, replaced by a moist sadness. Her lipsticked mouth compressed in sudden sorrow.

It wasn't the reaction I'd been expecting from the woman who had fired Madge.

"Oh, dear!" Eyes blinking rapidly, she fought to retain her composure. "I—I don't know how to say it. There was an accident . . ." Her hands fluttered awkwardly. "It happened up at Monarch Pass. Madge was *killed.*"

This time I let my surprise show. "No!"

Taking an uneven breath, Adrienne murmured, "It—it was such a shock for us all. She had so many friends in town." Fond smile. "*Everybody* liked Madge." Then she corrected herself. "Well . . . just about everybody. She was always so *alive.* I—I don't know . . . I just can't believe it."

"How long did Madge work here?" I asked.

"A couple of years," Adrienne replied. "She was so good with the customers. She didn't mind working weekends either. Unlike *some* I could mention! I really hated to lose her.

When she told me she wanted to quit, I begged her to reconsider."

Startled Angie expression. "Madge *quit?*"

The lady nodded. "Uhm-hmmm. A little over two years ago." Grimace of recollection. "I told her, 'Look, I know things are a little tight right now, but if you'll stay on, I'll give you a dollar raise by Christmas.' No such luck! Madge was determined to mosey on."

"Did she have another job lined up?"

"I'm not sure." Slender shoulders shrugged. "No one ever called here asking for a reference."

"Did you stay in touch?"

Regret touched the woman's face. "Well, she did send me a birthday card. But I'm afraid I never got around to writing back."

Time for a little prodding, Angie. "Did she mail that card from Malta?"

"Oh, no. From Leadville. Postal station two-oh-four."

"Leadville?"

"That's the nearest big town," Adrienne said helpfully.

"Any idea why she moved out there?"

"Not a one, honey." Quick glances in either direction, then she looked down her long nose at me. "Confidentially, though . . . knowing Madge, it probably had to do with some man."

"Very popular with the guys?"

Rueful shake of the head. "You should've seen her in action, hon. I'll never forget the time we got our noses wet at the Club Pub. This cowpoke walked in, and—I swear!—he was younger than *both* of us. He sorta looked like Mel Gibson. He could've had his pick of any gal in the place. I told Madge, 'Forget it. Gonna take more than a wiggle to get him over here.' Madge just smiled and said, 'He'll come over, gal. Don't you fret about that!' " Her nose wrinkled in mild amazement. "I *still* don't know how Madge did it. It's as if she sent out some kind of invisible radar. Next thing you know, there's that cowpoke staring right at us. Madge gave him a little here-I-am smile. Why, he grabbed up his long-necked bottle and scooted right on over."

"The two of you were friends?"

"About as chummy as a boss and an employee can get." She made a brisk gesture of dismissal. "Oh, I'd heard all about Madge's reputation. Sure, she was a little rough around the edges. So am I. Sometimes that's the way a woman's got to be." Tart smile. "Marriage taught me that!" Her eyes gleamed with a touch of envy. "When it came to men, though, Madge had a gift. That's the only way I can describe it."

"She seemed to enjoy meeting people."

"That she did. Madge Rooley was the best saleswoman I ever had," Adrienne said, folding her hands on the counter. "I don't mind admitting I was a little worried the first day she came to work. You know, her bein' an ex-convict and all. But Madge settled in just fine." Her lips tensed in irritation. "And when the word came down from on high, I paid it no mind at all!"

Bewildered Angie glance. "Excuse me?"

Adrienne's nose crinkled disdainfully. "That high-and-mighty Mrs. Longworth didn't approve of Madge working here. She made damned sure I got the message."

"Mrs. Cordelia Longworth?" I remarked.

"The same!" Adrienne cast an angry glance in the direction of Gunnison. "But like I said, I didn't pay her any mind. See, I know what it's like to be on the outs with Queen Dee."

"Oh?"

Nod of resentment. "I used to be a charter member of the Sew and Chatter Club. Soon as I divorced George, though, I stopped getting my weekly invitation to the Rafter L." Gray-green eyes narrowed. "That's when you find out how many friends you have, honey. When you get your divorce!"

If I'd let her go on, Adrienne would have cheerfully given

me the complete biography of Madge Rooley. But I knew
Sarah would be looking for me in just another hour, and I
knew my grandfather was patiently parked out there on
Gothic Avenue. So I cut it short. I shifted the topic to Aunt
Della's nonexistent quilt, spent another ten minutes admiring
Adrienne's collection of hand-crafted knits, and then left the
shop with my newly purchased Nuche scarf in hand.

On my way out, my gaze drifted toward the Gunnison Guaranty office. Computers bleeped behind the frosted glass.
Shifting the shopping bag to my left hand, I decided to play a
hunch.

The doorknob turned easily in my grasp.

A mahogany counter barred my way into the finance office.
I counted four desks in there—two of them unoccupied. Desktop computers, tall mint-green filing cabinets, and stucco
walls adorned with framed glass-covered ski posters. A short-
haired brunette, my age or thereabouts, manned a desk, having a very serious telephone conversation. Hmmmmm—must
be a client. Her partner, ten years older, watched the printer
spew its laser-spawned copies.

Glancing my way, the older woman cleared her throat.
"Yes?"

"'Afternoon!" Scintillating Angie smile. "I'm looking for
Madge. Is she in?"

Brown eyes blinked. "Madge Rooley?"

"That's her."

"Four doors down, dear. The sewing shop across the hall."
All at once the name's significance sank in, and a stricken expression crossed the woman's face. "Oh! Miss, wait—!"

Swiftly I closed the glass door. I already knew what she was
going to tell me. That Madge was dead.

Well, well, my little hunch had paid off.

Very intriguing reaction, Mrs. Printer Lady. I pop in out of the blue, looking for *Madge*—no last name!—and you come right back with *"Madge Rooley?"*

Why did I have the feeling Madge spent a lot of time here at the Gunnison Guaranty office?

Of course, it could all be perfectly innocent. Perhaps Madge and the Gunnison Guaranty ladies had often lunched together.

However, where Madge was concerned, I found I could no longer think in terms of innocent explanations. Like any good cop, I had begun looking for the angle on her every move, for the purpose lurking behind her each and every action.

And no wonder! I'd caught Sarah's mother in a flagrant lie. She hadn't been fired from the sewing shop—*she'd quit!*

But why? I asked myself. Why did she lie to her grand-daughter? Why did she want to conceal the truth from Karen? And why had she been in such a hurry to move to Malta?

That night, as the moon traced its path across the sky, a beam of silvery light streamed through my window. Open drapes and a raised venetian blind offered unhampered access. The beam slowly wended its way across the rug, up and over Madge's quilted coverlet. Moonlight splashed my face, and I jolted awake. My blinking gaze found the digital alarm clock's tritium readout. It was just after two A.M.

Of course, I could have just as easily set the alarm clock. But I couldn't take a chance on Sarah or Becky being roused by its insistent buzzing. They might wonder what I was doing, prowling around their house during the wee hours.

Bright moonlight offers a silent alternative.

Yawning, I pushed the blankets aside. Cold carpeting tickled the soles of my feet. I reached for my moccasins, slipped them on one at a time, then smoothed the wild cascade of raven hair away from my face. After donning my terry housecoat, I grabbed my Mustek scanner and made my stealthy way to the bedroom door.

Down the darkened hallway I padded, stopping at each door

to listen. Becky had an unusual snore. Sort of a *huh-huh-huh*, followed by a long, dreamy exhalation.

As for Sarah . . . well, have you ever heard a heavy-duty McCulloch chainsaw right after a logger pulls the lanyard?

Troy's door was the last one before the top of the stairs. Ragged baritone snoring serenaded me as I drifted past. Mischievous Angie grin. So far, so good.

I stopped briefly in the parlor and retrieved the *People* magazine I'd picked up in Gunnison twelve hours before. I needed to explore Madge Rooley's connection to Gunnison Guaranty. To con someone as sharp as Mr. Stockdale, I needed a cover a little more convincing than a business card.

Four handbags nestled on the counter of the redwood hutch. Feeling like a naughty little girl, I went straight to Sarah's, zipped it open, retrieved the wallet, and removed her South Dakota license.

Then I rifled the adjacent purse, which belonged to Merry. Deft and swift Anishinabe fingers removed her Colorado license.

Within minutes, I had the Wizard computer on line. A swivel-necked lamp cast its faint light over the keyboard. I hitched up the scanner, laid Sarah's license flat on the mouse pad, and slowly moved the lens over the laminate.

An exact copy of Sarah's license materialized onscreen. I blew it up to maximum, tapped a few command keys, and summoned my stored photo images.

Okay, princess, let's have a look at that rolldown menu one more time. Uh-huh. Overlay the smiling Angie photo onscreen. Massage the trackball, moving it to the left. Hit the maximize button, and *presto!*

Sarah's portrait vanished, replaced by the smiling face of my favorite Anishinabe princess. Whispered giggle. A definite improvement, if you ask me!

Quickly I rewrote the operator data.

| *License Number* | *Date of Birth* | *Sex* | *Weight* |
|------------------|-----------------|-------|----------|
| 84629367542      | 05  22  70      | F     | 105      |

Janet M. Wanagi
1267 South Coteau Street
Pierre, SD 57501

My grin widened. *Wanagi* is the Lakota word for *ghost.* Definitely one of my favorite aliases.

I found a wooden ruler in the desk's center drawer. After using it to measure Sarah's license, I entered the size into the computer's memory. Next I checked the font list and added to the print commands. Fingers trembling, I saved my bogus license as a separate file.

Copying Merry's license proved to be far more difficult. Sneaky Colorado puts their state seal right in the center of the card, making it nearly impossible to photocopy. Ah, but a computer is no mere copier. You can break down the driver's license into separate components and then build a facsimile on an empty template.

Poking about the desk, I found a flyer from the Colorado Division of Wildlife. The state seal appeared directly beneath the masthead. Like a diligent first-grader, I huddled over the page, my tongue protruding slightly. The scanner whined as it descended the page. The seal appeared onscreen in its original colors.

After saving that file, I scanned Merry's license and worked out the size configurations. Recalling my original file to the screen, I inflated the Colorado state seal to the proper size.

One by one, I filched elements from Merry's license and laid them out on the new template. Let's see now . . . name, address, sex . . . ooops, don't forget to put a letter in front of that six-digit license number, Angie. Ahhhh, very good! And now the signature of the director of the Motor Vehicle Division. Ah-*hah!*

I hammered the keyboard for two solid minutes, typing the proper print commands. Suddenly, I heard a strange sound in the hallway. Like pebbles skittering across a polished wood floor. *Snick-snick!*

I killed the desk light, then held my breath, waiting and listening.

Heavy breathing approached the darkened doorway.

Company, Angie! Whisking off my bathrobe, I draped it over the glowing computer screen.

The skittering noise halted. The intruder's labored breathing continued.

Quiet as a bobcat, I left my chair and ducked behind the old-fashioned desk.

The breathing quickened its tempo, becoming a low, moist panting. My features tensed in confusion.

I risked a peek over the desktop's horizon. In the doorway stood Ralph, the twins' Border collie, wagging a languid tail. Canine eyes peered in puzzlement, and he let out a quizzical murmur.

Trying not to laugh, I put out my arms. "Come here, boy."

Bounding over, Ralph accepted my embrace, content to let me stroke his fur. His energetic tongue lapped my face.

I ruffled the fur between his ears. "Sorry I woke you, boy. Sit right here and be quiet, okay? I'll get you a dog biscuit just as soon as I'm finished here."

Ralph made himself comfortable on a throw rug, watching with mild canine interest as I flicked on the lamp again, opened my *People* magazine, and extracted the staples. Flipping through the loosened pages, I hunted for a brief one-column story.

Once I had what I wanted, I removed that page from the magazine. Then I placed the page on the blotter and ran the scanner down its length.

I wondered what Joseph Weil, better known as the Yellow Kid, the dean of American con artists, would have thought of my portable computer. He's the one who dreamed up this phony magazine scam. The Kid used to bribe Chicago typesetters to reproduce magazines such as *Time* and *Collier's* with bogus news stories about himself inserted in the business section.

Once I had my *People* page loaded aboard, I blanked out a short piece on Nancy Kerrigan, inserted a photo of smiling Angie, and wrote a story of my very own.

### FLYING HIGH IN THE ROCKIES

With Global Investment Corp. riding tall in the saddle these days, financial wonder woman Janet Wanagi has gone looking for new worlds to conquer.

Global and Benson Fund Managers had been vying to handle a $500 million piece of South Dakota's investment portfolio. Jan recommended Global as the company best suited to reinvest the state funds in the booming money markets of South America.

Surprisingly, Jan turned down a seat on Global's board, pocketed a hefty broker's fee, and immediately took off for Denver. The Native American wunderkind is reportedly interested in ski condo development in the Aspen area.

There! I thought, hitting the Enter button. That ought to pique Mr. Stockdale's interest.

With Ralph tagging at my heels, I entered the kitchen and began snatching parkas and anoraks off the coatrack. Taking care to make no noise, I lugged a hefty armful back to the study. Unpleasant sensation of déjà vu. That's how I spent my workdays at the Springfield prison laundry.

Soon I had Sarah's printer well muffled by winter coats. I tap-tapped the keyboard, sorting my files and readying the machine to print. Then, biting the lower corner of my lip, I punched the tab.

*Screeeeee!* Down-filled parkas reduced the printer's ear-splitting whine to a whispery squeal. I cast an anxious gaze at the doorway. No lights had come on. So far, so good.

The printer lapsed into silence. Hastily I gathered my *People* facsimiles and phony driver's licenses. Just then I heard a muttered growl behind me. Ralph's sharp-nosed face swiveled toward the window. Canine ears immediately tilted forward.

Uh-oh! I thought, dousing the lamp. Someone's out there!

I knew better than to doubt a dog's sense of hearing. Switching off the computer, I sidled up to the window, moved the drape a quarter-inch to the left, and peered into the yard.

The stable's snow-covered roof gleamed in the pallid moonlight. Spruces quivered in the night wind. My gaze rode the snowdrifts up East Cement Mountain, past the stable and the barn and the milking shed, across deserted fields rimmed by half-buried barbed wire fences.

Ralph let out an excited bark.

My searching gaze scanned East Cement's snowy face, veering from spruce stands to granite balconies, and then I spotted it. About a half-mile up the mountain, a bright flash appeared on a lip of rimrock.

I frowned. A snowbank reflecting the moonlight?

And then it moved. The flash performed a perfect figure eight.

There's somebody up there, all right. Half a mile away, and the collie's keen-edged ears had still detected him. My grandfather was right. Compared to dogs, we humans are stone deaf!

The bright flash ceased its movements. Binoculars, I thought, holding the drape rigid.

Then the glimmer vanished. Must've lowered the binoculars, I thought. Either that or he's looking in another direction.

My free hand covered my mouth. I couldn't afford to let my

breath fog that frost-tinted window. Come on, fella. Where are you?

My plea was in vain. I watched for another ten minutes, but the glow did not return. Our hidden watcher must have called it a night.

A chill that had nothing to do with my proximity to the window began a slow journey up my spine. Returning to the computer, I showed Ralph a distinct fussbudget face.

Who is that guy? I wondered. What brings him to a Colorado mountaintop at three A.M. on a January morning?

Whatever it is, I mused, it must be a very compelling reason. The windchill out there has knocked the mercury down to sixty below!

And, of course, there was the big question. A question, I suspected, that had something to do with Madge Rooley's death.

Namely, why did he have the ranch under surveillance?

When I came downstairs the following morning, I found a Rooley quartet at the breakfast table. Troy and Merry, their faces ruddy from the early morning cold, sipping hot coffee from stoneware mugs. Becky in her emerald turtleneck and black stirrup pants, stirring the hash browns. Seated at the head of the table was Sarah, impeccably turned out in her lime woolen two-button suit. She didn't even notice me. Too busy thumbing through a hefty legal document.

Troy grinned at me over his coffee. "Sleepin' in, Angie?"

"Unh-unh! New hairstyle." I gave my French twist a pleased little pat, then took a seat. Actually, I'd just spent an hour running my phony driver's licenses through a laminator. A brief session with the scissors had reduced the plastic to the proper size. "What's for breakfast?"

"Eggs, bacon, and hash browns." Becky waggled her fingers. "Let's see your plate."

"No need to rush, Angie," Merry said, taking my empty

plate and passing it on. "We ain't leavin' for town for another half hour."

Sarah's document thumped the tablecloth. Her serious gaze found Merry. "Well, don't bother waiting around for Angie. She has enough to do today." She turned to me. "You'll be getting a fax from Pierre around ten. I left the response letters in the memory. Add my signature and get them right off to Mr. Hipple—pronto!"

"Okay." My fork captured a bit of fried potato. "Where are you off to, Sarah?"

"Gunnison." She dabbed at her lips with the napkin. "I've got some probate work to do on Momma's will. And I have an appointment with United Mountain Bancorp. I'll be gone all day."

Ferrying her steaming plate to the table, Becky muttered, "It's damn about time!"

Sarah cast her a look. "I'm not making any promises, Becky. I can only try to persuade them to renegotiate."

"Try real hard, Sally." Chair legs scraped the floor as she seated herself. "We're goin' to be up against it if we have to cough up sixteen percent."

"I'm doing the best I can." Sarah's voice began to creep upward in volume. "We don't have much room to manuever. UMB does hold the loan, so—"

"The poor-ass rancher has to dig deeper into her wallet," Becky interrupted. "Pardon me, sis, but I've heard this particular tune before."

Standing up, Sarah blurted, "Then why didn't *you* talk her out of it?"

Anger sparkled in Becky's green eyes. "I happened to think it was a fine idea."

"You should've known better. You *knew* what Momma was like. All those crazy money-making schemes . . ." Sudden shout of frustration. "You shouldn't have let her go through with it!"

Becky's fork clattered to the table. "You're absolutely right! I should've talked Momma out of it. But you know why I *didn't?* Because my big sister, the lawyer lady, read the fine print and told us we had nothing to worry about. That's why I didn't talk her out of it!" Her thumb jerked in the direction of the bathroom. "If you're lookin' for someone to blame, Sally, the mirror's in there!"

Sarah's expression reflected a kaleidoscope of emotions— anger, frustration, despair. She said not a word. She didn't have to. I read the heartache in her emerald eyes. Doing a brisk about-face, she marched out of the room, spine rigid and head held high.

One by one we drifted away from the table, leaving Becky to finish her breakfast in a sullen silence. I put in some time at the computer, pasting Sarah's signature to her E-mail, ready-ing them to fax out. Finishing up, I heard an aging pickup roaring down the canyon road. Troy and Merry on their daily milk run. I wondered how the middle Rooley girl was doing.

I found Becky at the washing machine. A plastic basket, bulging with wrinkled whites, sat on the dryer. Scowling, Becky yanked a child's wrinkled shirt from the basket.

"Hi." I leaned against the doorjamb. "How's it going?"

"For a woman with a shitload of laundry to do . . . *just fine!*"

"You know, if you're going to fight with your sister, you'd better learn a few Queensbury rules." Folding my arms, I showed her a conciliatory smile. "You know . . . padded gloves. Three-minute rounds. No hitting below the belt."

Despite herself, Becky's fearsome scowl gradually faded. Deep exhalation. "Don't pay us any mind, Angie. This has been buildin' for quite a while."

I helped her unload the lingerie. "What do you mean?"

"Sally's my sister, and I love her, and I'd do pretty near anything for that gal. But there are times when I feel like—" Her fist tapped the machine's upraised lid. "Pow! Right in the kisser!"

Suppressing a smile, I reached into the basket. Withdrew a white spandex body briefer—size ten. My brows knotted in puzzlement.

"Sally's," she announced, taking it from me and stuffing it in the bin. "Oh, we've had plenty of go-rounds, me 'n' Sally. Especially when we were kids. Drove Momma plumb loco, the way we fought." Grinning, she tossed in another blouse. "Momma sure kept the willow tree pruned, breakin' off switches every now and then. Believe me, we had more'n a passing acquaintance with the inside of that woodshed." Chuckle of reminiscence. "I remember one time . . . me 'n' Sally were hidin' under the bed. And there was Momma, switch in hand, jabbing it at the back door. 'Come on, you two! You know you got it comin'!' And there was Arthur, tryin' to talk her out of it."

I picked right up on the name. "Arthur?"

"Arthur Longworth." Bittersweet smile. "He lived with us for a spell. I kept hopin' he and Momma would get married, but it didn't last." Loose shrug. "He sure was a lot of fun, though. He bought us our first stereo. And he knew all the words to those songs by Earth, Wind and Fire. We'd be joltin' down 740 in the truck, and Arthur'd be behind the wheel, singin' away."

"Why didn't your mother marry him?"

"Same reason she never stayed in one place too long. Didn't want to get tied down." Becky upended the basket, dumping the remaining whites into the machine. "Momma spent most of her life runnin' away from responsibility. I know. 'Cause I was the exact same way . . . well, at least until I had the twins." She set it down. "It could've worked—I think—if Momma had stuck it out. No man ever made her happier. But it got to the point where they either had to tie the knot or forget the whole thing. And Momma said, 'Forget it.' Hand me that Wisk, would you, Angie?"

Picking up the squat red bottle, I remarked, "Did you move around a lot when you were a kid?"

"Uh-huh." Becky poured a capful of detergent. "About the only time me 'n' Sally ever stayed in one place was when Momma was in the pen."

Taking a careful breath, I added, "Karen tells me your mother moved to Malta a couple of years ago."

"Oh, yeah!" Becky's tone told me that here was an unpleasant subject.

"Did she have a job lined up?"

"Not that I know of."

"Did she ever mention why she wanted to move?"

Shaking her head, Becky capped the detergent bottle. "I reckon it was just another case o' Momma tryin' to find herself."

"Did you see much of her during that period?"

"Oh, she came back home now and then. Sundays, mostly. Momma said Saturday was their busy day at the mall."

"Mall?" I echoed.

Quick nod. "Momma worked in one of the stores at the Silver Kings Mall. She told me the name, but I forget."

I tried another approach. "Why didn't she take Karen with her?"

"Landlady didn't want kids around. That's what Momma told me. But . . ." Becky let the rest trail off. Her lips tightened as she closed the washing machine's lid.

Tread lightly, Angela. You're on sensitive ground here.

"But you don't believe that," I murmured.

"I'll be honest with you, Angie," she said, turning to face me. "For a long time, I was really worried. That move up north. That's the way it used to be when Sally 'n' me were kids. Momma would start gettin' restless. Complainin' about every little thing. Then, out of the clear blue sky, she'd say, 'Wouldn't you girls like to stay with Aunt Alice for a spell?' She'd stable us out at Gunsight Pass and come visit from time to time. But she never told us where she was or what kind of job she was workin'." All at once her voice became hoarse. "Soon after that, we'd get the word. Momma's in the pen." Halting fingers flicked the on-switch. Hot water cascaded into the machine. "I knew my mother, Angie. Knew her better'n *anybody*. When she moved up to Malta, I was so scared she was gonna pull another job. Just like the old days, you know? I used to dread it whenever the phone rang. I thought it was the law. Thought they were gonna tell me she'd been arrested." Relief filled her face. "Sure was wrong about that, though. And damned glad too! I don't know what was buggin' Momma, but she finally got it out of her system. She came on home the beginning of last summer, and things sorta got back to normal around here."

"I'm glad," I said softly. "Karen doesn't like to talk about it, but your mother's departure . . . well, it really hurt her."

Becky's eyes turned sympathetic. "I *know*. I know exactly what Karen's going through."

*Because you've been through it yourself,* I realized.

Holding the empty basket under one arm, Becky sauntered into the dining room. I followed at her heels. "If you don't mind a personal question . . . how did you feel about your mother leaving Karen with you?"

Sighing heavily, she faced me. "If you want to know the truth, I was glad. Between them, Sally and Momma have made a pretty thorough hash of Karen's life. That girl needs a stable home. Luckily, I was able to provide it."

"No second thoughts? No resentments?"

"Absolutely none! We Rooleys look out for each other. You oughta know that by now. Resentments? Well . . ." Becky displayed a saddened smile. "Maybe a little. Sometimes I think that big sister o' mine learned the wrong lesson from Momma."

"Such as shipping inconvenient daughters to the relatives?"

"Bingo!" Becky's index finger swiveled toward my nose.

"You are a pleasure to talk to, Miss Angie Biwaban. Do you know that?"

"Yeah . . . but it's still nice to hear it."

Becky chuckled, then showed me another bittersweet smile. "I loved that woman, Angie. Still do! But, I'm tellin' ya, if somebody gave me the means to do it, there's more 'n' one part of my mother's life I would've changed!"

Before I could comment, an off-key squeal erupted from the study. Our rented fax machine began disgorging correspondence. Hastily excusing myself, I set off at a trot.

As I arrived at the study, the last shiny sheet came curling out of the fax. I smoothed each sheet flat, gave it a hasty read, and then sorted them for Sarah. After that I hitched up the Wizard, summoned the boss lady's outgoing E-mail, and zapped it off to Pierre.

Shortly before eleven I heard the sound of laboring truck engines. After shutting down the computer, I walked into the living room and caught a glimpse of a familiar blue Sierra through the frost-rimmed window.

"Looks like we've got company," Becky remarked.

I knew who it was, of course, but I donned a puzzled expression as I followed her to the front door.

Up the front steps trod Merry, her cheeks reddened by the wind. Right behind was Chief, snug and warm in his evergreen Highlander parka, woolen scarf, brushpopper jeans, and black felt cowboy hat. A red-tipped eagle feather protruded from the hatband, denoting his status as an Anishinabe veteran wounded in action.

Pushing the door open, Merry cried, "Angie! Your grandfather's here."

"Chief!" I exclaimed, feigning a look of surprise. Vigorous Anishinabe bear hug. "What are you doing here? I—I thought you were headed for Utah."

"I was." Chief had no difficulty remembering his lines. "I

stopped in Pierre to say hi. Mrs. Sadowski told me you were out here. Figured to stop by on my way to Heber City."

"Am I glad to see you." One arm around his waist, I turned him toward my hosts. "Let me introduce you. Becky, Merry, this is my grandfather, Charlie Blackbear. . . ."

In no time at all, Chief and the Rooley sisters were chatting like old friends. Then Becky asked, "Where are you staying, Charlie?"

"Gunnison. The Water Wheel Inn."

"Not anymore you're not." Becky squeezed his shoulders. "No sense drivin' twenty miles to see Angie. You're welcome to stay here."

"Won't that be getting kind of crowded?" I observed.

"Not at all," Merry replied. "Guest room's empty. We can put Mr. Blackbear in there."

"Besides, the RJ Bar has a reputation for hospitality. I ain't one to let it slide." Becky turned to my grandfather. "You're stayin' for lunch, I hope."

Chief cracked a smile. "Ms. Rooley, I'd be delighted."

Smiling, she closed the front door. "Better keep it on a first-name basis, Charlie. Say 'Ms. Rooley' in this house, and three women are just liable to answer." Sidelong glance. "We'll be eatin' in another hour. Angie, why don't you show your grand-dad around?"

"Okay. Give me a minute to change, eh?"

A wintry gust ruffled my hood's fur trim as Chief and I reached the top of the rise. Loose snow swirled past us, streaming into the azure sky, whitening the top branches of the trailside spruce. As the chill numbed my face, I was very grateful to be wearing my Duluth snowsuit. Bulky game warden's parka with down insulation and a hood trimmed with fisher fur. Spruce-colored ski pants. Moosehide moccasin boots insulated with rabbit fur. Plus a pair of *mind-jikawanag*—fur-lined mitten-style gauntlets reaching all the way to the elbow. Back home in Minnesota, they're called choppers.

My bearpaw snowshoes kicked up a plume with every step. Good old Chief. He'd brought an extra pair with him, figuring I'd need them up here in the high country.

He figured *right*, too! Better than fifteen feet of snow covered East Cement's upper slopes. Vast snowdrifts, curling at the crest, smothered the groves of Engelmann spruce. Stalks of Gunnison mariposa were sheathed in ice.

Thigh muscles knotted and sizzled. My bearpaws began to feel like concrete blocks. Heart thumping, I signaled a halt. Looking over my shoulder, I spied the Rooley barn a quarter-mile below, a patch of red in the stark white snowfield.

"Almost there," I gasped.

Keeping his back to the wind, Chief joined me. "Take it easy, *Noozis*. You're not used to this altitude." Fond smile. "Guess you won't have to go jogging today."

"Guess not, *Nimishoo*." I had no breath left for inspired repartee.

Chief turned his gaze upslope. East Cement's snow-covered summit, crowned with cirrus, loomed above the trail. "Where exactly did you see that flash?"

"There!" I pointed out the snow-covered balcony at the foot of a vertical rock wall. Orange streaks stained the cliff face, the residue of glacial meltwater that had seeped through deposits of iron oxide. "Somebody's keeping tabs on the Rooleys, *Nimishoo*. I have a hunch it started before Madge's death."

Chief's gloved hand steadied his black Stetson. "Any idea who it might be?"

"Not a one," I replied.

"What about that big guy you saw at the gas station?"

Good point! I reflected. Perched on one leg, I brushed the caked snow from my bearpaw. Who was that guy? And why had he taken such a keen interest in Madge Rooley's wrecked pickup?

Chief and I resumed our uphill march. The spruce petered out the higher we climbed, giving way to dwarf alpine fir and snow-covered, wind-warped krummholz.

Snowshoes rustled the drift just behind me. "You know, I've been dropping that woman's name around town."

"Heard anything interesting?" I rasped.

"Yeah! C.B.'s legendary lady outlaw. In another twenty years, *Noozis*, they'll be adding a Madge Rooley exhibit to that museum."

"Not if Sarah has anything to say about it!"

"She's likely to be outvoted, girl. Her mother's as big a legend as Butch Cassidy himself." Sudden cough. "Everybody's in agreement about one thing, though. If you've got a question about Madge Rooley, your best bet is to talk to Chet Hurtig."

The name sounded familiar. Then I remembered those newspaper articles. "Any relation to Chester B. Hurtig?"

"One and the same, *Noozis*. He used to be sheriff."

"I know. And town marshal before that. He was the first cop to put the cuffs on Madge." Peering over my shoulder, I asked, "What's he doing these days?"

"Running a camping supply store on Elk Avenue."

I chose my steps with care. "Retired?"

"You bet. But it wasn't his idea."

"Oh?" Inquisitive Angie glance.

"He was defeated in the last election. Something strange happened to the deputies' retirement fund. The town auditor reported eighty-five hundred dollars missing. Hurtig denied it. The state treasurer's office sent down a team and found that someone had replaced the missing money in the fund's account, using eighty-five hundred in cashier's checks."

My eyebrows arched. "Interesting. Cashier's checks are untraceable."

"You bet. They couldn't prove who stole the money or who

engineered the coverup. Hurtig's opponent raised a stink during the campaign. Hurtig thought he could bluff it out, but the voters gave him the boot."

"The state attorney general didn't pursue the matter?"

Harsh chuckle from Chief. "Unh-unh! That Hurtig guy's been in town politics for over thirty years. He knows where *all* the bodies are buried!"

Perhaps that would work to my advantage, I thought. If Hurtig was on the outs with the current sheriff, he'd be highly unlikely to mention a visit from Angie. Using just the right approach, I might be able to pump him for more background information about Madge.

At last we reached the rimrock balcony. Krummholz and brittle stalks huddled against the cliff. A vertical rock chimney split the granite, wending its curvy way toward a broad band of diorite. I glanced in dismay at the blanket of pristine snow. Snowflake spirals danced over the edge with each strong gust of wind.

Fussbudget face. "Uh-oh!"

Chief sighed. "If there were any tracks up here, that wind has sure taken care of them."

Nodding, I stood at the brink. At this height, the Rooley ranch resembled a tabletop diorama. The rock balcony offered our friend the perfect observation post.

My parka fluttered in the mountain wind. Stepping back from the edge, I turned to my grandfather. "Maybe not, *Nimishoo.*"

"What do you mean?"

"The wind was blowing last night, too," I replied, nodding at the rock chimney. "Hard enough to rattle the windows. What do you suppose it was like *up here?*"

Sudden Anishinabe grin. "A windchill of seventy or eighty below, maybe?"

"Right! Meaning he would have wanted to get out of the

wind from time to time." Snowshoes whispered as I headed for the rock chimney. "Let's have a look, eh?"

Peering into the shadowy alcove, I spotted two large footprints at the rear. Blowing snow had partially obscured the tread pattern, but there was no mistaking those distinctive starbursts.

A chill that had nothing to do with the mountain wind rippled through me. I'd seen those footprints before. They were identical to the wet prints I'd seen at the Brown Palace Hotel.

Chief sensed my unease. *"Noozis?"*

"It's him," I muttered, stepping away from the cliff. "The guy who was spying on us at the hotel. The one who was gunning for Sarah."

"You sure?" he asked.

Vigorous Angie nod. "Same footprints, *Nimishoo*. He's followed us to Crested Butte."

Standing in the cliff's shade, Chief opened his mouth in reply. Suddenly, his obsidian eyes widened in alarm. Without a sound, he lunged at me. *"Mitchaii!"*

Quick as a lynx, Chief tackled me around the waist, dropping me in the snow. An angry supersonic hiss whizzed overhead as we splashed down. *Bweeeoww!* The bullet ricocheted off an outcrop of rimrock.

And then, like a peal of thunder, the roar of a high-powered rifle came tumbling down the mountainside.

## NINE

Gripping me in a bear hug, Chief rolled me over and over through the powdery snow. We tumbled out of the sunshine—into the cliff's frigid shadow. I slid over an outcrop, yelping as I plunged into a snowdrift. My grandfather landed beside me. His gnarled hand pressured my spine. "Stay down!"

A snow geyser erupted to our right. Again the hidden rifle roared. *KAAAAAROWWWWW!*

Flattening behind the stony outcrop, I hissed, *"Nimishoo!* The shooter! Where—?"

Chief pushed me under the rocky overhang, making me less of a target. "Farther up the trail." Another ricochet stung my ears. *"Noozis,* lie still!"

*KAAAAAROWWWWW!* The rifle's roar provided ample incentive. Huddled against stone, I turned to Chief. "How did you know?"

Anishinabe grin. "I saw the sun flash on the barrel."

Another rolling boom reverberated along the mountainside. *KAAAAAROWWWWW!*

Knowledgeable grunt from Chief. "Hunting rifle. Bolt-action model."

"C-c-could be semiauto," I murmured, my teeth chattering.

He shook his head. "Too long between shots, *Noozis*. It takes a few seconds to work the bolt."

My grandfather was right, of course. Those few seconds had provided us with just enough time to get behind cover.

Chief flashed an ironic glance. "Looks like your friend had the same idea, doesn't it?"

I nodded. The intruder must have been startled to find Chief and Angie nosing around his perch. And angry enough to risk a killing shot in broad daylight.

Crouched behind the outcrop, we were safe. But only for the moment. The sniper had the advantage. Squatting up there on the saddleback, peering through that scope, he could clip anything within two thousand meters. No chance of retreat. No way could we outrun a bullet.

Nor could we hold our position for very long. The snow's cold began to nibble my bones. Adrenaline had long since spent itself. My body shivered all over in an attempt to keep warm.

Grim frown. He didn't even have to *hit* us! With enough ammo, he could sit up there all afternoon, keep us pinned down, and let the frostbite finish us off.

Tense minutes passed. Facedown, I hugged the snow, keeping my hood well below the outcrop's horizon. The chill numbed my fingers. Breathing in long gasps, I nervously awaited the next gunshot.

And then my ears detected the start-up mutter of a pickup truck's engine. The sound drifted down from the saddleback, a monotone growl among the wintry gusts.

I started to rise, but my grandfather put a restraining hand on my shoulder. "What's your hurry?"

"*Nimishoo*, he's clearing out."

"There could be *two* of them up there." Chief jutted his chin toward the ridge. "One leaves in the truck. The other stays behind with the rifle, waiting for us to pop up." He patted my arm. "Rest awhile, *Noozis.*"

I took his advice. Now I understood how my grandfather had survived those three amphibious invasions fifty years ago. The wind brought us snatches of alpine sound. The skittering noise of sliding ice. The high-pitched warble of the mountain chickadee. But no more gunshots.

Chief nodded. "Let's have a look."

When we reached the saddleback, I found a depression in the snow. The spot where the sniper's knee had touched down. Off to the right, four lozenge-shaped holes marred a small windblown drift.

Grinning, I squatted on my snowshoe and thrust my mittened hand into the white stuff. Might as well have a look at the empty cartridges, I thought. Coming out of the rifle, the sniper's brass had been hot enough to melt the snow.

I withdrew a thin, tapered cartridge. It reminded me of a lipstick tube. Turning it over, I read the stamped legend on the base: 6.5MM X 55 REM.

"What did you find?" Chief asked.

"Remington cartridge." I handed it to him. "Six-point-five millimeter. That's a deer-hunting round, isn't it?"

Examining it, Chief let out a soft grunt. "You could knock down a caribou with this round. It's a 140-grain soft-point Remington Swede. This thing really flies, 2,560 feet per second."

Arch smile. "I suppose you can identify the rifle, too."

Obsidian eyes twinkled. "Of course! Bolt-action Remington Model 700 Classic."

"You sound very sure of yourself, *Nimishoo.*"

"I am! The M700 is one of the few rifles that can be chambered for a 6.5-millimeter Swede." Chuckling, he handed back the cartridge. "Now you've got a real clue. There can't be that many guys in Crested Butte toting a Remington M700."

"Oh, no?" Crooked Angie smile. "Have you seen all the pickup trucks with gun racks?"

"I guess we've got our work cut out for us at the gun stores."

Pocketing the round, I beckoned to my grandfather. "Come on. Let's do some tracking."

A line of familiar tracks slithered uphill to the rim. The impressions were oval, slightly longer than ours, with the same fishnet pattern on the sole. I frowned in recognition. Snowshoes! Of a style known as the Michigan bearpaw. The sniper had needed them to cross the deep snow beyond the ridge.

As we reached the skyline, my gaze followed the snowshoe trail fifty yards downslope. A broad snow-covered pathway, split down the middle by a parallel pair of tire ruts, meandered through the spruce forest. Surprised Angie blink. I hadn't expected to find a logging road this close to the ranch house.

I squatted beside the ruts for a closer look. The tread marks reminded me of a tractor's large rear tires. The vehicle's weight had packed down the snow.

Chief halted at my side. *"Eyan, Noozis.* Those are snow tires, all right. Michelin radials. He was driving a four-by-four." His forehead tensed thoughtfully. "Judging from the wheel base, I'd say a Chevy Silverado."

I pointed out the stirred-up snow beside the rut. To the immediate right was a size eleven shoe print identical to the one we'd found in the rock chimney.

"Here's where he removed his snowshoes and climbed into the cab." I grinned at the depth of the print. "Big boy!"

"Don't be too sure. You could read that two ways, *Noozis.*" Chief's grim expression lightened. "He could be a tall, rugged man weighing two hundred pounds. Or a fat man of medium height wearing a size eleven shoe."

Standing up, I extended my arms in a comforting stretch. "Well, at least we know he drives a Silverado."

"And totes a Remington M700. Don't forget that."

"I won't!" I shivered at the memory of that first gunshot. If not for my grandfather's vigilance back there, I'd be lying facedown in the snow. Thankful smile. "There's nothing more for us here, *Nimishoo*. Let's get back to the house."

On our way down the mountain, my thoughts drifted back to Mike's Mobil, to the hard-faced, heavyset man who put the grab on me. *Tayaa!* He certainly tipped the scales at two hundred.

Just then I heard a female voice calling my name. Peering downslope, I spied Merry and Troy. I felt my grandfather's grip on my shoulder. He flashed me a questioning glance. Should we tell them?

Fussbudget face. No, not yet, I decided. If I confided in them, Troy and Merry would be sure to tell Sarah. And she'd have the Colorado State Patrol here within the hour. No, I preferred to put off calling the Colorado Bureau of Investigation until I had some really solid evidence.

"Angie!" Troy hollered. "What's going on? We heard shots."

"So did we!" I made my own voice breathless.

Chief aimed his thumb upslope. "He was shooting at something up on the rim. Dall sheep, maybe. Angie and I found some tracks. He lit out when he heard us coming."

For a fleeting split second, Troy resembled his outlaw ancestor. "Poachers!"

"Are you two all right?" Merry asked, touching my sleeve.

"Just startled out of our wits." Reassuring smile. "We followed his tracks to a logging road up there."

"Did you see him?" Troy asked.

Shaking his head, my grandfather replied, "Afraid not."

"Shit." Troy lowered his Stetson against the wind. "Proba-

bly came up Rosebud Gulch. Where the hell are Quinn's deputies when you *really* need them?"

Folding her arms, Merry said, "They can't be everywhere,
brother of mine."

"Is that your logging road?" I asked.

"Nope!" Troy's gaze traveled up to the skyline. "Canaan
Lumber ran her through last March."

"They did some cutting?" I prodded.

Swift nod. "Momma let them trim a few acres of spruce up
there. That's how we got our down payment for the loan.
Eight thousand from the timber sale. The rest was Momma's
savings."

Chief spoke up. "How good are the local maps?"

Troy let out a belly laugh. "You're not going to find that
road on any map, Charlie. It's too new. County maps are usually a year or two out of date."

I exchanged knowing glances with my grandfather. If the
sniper knew about that logging road, then he had to be local.

Rubbing her mittened hands eagerly, Merry said, "Let's
get out of this wind!"

"Good idea." Her brother led the way. "Becky's cooked up a
batch of beef stew. That oughta melt the icicles." Country-boy
grin. "Let's move!"


Following lunch, my grandfather sat at the kitchen table,
nursing his cup of coffee, while Becky and I ferried the dirty
dishware to the sink. Pausing at the counter, Becky hefted the
beaker and asked, "Want any more, Charlie?"

Chief lifted his palm. "I'm fine, Becky."

"Well, if you're lookin' for a refill, there's a cup or two left."
Black liquid swirled as she gave the beaker a jostle.

"Thanks, girl, but I've got to get back to town." Amiable
grin. "Still got to check out of the Water Wheel."

I shot my grandfather a determined look. "You're going to
need help packing."

Good old Chief. He picked right up on it. "Sure am." He waved his cup in my direction. "You don't mind if I borrow my granddaughter for an hour or two, do you?"

"Not at all." Becky turned on the faucet. Hot water surged into the plastic wash basin. "And don't fret none, Angie. I'll tell Sally where you went."

"Thanks, Becky." Quickly I strode from the kitchen. "I'll be right down, Chief."

He chuckled. "Wardrobe change, eh?"

"Force of habit."

Change I did. Off with the ranch denims. On with my full-sleeved silken white blouse, weskit floral-print vest, and pleated spruce trousers. Ten minutes in the bathroom had my raven hair pulled back and uplifted in the ice-princess style made famous by Nancy Kerrigan.

Returning to my room, I lifted Madge's photo from the chest of drawers. The one showing Madge pushing eight-year-old Karen on the swing. I slipped it out of its wooden frame, then tucked it safely away in my purse.

Oh, I'd be helping Chief out of the Water Wheel, all right. First, though, we had to make a little side trip to Malta. . . .

"There it is, missy."

Chief's foot slowly pressured the brake. His Sierra rolled to a complete stop. Leaning forward, I peered out the windshield. A huge snow mound rimmed the side of the road, topped by a sign reading TURQUOISE LAKE ROAD.

"Turn left," I advised, tapping his sleeve. "The man said it was on the lakeshore."

"I sure hope so." Stepping on the clutch, Chief swiveled the stick shift. "There wasn't a whole helluva lot back there in town, Angie."

I grimaced. How right he was! Malta was a roadside village hanging a hundred yards back from Colorado 300. Well-kept ranch houses, bare-limbed cottonwood trees, and the steel tracks of the Denver and Rio Grande Western Railroad. A pair of Soo Line boxcars sat idle on a siding, their rusting wheels half buried in snow.

Chief pulled up in front of the combination cafe, grocery store, and gas station. The owner informed me that visiting ladies usually boarded with Mrs. Stalworthy at the Looseslipper House, a Victorian bed-and-breakfast on Turquoise Lake.

Rough going! The Sierra's tires slipped and spun on the road's icy surface. I let Chief concentrate on the driving, glancing at the dashboard clock. Two forty-five.

We'd had a long ride from Roaring Judy. From Gunnison to Poncha Springs, up and over Monarch Pass. We'd stopped briefly at the scene of Madge Rooley's death, but, after six days and fifteen inches of additional snowfall, there was nothing left in the way of trace evidence. So we'd continued on our way. Up Colorado 285 to Northrop, flanked on our right by the ice-rimmed Arkansas River. Then farther north on Route 24, skirting past the two most awesome fourteeners in the state, Mount Elbert and her sister, Mount Massive.

A sugarloaf peak sheathed in snow loomed on our left. At its foot lay Turquoise Lake, now a broad expanse of ice, virtually indistinguishable from the snow-draped valley. A sprinkling of dark green fishing cabins littered the lake's frozen surface.

Chief let out a laugh. "Remind you of anything, Angie?"

The sight brought a burst of contralto laughter to my lips. When I finally recovered, I gasped, "If I didn't know better, I'd think we were in Onamia."

"No mountains on Lake Mille Lacs, girl."

"Do you suppose they have *lutefisk* here?"

Shaking his head, he laughed again. "Only in Minnesota, Angie. Only in Minnesota!"

Just then a red brick house came into view. A trio of alders flanked it on the right. A snowplowed driveway met the main road. The sizable aluminum mailbox read STALWORTHY.

The house itself was an Italianate villa dating from the

Grant administration. A two-story home with peaked gables, a central chimney, a wraparound porch, and a large bay window. Slender hand-tooled Victorian columns upheld the porch roof. Cornices of gingerbread trim added to the aura of old-fashioned elegance.

Chief opted to remain in the truck. I didn't mind. For the con I had in mind, I'd do better working alone.

Stepping down from the truck, I cast a quick glance at the southern horizon. To the right of the frost giants, Elbert and Massive, reared the rugged peaks of the Sawatch range. Their clefts offered tantalizing glimpses of the more distant Collegiates. Thoughtful smile. It was strange seeing the two Cements from this side. Forty miles separated me from the Rooley ranch. Yet, packed within that forty miles was some of the most mountainous terrain in America. An eagle could have made it to the RJ Bar—no problem. Chief and I, however, had been forced to travel a hundred miles out of our way.

Huddled in my parka, I hastened up the shoveled pathway. Frosty vapors cuddled my face with every exhalation. Ancient stairs creaked beneath my spike-heeled boots.

I gave the pitted brass knocker a few raps. Light footsteps sounded on the other side of the door. An elderly voice sang, "Just a minute."

Squaring my shoulders, I watched the door swing open. On the threshold stood a petite lady in her early sixties, wearing a knitted red pullover sweater and a pair of bronze corduroy jeans. Thin shoulders and broad hips. Her hair was short and curly, its shade a Clairol light brown, just barely covering her prominent ears. She had a broad Teutonic face with low eyebrows, a sharp nose, a thin-lipped mouth, high cheekbones, and a noticeable chin. The lady smiled, showing a bit of silver. A bright smile, to be sure, but not as bright as her friendly, dark blue eyes.

"Mrs. Stalworthy?" I inquired.

"Yes, yes." Seizing my arm, she pulled me inside. "Come in,

dear, come in. Oh, please forgive the mess. Not many guests drop by in the wintertime."

My gaze traveled from the Victorian entryway with its hand-carved molding and Persian rug to the living room with its cozy upholstered chairs, low polished oak table, and plush, high-backed sofa. Blink of confusion. *Mess? What mess?*

Mrs. Stalworthy closed the front door. Unzipping my parka, I stepped off the mat. Then jumped at her sudden yelp of soprano alarm.

"*Aieeeee*—no, no, no, dear!" She shooed me back onto the mat. "The floor! It's varnished oak. Boots off! Boots off!"

And so, while I shed my high-heeled boots, Mrs. Stalworthy dropped to all fours, plucked a crumpled Kleenex from her pocket, and vigorously scrubbed the wet spot.

Now I understood why the living room resembled the centerfold in *House Beautiful!*

"I'm Rowena Stalworthy," she said, taking my parka and woolen scarf. "Welcome to the Looseslipper House, Miss—?"

"Lear. Judy Lear." My nyloned feet made no sound on the polished floorboards. "Is that really the name—*Loose Slipper?*"

"One word, dear. Looseslipper." Chuckling, she led me into the living room. "Sounds like a frontier bordello, doesn't it?" Deftly she hung my coat in a narrow hideaway closet. "That really is the name, you know. Mr. Looseslipper was a very prominent man. One of the richest in Leadville." Tone of reverence. "Dean Looseslipper."

How she said that name without cracking up I'll never know!

"Mr. Looseslipper built this house back in 1878," she informed me. "It was the first brick house in the county. He wanted to be close to the mine. And, of course, he always loved the lake. Come, Judy, let me show you around."

And so, Mrs. Stalworthy gave me the ten-cent tour, pointing out all the showpiece furnishings. Hardwood parquet floors, oak columns, and tall, arched windows. The dining room was decorated in stained cherrywood, a perfect match for the hand-carved mantelpiece above the Italian tile fireplace.

Even in Newport or Saratoga, the Looseslipper House would have raised eyebrows. So I was more than a little curious about the builder. Turned out that Mr. Looseslipper was one of the original silver kings of Leadville. A mining magnate in the same league with Meyer Guggenheim, Marshall Field, and James J. Brown, he who married the Unsinkable Molly.

Looseslipper had been a colonel in the British army, Rowena explained, and, having hunted elephants in Africa and tigers in India, he'd come to the land of the Awishi to have a crack at *Pijiki*. That's our word for *buffalo*. When his rambling two-year safari came to a close, the colonel found himself in Leadville one week before a pair of unemployed shoemakers, George Hook and August Riche, struck silver at Fryer Hill. When the Little Pittsburg Mine opened, Looseslipper purchased four hundred dollars worth of preferred shares. A wise investment, as things turned out, for within the month the Little Pittsburg had extracted fifty thousand dollars' worth of silver ore.

Flush with cash, Colonel Looseslipper sank a mine shaft of his own on Sugarloaf Mountain. The resulting strike sent silver shares skyrocketing on Wall Street. And Turquoise Lake, once the abode of Awishi medicine men, became the private pond of the nouveau riche colonel.

". . . His wife Adelaide did quite a bit of entertaining, Judy," Rowena explained, gesturing at the long, linen-clad table. "Oscar Wilde was a guest here. So was the Prince of Wales—"

Instant double take. "Prince Charles?"

"No, no, no! Edward the Seventh, Queen Victoria's son. He stayed for a week back in 1885."

Coy Angie smile. How would she react, I wondered, if I told her that her house was entertaining royalty yet again?

"Of course, it all came to a sad end." Mild sorrow pinched the lady's features. "Congress repealed the Sherman Silver Purchase Act in 1893. Silver stocks plummeted in value. Mr. Looseslipper became a pauper overnight. The same thing happened to many of the silver kings."

Sometimes it's best to go ahead and let them talk. It puts them at ease—makes them more amenable to questioning.

"What happened then?" I asked.

"He shot himself," Rowena said matter-of-factly. "When he realized he was broke, Mr. Looseslipper sent his wife by train to Denver. Then he dressed for dinner, putting on his white regimental jacket and cummerbund. After dinner he drank a little sherry and wrote a poem on the napkin. He didn't have a pencil, so he used a burnt-out match. Then he picked up his Webley, put the muzzle to his temple, and pulled the trigger."

I winced. A hundred years later, I could all-too-easily visualize the colonel's last moments. "How do you know all that?"

"The maid saw him do it. She ran three miles to town to fetch the sheriff." Rowena shrugged. "Of course, by the time he got here, it was too late." She tugged at my silken sleeve. "This way, Judy. I'll show you the poem."

Of all the strange things I've seen in my life, Colonel Looseslipper's final poem has to rank in the top ten. I kid you not, gang. There it hung, right in the parlor—a yellowing linen napkin pressed flat within its glass frame. Judging from the quatrain, the colonel was a fan of Kipling's.

*As I approach*
*the Gates of Heaven,*
*I ask myself,*
*Will it look like Devon?*

My gaze deliberately avoided the rust-brown stains at the bottom of the napkin. Somehow I didn't think they were gravy.

Change the subject, Angie, before she goes rummaging for the pistol! "Uhmmm—how long have you lived here, Mrs. Stalworthy?"

"My husband and I bought the house from the Hagerman family back in 1956," she replied, showing me a fond smile. "Ted passed away eleven years ago. I couldn't run the place all by myself, so I sold off the livestock and turned it into a bed-and-breakfast."

"You mentioned that you don't get many visitors this time of year," I remarked, waiting for an opening.

"There isn't much to do up here in winter." Wry smile. "Unless you enjoy ice fishing."

"How long do your guests stay?"

"Oh, a week or two. Sailing's the big thing in the summer. That and mountain biking."

"I understand you take boarders."

"Yes, indeed!" Dark blue eyes gleamed with sudden interest. "I'm renting to four women right now. In fact, I have a queen-size bedroom available on the second floor. You can take meals in your own room or eat right here in the dining room. I charge four hundred dollars a month, laundry service included. Would you like to have a look?"

"Uh, no thanks, Mrs. Stalworthy. I've already got an apartment." I slid the purse strap off my shoulder.

"In Leadville?"

"Denver," I replied. I did a passable imitation of Paul Holbrook. Exact same tone of patience and integrity. "I'm with the state Department of Social Services." I flashed one of the business cards I ran off on Sarah's printer. "Do you mind if I ask you a couple of questions?"

Disappointment softened her dark blue eyes. I guess I looked like a desirable tenant. "Not at all, dear."

Showing the Madge photo, I asked, "Do you know this woman?"

A flurry of emotions crossed Rowena's angular face. Shock,

dismay, irritation, and resentment. Not exactly the reactions I'd been expecting.

"Yes, that's Marjorie!" she said hotly. "Yes, she boarded with me for just over a year. And, Miss Judy Lear, I'm going to tell you exactly what I told Sheriff Whitaker *and* the Colorado State Patrol *and* the FBI back in June. That Monday was the last I ever saw of Marjorie Dexter!"

Blink of astonishment. *Marjorie Dexter?*

Her slender fingers curled into fists. "Just when is this persecution going to stop? I had no idea what that woman was up to. I've told you people everything! Here we are, seven months later, and you're *still* coming around!"

Rowena's outburst took me completely by surprise. She seemed to blame me for whatever had happened last summer. Trying to recover, I blurted out, "Marjorie!?"

"Of course! Who else would I be talking about? What do you think this is, young lady? A den of thieves?" Sudden confusion replaced the resentment in her eyes. "She *is* your client, isn't she?"

"Uh, no . . ." Frantically I concocted an alternate cover. "I represent the little girl—" *Tayaa!* Think of a name—quick! *"Sally Anne.* I'm a child care counselor with the DSS."

"I see." Suddenly contrite, she extended a hand. "May I?"

I gave her the photo. As she studied it, Rowena's expression melted in sympathy. "She looks just like Marjorie. How old is she?"

Little white Angie lie. "Twelve."

Handing back the photo, Rowena said, "I should have known. I had a feeling about Marjorie. She never talked about her family. Except that one time. The time she came home drunk. Lord, what a chatterbox! She went on and on about Sally." Slight shake of the head. "I had a feeling she was talking about her daughter."

"Sally had been staying with relatives in Steamboat

Springs." I tucked the photo away. "She disappeared about a week ago. We think she may have rejoined her mother."

"I—I see."

"I hate to bother you, Mrs. Stalworthy, but we have to check out Marjorie's last known address."

"Of course." Anxiety creased the woman's forehead. "You really think she took Sally with her?"

"It's a distinct possibility." Pulling a small notebook and pen from my purse, I added, "Anything you can tell me, ma'am, will be a real big help. When did Marjorie move in?"

"About two years ago." The landlady's face turned thoughtful. "She told me she needed a room. That she'd just gone to work at Trautmann's."

"Trautmann's?" I echoed.

"At the Silver Kings Mall." Her hand gestured at the arched window. "A couple of miles down the road."

"What kind of job?"

"Cashier. She worked the day shift, mostly. Except for Christmas, of course, when they work all those crazy hours. She had two days off a week—Tuesday and Sunday." Flustered look. "But I couldn't tell you anything about the robbery. All I know is, Marjorie had breakfast with me that Monday morning. Right here in the dining room. Perhaps you'd be better off talking to Sheriff Whitaker."

*Robbery?* I masked my surprise behind a professional counselor's demeanor. "What did she do on her days off, Mrs. Stalworthy?"

"That depends." Rowena smiled suddenly, overtaken by pleasant memories. "Marjorie was an outdoor girl. She took up cross-country skiing that winter. She told me she was determined to hold on to her schoolgirl figure. She did a lot of backpacking, too."

"Backpacking?"

"Yes, indeed. If the weather was clear, you'd find Marjorie tramping up there in the high country. I remember one weekend in June—a storm closed the Collegiate range. Marjorie was in the kitchen, swearing like a truck driver. 'Now, Marge,' I told her, 'What kind of language is that for a lady?' Oh, she hated it whenever she got rained out."

My ears perked. "Where exactly in the Collegiates?"

"I'm not sure. She did ask about Grizzly Peak one time."

"Did she go hiking alone?" I asked, taking notes.

"Not always. Sometimes she went with that bearded fellow."

I experienced a jolt of eerie familiarity. But I had to make sure it was the same man. "What did he look like?"

"Oh, about my age, I suppose. He had a beard like Yosemite Sam." Nostrils twitched in disgust. "I don't think he's changed his underwear since Kennedy was president. I remember, he came to the house one Sunday when Marjorie had to work." Dark eyes sizzled in indignation. "He had the *gall* to ask me for a drink! On the Sabbath! Just a little nip, he said, to help settle his arthritis. I told him to *git!*"

Smiling coyly, I kept right on scribbling. Well, well . . . *Pop Hannan!* What brings you up north, Pop?

All at once, my mind drifted back to our conversation at Kochevar's. Pop's raspy voice echoed in my memory. *Spent many a summer weekend up on Grizzly Peak. Me 'n' Madge 'n' Sally 'n' Becky.*

Right, Pop. And you're also the guy whose hand trembled when I mentioned Madge's trip to Malta. You knew she was here. You even dropped by the Looseslipper House on what you thought was her day off. Why did my mention of Malta upset you so?

"Did she have any friends in town, Mrs. Stalworthy?"

She shrugged. "Not that I'm aware of."

Tossing her a thoughtful gaze, I asked, "Any boyfriends?"

Thin lips puckered in disapproval. "A few!"

"Did you ever meet any of them?"

She shook her head. "Marjorie did all her socializing in

town, I'm afraid. She made a point of going out every Saturday night." Eyes narrowing, she added, "I did see her with a man, though. May, I think. I was driving down Harrison Avenue, and I saw them going into the Silver Dollar."

"What did he look like?"

"A hard-rock miner, I'd say. Big, big fellow." Touching her chin, she added, "He had a rather large jaw. And two deep lines across his forehead."

*Bingo!* I thought. The bruiser from Mike's Mobil!

"What made you think he was a miner?"

"His color," she replied. "He was wearing Tony Lama boots, but he was much too pale for a cowhand. He didn't spend much time in the sun. He looked as if he could handle a jackhammer, though."

"He never came to the house, eh?"

Another vigorous head shake. "The only man she ever brought here was that Indian . . ." Embarrassed wince. "Actually, it was the other way around. *He* brought Marjorie home." A faint blush descended from her hairline. "Now, I'm a God-fearing woman, but I'm no prude. I don't mind my tenants coming home a little tipsy now and then. But Marjorie! Honestly, that Indian had her draped over his shoulder."

"Describe him."

"In his early thirties, I'd say. Very tall and thin, with a narrow nose. Very, very short black hair. And he was wearing a black fringed vest. He showed up on the porch and asked me, 'Is this where Marge Dexter lives?' I had him put her on the sofa." Absentmindedly she gave her arms a rub. "I'm afraid he gave me a nasty turn, Judy. I didn't like that smile of his at all. It was as if we shared a dirty little secret."

My pen froze in midstroke. No! I thought. It can't be him. *He's dead!*

"When did this happen, ma'am?"

"The end of April. About a month before the robbery."

"And you saw, uh, Marge with the big guy in May?"

"That's right."

"Did she ever mention any names?"

"Not to me." Folding her arms, Rowena sighed. "What's going to happen to Sally Anne?"

Fortunately for me, unexpected questions serve as a stimulus to imagination. "She'll become a ward of the court. Her aunt has formal custody. I'll be the one taking her back to Steamboat Springs."

"I'm glad she has a family to go to." The landlady's voice quavered. "I'm glad it's her kin and not some foster home."

Closing my notebook, I said, "If you hear anything, you can reach me through the DSS in Denver."

She didn't appear to hear me. "Lord, how could she do it?"

Into the purse dropped my notebook and pen. "Excuse me?"

Those saddened eyes met mine. "How could she rob that store, knowing that sweet little girl was waiting for her somewhere?"

I thought of Sarah and Becky as children. Castaway Rooleys anxiously awaiting Mother's release from prison. Shunted off to the McCannell ranch while Madge pursued her outlaw career. Deep sigh. "I'm afraid I don't know, Mrs. Stalworthy."

"People like Marjorie . . ." Anger sharpened the landlady's soft voice. "They can't be satisfied with wrecking their own lives, can they? They always have to drag somebody down with them."

I couldn't argue with that. Neither, I might add, could Sarah, Becky, or Karen.

Regaining her composure, Rowena gave me a solemn glance. "I hope you find her."

"I'll try my best, ma'am."

The Silver Kings Mall occupied a one-time cow pasture on the outskirts of Leadville, just south of Mountain View Road.

It was a sprawling one-story shopping center, a cinderblock island in an asphalt lake, dwarfed by the surrounding mountains. The mall boasted two flagship stores, Bigelow's and Trautmann's, with a dozen specialty shops sandwiched in between.

Chief and I agreed to meet at the bookstore. He wanted to pick up a topographic map of the Grizzly Peak area. As for me, I headed straight for Bigelow's to take advantage of their January white sale. And, more important, to pick up a costume for my next scam.

After thirty minutes of agonizing deliberation, I settled on a Dawn Joy two-piece suit in mustard yellow. Long, shaped, single-breasted jacket and hip-hugging skirt. While the salesgirl did the folding, I scampered across the aisle and picked out a long-sleeved lace shell to go with it. One side trip to the jewelry counter for some pendant earrings, and another to the shoe section for a pair of Worthington dress pumps, and my costuming chores were complete.

Next I dropped in at the Rexall store. Up the narrow aisle to the stationery section. Ah, there's a likely-looking notebook. Love that handsome mock-leather cover. Let's see now. What else do I need? Oh, yes. Large gold stick-on letters. Small black adhesive letters. A stack of index cards. And one of those plastic name-tag covers.

I finished up in the ladies' room. After changing clothes, I applied three bright gold letters to the cover of my new notebook. Then, sitting on the vinyl bench, I painstakingly planted the much-smaller black letters to the blank white rear of an index card. Minutes later, well satisfied with my handiwork, I let out a ragged sigh. Then I slipped the card into the plastic holder, pinned it to my mustard jacket, stood up, faced the mirror, and touched up my Kerrigan hairstyle with a long comb.

Cradling the notebook, I gave myself the once-over. The mirror showed a bright-smiling raven-haired lass in a stylish wool-blend suit. The letters FOX gleamed on my notebook. The stark nametag read MELODY NAHTANHA.

Into the shopping bag went my other clothes. I ferried them to the Book Nook and left them with Chief. Then I set out in pursuit of my mark.

He was a mall vendor in his twenties, running a combination newsstand and coffee shop in front of Trautmann's. Tall and lanky with an outlaw mustache, sallow cheekbones, and languid brown eyes. Shirt cuffs hung loosely on his wrists. Hearing the sound of high heels, he cast a swift glance over his shoulder. Eyebrows rose in a gesture of masculine appreciation.

Displaying a scintillating smile, I extended my right hand. "Hi! Melody Nahtanha. I'm with FOX."

"Howdy!" He stood erect, nervously brushing his mackinaw shirtfront. His gaze flitted from my name tag to the notebook. Tenderly his hand enveloped mine. "Granger Simmons. Pleased to meet you."

"Granger, I have a little problem. You see, I'm a production assistant. I flew out with the advance team from New York, and I was supposed to meet the crew from KBTV. Mr. Holbrook just called and said they aren't coming. Connie Chung's flying in first thing tomorrow morning, and I've *got* to get this layout done."

Of my entire diatribe, only two words made an impression. Granger's brown eyes goggled. *"Connie Chung?"*

"Uh-huh." Prim nod. "We're doing a short segment on last summer's robbery." Gesturing at Trautmann's, I added, "Is that the store?"

"You bet! Biggest damned holdup ever here in Lake County." Resting both forearms on the countertop, Granger shot me a curious look. "Where are you from, gal?"

"Minnesota." Truthful Angie. "I'm afraid Mr. Holbrook didn't give me much in the way of preparation. When did it happen?"

"Ohhhh, Memorial Day weekend." His sidelong glance slid toward the huge department store. "See, Trautmann's had this big holiday sale. They were sure rakin' in the cash. Monday afternoon, Mr. Burns, the store manager—he called for the armored car. Jorgenson Armored Security. Same bunch they always use. Store policy is—keep ten grand on the premises, ship the rest straight to Denver." Grin of reluctant admiration. "Them boys sure knew what they were doin'. They had the Jorgenson routine down pat."

Pretending to consult some notes, I said, "I understand there was a woman involved—Marjorie Dexter."

Granger let out a guffaw. "Bet your ass, honey. They couldn't have done it without ol' Marge. She was their inside gal."

"You knew her?"

"Knew her? Hell, I talked to Margie Dexter every day. She used to come out here on coffee break and read the *Enquirer*. I never thought twice about it. But, you know, I'll bet she was settin' the whole thing up way back then."

"Not sure I follow, Granger."

Reaching for a pair of wire cutters, he added, "Miss Melody, those Jorgenson boys are supposed to go by the book. Whenever they make a pickup, one man sits behind the wheel—the other enters the store. Second guy's not supposed to talk to anybody. He walks in, keepin' one hand on his gun, and goes straight upstairs to the office." He snipped the wire on a bundle of newspapers. "Marge Dexter got to know that routine. First summer she was here, she commenced to takin' her break just before the armored car's arrival. Got to be a habit. Nobody gave it a second thought. Come Christmas, we had a big snowstorm one Saturday. Instead of buyin' one coffee from me, Marge bought *two*. She gave the second one to the Jorgenson guard when he came in. Fella was almighty grateful. Hot coffee tastes pretty good on a cold and snowy day." Sorting the newspapers, he flashed me a knowing smile.

"Next thing you know, it's a damned routine. There's Marge, waitin' by the door every day, holdin' that cup of coffee. She got to know all the guards—Londrigan, McAvoy, Goodwin, Ramirez." Chuckling, he shook his head. "Come March, she offered to bring an extra cup for the driver. That became part of the daily ritual, too. The guard would walk out of Trautmann's balancing two cups of coffee in his hand. Funny how easy a habit can take hold. Folks start doin' somethin' and the next thing you know, it's as if they've always been doin' it."

"How did they pull it off?" I asked.

"Well, like I said, it was Memorial Day. Londrigan and Ramirez made the run. Marge was waitin' in the doorway with the coffee, just like always. Only this time she had company. That Indian! Wearin' that gray uniform, he was a perfect match for Ramirez." Granger did a little pantomime. "Ramirez sees Marge smilin' at him and reaches for the coffee. Indian steps up behind him and sticks a pistol in his ribs. When Marge finished wirin' his wrists, the Indian cold-cocked him. Then they slapped some duct tape on his mouth and tucked him behind the trash bin."

I remembered Mrs. Stalworthy's description of Madge Rooley's Native American chaperon. The fellow in the black fringed vest.

"Nobody suspected a damned thing." Granger's voice held a touch of awe. "They strolled over to the stairway door. Marge took out her employee key. When they got upstairs, the Indian gave Marge a spare gun, turned his own on Mr. Burns, and advised everybody to get down on the floor."

"Then what happened?"

"After they finished fillin' the sack, they tied up Mr. Burns and the girls, quieted them with some of that there duct tape, and took their leave," he added. "Marge gave him the driver's coffee, and that Indian walked out of there, cool as you please. Used Ramirez's key to open the back of the armored car."

"What about Marge?"

"Well, she still had five minutes left on her break, so she headed back into the mall." Rueful chuckle. "And that's the absolute last anyone's ever seen of Marjorie Dexter . . . assumin' that's her real name, and I doubt it!" Tone of grudging admiration. "They must've spent over a year settin' it up! Puttin' Marge on the inside. Findin' a ringer for Ramirez. Thanks to Marge, coffee became a daily routine. The guard would climb into the back of the armored car, rap on the glass, and hand the driver his cup. They'd been doin' it for *months*. So when that Indian tapped the window, Londrigan slid it right open. 'Stead of his cup of joe, he's got a pistol muzzle on the back of his neck. I tell ya, Miss Melody, them boys were pros." Warning glance. "When you see Connie Chung, you tell her she can just forget about interviewin' Londrigan and Ramirez. They just don't want to talk about it. Can't say I blame 'em."

"Did they recover the truck?" I asked.

Granger nodded. "You bet. Sheriff Whitaker found it up in the San Isabel. Abandoned logging site just off Road 110. They found some tire tracks up there. Four-by-four. Figured there was a couple more boys waitin' for the armored car to arrive."

"Ms. Dexter was here over a year?"

"Fourteen months, by my recollection." He scratched the side of his neck. "Yeah, she was real patient. Put her time in, workin' as a cashier for six dollars an hour." Low whistle. " 'Course, that was one hell of a payoff at the end!"

Lift an eyebrow. "How big?"

"Four hundred thousand dollars, Miss Melody! Cold, hard cash. Ten, twenties, and fifties. And no way to trace it." He gave me a meaningful look. "Like I said, it was the biggest holdup ever in this here county. FBI figures it was a gang of four. Marge, the Indian, and them two at the logging camp. You cut that pie four ways, and it looks like ol' Marge made herself a hundred grand workin' at Trautmann's."

Pulling the pen from my purse, I glanced toward the store. "Could you do me a favor, Granger?"

"Name it."

"Could you give me the names of a few people I could talk to in there?" I asked, flashing a mendicant smile. "People who'd be willing to talk to Connie?"

"Sure!" And then his hand made a pushing motion. "Just don't go aimin' no cameras at me. Wife'll hang my hide on a barbed-wire fence if she sees me gabbin' with some cute little TV gal!"

Somberly I assured Granger complete privacy, and he provided me with half a dozen names. I thanked him for his invaluable assistance, then strolled into the huge department store.

Pausing at the cosmetics counter, I sent a surreptitious glance over my shoulder. Granger was no longer watching me. He was taking money from a pair of customers.

The counter girl asked if she could be of help. I pointed to the lipstick display and asked for a tube of Ultima II. After making the purchase, I ducked out the side door. Stood shivering on the concrete apron for a minute or two, buffeted by mountain winds. Then a familiar Sierra pulled up to the curb.

Chief pushed open the passenger door. Vigorously rubbing my sleeves, I slid onto the padded seat.

"T-turn on that h-heater," I said, teeth chattering.

He did so. Then reached down and pulled my parka out of the shopping bag. "Put this on." Engine gears grumbled as he let out the clutch. "How'd you make out in there?"

Donning the winter coat, I frowned. "I think we've found our motive, Chief."

# TEN

Light snowflakes spattered the Sierra's windshield. Ignoring the clacking wipers, Chief gave the mirror a thoughtful glance. *"Jack Sunawavi!"* Grunt of mild amazement. "Now, there's a name I thought I'd never hear again."

"Same here, Chief," I replied, glancing out the passenger window. A snowy overcast obscured the tops of the nearby radio masts. "But it was him, all right. Mrs. Stalworthy described every last detail, right down to the fringed vest."

"Can't be!" He flicked on our headlights. "Sunawavi's dead, Angie. You saw him yourself."

True enough! Sunawavi and I had crossed swords back in August, while I was in Utah, hunting my cousin's murderer. For a while there I'd suspected Sunawavi of killing Billy. In truth, however, Jack had been shot to death—and his identity usurped—by the real killer.

Yes, I knew he was dead. With my own two eyes I'd seen the killer haul Jack's moldering remains out of a granite fissure. But that was in August. Rowena Stalworthy had seen him in April—*three months* before his death at Dynamite Pass.

"Chief, remember when you talked to the people in Clover Creek? They thought Jack was on the dodge. That he'd pulled a job in another state."

Grunt of agreement. "Looks like they were right, Angie."

"Exactly! Jack was too sharp to rumble in Utah. He always scored out of state."

"So what do you think happened?"

Snuggling deeper into my parka, I took a deep breath. "Somebody put Madge on the inside. She worked there as *Marjorie Dexter*. Became friendly with the armored car boys. She must have found out Ramirez would be working the holiday. Sometime in April, Madge's boss recruited Sunawavi, knowing he was a rough match for Ramirez." Rueful smile. "Like Granger says, these guys were pros."

"Who do you think dreamed it up?"

"Hard to say, Chief." I shrugged. "Maybe it was Madge. Twenty years ago she pulled a similar job in New Mexico." Catching his surprised look, I added, "I read about it in the library."

He let out a hushed whistle. "Same M.O. as the Jorgenson armored car job?"

"The same! Only this mall heist went off without a hitch." Fussbudget face. "So that's what Madge meant when she talked about her *inheritance*. Her share of the loot!"

"One thing bothers me, Angie. Why didn't they split the money right away?"

"I don't know, Chief. That *is* the usual procedure. Hit, git, and split!" I chewed my lower lip. "Armed robbers usually don't stick together very long. Then again, there are the exceptions. This gang was small enough. Maybe Madge had worked with one or two of these guys on the Portales job."

"Couldn't have been Sunawavi," my grandfather commented. "He was twelve years old at the time."

"There's still two left, Chief. The guys who were waiting in the pickup when Jack showed up with the armored car."

Nodding, he adjusted the defroster. His expression turned curious. "What are you thinking about, young lady?"

"Hmmm? Oh, just wondering why Madge's friends needed that pickup truck." I turned in my seat. "What did you do with the shopping bag?"

"Behind the backrest."

While Chief guided the Sierra down into the valley, I grabbed the topographic map he'd purchased at the Book Nook. Folding it twice, I studied the country around Grizzly Peak, serenaded by the clacking of windshield wipers.

Finally, my grandfather spoke. "Find anything?"

"Interesting," I murmured, tracing my forefinger across the map. "To reach the logging camp, Jack had to go south on Route 24. He was only six miles short of the Chaffee County line. Why stop there?"

"Maybe they planned on doubling back?"

"Right past the mall?" I challenged.

Glancing quickly at my upraised map, he frowned. "So the only way out of that valley is back through Leadville." He made a quiet humming sound. "That explains the four-by-four."

Sudden comprehension! My free hand slapped the passenger seat. "Of course! *The logging roads!* They went over the divide into the Collegiate range."

My grandfather chuckled. "That's one way to avoid the state patrol."

"And it may explain what Pop Hannan was doing in Leadville," I said, thinking out loud. "He knows the backcountry as well as Madge did."

"*Beka!* You're way ahead of me, granddaughter. Back up a bit, will you?"

"Four people, Chief." Turning to face him, I raised four rigid fingers. "Madge, Jack, the guy who knew them both, and one other. I think it's Pop Hannan. He became visibly upset when I mentioned Madge's stay in Malta. According to Mrs.

Stalworthy, he was a frequent visitor to the Looseslipper House. And, whenever he showed up, he asked for *Marjorie Dexter* by name!"

"Meaning he was in on it." Chief exhaled heavily. "What are you thinking, Angie?"

"Pop and Madge went backpacking every chance they had." I explained, "They must have been scouting out an escape route." Daintily I folded the map. "So maybe now we have a motive."

"Not necessarily." Chief kept his gaze on the slush-covered road ahead. "We know for certain Madge participated in the robbery. We know someone tampered with her brakes *before* her trip to Denver. And that someone tried to run you down in a stolen car. But I'm not so sure we can tie it all together, girl."

I shrugged. "Maybe Sunawavi's the key."

"How so?" he asked.

"Try this on for size. Madge and the gang pull off the armored car job. Thanks to Madge and Pop, they have a hideaway for the cash. They drop it off and scatter." I flicked a tendril of raven hair away from my eyebrows. "That big a job always generates a lot of heat, but it never lasts. Madge and her buddies planned to go to ground for a bit. Later on they'd meet and split the loot."

My grandfather pondered my point. "Sounds like a batch of mighty trustworthy crooks."

"Or three people awfully scared of number four," I added, and thought instantly of the bruiser at Mike's Mobil. "Our friend Sunawavi went home to Utah, figuring to lie low for a while. Instead, he got himself killed. Suddenly we're talking about a three-way split instead of four."

Chief's backbone went rigid. Aged obsidian eyes blinked in understanding. "I see! Somebody heard about Jack's murder and decided to cull the herd."

"Right! Pop Hannan or Mister Bruiser."

"That's assuming the bruiser was one of the gang."

"Come on, Chief!" I glared at him. "He had to be. What about those size eleven footprints I found at the hotel?"

"Lot of men wear size eleven boots, Angie."

"But what about his gravelly voice! I'm pretty sure he's the guy who phoned our room, looking for Sarah."

"One question, missy . . ." Pensive smile on my grandfather. "If that was him in the lobby, then how did he get to the Mazda so fast?"

I became defensive. "It could've been parked right outside."

Chief made a face. "When's the last time you saw an empty parking space around a big-city hotel?"

"Welllll . . . maybe he had to run a few blocks."

"In a bad snowstorm?"

I wrinkled my nose in frustration. That grandfather of mine! Every time I come up with a great theory, he runs it through the shredder. Oooooh, I *hate* it whenever he does that.

"Face it, Angie." He flicked a switch on the steering column, and the wiper blades beat faster. "There were at least two people in Denver that night. Mister Bruiser and Pop Hannan. Or Mister Bruiser and somebody else. Or two perfect strangers, one of whom is a size eleven like Mister Bruiser." He shook his head slowly. "It's too damned early for theories, young lady. We need to know more about Madge's outlaw days."

"Then we'd better stop in Crested Butte before we head back to the ranch," I suggested.

"Reason?"

"If we need more info about Madge, we'd better ask the expert."

And I wondered what sort of scam would work best on a retired county sheriff like Chester B. Hurtig.

Six-thirty in good old Crested Butte. Thick snowflakes drifted down from the night sky, spiraling past the town's quaint streetlights. Victorian gas lamps now wired to carry electricity. Three inches of *jakagonaga*—what we Anishinabe call powdery snow—cloaked the narrow streets of the town. Lacking asphalt and automobiles, C.B. looked much the way it did in the days of the Wild Bunch.

Hurtig's store, The Old Muleskinner, was no exception. Plate glass windows, wooden-railed porch, and gingerbread trim. All it lacked was a cracker barrel beside the front door. Three giant steps put me on the porch. I took care to step inside existing footprints. The snow was already an inch higher than my heels. Pausing at the door, I brushed the snow off my brand-new pumps. And grimaced at the sensation of cold, damp nylon. Aaargh! Should've put the snowboots back on, princess.

Cowbells jangled as I pushed open the door. Once inside, I slipped off my parka, then folded it over my arm. "Hello?" My gaze darted from the empty counter to the numerous stacked displays to the frosted windows. "Anybody home?"

I skirted the dome tent in the middle of the room, casting a hasty glance at the camping gear lining the shelves. Mr. Hurtig had quite a selection of outdoor equipment. Mountaineer sleeping bags, propane stoves, and crank-powered emergency radios. Steel racks boasted the latest in denim and canvas trail shirts for women. Behind the counter, built right into the wall, was a jumbo-size gun case containing two dozen hunting rifles.

I learned all about guns when I was seventeen. Bob Stonepipe gave me a summer job as a guide on the Gunflint Trail. His guests did a lot of target shooting up there at Little Pancake Lake. I learned about muzzle velocity and trajectory and bore size. And so recognized the firearms behind the glass. Weatherby Mark V in .300 Magnum. Bolt-action Ruger Model 77. Plus something of a rarity. A long, elegant Harrington & Richardson Model 300. My eyebrows rose slightly. Hurtig must be doing well if he's retailing expensive hardware like that.

Just then I spied a framed photograph of a youthful smiling uniformed patrolman on a sunwashed city street. Beneath the photo was a small bronzed plaque reading

PHOENIX POLICE DEPARTMENT
DISTINGUISHED SERVICE AWARD
PATROLMAN CHESTER B. HURTIG
RAPID RESPONSE TEAM

"Can I help you?"

The voice was deep, rich, and baritone, projecting an aura of power and authority. The voice of a top sergeant. I spun at once, instantly aware of the rugged, short-haired man in the storeroom doorway. The officer in the photo thirty-odd years later. Awkward Angie smile. "Mr. Hurtig?"

"That's right," he said, ambling past the counter. He reminded me a little of J. Edgar Hoover with his bulldog face, slitted sable eyes, solid chin, and thick eyebrows. His head was blunt, square, looking as if it had been struck from an Arizona quarry. Wiry ash-gray hair covered the top, rising on the left in a timid and unlikely pompadour. Short, flat ears pressed the side of his head. A Bismarckian mustache graced the upper lip. With most people, lines run across the forehead. Not Chester B. Hurtig. His wrinkles radiated outward from the point where those craggy eyebrows met, straining for the high hairline, looking like rilles in a dry lakebed. His flinty gaze took in the case. "You interested in guns?"

I waggled my palm. "A bit." Sidelong glance. "I see you carry the Remington M700."

"Sure do! It's a favorite around here." The corners of his mouth moved upward slightly. A smile, I think. Or as much of a smile as an ex-cop could manage. "Are you a shooter, miss?"

Shaking my head, I replied, "Not me. My cousin Wayne."

No lie there. He and his brother Wyatt are qualified Marine sharpshooters. "Have you sold many of those?"

"Maybe a dozen or so. Most people buy just before elk season."

"What round do they use?"

"Seven-millimeter Magnum." His blunt head tilted in curiosity. "Why do you ask?"

Schoolgirl Angie. "Oh, just wondering if anybody uses 6.5-millimeter Swedish. That's Wayne's favorite round."

"*Swedish?*" Hurtig's chuckle resembled a bandsaw. "Sorry, hon, I don't carry that foreign shit. Nothing but good old American ammo here."

"Do you know anybody in town who sells that round?"

"Not off the top of my head." The shrug moved his entire upper torso. He wasn't very tall. Even in a Stetson, he wouldn't reach six feet. But he was broad, durable, and muscular. The mackinaw shirt seemed to stretch across his meaty chest. "But I could ask around." Authoritative bark. "What's your name?"

A civilian might have responded instinctively to that stern tone, but I'd heard it too many times from those Springfield screws. Completely unruffled, I dipped into my shoulder bag.

"Heather Nahni," I replied, presenting a phony business card. *Nahni*, of course, is Awishi for *princess*. My heartbeat quickened as he studied the card's computer icon and the neat black lettering.

"Author, eh?" Muted grunt. "What brings you down from Denver, Miss Nahni?"

"Heather," I corrected him, showing a warm smile. "I'm doing a book on Madge Rooley. I was wondering if I could talk to you for a few minutes."

Cop eyes met mine. Hard, cold, and disbelieving. "Who's your publisher?"

"Pinnacle Books."

"They're in New York, ain't they?"

I nodded, wondering where he was going with this.

"Which editor are you working with?"

Sudden Angie chill. I could feel the scam coming apart. I didn't dare give him a name. No doubt he'd be calling New York one minute after I walked out the door.

Improvisation time! Flicking my wrists, I replied, "Well, I don't exactly have a contract—*yet*. Right now I'm doing a proposal. You know, a few sample chapters." Dodge the issue. "True crime paperbacks are really hot just now." I made a frame of my hands. "That's what I'm calling it—*The Border Bandit Queen*. People said I ought to talk to you, Mr. Hurtig."

"Make it Chet." Another rictus-like smile. "Yeah, I knew Madge. Our paths crossed a few times."

"I understand you were the first lawman who ever arrested her."

"Yeah, I guess so." He seemed singularly disinterested in Sarah's mother. " 'Course, Madge was just a kid back then. Nineteen years old. She was workin' at Apex here in town." Flinty eyes narrowed. "Let's see, Sally must've been about two then. Madge filched some blank checks from the company. Poor dumb kid didn't even know how to cover it up. She signed her own name to the checks. Judge Boyle gave her ninety days."

"That was the start," I commented.

He nodded sadly. "Yeah, I guess so. Madge pulled some mighty big scores in her day."

"What about the people she worked with?"

"Most of 'em are either dead or stampin' out license plates, Miss Heather," he replied with a grim chuckle. "Brownlow— that fella she worked with in Montana. He's doing twenty to life up in Deer Lodge. The Portales bunch . . . well, let's see, Kirby and Ziegler are dead. Blodgett's on the inside. And I know Madge was the sole survivor of that Deadwood shoot-out. Blanchard, Davis, and Stirewalt—they're all buried in that Mount Moriah cemetery."

His memory impressed me. "You do keep track."

Self-conscious grin. "I read up on it some, that's all. Can't tell you much about Madge's travels, hon. Most of our business was transacted right here in C.B."

"What kind of business?" I asked.

"Ohhhh, D & D mostly." His gaze softened a little. "Every so often, Madge decided to get her nose wet, and I'd have to haul her down to the jail to sleep it off."

"She had a drinking problem?"

His bulldog face tightened thoughtfully. "Nahhhhh, I wouldn't say that. Those female alkies—they tend to hit the bottle every day. Madge was more of a binge drinker. Go without for weeks on end, then fall off the wagon." He nodded suddenly in the direction of Kochevar's. "Madge used to get bored. Then she'd go downtown and tie one on. She'd complain, 'Those kids are drivin' me crazy.' Then she'd get surly and start bad-mouthin' the other customers. That's when I got called in."

His expression became even more pensive. "Madge just never found what she was lookin' for, I guess. Maybe it'd been different if the right man had come along."

"And maybe not," I commented.

Chet stiffened at once. Anger smoldered in those gimlet eyes. "You know, you kids have no respect for anything," he snapped. "It's the family that holds this society together. If Madge'd had a good husband, then maybe she wouldn't have run off on those damned-fool adventures." The small mouth hardened. "People can't hack it on their own. They need to know what's expected of them. Leave 'em to their own devices, and they screw up every time. Every fucking time! Madge is a perfect example. No different'n any of the others I've busted." His thick forefinger stabbed at my nose. "Just another loudmouth who screwed up and then got sent up. I've never seen it to fail, honey. They take one step off the path, and next thing you know they're livin' out on the edge."

There was no mistaking the contempt in his tone, but I couldn't tell if it was directed at Madge in particular or at people in general.

Trying to soften him a bit, I asked, "Are you married, Mr. Hurtig?"

"Used to be." Resentment turned his voice into a guttural undertone. "The old girl couldn't hack it. She left."

"I'm sorry to hear that."

"Don't sweat it. Marlene knew what she was getting into when we tied the knot." Brutal hands curled into fists. "She always did have a problem dealin' with reality. A cop's wife knows he ain't gonna be home at seven, ready to chat about his day. Marlene never got that through her squirrely head."

I made no comment, but Hurtig reacted as if I had. "They don't know what it's like. They're nice and safe back in the herd. Your ass is on the line every fucking day. You're nose-to-nose with the losers and the dirtbags. Did she care? Shit, no!" His hand made a savage gesture of dismissal. "Ahhhhh, I'm better off without that broad."

I decided to change the subject. Nodded at the plaque. "How long were you a cop in Phoenix?"

Harsh chuckle. "Couple of years. I helped put the team together when I got out of the army." His eyes narrowed. "Ain't much in the way of advancement on a big-city force, Miss Heather. It's all politics. Most of the old-timers get the good jobs on daywatch. You've gotta cart your ass around fifteen years on street patrol before you can ditch the blue."

"I guess a sheriff is more his own man," I remarked.

He shot me a flustered look, then burst into raucous laughter. "Don't you believe it, honey!" His smile turned brittle. "A sheriff can't go to the shitter without clearin' it first with the county board. Only thing those bastards care about is the bottom line. 'Gasoline bill's kind of steep this month, Chet.' Yeah, well, maybe I burned a little extra gas, rushin' some injured rancher to the hospital. Sue me! And how come you want my budget cut, Mister Board Member? Are you really tryin' to save some money? Or maybe you just don't want me chasin' that hot-roddin' drunk you call your son the next time he goes tear-assin' down to Gunnison." His fist lashed out suddenly, thumping the countertop. "Fuckin' politicians! What the fuck do they know!"

Swallowing hard, I aimed my prettiest smile at the volatile ex-lawman. Hurtig was a strange one, an odd blend of deep insight and caustic resentment. His forced resignation still rankled. Best to handle him with kid gloves.

He gave me a long, hard look. "Didn't I see you at the funeral, Heather?"

"Uh-huh." So he'd been there too. Given his interest in Madge, that was not unexpected.

His gaze turned suspicious. "How'd you find out about it?"

Bland gaze. "I read about Madge's accident in the *Denver Post*."

"You were sittin' with somebody. Who?"

Actually, I'd been sitting with Sarah's uncle. But I needed to quiz Chet about Madge's other acquaintances. Expression of girlish innocence. "He didn't give his name. Big guy. Big in the chest and shoulders. Large jaw. Some acne scars on the upper cheeks—"

"Jesus!" he exclaimed, cutting me off. "*Frank Blodgett!*" Muscled hands gripped my shoulders. "What did he say to you?"

Caught off guard, I blurted out, "N-nothing much! He, uh, he saw me taking notes in church, and he wanted to know why. I—I told him I was writing a book about Madge."

Chet seemed to buy it. Releasing me, he muttered, "What the hell is he doin' here!"

Rubbing my shoulder, I asked, "Who is he?"

"Old buddy of Madge Rooley's. They pulled plenty of jobs back when you were in nursery school."

"Like that one in New Mexico?"

Firm nod. "Yeah, Frank drew fifteen to twenty for that score. Madge pulled ten and served six." Thick eyebrows knotted anxiously. "Frank Blodgett . . . Christ! Last I heard, he was in Nebraska."

"Doing what?" I inquired.

"Swingin' a sledge on the rock pile." Looking far beyond me, he slowly thumbed his chin. "I hear some shitbird rolled him over on that Northport job. FBI busted him last summer. He was holed up at a motel in Scottsbluff."

My ears perked at the word *summer*. "Exactly when did the FBI make the arrest?"

"End of August."

Of course! I thought. That's when Jack Sunawavi's death hit the headlines.

His gaze showed amusement. "Thinkin' about writin' him up in your book, Miss Heather?"

"Should I?"

"Ahhhh, you'll probably have to devote a whole chapter to Frank. He and Madge go back a long way." He hitched up his rodeo belt buckle. "So Frank's back on the street, eh? Reckon that's no surprise. It was an old beef. He boosted that hardware store a couple of years ago."

"Isn't that about the same time Madge Rooley left the RJ Bar?" I remarked.

Chet's alert gaze zeroed in on me. "You think she was with Frank?"

Of course, I already knew where Madge had gone, but I didn't dare share that knowledge with him. I didn't want the former sheriff carrying tales to his successor.

"I hear she had a good job here in town. Suddenly, she chucked it all and headed for parts unknown. How come?"

Making a cavalier gesture, Chet sighed. "Knowin' Madge . . . yeah, she could've been shackin' up with Frank. Or some other guy." Chuckle of reminiscence. "For a lady with four grown young'uns, she never had much trouble gettin' a date for Saturday night."

Grinding one heel against the floor, I remarked, "That particular talent got her into trouble, I hear."

"On more'n one occasion!" And he laughed.

"Do you mind a personal question?"

He spread his hands expansively. "Not at all."

"Did Mrs. Longworth ever ask you to keep an eye on Madge?"

He gave me a long, flint-eyed look. Blunt lips quivered, and he broke into a gale of basso profundo laughter. Slapping the countertop, he replied, "Miss Heather, if I was still wearin' the badge, I'd have to walk you right out to your car. And, sure as shit, I'd find something wrong with it. Broken taillight, maybe. Or missin' an insurance sticker. Then I'd have to march your pretty ass right on down to the jailhouse. Word of advice, honey, there's just some questions a lady doesn't ask. And that means any question with the words *Mrs. Longworth* in it."

Tilting my head, I drawled, "Is the conversation over, Mr. Hurtig?"

Deep-throated chuckle. "Nawww! Unlike that pissant Quinn, I don't have to jump anymore when the old bitch snaps her fingers." Resting his forearms on the counter, he added, "Seein' as how you're just startin' out in the book business . . . why, I'd be delighted to answer your question, Miss Heather." Chet's gaze swiveled southward. "Once a month I had to drop by the Rafter L and tell the old girl what the Rooley clan was up to. I had to report on all of 'em—Madge, Becky, Merry, Troy, the grandkids . . . hell, even Sally whenever she showed up for a visit. Lord, did that ol' bitch hate them Rooleys! Worst of it was standin' there in the parlor, listenin' to Queen Dee rant and rave. She wanted that bunch rousted clear out of Gunnison County, and she didn't want me bein' gentle about it."

"And you disobeyed Mrs. Longworth?"

Sly smile. "Let's just say I had an endless number of excuses." It became a grin. "Learned a lot from those old shitbirds on the county board."

"What happened when Madge up and left?"

Casual grunt. "Nothing. Once she was over the county line, she was out of my jurisdiction."

"And when she came back?"

"I was no longer sheriff." Bitterness put a keen edge on that guttural voice. "By then it was somebody else's problem."

"Any idea whose?"

"One or two." His tone hinted at conspiracy. "I hear the RJ Bar's out at the edge of a limb."

Sudden scowl. What did Hurtig know about Madge's troubled finances? Playing dumb, I replied, "I don't follow."

The lawman's eyes held a vengeful gleam. "You know Matt Stockdale?"

"I've heard the name."

Chuckle of triumph. "He persuaded Madge to take out one of them Quick Start loans. Put her better than a hundred grand in the hole. When his company went belly up, his creditors went howlin' after the Rooleys." Knowledgeable look. "Could be the firm's collapse wasn't all that much of a surprise to Matt."

"Really?" I tilted my head to one side. "Why would he want to do that?"

"Answer's obvious, gal." Slow feral grin. "Cordelia Longworth's maiden name is *Stockdale*."

Six-thirty found me at the Dry Gulch, the site of my planned rendezvous with Chief. The Gulch was a few doors down from Hurtig's store, a walk-in saloon with dark rosewood paneling, a narrow bar fronted by half a dozen admiralty chairs, thick oak ceiling beams, and a detailed walnut fireplace front. Beneath the wall-to-wall mirror was a venerable Victorian backbar, a hand-tooled mahogany hutch with separate glass cabinets for the whiskies.

This was the bar's dead time, halfway between happy hour and the first arrival of the swinging skiers. Four cowpokes perched their lean backsides on the chairs, upending short-necked bottles of Coors and jeering at the hockey game on TV. I selected one of the plush velour easy chairs by the fireplace, put in my order for a Lowenbrau, and settled back to wait for my grandfather.

Sipping my chilled beer, I gave some thought to the former sheriff. Strange guy, that Hurtig. At first he'd been really suspicious of me. However, once assured that I was indeed an author, he'd been quite willing . . . no, *eager* . . . to sell out Matt Stockdale. Why?

Another ladylike sip. Hmmm, perhaps Mrs. Longworth, not Stockdale, was his intended target.

I remembered what Chief had told me about the cashier-check scandal. If I had to make an educated guess, I'd say Hurtig must have appealed to Mrs. Longworth to keep his job. The old girl must have turned thumbs down. So now, eager for revenge, he had no qualms at all about siccing me on Queen Dee and her slippery nephew.

One thing for sure, I mused, Chet Hurtig was certainly carrying a king-size chunk of resentment around.

Hearty masculine laughter sounded behind me. Turning, I fired a surreptitious glance at the barstool quartet. Two of the punchers were arm-wrestling. One was a lanky, horse-faced guy in his late twenties. His opponent was the same age but much more solidly built. Bull neck, big biceps, trail sideburns, and wiry hair the same shade of brown as the backbar. Crimson flooded their quivering faces. Bull Neck's older brother cheered him on. The fourth man was a thick-waisted rancher in his middle thirties, wearing a checkered shirt and a wide-brimmed Stetson pushed back on his head.

Just then a familiar emerald-eyed blonde walked through

the doorway, the folds of her unbuttoned Chesterfield coat brushing her thighs. My heartbeat doubled. *Sarah!*

She spotted me before I could duck out of sight. Her lovely face tensed in puzzlement. Unruly sheepdog bangs concealed her eyebrows. I steeled myself for the inevitable questions.

Then I noticed Sarah's unusual stride. She walked with a queenly deliberation, chin high, her gaze slightly out of focus, planting her feet with extreme care, one in front of the other. She might have been a soldier traversing an enemy minefield. Or Blondin teetering high above Niagara Falls. She was doing just fine, too. Right up to the moment her hip bumped my table. She slapped both palms on the linen in an effort of steady herself. And then, with an air of matronly dignity, she slumped into the chair across from mine.

She closed one bleary eye. "Angela . . . why are you all dressed up?"

"I'm meeting my grandfather." My nostrils detected the whiskey tang on her breath. "How did it go at the bank?"

Ragged sigh. "Rotten!"

"Ladies?" The bartender stood attentively beside Sarah's chair. Slender fortyish woman with an auburn hairstyle that reminded me of Peg Bundy. "Can I get you anything?"

Tugging at my hem, I smiled. "Mrs. Sutton will have a cup of coffee—"

"Mrs. Sutton will have a stinger," Sarah interrupted. "A double. Easy on the crème de menthe." Broad, foolish, dreamy smile. "I'm not breaking the habit of an afternoon."

After the bartender left, I said, "So what have you been doing with your day, Sarah?"

She sank deeper into her plush chair. Peering at me between the upraised collars of her coat, she murmured, "I believe the phrase is *bar-hopping*, kiddo. Haven't done that since I got married. Completely forgot what it was like." Brushing the bangs away from her eyes, she mumbled, "I renewed many an old acquaintance today, dear. You know, some of them thought I was still living in Colorado. Imagine that."

I couldn't! I was too busy trying to absorb the reality of Sarah Sutton with a snootful.

Blinking sleepily, she remarked, "Did you just say your *grandfather?*"

Pert Angie nod. "Uh-huh."

"Guess I'm not as plastered as I thought." Her gaze turned serious. "Doesn't he live in Minneapolis?"

"Unh-unh. Duluth." I could've given her an argument about her level of inebriation, but I held my tongue. "He was out in Utah visiting my aunt. Dropped by on his way home. Your sister Becky invited him to stay at the ranch."

"She would." Series of slow eyeblinks. "Of course, it may be a very short visit. Especially if the United Mountain Bank Corporation has its way."

The bartender's tray sported an amber-colored drink in a highball glass. Smiling, she set it on the table between us. Eyes gleaming with tipsy pleasure, Sarah reached for the glass. It wobbled in her grip, staining her wrist with fluid. Mournful moue. "Shit!"

She drank as if it were orange juice. Bottoms up! I touched her forearm. "Hey! Take it easy!"

"I'm fine." Bourbon gave her instant laryngitis. Sassy Rooley grin. "I grew up with the family vintage, dear. Mother's white mule. This stuff's like soda pop."

"Ninety-proof soda pop!" Wincing, I watched her drain the glass.

Her smile became even more ethereal and foolish. "The amazing thing about bourbon, kiddo, is that the more you drink, the easier it goes down."

"You're going to regret it tomorrow morning."

Her zombie smile wilted. "I'll worry about *that* then. Right now I'm getting smashed."

"Any particular reason?" I asked.

Dismal sigh. "In a little while I've got to go home and tell them I've failed. We're losing the ranch. I want to be numb when it happens."

"The bank refused to renegotiate?"

Nodding slowly, Sarah touched the bridge of her nose. "I—I don't know what I'm going to tell Becky. I tried my *best*. They wouldn't even listen. They gave me the same damned line they gave her. Pay off the damned loan immediately or take out a new mortgage at sixteen percent. What is the matter with those people, anyway!"

Could be Mrs. Longworth is putting the squeeze on United Mountain. I thought. But I kept that to myself.

"Dammit! It isn't fair!" Impending tears lightened Sarah's tone. "My own family! I can't even *help* them."

Sympathetic Angie smile. "It's not your fault, Sarah."

"Yes, it is." Brooding, she studied the empty glass. "I should have known better. It was just another one of Mother's crazy schemes. Why couldn't I have seen that?"

"You wanted her to make a success of it," I said, patting her hand. "Besides, she's not the only one who was left holding the bag. I hear a lot of ranchers got stung when that bank folded."

"You don't understand." Her words ran together in a sing-song contralto. "Mother asked *my* advice. She came to *me*. She never would've signed if I—if I hadn't—"

"I've been meaning to ask you about that, Sarah," I interrupted. "When did your mother first come up with the idea for a stable?"

Any other time Sarah would have wanted to know the reason for my question. But the bourbon had tarnished her sharp legal mind. "A couple of years ago, I think."

"Before she moved to Malta?"

Slow nod. "That's right."

"I don't understand. She was all fired up about building a stable. She went to the trouble of getting a loan. Then she dropped the whole project in Becky's lap and took off for the tall timber."

Her lips curled in a pained smile. "Believe me, Angela. For Mother, that was standard operating procedure." Her hand signaled the bartender. "Bring me another one."

"I assume she had a reason for going up north."

Unpleasant memories put a scowl on Sarah's face. "His name was Jack. She never told me his last name."

"Weren't you the least bit curious?"

"Angie, I stopped interfering in my mother's love life long, long ago. Nothing I ever said or did made a damn bit of difference, anyway." Deep sigh. "Mother never listened. Not to me. Not to Becky. No . . . she never listened to us."

I grimaced as half the amber liquid disappeared. I swear, the ladylike Mrs. Sutton could drink a Cossack under the table. A warm flush flooded her face, creating an impression of queenly serenity.

"I take it there was more than one man in your mother's life," I prodded.

She peered at me over the glass. "You can say that again!"

"Frank Blodgett?"

Sarah made a pretty good fussbudget face. "Did I tell you about him?"

"A little," I lied, making a steeple of my fingers.

"Frank Blodgett . . ." Her tongue stumbled over the last name. "Lord, I haven't thought about him in years." Tipsy sigh. "He stayed with Mother the longest, I guess. Four or five years. Becky's too young to remember." Lengthy sip. "She was still in diapers when he went to prison. I—I remember . . . Mother took the bus to Canon City to visit him. That was the first time we stayed with Aunt Alice."

"Did Blodgett live with her?"

"Uhm-hmmmm. Before he went away. And a few times after he returned, too." Blinking at me, she swayed slightly in her seat. "It didn't take, though. It never took. Not with him.

Not with Arthur." All at once she revealed a glimpse of her own personal pain. "M-my mother just never wanted to be tied down."

"How did Blodgett take it when your mother walked out on him?"

"Angela, I have *no* idea!" Another hefty swallow. It restored her giddy smile. "I haven't seen Frank Blodgett since I was ... oh, Karen's age."

I did some quick mental arithmetic. Assuming Sarah was five when the law carted Frank away, that meant Madge's live-in boyfriend had been ten years away from the RJ Bar. No doubt doing time for a weighty felony rap.

"You were in kindergarten when Frank was arrested?"

"That's right." Sarah finished her drink.

"Who arrested him?" I inquired.

"Chester Hurtig. He was town constable back then."

Small world! I thought. No wonder Hurtig had pressed the panic button. "What was Frank wanted for, Sarah?"

"Bank robbery." Her voice developed a slight slur. "H-he knocked over some bank in Fort Collins. Couple of people got shot. One of them was a state t-t-trooper." Her tongue tripped over the word. Head bowing, she mumbled, "Frank wanted to get together with Mother again. She was willing, too. But it didn't work out ... no ... no ... didn't ..."

Tense Angie frown. I had a strong feeling Sarah's mother had been seeing her first love off-and-on during the past quarter century. They had collaborated on the Portales department store job. Hijacking the armored car was a variation on the same M.O.

Just then Sarah let out a hushed sob. A solitary tear began streaming down her face. Awkward fingers fumbled for her purse.

Handing her a paper napkin, I whispered, "What's the matter?"

"Everything!" Delicately she blew her nose. The slightly

shrill tone sounded familiar. That's the way I get whenever I flop down for a good long cry. "I never should have let Mother sign that loan agreement. That's the biggest mistake I ever made!" Frowning, she dabbed at the tear stains. "No . . . *second* biggest!"

I should have dropped it right there, but I had to ask. "What was *the* biggest?"

"A man asked me to marry him." Moist emerald eyes gleamed. "W-we met while I was divorcing Pete. It was *glorious*. About a year after the divorce, he proposed, and . . . well, like an idiot, I turned him down. I—I guess I thought it was too soon. Maybe I was afraid people would think I'd grabbed him on the rebound. I had just started practicing in Pierre, you see, and . . . damn! How did my career get to be so important?" Sniffling, she rubbed her forehead. "I never should have let my pride come between us."

My mouth dropped open. *Paul!* I thought, suddenly sick at heart. She's talking about Paul Holbrook.

A sudden chill enveloped my heart. Oh, I knew Sarah and Paul had had a fling. But I hadn't realized they'd become so involved. He'd asked her to *marry* him?

A taut invisible band suddenly tightened around my chest.

Drunk as she was, Sarah sensed my reaction. Shakily putting her glass down, she avoided my sizzling gaze. "You didn't know that, did you?"

Well, I could play the grande dame, too. "No, I didn't."

"I—I should have married him."

Had I been a little bit calmer, I would've left then and there. But Sarah's tipsy confession had me steaming, and I couldn't resist the impulse to twist the knife. "I see he had the good sense not to ask *twice*."

Sarah's eyes goggled. "How dare you!"

"Yeah, you're a real prize, Sally," I interrupted, reaching for my shoulder bag. "Next time I see Paul, I'll congratulate him on his narrow escape."

She seized my forearm. "You stay away from him!"

Shaking off her grip, I snapped, "Don't start something you can't finish, Mrs. Sutton!"

"You think I haven't seen the way you look at him?" Sarah's voice rose sharply. "Those sly glances you give him at the office! I know what you're thinking. I'll tell you right now, Angela Biwaban, it's *not* going to happen! Not as long as I have anything to say about it."

"Well, you've got *nothing* to say about it, Mrs. Sutton ma'am!" I replied. "Because my relationship with Paul Holbrook is none of your goddamned business!"

"I'm making it my business, Angela!" Jealousy nearly choked her lovely voice. "He's a good man. He has a great future ahead of him. And I'm not going to let some short-skirted convict ruin it!"

In an eyeblink, I found myself nose to nose with the boss lady. Fierce Anishinabe scowl. "Why don't you go home and sleep it off, Sally Anne?"

"You stay away from him." Her drunken gaze met mine. "You're nothing but trouble! You and your cavalier attitude and your tongue-in-cheek wit. You may have Becky and Merry and Karen fooled, but you don't fool me. You insinuate yourself into our lives, brimming with friendship and good cheer. Yet, all the while, you hold back a portion of yourself. It's as if you're secretly laughing at us all."

My scowl deepened. "Better stick with filing torts, Sally. Your bedside manner definitely stinks!"

Sarah let out an indignant gasp. Then her green eyes narrowed. "You're a manipulative little minx, Angela. I can't quite decide if you really are trying to be helpful, or if we're simply the pawns in some private little game of yours." Her mouth twisted. "You've already ruined your own life. Don't you *dare* ruin Paul's!"

As I opened my mouth to rebut, a cowpoke's laconic drawl intruded. "Well now, I reckon you ladies could use a referee."

Turning, I confronted two of the bar patrons. The younger pair—Horse Face and Bull Neck.

Ignoring me, Sarah glanced coyly at the pair. "I could use another drink."

"You've had enough," I said sternly.

Bull Neck flourished his black Stetson at the bar. "Why don't you ladies join us?"

Girl Scout smile. "Thanks, fellas, but Sarah and I really have to be going."

While I chattered away, Sarah carried on her own unspoken conversation with the men. Somewhere in my prim boss lurked a major-league seductress, and her two double stingers had unlocked the gate. Lowering her lashes demurely, she set her lips in a sultry smile. Grinning, Bull Neck nudged his lanky pal.

Of course, I'd never seen the legendary Madge Rooley in action. However, if the oldest daughter's performance was any indication, Madge had been one hot number, indeed.

"Oh, come on, gal. One more drink," Horse Face said, his voice a wheedling tenor. "At least stay and say howdy to Cy and Homer."

The older punchers waved to me from the bar.

Standing, I shook my head. "We'd love to, but we really have to go—"

"You go!" Displaying a dreamy smile, Sarah undulated out of her seat, hips gently swaying. Her fingertips coyly touched the underside of Bull Neck's chin. "I think I'll stick around—"

His expression reminded me of a bull buffalo during the rut. "You won't regret it, darlin'."

Moving away from the chair, Sarah wobbled on her high heels. She took three awkward steps toward the bar, then toppled sideways into Bull Neck's willing embrace.

"Whoa! That first step's a dilly, ain't it, gal?"

No response. Sarah was too busy fighting the effects of the

bourbon. Sighing heavily, she looped her arms around his neck.

Bull Neck took immediate advantage. Work-roughened hands lifted the hem of her coat, then massaged her shapely stern. Eyes shut, Sarah let out a murmur of protest. "C-cut it out!"

Winking at his pal, he chuckled. "Lord have mercy! We've got us the meat and potatoes this time, ol' buddy."

For a moment I was half tempted to leave her there. Valid or not, Sarah's angry words had cut deeply. As for her predicament . . . well, really, she had only herself to blame!

Still, I couldn't leave a woman—any woman—with those two clowns!

Certain that Sarah was headed for a vile and humiliating experience, I rushed forward. "We'd better be going, Sarah! Becky's expecting us—"

"Not so fast, little darlin'!" Horse Face barred my path. "You heard your friend. She's stayin'."

"We have to go—"

"Then go!" Annoyed glance from Bull Neck. "No one's blockin' the door, Cochise."

Ignoring the racist taunt, I snapped, "Not without Sarah."

"Then my advice is to *run along*, sweetie." Coming up beside me, Horse Face grabbed my wrist. "Sarah's stayin' with us."

Bull Neck nuzzled her throat. Gasping in indignation, Sarah put up a struggle. Splayed fingers pawed his grinning face. She squirmed and wriggled but couldn't quite break the masculine grip. "Let go of me!"

Bull Neck chuckled. "Got us a live one this time, Grant!"

"Leave her alone!" I shouted.

Horse Face grabbed my shoulder. "Why don't you and me just sit this dance out, Injun gal?"

Instantly I whirled, letting fly with a quick Rockette kick. My pump's pointed toe tagged him squarely on the shin. The expression on his equine face shifted from giddy amusement to wide-eyed anguish. "Owwww! Owwww!" Grimacing, he did a one-legged hornpipe. "You little—"

"Let me guess. Hopalong Cassidy, right?" Shaking free of his grasp, I shot Bull Neck a threatening glare. "Let go of her this instant, or I'm calling the sheriff!"

Bull Neck was far from impressed. Lascivious grin. "Phone's over yonder, gal."

Gales of laughter drifted over from the bar. One cowboy slapped the bartop, cackling, "Hey, Grant! That Injun gal teachin' you the Love Dance?"

"No!" Up came Grant's bony fists. "But I'm teachin' *her* something. A lesson she won't ever forget!"

# ▼▼▼▼▼▼ ELEVEN ▼▼▼▼▼▼

Grant rushed me. I had two options—fight or flight. And I definitely preferred flight. I had my fill of fisticuffs in the Big Dollhouse.

My gaze flitted from side to side, seeking an escape route. That fine old fireplace was right behind me. Chairs hemmed me in on the left. To my right stood Bull Neck. So much for an escape route . . .

Swallowing hard, I showed Grant my combat stance. Arms raised in supplication. Wide obsidian eyes. Expression of dismay. "No! Please . . ."

Another catcall from the bar. "Awwwww! Give her a kiss, Grant."

Judging from the expression on Grant's equine face, smooching was the very last thing on his mind. Seizing my outstretched arms, he hauled me in.

My right knee snapped upward, bashing him on the thigh. Grant reacted like any man, bending instantly, turning his leg inward, trying to protect the groin. The motion tipped him off balance. I struck a bit higher, crunching the base of his rib cage. Gasping for breath, he toppled past me like a cut spruce.

I added some velocity to his fall, spinning to the right, slapping one hand on his outflung arm and the other across his shoulder blades.

Grant hit the hardwood floor like a hay bale coming out of the loft. Our empty glasses leapt off the table and shattered. The bartender let out an anguished groan.

Shoving Sarah aside, Bull Neck advanced on me. "You like ass-kickin', eh? Try this on for size, Cochise!"

If anything, he was quicker than Grant. His brawny hand lashed out, seizing a sheaf of Anishinabe hair. Gritting my teeth against the pain, I reached up and grabbed his wrist. And my left leg pistoned upward. For a split second, it looked as if I were trying to do the Highland fling. Then I performed a flawless snapkick, my foot driving deep into his abdomen, folding him like a jackknife.

As he plunged forward, I gave his wrist a savage twist, following up with a stiff-armed shove to the shoulder. Wrenching pain spurred him into a forward roll that would have warmed the heart of any *sensei*.

The resulting crash splintered the low table. Bull Neck's flailing legs sent chairs careening across the floor. I had hoped to put him down with enough force to render him senseless. But he was too big—too rugged. The impact failed to stun him.

Rising to his knees, Bull Neck cast me a murderous glance. My first impulse was to run . . . but I couldn't leave Sarah!

Suddenly, a brutal shove sent me hurtling toward an empty chair. I landed facedown over the armrest, vaguely aware of a human juggernaut streaming by. Righting myself, I swept the raven hair out of my face. There was no mistaking that familiar quilted ski jacket. Or those yard-wide shoulders. *Frank Blodgett!*

Bull Neck waved him aside. "You're in my way, hoss!"

"Not for long, asshole."

Frank punctuated the reply with a sharp overhand right. I

flinched at that loud, meaty smack. Bull Neck's head snapped backward, and he stumbled against an empty table, clutching his pulped eye. Then he doubled his fists and charged.

If you ask me, either one of them could have held his own with Evander Holyfield. They confronted each other like seasoned heavyweights, ready to block with shoulders and forearms, circling each other slowly, feinting and weaving.

Head down, Bull Neck pounded away at Frank's durable middle. He might as well have tried to chip concrete with a straw. Frank absorbed each blow with a simian grunt. Fleeting grimaces hinted at the sizzling pain. But the tempo of his punches never flagged. Again and again Frank let him have it. Always the same one-two-three combination. Right hook, left jab, right cross. He hammered away as hard and as tirelessly as a pile driver.

At last Bull Neck's counterpunches lost their zip, and his shoulders began to sag. Frank opened him right up, driving a hard left deep into his middle and following up with a roundhouse right to the jaw. If he hurt those thick knuckles walloping bone, his expression gave no sign. I expected him to let his opponent drop. Instead, locking an arm around his opponent's neck, Frank ran him headfirst into the bar.

*Wham!* My stomach flipped at the sound of impact. Bull Neck's buddies howled in protest. Again Frank used that skull for a battering ram. This time Bull Neck went completely limp. A noticeable dent marred the bar's polished wood.

*Click-chock!* I flinched at the sound of a shotgun's slide. Standing behind the mahogany was our lady bartender, cradling a Mossberg twelve-gauge.

"That'll do, mister!" she barked. "I'm still makin' payments on this place." The muzzle tilted in the direction of the door. "You two want to do-si-do, you take it on outside."

Just then I heard a woman's voice. "Omigawd!" And spied a

quartet of skiers in the doorway. The wide-eyed speaker covered her lips with a mittened hand.

Yes, it was quite a tableau for the après-ski crowd. Frank at the bar, reaching for his wallet. Bull Neck snoozing on the floor. Cowpokes hastily downing their drinks. A groaning Grant on his knees. And then there was my boss, the demure lady lawyer. Still flashing her tipsy smile, she lay sprawled across a chair, her lovely legs slung over the armrest.

Leaning forward, I examined Sarah's face for bruises. Gasp of relief. No damage. The booze, not Bull Neck, had rendered her unconscious.

I helped her sit upright. The skirt rode high, exhibiting a long expanse of nyloned leg. Male skiers looked on with interest. Giving Sarah's hem a sharp tug, I put an end to the show. Her dignity had suffered enough for one night.

Lightly I stroked her cheek. "Sarah! Wake up! Come on. We've got to get out of here."

Heavy footfalls sounded behind me. Frank's grim chuckle sent a tremor up my spine. "I thought you were just passin' through."

Pretending not to have heard him, I stood and did a hasty about-face. "I'd better call a doctor—"

"Not so fast!" Frank's big hand circled my bicep. He had a grip like a hydraulic clamp. "You got me curious, dolly. Whatcha doin' here with Sally?"

"Owwww!" Clenched teeth. "Let go, Blodgett!"

"Knows my name, too." Dutch-chocolate eyes glittered with rank hostility. "That settles it, hon. You 'n' me got to have a little talk."

I glared right back. Angie the Defiant.

"You know, you didn't even yell when that asshole grabbed you. Where'd you learn judo? In the service?"

Actually, my fighting style is a blend of the Big Dollhouse and the Park Point playground. Whenever we second-graders played superhero, Angie was always the Black Canary. But I wasn't telling Frank that. I wasn't telling him *anything!*

"You didn't even flinch." His eyes narrowed in speculation. "Let me guess. Undercover cop, right?"

I shook my head. "Not even close."

Our conversation roused Sarah. Her eyelids fluttered upward. Blinking like a sleepy toddler, she murmured, "F-Frank? We—we were jus' talkin' 'bout you . . ."

His grin turned feral. "Is that a fact?"

My stomach froze over. Just the thing to tell a hardcase like Frank Blodgett! *Thanks a lot, Sarah!*

Snarling lips formed a single word. "Sit."

I sat. Knees trembling, I waited for his next move, but Frank seemed more interested in my boss. "Sally? Hey, Sal!" Showing a churlish scowl, he cradled her chin. "What's the matter with her?"

"Too much bourbon, not enough crème de menthe," I replied.

"Ahhhhh, she never could handle the stuff." His scowl deepened. "Takes after her old lady." Letting Sarah doze, he turned to me again. "Last time I saw you, sweetie pie, you were pokin' around Madge's truck. Now, here you are, chummin' it up with Sally. What gives?"

I licked dry lips. "Long story, Frank."

"We got time."

"Not that much time!"

"I could *make* you tell me."

Suppressing a shudder, I tried a bit of outlaw bravado. "That could play hell with your parole."

Frank's hard eyes blinked suddenly. "Parole?"

"Don't try to shit me, Blodgett." I thought of a way to mislead him. Sidestepping into my convict persona, I added, "You just finished six months swinging a sledge in Nebraska. Get busted out here, and it's straight back to the quarry."

"Where'd you hear that?"

I shrugged. "Around."

Blunt fingers tap-tapped the tablecloth. "You're beginnin' to get on my nerves, dolly."

"Relax, Frank." Saucy Angie smile. "I'm not looking to roll you over. I just want my share."

Gleam of suspicion. "Share of what?"

"One word . . . *Trautmann's.*"

Frank's gaze turned lethal. "No more games! You tell me everything you know—*right now!*" His hand pounced like a hungry cat. An agonizing fireburst traveled up my arm. "Who told you about that?"

"Jack!" My reply exploded in a shrieking whisper. "J-Jack Sunawavi! H-he told me. Honest! Owwwww! Let go!"

*That* gave him pause. So I pressed my momentary advantage. "I knew Jack in Utah—"

"Where in Utah?"

"Clover Creek. Jack's hometown," I replied. "He visited me last summer while I was in Draper. Told me about the big score he pulled in Colorado. Said his share was two-fifty large."

Frank's face tensed suddenly. Sunawavi's reputation for womanizing made my tale sound convincing, but he didn't quite buy it. "You knew Jack, eh? Where was he killed?"

Oh, boy, could I answer that one! "Dynamite Pass. Up near the Idaho state line."

He grunted in satisfaction. Correct answers always instill confidence. Releasing my arm, he asked, "What were you doing in Draper?"

Penitentiary scowl. "A shitload of laundry!"

"So what brings you to Colorado?"

"Same reason as you, Frank. The money."

"You just figured to mosey off with Jack's share, eh?"

Folding my arms, I smiled. "Jack told me you people hadn't made the split yet. We were . . . well, you know how it is. He would've wanted me to have it."

"Jack's little heiress." Frank let out another harsh chuckle. "And, if you come across the money, I suppose you're gonna confine yourself to Jack's eighty large."

"Eighty large!" Adrenaline helped me put across a valid impression of indignant outrage. "Fuck you, man! He said his cut was a quarter mill."

Guttural laughter. "He lied, sweetie. Jack's been known to do that from time to time." Releasing my wrist, he smiled. "So you were aimin' to help yourself, eh?"

Demure Angie smile. "I didn't know you were in town, Frank."

"What were you doing at the garage?"

I swallowed hard. Well, Biwaban, now we find out if you're right about the robbery.

"Jack said you planted a woman on the inside—Madge Rooley," I said, keeping my voice low. "She helped him tie up that guard—got him into the Trautmann's office. Jack mentioned only two names, Frank. Yours and hers. I read about you taking the fall in Nebraska. Few months later, when I got out of the Big Dollhouse, I figured to pay a call on Ms. Rooley."

Suspicious glower. "That doesn't explain what you were doin' at the garage."

"Okay . . ." Lifting my hands, I sighed. "I was poking around. I thought it was kind of suspicious, that's all. Her having an accident up at Monarch Pass. I wanted a closer look at her truck."

"What for?"

"I think someone's thinning the field, Frank."

He smiled. "We seem to be thinkin' along the same lines, dolly."

"Then you don't think it was just good fortune that the Bureau tumbled to your Nebraska hideout."

"Somebody dropped a quarter. I know that."

"Putting you out of circulation," I added. "Then Madge got

killed up at Monarch Pass. Suddenly, there's three fewer people to split with."

"Somebody mighta had that in mind, yeah."

"Has *somebody* got a name, Mr. Blodgett?"

"None that I'm givin' out."

"And the money?" I asked.

His mouth hardened. "Let's just say it ain't where it's supposed to be."

Instant fussbudget face. I didn't know what to make of Madge's old boyfriend. If the money had indeed been moved, then that explained Frank's presence here in town. He'd come for his share.

On the other hand, it could be Frank himself doing the weeding. The missing four hundred grand offered a compelling motive, indeed.

Just then I spotted my grandfather in the crowd at the bar. Fortunately, Chief had had the good sense not to join us. He avoided a direct stare, keeping his gaze fixed on our mirror reflection. I could see that he was concerned about my choice of drinking companions.

Coy Angie smile. "So what do you say, Mr. Blodgett?"

Acerbic glance. "To what?"

"To cutting a deal. You and me. We find the money, and we split fifty-fifty."

Frank made a wry face. "You gotta be shittin'!"

"We could help each other out."

"Hey!" His upright forefinger flashed in front of my nose. "Just 'cause we think alike don't make us partners." He gave me a long, shrewd look. "Yeah, I can see why Jack took a shine to you. He always was a sucker for a sharp little skirt." Brows lowered in deadly earnest. "Well, forget it. I'm gonna give you some free advice, honey. Plunk your ass on the first bus back to Salt Lake."

"And leave without Jack's share?" I challenged him.

"Jack's dead. Same thing could happen to smart-mouthed little Injun gals, too."

Lifting my chin, I asked, "Is that a threat?"

"Just statin' an everyday fact, Miss . . . you know, you never got around to tellin' me your name."

"Janet Wanagi," I snapped, using my Lakota alias. "You can't just run me out of town, Blodgett."

"Watch me!"

"What about your parole?"

Deep-throated chuckle. "That's a double-edged blade, dolly. You ain't so long out of the pussy palace yourself."

Feigning indignation, I added, "Chet Hurtig might be interested to hear you're back in town."

The notion amused him. "Awwwww, you don't wanna spoil Hurtig's day. Poor guy'll have to run home and change his skivvies." Wry chuckle. "Don't you worry, hon. He'll find out soon enough."

Curious, I thought. I'd already inadvertently mentioned Frank's presence to the former lawman. And Hurtig had been as distraught as Frank had just described. It didn't make sense. Hurtig had friends and allies all over the political map. Why should he be frightened of Frank Blodgett?

Just then Sarah turned in her chair, pillowing her face against the padded backrest, making a small sound of contentment. Frank's reaction intrigued me. Gone was the tough-guy smirk, suddenly replaced by genuine affection. Then his gaze shifted my way once more.

"How'd you get hooked up with Sally?" he asked.

Scheherezade Angie strikes again! "We, uh, met the other day. I heard the Rooleys were having real estate trouble. I offered to help. Sarah thinks I'm a developer."

"Figured to have a look at Madge's papers, eh? Smart girl." Stroking his stubbly chin, he asked, "What do you mean by real estate trouble?"

"A bank's putting the squeeze on Becky and the kids. I hear Cordelia Longworth might be behind it."

Grunt of disgust. "So Dee's up to her old tricks again. Christ! Talk about beatin' a dead horse." His expression became troubled. "How much does Sally know?"

"About her mother's role in the Trautmann's job? Nothing!"

He seemed relieved. "Let's keep it that way, eh?" His thumb pointed at the doorway. "If I pay the cab, will you see that Sally gets home all right?"

Frown of uncertainty. Did Frank know I was staying at the RJ Bar? "Sure. No problem."

"This changes nothin'! Understand?" Frank's expression soured. "I want you *out*, you read me? Outta CB, outta my hair, outta Sally's life!" His voice rose angrily. "Next time I find you underfoot, dolly, you're gonna get stepped on!"

Showing a skittish smile, I babbled, "Okay, okay! Consider me gone. Look, you can't blame a woman for trying, can you?"

Hearty chuckle. "It's damned easy for me, hon!" Rising from the chair, he added, "See if you can get some coffee into Sally. Lemme go call that cab."


Shortly after nine-thirty I coaxed a certain lead-footed lawyer out of the warmth of our taxicab and, slinging her arm across my shoulders, helped her toddle up the snow-covered driveway.

"Are we home yet?" Sarah murmured, lurching against me.

Staggering under the shifting weight, I fought to keep my footing. With any luck, we might reach the front porch by sunup.

"We're making progress, Sarah."

"Next round you're buying."

High beams spread their light over us. I grinned with relief as the Sierra rolled past. Heard the driver's door slam. My grandfather's voice emerged from the darkness. "Need a hand there, *Noozis?*"

"Please!"

Chief shifted Sarah's loose-limbed body onto his own shoulder. Together we helped her negotiate the path leading up to the porch. Sarah pronounced him a gentleman. Me, she referred to as "the party pooper."

Fussbudget frown. Well, the evening hadn't been a complete waste. I'd learned two important facts. Frank Blodgett, Madge Rooley, and Jack Sunawavi hadn't pulled the heist on their own. Other parties had been involved. Pop Hannan, for one. He'd been to Leadville, and he knew the Collegiates as well as Madge. And there had been others, too. People from Crested Butte?

Conscious of Sarah's presence, my grandfather hailed me in our language. "What are you thinking about, *Noozis?*"

Briefly I told him about Frank, adding, "If he's telling the truth, *Nimishoo*, then one of the gang must have moved the money two or three months after the robbery. Frank headed for CB as soon as he was paroled from prison. Boy, was he pissed off when he found the loot gone!"

Chief's lips puckered thoughtfully. "There's our motive. After Sunawavi died, the killer decided to double-cross his partners. Frank's the most dangerous, obviously, so he ratted him out first."

Helping Sarah climb the steps, I murmured, "There's something I don't understand, *Nimishoo*. What did the killer have on Madge? Her role in the Trautmann's job? And if he rolled her over, then what was to prevent her from fingering *him?*"

"That could be why he killed her, *Noozis.*"

Scowling, Sarah contributed to our conversation—in English. "Say . . . are you people talking about me?"

"Absolutely! We both think it's high time you went on the wagon, Sarah," I replied, then switched back to Anishinabemowin. "I'm not so sure, *Nimishoo*. My question is—

can we believe Frank Blodgett? We have only his word for it that the loot was ever moved."

"What wagon?" Sarah mumbled, staring blearily at me.

Chief cleared his throat. "What are you getting at?"

"Suppose it was Madge who made that phone call to the FBI. Maybe she was scared of Blodgett. Scared that he might hurt her family. She knew he was wanted in Nebraska, and she tried to trip him up. What have we got then?"

My grandfather nodded. "A dandy motive for Blodgett to kill Madge Rooley. And it might also explain why Pop Hannan is still alive and Madge isn't." Wry scowl. "I don't know. You could read it either way, *Noozis.*"

Once on the porch, Chief supported Sarah while I rummaged through her purse for the house keys. She clung to my grandfather like an old-time marathon dancer, muttering about impertinent secretaries. After opening the front door, I helped him seat her on the sofa.

At first I'd planned on hunting up Becky. And then I thought of someone else who would benefit more from seeing the unruliest Rooley in that particular condition. Stifling a giggle, I trotted upstairs, selected the proper bedroom door, and gave it a brisk knock.

Muffled teenage voice. "Who is it?"

"Angie," I replied. "Got a minute? I need your help downstairs."

Sarah will never forgive me, I thought. But if those two are ever going to restore their relationship, then Karen has to stop seeing her mother as some sort of unapproachable monarch.

Down the stairs she came, Sarah's darling daughter, coltish blonde in her oversized football jersey and white leggings. Rounding the banister post, she came to a sudden and complete halt, her jaw dropping open. *"Mother!"*

I made a little gesture of presentation. "I thought you could give me a hand with the world's most perfect woman."

Karen's eyes blinked in disbelief. "She's drunk."

"Uh-huh." I folded my hands in front of me. "Or to use her own lovely phrase—*thoroughly smashed.*"

Dignified as a dowager, Sarah mumbled, "Thass right!"

Karen sat beside her on the couch. "What happened?"

"Don't ask me." Mild Angie fib. "That's the condition she was in when I ran into her at the Dry Gulch."

Teenage eyes goggled. "Mother was at the Dry Gulch?"

"Whooping it up with a pair of cowboys." I gestured at the stairway. "She's all yours, honey."

"Me?" Karen bleated.

"Well, she's not *my* mother."

Together we pulled Sarah to her feet. Karen took the supportive position beneath her mother's arm. My grandfather moved in to assist. "I'll give you a hand, Karen."

"That's okay, Mr. Blackbear." Karen's grin was almost as silly as her mother's. "I've done it before . . . with Nana. Thanks for seeing her home."

Up the stairs they went, with Karen holding her mother firmly about the waist. Karen had slipped easily into the role of guardian.

That's a fine girl you have there, Sarah, I thought. I only hope you realize that before it's too late.

As soon as they were out of earshot, Chief turned to me. "Not *my* mother! What are you trying to pull, Angie?"

"*Moi?*" Delicately I touched my collarbone.

"Sarah is going to be mortified."

"Hey! At least they're talking to each other. That's a start."

He shook his head. "Sarah's going to want to talk to *you*, missy."

"Like Scarlett said, tomorrow is another day." I gave my grandfather's arm a playful squeeze. "Come on. Let's grab some supper."

----

The long drive to Leadville had really taken its toll on us. I slept late the following morning. The sound of a pickup's engine roused me from slumber. Tossing the blankets aside, I yawned, toddled over to the bedroom window, and looked out the frosted windowpane. Just in time to see Troy's truck backing down the driveway past my grandfather's Sierra. Lashed-down milk cans lined the truckbed.

Following a leisurely shower, I lifted a brush and removed the snarls from my raven hair. Selected a long-sleeved blue turtleneck and a pair of stonewashed khaki slacks from the closet and gray woolen ski socks from my suitcase. Got dressed, pulled on my moccasin boots, and headed for the kitchen.

I found the Rooley twins munching Apple Jacks and sipping Tropicana. Both acknowledged my arrival with smiles and giggles. Then Laura put her finger to her lips.

"We've got to be quiet, Angie," she whispered. "Aunt Sally's got a headache."

"I'll be as quiet as a little mouse." Keeping my voice down, I seated myself. "Where's Mommy?"

Just then the back door swung open, and Becky entered the kitchen. Peeling off her sheepskin jacket, she grinned. "Morning! You're just in time for some raisin cinnamon rolls. Interested?"

"Definitely." I poured myself a glass of orange juice. "Uhm, how's the patient?"

Becky glanced toward the parlor. "She'll live." Tried very hard not to smile. "Hopefully, she'll learn from the experience."

I thought of the item I'd put in the freezer last night. "I've got a little something that'll make her feel better."

"If I were you, Angie, I wouldn't go in there."

"I'll risk it." I smiled over the rim of my glass. "Is Chief up yet?"

Becky informed me that my grandfather had been up since

dawn, helping out in the barn. Over breakfast I explained how I'd run into Sarah at the Gulch, and then we spent a good twenty minutes on family chitchat.

After breakfast Becky shepherded her young into the rumpus room, and I went to the refrigerator to retrieve my makeshift icepack. Aunt Della taught me this trick. She learned it in the Air Force. I gather it came in handy after a rough night at the officers' club. You take a plastic Ziploc bag and fill it with three parts water and one part rubbing alcohol. Then you stuff that bag into another Ziploc bag and place both in the freezer overnight. The water becomes chilled, but the alcohol prevents it from turning into ice. Come morning, you have a semi-plastic icepack that can be molded to fit the forehead.

I wrapped the icepack in a dish towel, then made my way to the parlor. Just in time to hear Karen's voice, hurt and angry.

"All right! All right! See if I care!"

Into the dining room she came, her features simmering. Snapping a look at me, she blurted out, "You can't talk to that woman! I don't know why I even try!"

I reached out. "Karen . . ."

"Look, I have *had* it with her. If she doesn't want to talk to me . . . *fine!* I have other things to do."

"Karen, it isn't you she's mad at. She's—"

"She just never lets up. Everything I do is wrong, even when I try to help." Biting her lower lip, she grabbed her plum-colored ski parka. "Well, no more! *You* deal with it. I'm out of here!"

Heartsick, I watched her wind a knitted maroon scarf about her neck. "Where are you going?"

Zipping up her parka, she snapped, "Out!"

I flinched at the deafening door slam. So much for my planned mother-daughter reconciliation. From the parlor came a muted contralto groan. "Ohhhhh, my head!"

Hefting the icepack, I tiptoed through the doorway. Sarah lay on the sofa, one hand clasping a damp facecloth to her brow. Suffering lady lawyer in her flannel nightgown and powder-blue bathrobe. Judging from her facial expression, Sarah's hangover was somewhere around ten on the Richter scale.

"Ouch!" I remarked, trying not to giggle. "I can feel that headache all the way over here. You poor thing!"

"Owwwww! Will you please keep your voice down?"

"Sorry." Sympathetic whisper. "Big head?"

"Out to here!" Sarah's palms hovered five inches away from her temples. Agonizing grimace. "Ohhhhh! Never again!"

I could have gone right on playing Florence Nightingale, but, vixen that I am, I couldn't resist the temptation to do a bit of teasing.

Folding the icepack into a half-moon shape, I remarked, " 'The amazing thing about bourbon, kiddo, is that the more you drink, the easier it goes down.' Quote, unquote."

"Who came up with that!?"

Delicately I laid the icepack across her forehead. "A South Dakota lawyer named Sarah Sutton."

Her emerald eyes were slightly bloodshot. "I suppose you're here to gloat."

"Wouldn't dream of it, dear." I seated myself on the sofa's edge. "Hurry up and recuperate, eh? You've got some apologizing to do . . . to your daughter!"

Her teeth gritted. "I'm afraid I'm not in the mood for company just now."

"Well, that's a switch." I shrugged, folding my arms. "You were the life of the party last night."

Sarah's face quivered in alarm. "I—I was?"

"You bet! A real hit with the cowboys," I replied innocently. "Especially when you jumped up onto the bar. You hiked your skirt up to here." Quick chop at mid-thigh. "Me, I *never* would've had the nerve."

"I didn't!" Her features blanched in horror. "Did I?"

"You don't remember much about last night, I take it."

Touching her eyebrow, Sarah groaned. "It's all a big blur. I remember talking to you. And Frank was there—"

"Frank?" I interrupted.

"Frank Blodgett. An old boyfriend of my mother's." She shook her head slowly. "I haven't seen him since I was a kid. Ohhhhh, I must've been dreaming."

"You probably were," I added. "You conked off the minute I got you into the cab."

Bright scarlet swept across her face. "I—I don't usually drink like that."

"Did I say anything, Sarah?"

"You didn't have to." Eyes shut, she massaged both temples with her fingertips. "Ooooooh! I haven't done this in *years*. I—I don't know what came over me."

"I do!" Blunt Angela. "You failed to persuade United Mountain to renegotiate your mother's loan, so you decided to punish yourself by getting drunk."

"You think you're so damned smart!"

"No, just observant," I replied. "That's quite the image you've built for yourself. Sarah Sutton, attorney at law. Proud, regal, competent, ladylike, and tough. Most people find it hard to believe you're Madge Rooley's daughter. But I guess that's the whole idea, isn't it?"

"I have nothing to say to you!"

"Fine! Then you can do the listening." I peeled back a wing of long, raven hair. "Your pride has carried you a long way, *Sally*. It got you through college and law school. But it's gotten out of hand. You've let it come between you and Karen."

Wince of humiliation. "You never should have let her see me like that!"

"Why not?" I snapped. "What are you afraid of? That she might find out you're not the world's most perfect woman? That she might actually see—God forbid—that you sometimes get depressed and feel sorry for yourself? The knowledge isn't going to shatter her psyche, dear. Karen's a big girl now. She can take it."

"I never claimed to be the world's most perfect woman!"

"Maybe not, but that's the impression Karen gets. And you won't let her come close enough to find out otherwise."

"Angela, my relationship with my daughter is none of your damned business!"

"I'm making it my business. You've got a fine daughter there, Sarah. I just wish you'd open your eyes to that."

Clutching the icepack, Sarah shot me a furious look. "I can manage my own life, Miss Biwaban, thank you very much!"

"Oh, yeah! You're doing a bang-up job, Sally! Whenever Karen's growing pains get a little too troublesome, ziiiip . . . off she goes to Crested Butte."

"I've had a lot of trouble in my life—"

"And I see you've handled it the same way as your mother," I interrupted. "Ship the daughter off to the relatives."

Enraged, she sat up suddenly. "How *dare* you!"

"Madge turned her back on you. So what do you do? You turn your back on Karen." Facetious nod. "I reckon you really showed Madge, didn't you?"

"Ohhhhh! You little—"

"Listen to me," I snapped. Sarah's furious face hovered two inches from mine. "I don't know what kind of resentment you're still carrying around against your mother, but you're better off dropping it. I can't give you your childhood back. Nobody can. All you can do is pick up the threads and go on."

Sarah's lower lip trembled. Turning her gaze away, she replied, "It's very easy for you to talk, isn't it? You have no idea what my life has been like."

"So you intend to spend it running away, eh? Just like your mother."

Shrill denial. "I am *nothing* like my mother!"

"Can't prove that by last night," I replied, my voice low. "That's something Madge would have done. You want to punish yourself, Sally? Fine! Be my guest. But leave your daughter out of it. Karen deserves better than the same old Rooley crap."

Just then an off-key yowl erupted in the rumpus room. Two parts human and one part canine. The din struck Sarah like an invisible fist. She doubled instantly, her face tensing in anguish, clapping both hands over her ears. The icepack landed in her lap. "Owwwww! Owwwww! My head!"

"Lie down," I murmured, putting the icepack back on her forehead. "I'll keep them quiet."

Arriving in the rumpus room, I found Becky's twins and Ralph the Border collie sitting on the rug, watching TV, and singing along with a purple dinosaur. Musical enthusiasm in three-part disharmony. *"I love you . . . Arrrooooo!"* Laura had her arm around the dog. Ralph went at it with operatic vigor. Canine howling numbed my ears.

I shushed the collie by giving his nose a rub, then smiled at the twins. "Tone it down, you two. Aunt Sally's trying to sleep."

"We're singing with Barney," Laura explained.

"It's too nice a day for a singalong," I said, resting both hands on my knees. "Why don't we go outside and build a snowman?"

Toddler shouts of joyous affirmation. The twins galloped into the kitchen. I grabbed ahold of Ralph's collar. Low-throated whine of inquiry. Ruffling the fur between his ears, I whispered, "Howling when your aunt has a hangover? That's the express ticket to the pound, Pavarotti!"

Suitably chastened, Ralph wagged his tail and looked on as I wrestled with the twins' winter clothing. Pull up the ski pants. Zip the parkas. Wiggle the boots onto wriggling four-year-old feet.

Outside, Luke, Laura, and I built a lopsided snowman. The kids rolled their snowballs along, squealing with laughter, taking an occasional spill, and bursting out of the powder like frosted elves.

Glancing at the house, I gave some thought to the twins' ailing aunt. Okay, princess, maybe you were a little rough on Sarah. There is such a thing as moderation, you know. One can be frank without being brutal.

Fussbudget frown. I wondered how much of my own anger had been stoked by what she'd said about Paul last night.

Conscience is an inconvenient thing.

Well, perhaps I could make it up to her . . .

When the kids were finished, I took them for a short stroll along the snow-covered bank of Roaring Judy Creek. They asked where we were going. I explained that we were going to find some Indian medicine for Aunt Sally.

And we did. The sun had melted the waist-deep snow on the creek's south side, exposing a narrow mossy path about twelve inches across. Enough to expose the dessicated stalks of honeysuckle and wild ginger. I pulled two of each, snapped off the stalks, pocketed the frozen roots.

Finding the yarrow was quite a bit harder. With the kids in tow, I followed the creek fifty yards upstream, then halted beside the frozen remains of a marsh. Fuzzy brown stems poked through the fragile ice. In six months they'd be sporting delicate white blossoms. At the moment, however, I was far more interested in their tiny mud-caked bulbs.

When we returned to the house, Becky took charge of the twins. I cleaned the roots beneath a streaming faucet, dropped them into a porcelain teapot, and added enough water for one steaming cup.

While waiting for the water to boil, I glimpsed Madge's antique rolling pin nestled in its varnished cedar cradle. Yielding to curiosity, I gave it a lift.

Aunt Della would've loved to have had this in her collection. A solid, hand-molded ceramic rolling pin about fourteen inches long. Genuine Meissen pattern, all right. The surface looked like a checkerboard drawn with upraised blue lines. Each square contained an upraised symbol. Sunbursts, tulips, hearts, and hex signs. The latter gave me a start, and then I remembered what Karen had told me. An Amish family from Gothic had cast it.

Turning the rolling pin over, I blinked in surprise. Marking the cylinder's middle was a rectangle measuring three by five inches. Instead of the usual hex signs, the rectangle contained thirteen tiny blue pyramids. They crammed the right-hand side, strung out in the shape of an irregular 7. A white dot marked the third pyramid in the upper row. To the left of the 7 was a jagged blue line running from the upper left to the bottom right corner. At first it looked as if the artisan had filled in and painted over a crack. Then I ran my thumbnail down the line. Nope! No crack. The blue line was definitely part of the design.

Scowl of confusion. What is this, anyway? Some kind of trademark?

The teapot's shrill whistle put an end to my ruminations. I replaced Madge's rolling pin in its cedar cradle. Perhaps it was an Amish custom. You know, like painting false doors on the barn to trick the devil.

Minutes later, balancing a tray on one hand, I gave the parlor door a quiet rap. Sarah's eyes winked open. Turning her head on the pillow, she offered a questioning glance.

Smiling, I set the tray on the coffee table. "Got something here that'll help you feel better."

"What is it?" she murmured.

"Nuche hangover cure. Guaranteed to soothe that splitting headache or your money back." Lifting the teapot, I added, "Mother Shavano taught me this recipe."

Anything to keep Angie's mind off those good-looking Mormon boys!

Saffron tea spattered out of the spout. Handing the cup to Sarah, I said, "Bottoms up, dear."

The pungent scent crinkled Sarah's nose. "What is this stuff?"

"Wild ginger and honeysuckle for the headache. Yarrow to settle your stomach. Drink up!"

Soft groan. "Do I have to?"

"Come on! Take your medicine like a big girl."

Slowly she lifted the cup. Her first taste triggered a hellish grimace.

I had the good grace not to chuckle. "Not very yummy, is it?"

Sip by sip, Sarah bravely knocked it down. Meanwhile, I hunted up a blanket for her. In thirty minutes she'd be fast asleep. Honeysuckle root does that to a woman.

Looking a little shamefaced, she put the empty cup on the saucer. "I—I did some thinking while you were outside." Troubled sigh. "You were right, Angela. About Karen. And about last night."

"Drink your tea, dear. We can discuss it later."

She took a timid sip. "You were even right about the image. But it wasn't some old biddy in Gunnison." Glum smile. "Guess I modeled myself after Mrs. Longworth."

"Cordelia Longworth?"

Sarah blinked. "You've heard of her?"

Seating myself on the sofa, I shrugged. "People talk."

"She . . . well, she has quite a bit of money. And—" Sudden downcast gaze. "I—I guess I wanted to be just like her. So poised and gracious and self-confident."

"So much unlike your mother?" I prodded.

A solitary teardrop rolled off her eyelash. "You have no idea what it was like, Angela. Becky does. Strange men moving in from time to time. Landlords pestering Mother for the rent. I—I wanted her to *change*, and she never did. We'd live with Aunt Alice till she made parole, and then we'd be on the road again." Hushed sob. "I swore someday it was going to be different. If not for me, then for my children!"

"So, when you had the chance, you bundled up Karen and headed for South Dakota."

Slow nod. "I d-didn't have much of a choice. You know what a small town is like. If I'd stayed in C.B., I never would've gotten away from it. Madge Rooley's daughter! I had to change it, Angela. I—I had to change *everything*."

"Isn't Mrs. Longworth the one who had you kicked out of school?"

"Because of Arthur." An old resentment hardened her lovely face. "I'm afraid the admiration wasn't mutual, Angela. I never *dreamed* Mrs. Longworth was so vindictive."

"Becky's told me some of it."

"Then she must've told you how Terry took off with the rodeo. Some father! I haven't heard from him since the day I learned I was pregnant." She looked up at me. "I won't kid you, Angie. It was rough. But I did have some support. Aunt Alice was a jewel. And Mrs. Tarkian at the high school—she went to bat for me."

"Mrs. Tarkian?" I echoed.

Brisk nod from Sarah. "My English teacher. I thought about dropping out, but she encouraged me to stay on. So I went with her to the school committee meeting."

"Which old lady Longworth turned into a court-martial."

Sarah's voice turned bitter. "She humiliated me, Angie. I was seventeen years old, for heaven's sake! My mother was in prison. I was scared and pregnant, and she didn't give a damn. She had Madge Rooley's daughter sitting in that chair, and she couldn't resist the opportunity to make Mother pay." Green eyes glittered angrily. "She stood before the microphone and made this big speech about 'white trash mountain girls' getting pregnant. She made me feel like the town tramp, which is exactly what she wanted." Her tone cut like a razor. "You know, I've always wanted to meet that bitch again. To face her as an equal. Perhaps at the Inaugural Ball in Denver.

I'd walk right up to her and in her own ladylike way I'd tell that woman *exactly* what I think of her!"

"What about your friend Mrs. Tarkian?"

Smile of fond remembrance. "Well, she really went to bat for me. Pointed out all those A's on my report card. She was very persuasive. But the vote was a tie—three in favor, three against. Mrs. Longworth was the chairperson, and she cast the deciding vote. So I was out."

"Your mother tried to break out of prison right after that, didn't she?"

Sarah nodded. "Uh-huh. A couple of days later. She was shot while trying to climb the fence." Mild shake of the head. "Good Lord, what a summer that was!"

"Did you tell Madge about the hearing?"

Wry grimace. "Are you kidding? I was still trying to work up nerve enough to tell her I was pregnant."

"Your aunt?"

"I don't think so." Sarah's lips tightened. "Aunt Alice and I were in Springfield only a couple of weeks earlier. We planned to tell her everything during our next visit."

I frowned. "Then how did your mother find out about the hearing?"

"I don't know, Angie. Mother never told me." Stroking her temple, Sarah murmured, "Although I do have my suspicions."

"What do you mean?"

"I think Mrs. Longworth sent word to Mother. That was her sneaky little way of rubbing it in."

Expression of disbelief. "Don't tell me Mrs. Longworth had clout with the Springfield warden!"

"Hardly! Her influence doesn't extend that far. She does have friends in the sheriff's department, though."

"Such as?"

"Sheriff Hurtig, for one."

"Hurtig?" I echoed. "She's chummy with *him?*"

"Of course." Sarah looked at me as if I were the village idiot. "Who do you think put up the money for his first election campaign?"

# ▼▼▼▼▼ TWELVE ▼▼▼▼▼

"Señorita Wanagi?" said the maid.

She was petite, Mexican, and about twenty years old. The old-fashioned black-and-white uniform complimented her curvy figure. Flashing dark eyes and a no-nonsense expression. Cordelia Longworth had trained her well.

"The señora is on the telephone." Faint Guadalajara accent. "She'll see you in a few minutes."

"Thanks."

Arms folded, I stood at the parlor window, peering through the frost-rimmed glass. A zigzagging split-rail fence broke the monotony of drifting snow. A mile beyond, an evergreen forest began its relentless climb up Whetstone Mountain. A high haze wreathed the skyline, hinting at an impending snowfall.

I glanced at the corner grandfather clock. Three thirty-five on the first day of February. For my meeting with Madge Rooley's nemesis, I'd put together a stunning Corporate Angie outfit, beginning with every woman's wardrobe staple—the black skirt. To that I'd added a black satin camisole, a gold-plated chain necklace, and a white double-breasted cutaway blazer with matte piping. Just what you'd expect from my alter ego, Janet M. Wanagi, that high-powered developer from South Dakota.

The Longworth home surprised me. It had seen less than twenty Colorado winters. A large chalet-style house built of native lodgepole with tall southern windows and a rooftop observation deck. From Sarah's description of the woman, I'd been expecting a Queen Anne mansion on the order of the Looseslipper House.

Beside the window stood a prodigious fireplace. The hefty stones looked as if they'd been fished out of Carbon Creek. The chimney soared to meet a redwood cathedral ceiling. The decor was aggressively Western. Antique pioneer furniture, wood-paneled walls, hand-stitched throw rugs, and a wagon-wheel chandelier.

I thought of Sarah, fast asleep back at the RJ Bar. With any luck she'd sleep through supper, giving me plenty of time to interview the formidable Mrs. Longworth.

I had to learn more about Madge and Arthur. Just about everybody I'd spoken to had a tale to tell. They'd all been remarkably consistent, too. Dee Longworth had been humiliated by her husband's affair with Madge. Years ago she had struck at the teenage Sarah. Was she also behind the financial misfortunes of the Rooley ranch?

Sarah had raised an interesting point. Neither she nor Alice McCannell had contacted Madge at the Big Dollhouse. Had Mrs. Longworth sent word to the prison, hoping that Madge would be killed trying to escape?

And, having dabbled in attempted murder once, could she have tried it again? Could she be the one who tampered with Madge Rooley's brakes?

My window reflection showed a fussbudget face. It had been fifteen years since Sarah was drummed out of high school. If Cordelia was behind the murder attempt, then why had she waited so long before trying again? Had something set her off? If so, what?

"Miss Wanagi?"

The lady's voice was a crisp contralto, accustomed to instant obedience. Reminded me of the assistant principal at Central. I turned at once, just in time to accept Cordelia Longworth's outstretched hand.

My first glance put the lady at age forty-five. Tall and slender, with delicate cheekbones, bright blue eyes, a sharp aquiline nose, and a forthright chin. Her hair was the russet hue of a thoroughbred Irish setter, and she wore it in the short style so popular thirty years ago. Twin auburn commas brushed the upper corners of her brow. As we shook hands, however, I felt the dry, papery skin and noticed the telltale age spots behind her knuckles. My second glance found more evidence of skilled cosmetology. Pancake makeup obscured her crow's-feet, concealed the neck wrinkles, and subdued the laugh lines on either side of her chin. I added another decade to my estimate.

"My apologies. I was on the phone." Cordelia had a rancher's smile—warm, wide, and hospitable. "Sorry to keep you waiting."

"That's okay, Mrs. Longworth. I appreciate you seeing me on such short notice."

"No problem at all. Would you care for some coffee?"

"That'd be nice. Thanks."

Glancing at the doorway, she snapped, "Juanita! Coffee for two in the family room."

The maid nodded. *"Si, señora."*

I fell into step behind Cordelia as she headed for the door. She had a very brisk, aggressive stride, moving very swiftly on her too-high heels. Shoulders squared, backbone perfectly straight. Her meaty derriere hardly wobbled. Her feet were small, and, perched in those narrow hunter's-green dress pumps, they looked even smaller.

The lady's woolen suit must have come straight from Neiman-Marcus. And I don't mean the bargain basement. It was a tailored two-piece suit in a subdued shade of celery.

Lengthy, double-breasted, shawl-collar jacket and a knee-grazing slim skirt. Four strands of perfectly matched pearls nestled against her chemise. On anyone else they would have looked gaudy and pretentious. But not on Mrs. Longworth.

I spoke up. "I hope I'm not interrupting anything."

"Not at all, dear," she replied. "I was just talking to my attorney. We've run into a bit of a snag with the pipeline, I'm afraid."

"Pipeline?"

"This year's big project. We're building an LNG pipeline from our Lake City field clear on out to Colorado Springs."

"LNG?" Angie the Echo.

"Liquid natural gas." Satisfaction added a vibrant tilt to her voice. "We'll be running one hundred and twenty miles of twenty-inch insulated pipe right over the divide. *And* building two large storage tanks off Wigwam Road. With any luck, we'll finish in October."

"Sounds expensive."

"It is! About a hundred million, all told." Her tone chilled suddenly. "Of course, it'll go much higher if our friends in Washington have their way." Showing me an irritated glance, she added, "Does Hillary really expect me to provide full medical coverage to *temporary* employees? Those Texans don't live here, you know. They're roustabouts. They drift from field to field. I have enough expenses to worry about without *that!* Whatever happened to free enterprise?"

"Well, roustabouts do have families . . ." I began.

"True, and it's *their* responsibility to pay for a doctor—not mine!" She cast me a suspicious glance. "Where did you go to school, Janet?"

I gave her an answer I thought she'd like. "Brigham Young University."

"Good choice." Cordelia seemed more at ease. "Thank God your mother had the good sense to send you there and not to some bastion of socialism . . . like Radcliffe!"

The family room was about one-third the size of the parlor, a spacious den with a fieldstone fireplace and a peaked ceiling. Twin sofas faced each other across a low rosewood table. A vintage Henry rifle was mounted on the cedar-paneled wall above the mantelpiece. Just above that was an oil painting of a distinguished-looking white-haired rancher.

"Who's that?" I asked.

"My great-grandfather." Eyeing the portrait, Cordelia gave her chin a sudden languid lift. "Linus Stockdale. Daddy gave me that painting. It used to hang in the old house."

Strange feeling of déjà vu. How many times have I seen Sarah lift her chin that way? You know, had I never seen that photo of Madge Rooley, I might have thought *Cordelia* was her mother.

Sarah had done more than borrow Mrs. Longworth's style. So determined was she to break with her family's past that she'd unconsciously imitated the woman's very mannerisms.

Juanita arrived with the coffee, and we took our seats. I spread the linen napkin across my lap, then smiled thankfully as the maid offered me a steaming cup.

"Linus ran quite a herd in the old days," Cordelia said, stirring her coffee. "Two thousand head. And he did it all without any help from some damned liberal social worker. Do you know what's wrong with this country? Too much welfare! Those liberals keep pushing all this 'entitlement' nonsense. Americans used to say '*I can.*' Nowadays it's '*I deserve.*' Can you imagine! Trashy people thinking they *deserve* to live in a house my taxes built instead of getting a job and buying their own like Great-gran—*ohhhhh!*"

Cordelia's fingers trembled suddenly, knocking over the sugar bowl. White cubes clattered across the tray. Wincing, she put down her coffee and clenched her quivering hand.

"Are you all right?" I asked, leaning forward.

Nodding curtly, she grimaced. "Neuralgia. It comes and goes. I'll be fine." Anger crept into her voice. "The price of growing old, I suppose." Infuriated by this public display of weakness, she showed me a bland look and tried to change the subject. "Now then, girl, what brings you to the county?"

So I treated Mrs. Longworth to an abbreviated version of the Janet Wanagi biography, adding in conclusion, ". . . So that's it, basically. I pocketed my comission from Global Investment Corp. and flew down to Denver. I've heard rumors of future development on the Western Slope."

Coy smile. "You heard right, girl."

"Care to share any particulars, Mrs. Longworth?"

She cleaned her lips with the napkin. "Are you familiar with the Cottonwood Pass project?"

I shook my head.

"Some of us have prevailed upon the legislature to free up ten million in highway funds," she confided. "The state will be paving the old Forest Service road from Almont to Buena Vista. The road runs straight through Cottonwood Pass." Dimples appeared at the corners of her smile. "That is prime land for cross-country skiing."

"So you're buying real estate up in Cottonwood Pass."

"There have been several transactions during the past few months."

"What do you have in mind, Mrs. L? Ski condos?"

"For a start." Inquisitive blue eyes gleamed. "Is that what you're looking to build?"

"Uh-huh." My hands performed a spirited pantomime. "I'm thinking of seven houses on a fifty-five-acre spread. Six condo units to each house. Two big stables and plenty of trails for skiers, snowmobiles, and horses."

"I assume you have a name for this development."

Sudden grin. "Sunset Ridge."

"Bottom-line construction cost per house?" she snapped.

I'll say this for Cordelia Longworth. She definitely knew the real estate trade. Which had me wondering how closely she worked with her developer nephew, Matt Stockdale.

"Ohhh, let's say three hundred K per structure," I said, trying to stay in the ballpark. "Of course, I haven't yet filed with the subdivision board."

"What's your projected retail price on the individual units?" she asked, her gaze growing sharper.

"A hundred and twenty K." Disarming smile. "I'm aiming at the upper-income market."

"So you'll gross four hundred and eighty K per house. Which means that after initial property taxes, consultant fees, and other sundry closeout costs, you should walk away with one-point-three million." Dry chuckle. "Not too shabby, dear." Neuralgic fingers trembled on her knee. "Have you selected a site for this proposed development?"

Slow nod. "I understand that the United Mountain Bank Corporation may soon be putting a few ranches on the auction block."

"True enough. Which ranch are you looking at?"

"The RJ Bar."

Cordelia looked at me as if I'd just told her where to find the Fountain of Youth. Chuckling with undisguised glee, she slapped the sofa cushion. "Wonderful!" Then, remembering my presence there, she put a cap on her enthusiasm. "It's a fine property, Janet. You'll be quite pleased with it."

Awaiting a reaction, I asked, "Do you know the owners?"

"You bet I do!" Venom laced her rasping voice. "The Rooleys! Believe me, this county will be a lot better off without *that trash!*"

"I'm not sure I understand, Mrs. Longworth."

"There isn't one of them who hasn't been in jail!" she blurted out, her eyes ablaze. "White trash! All of them! Old Tom Rooley was a bank robber. And so was his daughter, Madge!" Just saying the name set her teeth on edge. "Why, Madge Rooley was nothing more than a slut. She got knocked up when she was fifteen. Never did get around to naming the father! Ohhhhh, that cheap little tramp!" Fury hardened her features. "Her *daughters* aren't any better! I remember the time Sally came before the school committee. With her stomach out to here! Pregnant in her teens—just like her mother! She actually had the gall to ask us to let her finish her senior year." Glare of indignation. "No *way* was I going to let some trashy Rooley girl disgrace our school! I made damned sure of that."

Seeing that Madge had once run off with Cordelia's husband, I'd expected a good deal of animosity. But the depth of her hatred took my breath away.

"Marsha Randolph told me I was being unfair. But I was right about those Rooley girls. Look at Becky. She had twins. There's not an ounce of decency in the entire family."

At that moment I felt like shampooing Cordelia's bogus auburn curls with the remains of my coffee. Somehow I managed to stifle the impulse. After all, I needed the sanctimonious old bitch to get at her nephew.

"Is there any way they could avoid eviction?" I asked.

"I doubt it." Gradually she brought her temper under control. "Madge left a debt of just over one hundred thousand. They can't possibly cover it."

And how would you know *that*, Mrs. Longworth?

"I understand the oldest girl is a lawyer," I said.

"No problem. Sally doesn't have that kind of money. She'd have to raise it somehow." Sudden ferocious smile. "She won't be successful. I can guarantee that."

I didn't doubt her for a second. Seeing the Rooleys run off their ranch would be the happiest moment of her life. One final slap at the hated Madge.

Rubbing her sinewy hands, Cordelia asked, "Have you seen the property yet?"

"Not yet," I replied. "I just got the directions from a guy in town."

"If I may be so bold . . . *who?*"

I tossed out a familiar name. "Chet Hurtig."

All at once the lady's features softened. "Really? And how is Chester?"

"Uhm, fine. Pretty busy with the store and all." I turned the tables on her. "Do you know him?"

"Of course." Her smile was genuine. "Chester Hurtig was our sheriff for a good many years. He was a frequent guest here. My late husband and I both served on his campaign committee." Mild sigh. "I haven't seen too much of him lately, though. He spends quite a bit of time up in the high country, I'm told." Her slender shoulders shrugged. "Strange how people drift apart, isn't it?"

Wait a minute! My eyes narrowed suddenly. I thought Mrs. Longworth and Hurtig were supposed to be enemies.

"How often did he visit the Rafter L?" I inquired.

"Once or twice a month. If you ask me, Chester was the finest sheriff we ever had. It's such a shame he was implicated in that scandal." I detected a note of sincere regret. "I haven't seen him since he and and Marlene divorced. He stopped coming around. A pity, that. I always enjoyed his company." All at once her forehead wrinkled in confusion. "One thing bothers me, Janet. Why did you approach Chester about the Rooley ranch?"

Schoolgirl Angie. "I heard he and Madge were chummy."

Blue eyes blinked. "Who told you that?"

I tossed out another name. "Pop Hannan."

Exasperation colored the lady's features. "Oh, for— Janet! He's the town drunk."

"Well, he did look like he had a few—"

"I wouldn't believe a word of his!" Cordelia advised. "Chester and that—*that woman!* Ridiculous! Why, he's the first man who ever arrested her."

"Pop seemed to know what he was talking about."

"Nonsense!" she snapped. "Hannan is a hopeless drunk. Chester's arrested him a dozen of times. He was probably trying to stir up trouble."

Chastened look. "I guess I shouldn't have given him that ten dollars, huh?"

"Certainly not!" Cordelia gave me a stern look. "If it's information you're after, young lady, you'd be better off making discreet inquiries at the chamber. A girl can get into all sorts of trouble talking to disreputable characters on the street."

"I'll keep that in mind, ma'am."

"See that you do." Just then her gaze found the Edwardian clock on the mantelpiece. "Tell me, have you any other appointments this afternoon?"

"Not a one, Mrs. L."

Warm smile of invitation. "Then I'd very much love to have you as my dinner guest. I'd like you to meet my nephew, Matthew. My brother's son. I'm sure he'd love to be a part of this discussion."

"Is he a realtor?" I asked, tongue in cheek.

She nodded. "Twelve years now. He owns Gunnison Guaranty Corp. You may have seen him in Denver."

"Maybe. I'm a newcomer to Colorado." Couldn't resist the temptation. "How often does he visit Denver?"

"Once a week, usually. He has quite a few friends on the state board of realtors."

"When's the last time he was up north?" I asked.

Her lips puckered thoughtfully. "A week or so ago, I believe. Thursday the twenty-second."

Small tingle of excitement. Stockdale was in Denver the same day Sarah and I were at the conference. The day Madge was killed at Monarch Pass.

Hiding my reaction, I asked, "Is he coming here?"

"No, I thought we'd join him in town," she said, standing up. Her fingers suddenly curled into fists. Another neuralgic spasm set them trembling against her skirt. "You don't mind driving, do you?"

Polite smile. "Not at all."

While Mrs. Longworth went to freshen up, I did some hasty

thinking. There was no way I could reconcile her version with what Chet Hurtig himself had told me.

Could Hurtig have lied?

Tart fussbudget face. Why would he lie to a total stranger about his friendship with Cordelia Longworth?

Cordelia knew about Hurtig's divorce, but she seemed unaware of his continuing bitterness. Perhaps Hurtig held her responsible for the loss of his badge. That made sense. There could be a lot of animosity on his part—rancor Mrs. Longworth was completely unaware of.

Well, at least I was certain of one thing. Cordelia Longworth may have hated Sarah's mother, but she hadn't committed the actual murder. Her small feet could never have left those size eleven footprints I found at the hotel and up on the mountain.

Nor was there any way the woman's afflicted fingers could have disassembled a truck's master cylinder and sabotaged Madge Rooley's brakes.

Cross the lady off your list, princess. At least for now. But keep your eyes and ears open around her nephew!

"Park over there, Janet."

Cordelia's forefinger pointed out a vacant parking space in front of a distinguished old Victorian home. Stepping lightly on the brake, I eased the Sierra out of the traffic stream and nosed it up against the high sidewalk.

"Where are we going?" I asked.

"Penelope's." Her nod targeted the upscale restaurant neighboring the aged, well-kept house. "I highly recommend the steak, dear. It's superb." Mischievous smile. "But you may find the decor a bit . . . unusual."

Well, Mrs. Longworth was certainly right about that. As I stepped through the doorway, moisture-laden warmth washed over me. A hanging palm frond swatted my hair. I looked around in amazement. Dwarf palms, tree ferns, and tropical plants smothered the interior. Sort of like walking through the Everglades. I almost expected to see Tarzan in a white tux come swinging down from the ceiling, carrying a wine list.

Moving ten times quicker than Tarzan, the maître d' rocketed across the room, his vulpine face split in an eager smile. "Ah, Madame Longworth! How good of you to come."

"Hello, Jules." Showing a gracious smile, Cordelia peeled off her kid gloves. "My usual table?"

"Available, of course." Precise Gallic bow. "Will you follow me, please?"

So we trooped through Tropical Colorado, with Angie in the rear. Only a handful of diners. The supper crowd hadn't arrived yet. I swear, Cordelia could have given Princess Di tips on how to make an entrance. Her regal passage drew nearly every glance in the room.

Then they looked at me, and their expressions said it all in two words. *New secretary.*

Mrs. Longworth's favorite table occupied an alcove screened from the main floor by luxurious stands of fern and bamboo. Two large tinted windows looked onto Elk Avenue. After we took our seats, Jules handed each of us a wine list bound in maroon leather. Cordelia recommended the Badia à Coltibuono, and I bowed to the lady's expertise.

While we waited for the entree, Mrs. Longworth chattered on and on about the cornerstone of her fortune, Mineral Mountain Natural Gas Corporation. The new pipeline, she told me, would make them competitive with the big boys up in Edmonton.

"Our share of the energy market is growing, dear." She paused for a hasty sip. "This year the industry plans to market twenty *trillion* cubic feet of natural gas to an estimated sixty million customers nationwide." Sudden frown. "So long as those pinheads on the Potomac don't mess it up!"

"Did some new regulations come down?" I asked.

The frown deepened her wrinkles. "Oh, those wretched liberals are always harping about something. Now they're pushing for more frequent inspection of our lines. *To check for possible corrosion*, they say. Nonsense! Why, gas is the safest form of energy there is. In all the years I've owned Mineral Mountain, we've had only . . . oh, seven or eight leaks. And only three of those ever resulted in an explosion!"

I remembered a recent gas explosion that had nearly leveled a housing project in New Jersey. "Well, a lot of those gas transmission lines run through populated areas, Mrs. Longworth."

"The danger is highly overrated, Janet," she said tartly. "Have you any idea how many pipelines actually succumb to corrosion?"

Ever the polite dinner guest, I shook my head.

"One in five." Smug look. "That means the odds against any kind of explosion are four to one." Jovial wink. "Try to beat those odds at the racetrack."

True enough, Mrs. L, I thought. Yet, there are a whole lot of gas lines running through American soil, 1.7 million miles of pipeline, to be exact. And with twenty percent of them yielding to age and corrosion, what happens to the odds then?

In the next decade, I fear, gas line explosions could become as commonplace as fender benders.

While I picked at my salad, Cordelia went right on singing the praises of the natural gas industry. Every so often, I smiled and made humming sounds of assent, all the while hoping that she'd give me an opening.

My wandering gaze drifted out the window. Across the street stood Kochevar's, its doors open to the après-ski crowd. Right next door was the Forest Queen Hotel. Just then I spotted a girl waiting at the bus stop in front of the hotel. A familiar coltish teenage blonde in a plum-colored ski parka with a canvas tote bag slung over her shoulder. She waited patiently at curbside, occasionally shooting an expectant glance up Elk Avenue.

I blinked in recognition. *Karen!*

"Janet!" Cordelia's voice broke into my reverie. "Would you care for a roll?"

Turning, I saw the waiter setting down our steaks. Cordelia offered me the breadbasket, and I helped myself. My plate definitely looked inviting. Sirloin steak, done to a choice medium rare, quick-fried potatoes, and a dollop of spinach.

Glancing at her watch, she remarked, "I wonder what's keeping Matthew?"

"Oh, he'll be along soon enough."

I sneaked a glance out the window. Across the street, a Greyhound bus obscured my view of the hotel. The sign above the windshield read DENVER. All at once, its diesel engine rumbled to life, and it lumbered away from the curb. The sidewalk was empty.

What happened to Karen? I asked myself. Did she board that bus?

I remembered this morning's altercation—the recent threat to leave home! Ohhhhh, Karen, I thought, slicing my steak. Please don't do anything rash.

"Ah, here he is." Satisfaction smoothed Cordelia's sharp voice. "I'm waiting for an explanation, young man."

"Sorry, Aunt Dee. I got tied up on the phone." Removing his cream-colored Stetson, Matt Stockdale bent and gave his aunt's cheek a perfunctory kiss. "Hope you ladies haven't been waiting too long."

Flashing us both an apologetic smile, Matt drew one of the empty chairs. Same square, boyish face and De Gaulle nose and bristling outlaw mustache. His tailored Western suit was a shade too loud for the banking industry. Medium gray sportcoat with a white pinstripe and suede yokes. Matching dress slacks. Dobby-pattern dress shirt and a dark gray Apache tie.

Cordelia gestured my way. "Matt, this is the woman I was telling you about—Janet Wanagi."

"Howdy, Jan. Welcome to C.B." He had a hearty salesman's handshake. Dark brown eyes gave me a quick but thorough once-over. "Say . . . have we met?"

I masked my sudden anxiety behind a sparkling Angie smile. Cordelia's nephew had a good memory for faces. He must have seen me in the crowd at Madge's funeral.

Matt's smile turned pensive. I realized he was trying to remember where he'd seen me before. Unwilling to let him grasp that memory, I blurted out, "Most likely in Denver, Mr. Stockdale."

He took a seat. "You're from Denver?"

Shaking my head, I replied, "Rapid City. I just moved to Denver last month." Remembering what Mrs. Longworth had told me, I added, "Most likely we've passed each other in the hall at the board of realtors."

"Oh, yeah." He seemed satisfied with my answer.

The waiter returned, ready to take another order, and Matt put in a request for Coors. During dinner he quizzed me about my . . . uhm, Janet Wanagi's background. Fortunately, I'd had a couple of days to dream up a plausible biography. Four years at Brigham Young, leading to a degree in business. Two years running a low-income housing program in the Dakotas, followed by a highly successful jump into the private sector.

"So what brings you down here?" Matt asked, sitting back and resting a shiny Dan Post boot on his knee.

"Opportunity," I replied, pushing my empty plate away. "Like I told Mrs. Longworth, there's a big demand for ski condos these days. Gunnison County isn't exactly overbuilt yet."

"So . . ." Nimble hands searched the pockets of his sportcoat. He withdrew a matchbook and a rumpled package of Camels. "Are you thinking of building?"

"If I can get the lots and the permits."

He struck a match on the boot's sole. "How are you fixed for financing?"

Nonchalant shrug. "I haven't gone shopping yet."

Cracking a grin, he dangled the fiery match between two fingertips. "Keep me in mind, okay? Gunnison Guaranty handles quite a few real estate transactions."

I cocked an eyebrow. "Such as the Quick Start program?"

Matt's smile instantly vanished. Brown eyes narrowed in irritation. "Now, what would you mean by that, Jan?"

"People said some nasty things about it back in Denver."

Cordelia gasped. *"What people?"*

The old girl looked ready to take names!

Patting her arm, Matt said, "No need to get riled, Aunt Dee." He blew a thin stream of smoke. "I'm not ashamed of it. Quick Start was a damned good program. It made a lot of money available to small ranchers. Too bad it didn't work out."

"I've heard another version," I said.

"Whose version? Some range county state rep's? What the hell does he know about the industry?" Matt's expression radiated utter sincerity. "What did he tell you? That I left those poor folks in a bind? Hey, I didn't take the money and run. I'm still here. I was born in Crested Butte. This is my hometown."

"They say there are quite a few ranches heading for the auction block."

"That's not Matthew's fault," Cordelia said, drawing herself erect. "He worked out very favorable terms with United Mountain."

"Janet, while it was running, Quick Start was a great success." It sounded as if Stockdale was trying to convince himself. "We had a loan portfolio totaling twenty-two million. I don't remember anybody bellyaching back then."

"What happened?" I asked.

He tapped his cigarette against the ashtray. "We had a good portion of our capital tied up in bonds and debentures issued by the Bristlecone National Bank. They went belly up last April. The feds took over. You know, Resolution Trust Corporation. We were losing sixty cents on every dollar on those Bristlecone bonds. I admit it—Gunnison Guaranty was hurting. I was forced to sell a few assets. Quick Start was a very attractive asset, and United Mountain made me a good offer."

Translated from the bullshit, Stockdale was telling me that he'd sunk a shitload of money into Bristlecone's junk bonds. When the bank failed, those bonds really did turn out to be junk. To save his own ass, Matt had stacked all his Quick Start loans in a neat little bundle and sold them to the first buyer who ambled along.

This, of course, had left the Rooleys at the mercy of the buyer, United Mountain Bankcorp. As a banker himself, Stockdale must have been aware that an acquirer always has the option to call in old loans. Even if they were only a week or two old.

"Sounds like a rough year," I remarked.

"That it was." And he took another drag on his cigarette.

"So, if you don't mind a personal question, can you tote the load?"

Dark brown eyes sizzled. "Don't worry, Miss Wanagi. It can be done."

Aware of the growing antipathy between us, Cordelia gave him a gentle nudge. "You know what your trouble is, boy? You talk when you ought to be listening. Why don't you let Janet have her say?"

He put together a reasonably friendly smile. "Just explaining what happened, Aunt Dee."

"You listen to this girl, Matthew. She's got some great ideas. Ideas that'll get those trashy Rooleys off that mountain once and for all!"

He sighed. "That ain't exactly a priority for Gunnison Guaranty, Aunt Dee."

"Well, it ought to be!" Disapproving look. "You know, you had the perfect opportunity to run that—*that woman* out of this county, and you blew it!"

"Aunt Dee—"

"You listen to her." Cordelia's lacquered fingernail jabbed my way. "And don't go wasting any more time trying to impress her with what a big shot you are. Her idea's going to put Gunnison Guaranty right back in the black." Shouldering her purse, she stood slowly. "Now, if you two will excuse me ..."

Both Matt and I watched her traverse the now-crowded restaurant, heading for the ladies' room. Then, emitting a humorless chuckle, Matt turned to me. "So you're interested in the RJ Bar."

"It's a very attractive property."

"Can't dispute that.." He stubbed out his cigarette. "But I wouldn't count on getting ahold of that ranch anytime soon, Jan. Madge Rooley's the owner of record. I can't see United Mountain beginning foreclosure until after the will's been probated."

I feigned a tone of surprise. "Ms. Rooley passed away recently?"

Matt nodded. "Got killed last week in a traffic accident. The kids'll inherit the ranch . . . and her debt."

"Your aunt tells me it's a sizable debt."

"For a local rancher, yeah." His expression turned somber. "Madge took out a Quick Start loan for just over a hundred thousand."

I made a fussbudget face. "What did Mrs. Longworth mean by that remark?"

"What remark?"

Quoting from memory, I added, " 'You had the perfect opportunity to run that woman out of this county . . .' "

Matt's hand rose in an exasperated flourish. "Ahhhh, Aunt Dee's still pissed off at me for selling Madge's note to United Mountain. I think she was fixing to buy it herself." Arch smile.

"Just so she could have the pleasure of foreclosing on Madge Rooley."

"What's she got against Ms. Rooley?"

"It's a long, long story, Janet."

"I'll gladly settle for the *Reader's Digest* version."

"Ahhhh, it's all because of Uncle Art." He kept his voice low, as if afraid Cordelia might overhear. "Aunt Dee gave him the boot twenty-five years ago. Planned on divorcing him. Hell, she even spent three weeks out there in Reno. Then she changed her mind. 'Course, by then Uncle Art had taken up with Madge." He shook his head in exasperation. "My aunt's a proud woman, Jan. She never could admit the truth. For a while there, Uncle Art just plain didn't want to come back. Aunt Dee couldn't accept that. Way she sees it, Madge stole her husband, pure and simple."

"Is that view shared by the rest of the family?"

"'Course not!" He resumed his normal tone. "In fact, we sort of wish she'd get over it. Uncle Art's been dead fourteen years now." He looked up suddenly, as if the reality of death had only just penetrated. "Madge is gone, too." Quick nervous glance toward the lavatories. "And here's Aunt Dee, still muttering about 'those trashy Rooleys.' She's my dad's sister, and I love her dearly, but . . . Lord, how long's she going to hold a grudge?"

On to the magic question. "Did you know the lady?"

"Madge? Sure! She used to work for me."

*Really?* Somehow I veiled my startled reaction. Expression of polite curiosity. "In what capacity?"

With a suave smile, he touched his conch tie clip. "Madge was sort of an unofficial hostess."

"Not sure I follow, Matt."

"I've got an office at the Ore Bucket Building," he explained, gesturing eastward. "That's where we met. Madge's parole officer got her a job at the Little Sew 'n' Sew. She used to get bored with standing behind the counter all day long, so she'd mosey on down for a visit." Brown eyes gleamed at the onset of pleasant memories. "Sometimes we went out for lunch together. Then one day I was trying to sell this ol' boy some commodities futures. He was a tough old cuss. Rancher from Poncha Springs. You'd have had an easier time getting a boulder to crack a smile. Then Madge came in and gave him the old come-on. Some of that mountain-gal flirting she was so famous for. Next thing you know, that ol' boy's smiling and laughing and asking if she likes rodeo. Madge had that effect on a fella."

I didn't doubt it. Having seen her daughter in action at the Dry Gulch, I could easily imagine the effect Madge must've had on that tight-fisted rancher.

"After that, if I had any tough selling to do, I used to give Madge a call. Ask her to play hostess at one of my Sunday barbecues." A knowledgeable smile appeared beneath Matt's mustache. "I'd give her an hour to butter him up, then slide right in and make my pitch. That gal helped me sell one hell of a lot of futures." Sudden anxious glance. "Don't ever mention that to Aunt Dee, though. She'd hang my hide on a fence if she ever found out I was chumming it up with Madge Rooley."

So Madge had once worked as a shill for Stockdale, eh? That opened a whole new avenue of investigation.

"How long did she work for you?" I asked.

"Three years maybe." Insouciant male shrug. "Then she quit her job at the sewing shop and moved up north."

"Where up north?"

"Leadville."

Excitement had my nerves tingling. I'd asked a lot of people that question, and everyone else had answered *Malta*. Not Matthew! Had he seen Madge working at the Silver Kings Mall?

"What was she doing up there?"

Matt's gaze deliberately avoided mine. "I don't know.

Whatever it was, Madge sure didn't cotton to it. She came back to C.B. last summer."

"Is that when she took out the loan?"

Stiff nod. "Right. Madge told me she wanted to build a boarding stable."

I gave him an arch look. Soft tones of disbelief. "And with her work history, you lent her a hundred thousand dollars?"

A flush rose from his shirt collar. "Madge was good for it. She told me she was coming into some money soon. That she'd have no trouble keeping up the payments." His sincere tone began to waver. "Besides, a Rooley's handshake is the best collateral there is. Everybody in C.B. knows that."

I found Matt's version intriguing. When Madge and I spoke on the telephone, she coyly mentioned that she might be coming into some money. No one else around here had mentioned that. Not her children. Not her friends. Only Matt Stockdale, her sometime business partner.

That, and his mention of Leadville, had put a whole new spin on things. I had a feeling Matt was telling the truth about the loan. Mrs. Longworth's disapproval was proof positive of that. But would anyone—even a high-risk banker like Matt Stockdale—lend money to an ex-convict who had quit two jobs during the previous year?

Of course not! Lenders just aren't that sentimental. If Stockdale had lent Madge the construction money, then he must have been pretty certain of repayment. I could think of only two explanations. Either Matt believed Madge's story about the supposed inheritance. Or else he knew of her participation in the armored car holdup.

Suspicion altered the set of his eyes. "You've been asking a lot of questions about the Rooleys, I take it."

Gracious smile. "I like to know a little about the seller before I make an offer."

"Who else you been talking to besides Aunt Dee?"

I knew he'd check with Cordelia, so I made sure I used the same name. "Chet Hurtig."

Matt blinked in mild surprise. Let out a muted chuckle. "So he still keeps his hand in, eh?"

"Your aunt thinks very highly of him."

"He's done us a few favors over the years."

"Such as keep tabs on Madge Rooley?"

He tried without success to smother his grin. "Yeah, I guess you could call ol' Chet our resident Madge expert."

"How so?"

"Honey, if anybody was ever going to write a book about the Border Bandit Queen, it'd be Chet Hurtig." Absentmindedly he buttoned his sportcoat. "He's got a scrapbook on Madge this thick." Held his thumb and forefinger two inches apart. "Newspaper clippings, magazine articles, old FBI advisories—you name it. You'd have thought he was her biggest fan."

I caught the undertone of dislike in his voice. "You don't sound like much of a Chet Hurtig fan."

"I'm not!" Matt's baritone developed a distinct chill. "I know his type. Always hanging around, willing to do favors. Can't do enough for you. Yet, all the while, he's building his file on you." Spat out the last word. "Cops!"

Knowing Matt's penchant for dirty deals, I could understand his underlying enmity toward policemen.

"He doesn't seem to be enjoying his retirement," I said.

"Yeah?" Matt's eyebrow quivered. "Well, he'd better get used to the idea. I don't care how much clout he has with certain board members—he ain't making a comeback!"

"Has he attempted one?"

"Yeah." Glum smile. "Last summer. Way I heard it, ol' Chet showed up at a mountain search run by the state patrol. As usual, he was throwing his weight around. And those damned troopers—they were treating him like an elder statesman!"

I grinned. "Brotherhood of the badge."

"You can say that again." Matt's gaze sailed over my head. "Ah, here comes Aunt Dee. What do you say to another cup of coffee, Janet?"

I agreed, and Cordelia's nephew signaled a passing waiter. Then the three of us spent another twenty minutes chatting about the local real estate market. I could tell Matt wanted to learn more about me, so I casually mentioned that article in *People* magazine.

Hopefully, Chief had been able to plant one of my doctored copies at the library.

As he paid the check, Matt offered to drive his aunt home. No doubt he wanted to compare notes with Cordelia. I told him he could reach me at the Water Wheel Inn. Flashing a bright country-boy smile, he touched my hand, invited me to phone his office in the morning, and wished me a pleasant evening.

So there I was, alone at the table, frowning at my reflection in the glass pitcher. And gave some thought to this unlikely acquaintance of Madge's.

So Madge and Stockdale had often lunched together. Well, that explained why her name was instantly familiar to those women at the Gunnison Guaranty office.

Also, Matt Stockdale had known of Madge's presence in Leadville. As near as I could tell, the only other person who knew about that was Pop Hannan. And he'd lied to me.

By my calculation, there were four participants in the armored car holdup. Madge Rooley, Jack Sunawavi, Frank Blodgett, and the fourth man. The one who helped Frank load the money into the getaway truck. I had a feeling that was Pop Hannan.

Frank Blodgett had hinted that one of the others had moved the money. It wasn't at the agreed-upon location when he returned to Colorado.

Okay, that could have been Madge. Or Pop. Or the two of them working in partnership. They'd spent a lot of time together, hiking the upper trails on Grizzly Peak. Sure! First Jack Sunawavi dies. Then one or the other moves the money to a new locale. And drops a quarter on the Bureau, telling them where to find Frank Blodgett.

My lips compressed in frustration. So many conflicting possibilities . . .

Possibility number one: Madge and Pop move the money. Frank gets out of prison a little earlier than expected and kills Madge. Now he's hunting for Pop.

Possibility number two: Madge moves the money. She refuses to tell Pop where it is. He goes crazy searching for it and then decides to kill Madge.

Possibility number three: Pop decides to double-cross his partners. He buries the Trautmann's loot in a new cache, rolls over Frank Blodgett, and then cleverly sabotages Madge's truck.

Now, that would have been quite easy for Pop. Whenever mechanical equipment breaks down on the claim, the prospector quickly learns how to become his own repairman.

Hmmm, on the other hand, if Pop Hannan did have access to all that money, would he still be hanging around C.B., bumming drinks from the tourists?

There was one final possibility, though, and it had just occurred to me. What if a *fifth* man had participated in the robbery?

Were that the case, then the motives all remain the same. Our fifth man could be the murderer . . . or a target.

Fussbudget frown. I really couldn't see Matt Stockdale as an armed robber. He was your classic white collar criminal. He might stiff neighboring ranchers in a sleazy and questionable loan program. But I didn't think he had the stomach to sit next to Frank Blodgett, waiting for a hijacked armored car to arrive.

However, based on what he'd just told me, Gunnison Guaranty had been teetering on the brink of Chapter Eleven. In-

deed, Matt was still trying to recover from the junk bond de-
bacle. He'd needed money desperately, and his share of the
loot would have netted him eighty thousand in cash.

Then again, perhaps Stockdale *wasn't* a participant. Maybe
he'd only been talking to Madge. Sure! Sarah's mom might've
had a few too many and let something slip. Matt could have
done some checking in Leadville and then put two and two together.

A new scenario hurriedly took shape. A variation of possi-
blity number one. Maybe Madge and Pop had double-crossed
Frank Blodgett. Perhaps they were planning to split the
money and hightail it in the spring. But then Matt Stockdale
found out about the money, and he wanted the entire four
hundred thousand for himself.

Great theory, princess! Only how do you draw him out? You
can't very well ask, "By the way, Mr. Stockdale, did you ever
study auto repair in high school?"

Memo to myself: Find out what Stockdale was doing in Denver the day Madge was killed. Get times and places out of him.
Any information I'll be able to corroborate.

Oh, and work on *the tale*, princess. If you can't con him out
of a hundred thousand, the Rooleys are going to lose their
ranch!

Hmmm, I wonder what game works best on a conniving
Western Slope banker?

# THIRTEEN

"Will you be staying long, miss?"

Showing a neighborly smile, the clerk returned my Sun-West credit card. He was a lanky guy in his twenties, with short chestnut hair and a noticeable Adam's apple.

"Not more than a week," I replied, putting away the card.

"Will you be doing any skiing?"

Eager Angie smile. "If I can work it in."

"Well, you'll probably want to give Mineral Point a try," he said, savoring his own memories of the slopes. "Stay away from Paradise Bowl, though. They've got better'n thirty feet of snow up on the Headwall, and they're worried about a slide."

"How worried are they?" I asked.

"Ohhhhh, little bit, I guess. Not enough to post avalanche flags, but they're keeping an eye on it."

He put the guest register on the counter. His lean arm was a shade too long for the motel's cranberry blazer. Two inches of hairy wrist showed beneath the cuff.

"Fill out the card, please." Planting a ball-point pen on the clipboard, he said, "I can run the payment through now, Miss

Wanagi, or you can wait till you check out. Which would you prefer?"

"Let's make it the last day, shall we? I'm not sure how long I'll be staying in Crested Butte."

Looking over the Water Wheel Inn's registration card, I reached for the pen. One by one, I filled in the boxes. Name, address, zip code, company affiliation. The bottom box requested my license number and the make and model of my car. I hesitated. But only for a moment. Which is how long it took me to remember the license number of the green Dodge I'd seen parked in front of Penelope's.

If ever you're on the dodge, gang, always be sure to fill in that automotive ID box. State troopers and sheriff's deputies have the nasty habit of visiting motels at three in the morning to check the register.

My old mentor at Springfield, Toni Gee, had taught me how to avoid attracting the law's attention. First, always show up at the motel at six P.M. Before you check in, go for a quick spin around town. People are usually home having supper at that time, which makes it easy to find a car parked in a driveway. Memorize the make, the model, and the license number, and then use that information to fill out your registration card. Local cars are much less likely to arouse suspicion.

"Would you like some help with your luggage?" he asked.

"Thanks, but I can manage." I slid the clipboard across the polished counter. The clock behind the desk clerk's shoulder read seven-fifteen. "Uhm, I've got a lot of meetings in the next few days. Probably be in and out of here. Do you—?"

"No problem, miss." The clerk's smile showed a slightly crooked eyetooth. "The switchboard has twenty-four-hour coverage. We'll be glad to hold your messages for you."

"Thanks."

Of course, that was the reason I'd rented the room in the first place. I needed a place where Matt Stockdale could reach my alternate identity. After all, I couldn't very well give him the phone number of the RJ Bar.

My room overlooked the parking lot. Queen-size bed with a quilted comforter. Thick drapes and pastel walls. Color TV, refrigerator, and microwave. I took a quick look around, dropped my shoulder bag on the desk, and went digging for my wallet. The motel offered a direct-dial telephone, but I preferred to use the pay phone in the lobby. Couldn't risk my call showing up on the motel bill.

Minutes later, there I was in the lobby, leaning against the wall, the receiver nestled against my ear. Two sharp ringings, and then Sarah's voice came on line. "Hello?"

"Hi, Sarah! It's Angie—"

"Angela!" She cut me right off. "Where have you been? It's nearly seven-thirty."

Judging from the anxiety in her voice, she must have been waiting to hear from Karen. I kept my own tone cheery. "Down in C.B. How's your head?"

"Much better, thank you." Twinge of irritation. "What are you doing in town?"

Think fast, princess! "Oh, I had some trouble with my grandfather's truck. Carburetor trouble. Took it to Mike's Mobil."

"Angela, you didn't tell me where you were going."

"You were asleep," I pointed out.

"You could have left a note." Uh-oh! Sounded as if Sarah was on the warpath. "You and I need to have a little talk, miss. I don't mind you heading into town. But I would appreciate it if you asked permission first."

"Yes, Sarah." Humble Angie.

"I like to know where my employees are during the work-day."

"Yes, Sarah." I cleared my throat. "Uh, could you put my grandfather on for a minute?"

"All right."

The receiver changed hands. Chief's gravelly voice came on. *"Noozis?"*

I made the switch to my people's language. *"Watchiya, Nimishoo.* Quick question—has Karen come home yet?"

*"Gawiin, Noozis.* No sign of the girl. I think that's why Sarah's on the prod." Bass chuckle. "I wouldn't want to be in that girl's moccasins when she comes home."

"That's just it, *Nimishoo.* I don't think she's coming home."

"What do you mean?"

"Mrs. Longworth treated me to supper at Penelope's," I replied. "While I was there, I spotted Karen at the bus stop across the street. Just before the Denver bus arrived."

*"Tayaa!* Did you see her board the bus?"

*"Gawiin, Nimishoo."* Rueful grimace. "I got distracted. When I looked again, the bus was pulling away from the curb." Took a deep breath. "What should I tell Sarah?"

"Nothing! Poor gal's anxious enough as it is," Chief said. "Before you head back, find out for certain if Karen bought a ticket, okay? Let's give the girl the benefit of the doubt."

"All right. See you in thirty minutes."

"Not so fast, *Noozis.* How did the interview go?"

"Very well," I replied. In brief, I summed up my chat with Cordelia Longworth, Matt Stockdale's prickly defense of the Quick Start program, and his unexpected collaboration with Madge Rooley.

When I finished, Chief asked, "What makes you think it might be Stockdale?"

"The man is a sleaze, *Nimishoo.* He has a very glib explanation for handing off the loans to United Mountain. But it's bullshit. He was in trouble *before* he launched the Quick Start program."

"Why do you say that?"

"Commodities trading is a very volatile market, *Nimishoo.* If a futures price comes in ten cents under the estimate, an investor can get clobbered," I explained. "That's what happened to Stockdale. But it doesn't happen overnight. He pumped most of Gunnison Guaranty's assets into the commodities market, figuring to make a killing. Instead, the commodities prices took a dip, and he was wiped out. To keep his own firm afloat, he had to put together a very attractive asset package and then peddle it to a bank."

"In other words, he suckered those ranchers."

"Afraid so, *Nimishoo*. He lured them in, sold the program to United Mountain, and then used the proceeds of the sale to cover his ass. I think that was the main idea all along."

Chief's tone turned thoughtful. "You say Madge worked for him. Do you think she tumbled to the scam?"

"It's possible, *Nimishoo*. But, if he did it, I don't think that was his motive," I replied, my spine at rest against the cinder block. "Stockdale said the magic word—*Leadville!*"

All at once my grandfather hummed in understanding. "He knew she was involved in the robbery?"

"*Eyan, Nimishoo.*" I nodded. "At least that's what I think. We know the money's been moved. Madge might have inadvertently tipped Stockdale to its hiding place. Killing her in a rigged accident eliminates the only other person who knows where it is."

"So you're pretty certain that's the motive?"

"*Eyan.* We can forget about Mrs. Longworth. Oh, she hates Madge, all right. Hates her with a vengeance! But there's no way she could have tampered with those brakes."

"Well, don't bet all the rent money on Stockdale, *Noozis*," he cautioned. "Frank Blodgett has the same motive. Grab the loot. And he also owed Madge for ratting him out."

"You think she did that?"

"Stands to reason, child. Madge wanted Frank tucked safely away behind bars while she moved the money. Only one of the gang could've known Frank was on the dodge in Nebraska."

"Point taken. Anything else?"

"Pop Hannan," my grandfather reminded me. "He came calling for Madge at Turquoise Lake. Asked for *Marjorie Dexter*. And do you remember that day you bought him a drink at Kochevar's? He started muttering about Madge holding out on him. We thought he was talking about Dutch Bohle's treasure, but he could've been talking about his share of the Trautmann's loot."

"So we've narrowed it down to three," I remarked.

"And we have physical evidence that Madge was murdered—the truck's master cylinder," he added. "I think it's time we leveled with Sarah. We'll let her bring the evidence to the state patrol. They can take it from there."

Anxious fussbudget face. "*Nimishoo*, what about the ranch?"

"What about it?"

"If United Mountain insists upon renegotiation, the Rooleys are finished. They won't be able to make the payments. They'll lose *everything!*"

Sigh of exasperation. "*Noozis*, that's not our problem."

"But they're our friends."

"Right! And Sarah is a very capable woman. I'm sure she'll be able to come up with something."

"What if she can't?" I challenged. "If the Rooleys had a hundred thousand dollars, they could pay it off all at once."

"And if I could sing, I'd be the new Conway Twitty! How are we supposed to come up with a hundred thousand—?" Moment of stunned silence. "*Noozis!*"

Holding the receiver away from my ear, I grimaced. "Come on, *Nimishoo*. Stockdale's got it coming. He conned all those ranchers, didn't he?"

"Isn't that a matter for the grand jury?"

"He's too slick, *Nimishoo*. The law can't touch him. But we can give him a dose of his own medicine. And save the RJ Bar at the same time." Mischievous Angie smile. "Matthew is a natural for the old drop game."

"*Tayaa!* The FBI's hunting all over the West for Pocahontas, and you want to run another con?"

"It's risky, I know, but it's the only way to save the ranch," I replied. "Stockdale got them into this mess. It's only fair that his money should get them out."

"That ain't the way the judge is gonna look at it!"

Making a face at the receiver, I muttered, "You're such an optimist, *Nimishoo.*"

"Besides, what makes you think Sarah would even accept that kind of help?"

"She won't, of course. That stiff-necked pride of hers wouldn't let her. That's why we're giving the money to Becky."

"What makes you think Becky'll go along with it?"

"Becky isn't a starch girdle like her big sister," I replied. "If it means saving the RJ Bar, she'll do it."

He still sounded a bit leery. "Drop game?"

"I'll explain it when I get back," I said, toying with the telephone cord. "In the meantime, not a word to Sarah. Okay?"

"Ought to have my damned head examined!" he muttered. Then a deep, calming breath. "I'll talk to you later."

"*Miigwetch. Nimishoo.* Bye!"

On my way out of town I spied an empty parking space a few doors down from the Forest Queen Hotel. My rearview mirror showed a pensive Anishinabe face. Had Karen left on that bus?

I thought of one way to find out.

Minutes later I sauntered into the hotel lobby. A wiry, gray-haired woman sorted mail behind the reception desk. Hearing me, she reacted like a spooked squirrel. Sudden turn of the head. Crow's-feet, wire-rimmed glasses, and a toothy grin. "Howdy!"

"Hi!" I gave the lady my friendliest Northland smile. "It's getting a little snowy out there."

"Tell me about it. We've already got sixteen inches up by

Taylor Park." Facing me, she put down her handful of envelopes. "Todd and me got a spread just north of there. He's my husband. I'm Lainie Winslow. What's your name?"

I sailed right into my impromptu cover story. "Janice Kanoshe. I'm a substitute teacher."

"New to C.B., ain't you?"

"You bet!" I brushed melting snowflakes from my shoulders. "Just rented a condo at Elk Ridge. I'll be teaching here till June. Figured it was easier to rent."

"What do you teach?"

"Social studies." Tilting my head toward the door, I changed the subject. "Is this where you catch the Denver bus?"

"That's right, Jan. Express goes through twice a day. Six in the morning, six at night." Lainie put a small tin box on the hotel register. "You looking to buy a ticket?"

"Friday, maybe. I've got a boyfriend in the big city." I feigned an uncertain look. "You know, I could have sworn I saw one of my students out front a little while ago."

The lady's features brightened. "Karen Rooley, you mean."

"That's right. Do you know her?"

Feminine chuckle. "Oh, yeah! There's no mistaking a Rooley girl. My daughter Dawn went all through school with Merry."

"Was Karen waiting for the local?"

Shaking her head, Lainie replied, "Nope! She asked me about the fare to Denver. I think she was fixing to buy herself a ticket, but she just didn't have the cash." Curious glance. "How do you happen to know her, Jan?"

I fielded the query with ease. "Karen's in my World History class at Gunnison High. A very bright girl."

"Well, she takes after Sally, you know. That's her mom." Lainie appeared to have a passion for genealogy. "That Sally's a sharp one. She's a lawyer now. I hear tell she's back in town, so you'll probably be seeing her at parents' night."

*I certainly hope not!* Backing away from the counter, I remarked, "Thanks for the info, Lainie. I'll be back Friday." This time there was no need for me to fake an expression of anxiety. "I'm going to go see if I can find Karen. She could probably use a ride home."

"You do that." She fired a glance at the front window. "Yeah, it really is starting to come down." Broad smile of farewell. "Nice meeting you, Jan."

"Same here, Lainie. Take care."

As I headed back to the truck, I treated myself to a mammoth frown. So Karen had been planning to leave town. If not for lack of funds, she'd be aboard the Denver bus at that very moment.

Heartsick, I levered open the driver's door. I hoped Karen had changed her mind. That she'd come to her senses. That she'd be safe at the RJ Bar when I returned.

Deeply worried, I switched on the truck's ignition. A question bounced around the shadowy corners of my mind. A disturbing query that refused to go away.

Had Karen Rooley run away from home?

One way or the other, I would soon have an answer.

Ten o'clock found me back at the RJ Bar, huddled over the Wizard subnotebook, hurriedly typing a phony prospectus for Matt Stockdale's review. Feminine footsteps sounded next door. The sound of Sarah pacing the parlor.

Not that I blamed her, I reflected, glancing at the window. Wind-driven snowflakes pelted the glass. The Weather Channel was predicting a five-inch snowfall . . . and more to come!

Frigid mountain gusts buffeted the house. Shivering, I turned back to the computer screen. Wherever she was, I hoped Karen had sense enough to remain indoors.

My fingers hovered above the keyboard. Glum Anishinabe frown. Maybe I ought to tell Sarah what her daughter was up to.

Yeah, right! Only what happens when Sarah asks how I came by this important information? I can't very well tell Sarah I spotted her daughter while I was working a con on Mrs. Longworth!

And if I mention my chat with Lainie Winslow, and Sarah calls the hotel, she's going to wonder why I was using an assumed name.

Ohhhhh, princess, how do you get yourself into these jams?

I resumed my typing. One tale at a time, Biwaban. After I finish Matt's prospectus, I'll cook up a plausible story for Sarah. Let her know where Karen was last seen. Hopefully, that will help to ease her anxiety.

Just then, feminine footsteps sounded behind me.

"That does it!" Sarah snapped. "It's after ten. I'm calling the sheriff."

Her sudden entry rattled me. My hand darted instantly to the Save button.

"Wrap it up, Angie. I've got to use the phone." Reaching for the receiver, Sarah aimed a curious glance my way. "What's that you're working on?"

"Nothing important," I replied, shifting back to the Program Manager. "Just sending out some E-mail."

Pretty features tense with anxiety, Sarah tapped out the seven-digit number. Then she stood up straight, biting the corner of her lower lip, waiting for the dispatcher to pick up.

"Sheriff Quinn, please." Her hand trembled as she held the receiver. "Sheriff? Hi, it's Sally . . . Yes, I got the card . . . Thanks for coming to the funeral . . . Listen, we have a real problem out here . . . It's my daughter, Karen. She hasn't come home . . . ." A tone of apprehension entered her voice. "We've *called* all her friends. They don't know where she is . . . Becky says she's never stayed out this late before . . . Would you? Thanks, Sheriff, I really appreciate it . . . No, no, go right ahead and call. Someone will pick up. And it'll probably be me! . . . Yes . . . Yes . . . How can I possibly sleep when my daugh-

ter—! . . . All right, all right. I'm calm now. See? . . . Thanks
again. Bye."

I shut down the computer. "He's put the word out?"

Sarah nodded. "To all the cruisers. And the state patrol, too.
If she's out on the road, they'll find her." Whisper of worry. "*I
hope!*"

"They'll find her," I said. After all, if Karen didn't have
enough money for bus fare, she still had to be somewhere in
Crested Butte. But where? And with whom?

Lingering in the doorway, I murmured, "Sarah?"

She cast me an inquisitive glance. Folding my arms, I
added, "Given any thought to what you're going to say when
she gets in?"

With a sudden exhalation, she went into her lady-lawyer
routine. "Believe me, I'll have *plenty* to say."

"Maybe that's part of the problem."

Emerald eyes blossomed wide. "Excuse me!"

Well, I could kiss this job good-bye, but it had to be said.
"Any idea why she hasn't come home?"

She sucked in her breath as if to shout, then thought the
better of it. "No."

"Could be she's decided to run away."

A stricken look crossed Sarah's lovely face. "Th-that's ridiculous."

"Is it?" I challenged her. Might as well drop the lady a broad
hint. "You two were going at it pretty hot and heavy this
morning. Maybe Karen's decided she's had enough."

"Listen, my daughter has no reason to run away."

"How do you know that?" I said in defiance, whether wise
or not. "Have you ever talked with Karen?"

"Of course I have!"

"I'm not talking about a lecture, Sarah. Or one of these ses-
sions where you stand up and pontificate like you do at the
office. I mean a real mother-and-daughter conversation."

Sarah stiffened suddenly. "We-we've talked—"

"When?" I prodded Sarah. "You two weren't even speaking the first three days we were here."

Irritation reddened her lovely face. "Angela! I'll thank you to stay out of my personal affairs!"

Too late for that! I thought. One final backward glance. "There's a lot happening in your daughter's life, Sarah. Maybe it's high time you became part of it."

The lady's outraged gasp pursued me out the door. On my way to the stairs I gave myself a swift mental kick. Well, I sure didn't make any friends back there.

Still, it had to be said. Once before Sarah had let that stiff-necked Rooley pride of hers come between herself and her daughter. I couldn't allow it to happen again. For both their sakes.

I paused on the landing, peering out the snow-rimmed window. Better give some thought to the scam, princess. You have plenty of work to do. Steal a hundred grand from that slimeball Stockdale. Flush out Madge's killer. With any luck, I just might be able to accomplish both objectives tomorrow.

*In the meantime* ... Rubbing my sleeves, I watched the falling snow. Wherever you are, Karen Lynn Rooley, hurry on home! Your mother needs you ... more than ever!

Monday, February 2. Had Mr. Groundhog been up and about, seeking his shadow, he wouldn't have had much luck. Snow-laden clouds blanketed the skies above Crested Butte, making for a dour gray morning. But he would have seen my grandfather's Sierra speeding north on Route 135.

Karen had not returned home.

Our game plan was simple. Two search parties. Troy and Merry in his truck. My grandfather and I in the Sierra. Becky would stand by at the ranch. And Sarah ... well, over her vigorous protest, Becky had ordered her back to bed. Judging from the bags under her eyes, Sarah had managed a total of maybe twenty minutes of dozing during the entire night.

Chief dropped me off in front of Kochevar's. I felt a bit like a deserter, taking time off from the search, but Chief assured me he could handle it. "Launch the game," he told me. "Stockdale will be looking for you. I'll meet you at the Paradise Cafe at noon."

And so I did some hasty clothes shopping at Something for Everyone, a stylish boutique at the corner of Second and Elk. Thirty minutes later, an Alpine Express taxicab shuttled me out to the Water Wheel Inn. Arms laden with bundles, I climbed the outdoor stairs to the mezzanine. Small smile of relief. The cleaning ladies were still on the first floor. No one had been into Room 248 yet.

Once inside, I dropped my bundles on the easy chair, hung the Do Not Disturb sign, and turned the deadbolt. To work, Angela! I crumpled the sheets and blankets, giving the bed a slept-in look. After pulling on a pair of rubber gloves, I began staging the scene. I deposited several jars of cosmetics in the bathroom, then left a copy of *Vogue* on the night table. Sooner or later, Sheriff Quinn would show up there, and I didn't want the law wondering where I'd spent the previous night.

Following a leisurely shower, I patted myself dry with the thick bath towel, donned fresh lingerie, and reached for my newly purchased outfit. Woolen single-breasted bouclé jacket and navy-blue slim skirt. Then I spent fifteen minutes in front of the mirror, brushing my dampened hair.

Promptly at nine-thirty, I put in an appearance at the front desk. Showing a cheery smile, I dangled my room key. "Hi! Janet Wanagi. Room 248. Any messages for me?"

"One minute, Miss Wanagi." The clerk pivoted toward the mail slots. Sinewy fingers withdrew a cluster of pink slips. Soft whistle of surprise. Grinning, he handed them to me. "Here you go."

"Thanks." I gave them all a fleeting glance. Five calls. All from Stockdale. He must have been impressed by that *People* magazine article.

"Will you be checking out later this morning, miss?"

Brisk shake of the head. "No, I'll be staying another night. Thanks again."

Returning to my room, I plucked a tissue from the Kleenex box, covered my fingers, and reached for the telephone. No sense leaving recoverable fingerprints for the FBI. My Bic pen tapped out Stockdale's office number.

A woman's voice answered. "Gunnison Guaranty."

"Good morning." Secretarial Angie. "Could I please speak to Mr. Stockdale?"

"Whom shall I say is calling?"

"Janet Wanagi."

While on hold, I ran the tale through my mind one more time. Ten seconds later, my rehearsal was cut short as Matt Stockdale's enthusiastic baritone intruded.

"Janet! Thanks for calling back."

"No problem, Matt," I said nonchalantly. My, was he eager! "What can I do for you?"

His voice tense with excitement, Matt said, "Listen, if you have time today, I'd like to sit down and talk. Just the two of us."

I played hard to get. "Well, it is kind of a busy day."

"What about lunch? Drop by around noontime. My treat."

"I have a luncheon appointment with a client." Smiling to myself, I tossed him a dollop of hope. "But I am free at eleven o'clock. Why don't I pencil you in?"

Sounding highly relieved, he said, "Do that! My office is in the Ore Bucket Building on Gothic Road. East end of town. Can't miss it. See you in thirty minutes."

My smile turned feline. "I'm looking forward to it, Matt. See you then."

Promptly at eleven o'clock, I strolled into the Gunnison Guaranty office. Matt Stockdale stood behind the counter, idly thumbing through a manila folder. As I closed the door, he glanced my way, his rugged features beaming with pleasure.

"Hi, Janet! Glad you could make it."

Quickly I tucked my manila envelope under my left arm. "Hello, Matt."

I winced as Stockdale's hand closed around mine. Enthusiasm added might to an already firm grip. What a change in attitude! Yesterday he'd been standoffish, defensive. Today he was greeting me like a long-lost sister. That phony *People* article had certainly upgraded my image!

"We can talk in here." Placing a brotherly arm across my shoulders, Matt led me into his office. "I've got some ideas you may be interested in."

And so, I seated myself in Matt's comfortable leather guest chair and listened politely to his proposals. All of which had Gunnison Guaranty brokering the sale of the RJ Bar. I let him talk, showing an expression of keen interest. And readied myself for the scam.

". . . a no-lose proposition, Jan," he said, his eyes gleaming with avarice. "We'll know exactly when United Mountain's putting the RJ Bar on the auction block. And we'll adjust our financing to ensure a winning bid. What do you say?"

"I'll keep it in mind, Matt," I said, opening my manila envelope. "But the ranch isn't really a priority just now. It'll be *months* before United Mountain forecloses. To be perfectly frank, I'm interested in Gunnison Guaranty for another reason."

"Oh?" He sat up straight. Expression of mild bafflement.

"I have a prospectus here I'd like you to take a look at. Read it over and let me know what you think."

I handed Matt a thin booklet with a clear plastic cover. Emblazoned across the title page was the legend RANCH OWNERS' SAVINGS AND LOAN ASSOCIATION—STATEMENT OF EARNINGS.

My friend Ramon had done a fine job on the packaging. Originally, I'd planned to print the booklet myself. But, with a distraught Sarah roaming the house, there'd been no chance of that. So I'd downloaded my copy onto a disk, tucked it into my purse, and dropped in at Mainframes Plus on my way to Stockdale's office.

There really was a Ranch Owners' Savings and Loan Association. Their home office was way up north in Steamboat Springs. Far enough away so that Matt Stockdale couldn't possibly be familiar with their financial health. For all I knew, ROSLA was doing just fine. But that's not what I wrote in the booklet.

Pulling on a pair of glasses, Matt settled back in his swivel chair. He took his time reading. Paid particular attention to the columns of figures.

"Now, that's interesting," Matt remarked, dropping the booklet on his desk. "Their stock price fell from twenty-one dollars to fourteen dollars a share. And all in one month." He cast me an inquisitive look. "What's going on up there?"

Demurely I crossed my legs. "There have been changes in the federal tax laws, Matt. Congress removed many of the incentives for buying new property. Ranch Owners' got caught in the crunch."

His forefinger tapped the plastic cover. "How'd you get your hands on this?"

Smug little smile. "I have my sources."

Intense curiosity altered Matt's expression. "What's your interest in ROSLA, Jan?"

Now that I had him hooked, I spun my contrived tale. Angie Biwaban, the Scheherazade of high finance.

"Any idea how much business the mortgage-banking industry does nationwide, Matt?"

Broad shoulders lifted in a slow shrug.

"Seven hundred and fifty *billion* dollars," I replied, leaning back in my chair. "And the key word these days is *consolidation*, Matt. During the next few years, about fifty percent of the mortgage-banking business will be coming under the control of a few giant corporations. It's starting to happen. I'm trying to get in on the ground floor."

Brown eyes showed keen interest. "You're in touch with such a group?"

Ladylike nod. "Uh-huh. Prairie Investors, Inc. They're based up in Sioux Falls. Try to picture the real estate trade when Century 21 and Coldwell Banker moved in. That's what our group wants to do in mortgage-banking."

"What's your interest in ROSLA?"

"They're particularly vulnerable just now," I explained, brushing a wing of dark hair away from my cheek. "Investors used to chase their stock. Now they're shying away from it. Prairie wants to move in before those Wall Street sharks begin their feeding frenzy."

"Short-selling has become a problem, eh?"

I nodded. "We have to bring it into the fold before the price drops through the floor."

"So why don't you simply make them an offer?"

"It's not that easy, Matt." Primly I folded my hands. "To make the purchase, my friends would have to incorporate here in Colorado. The minute the Denver banks get wind of that, they'll throw all kinds of obstacles in our path. They don't want the competition."

Baritone chuckle. "Well, they do enjoy holding the lion's share of the mortgage business."

"Bottom line, Matt. Prairie needs an ally in Colorado. A company already in the mortgage trade that's willing to serve as our acquisition agent." Sublime smile. "Interested?"

I saw the sudden tremor in Matt's hands. Oh, he was ripe for it, all right. For months he'd been struggling to survive, and then in walks little Angie, offering to resolve his financial troubles with one sweet deal.

Still, he managed to hold on to his poker face. "I'd say that depends."

"On what?"

"On the role you have planned for Gunnison Guaranty."

So he wanted to hear it all, eh? So far, so good.

"It's very simple, Matt," I said, my agile hands outlining a rectangle. "Gunnison Guaranty borrows money from our bank in South Dakota. On very *generous* terms. Then you turn around and buy shares in ROSLA. And I'm not talking nickel-and-dime here. I'm talking about hundreds of thousands of shares. We'd like Gunnison Guaranty to buy controlling interest in ROSLA."

Hushed whistle. "We're talking about a lot of money, Jan."

"Indeed we are!" Thoughtfully I touched my chin. "Let me guess. Gunnison Guaranty's asset total is about thirty million, am I right?"

His brown eyes flickered suddenly. "Close."

"How would you like to pyramid that up to *three billion?*"

Licking dry lips, he rasped, "What's the ceiling on the loans?"

"There is none," I answered. "You file a loan application, and it'll be approved. No questions asked. Spend whatever you need to buy ROSLA stock. Whatever's left over is yours to keep." Grinning, I made a dainty steeple of my fingertips. "Of course, we'll expect to see photocopies of your stock purchases once a month."

Matt was nearly panting. Ohhhh, he definitely wanted access to *this* money store! "That's all there is to it?"

My smile turned rueful. "Well, there is the little matter of your facilitation fee."

"Facilitation fee?" he echoed.

Quick Angie nod. "My friends are expecting a good-faith offering on your part. Sort of like buying a membership in an exclusive club."

Matt nodded in understanding. "How much?"

"One hundred thousand . . . cash!"

Cowpoke features winced. "That's pretty steep, Jan."

My heartbeat quickened. Uh-oh! What if he couldn't come up with the cash? Gunnison Guaranty might be in worse trouble than I thought.

Sheepish smile. "Sorry, Matt, I don't make the rules."

"I suppose Prairie wants the money up front."

Another nod. "I'm afraid they're insisting on it."

He fell silent all at once, stroking his chin. Eyebrows dipped in a fearsome scowl. He was thinking it over.

I swallowed hard, realizing it could go either way.

Matt gave me a leery sidelong look. "It's an awful lot of money to come up with all at once."

Better play your ace, princess.

"I agree, Matt." Hastily I snapped my person open. Frantic fingers sought the bogus check I'd run off at the computer store. "Maybe I can be of help with that."

Features hopeful, he swiveled to face me. "How?"

I gave him the oblong pastel-green check. "If you can have the cash here first thing tomorrow, I'll open an account with Gunnison Guaranty in that amount. Do we have a deal?"

Brown eyes opened wide. "Fifty thousand?"

"Colorado's a wide-open state, Matt," I said, holding my purse strap. "Your aunt told me about the new road through Cottonwood Pass. The market for ski condos is going to boom, and I want to be in on the ground floor. The recovery seems to be taking hold. Construction is on the rise. There'll be a big demand for mortgage loans." Touch of urgency. "We can't afford to get bogged down in a protracted struggle with the Denver banks. We need a man on the inside . . . right now!"

Matt stared at my bogus check as if it were solid gold. "You're willing to put your own money at risk?"

"Absolutely!" Confident smile. "Think of it as an investment, Matt. My contribution cuts your requested fee in half. All you have to do is have one hundred K ready for me at nine o'clock tomorrow. Put down one hundred—get *eight* hundred in return."

Knuckles whitened as he squeezed the check. "Eight hundred thousand!"

"Or higher!" My smile showed dimples. "You can negotiate directly with Prairie Investors."

"How soon can I apply for one of these loans?"

"A week from Wednesday."

Cupidity filled those dark brown eyes. Letting out a bark of laughter, he drawled, "Little lady, you've got yourself a deal."

"Fine!" Polite extension of my hand. "I'll be back tomorrow."

"Listen, why don't we do the application paperwork right now?" he suggested. No way was he relinquishing control of my bogus check. "It'll put us a few steps ahead of the game. You don't mind, Jan, do you?"

"Not at all." I could afford to be gracious. After all, Matt Stockdale was accepting a check that would soon bounce higher than the space shuttle.

While he went to fetch the application forms, I leaned over his desk and consulted his appointment calendar. Flip the pages back. Ah, here we are—January 22. The day Madge Rooley was killed at Monarch Pass.

Oh-ho! So you were in Denver, Mr. Stockdale. The page lists a Board of Realtors meeting at two P.M. Plus this intriguing entry . . . Dinner—Buck Snort Saloon.

Well, I couldn't forget a name like that, but I was taking no chances. Giving Matt's Rolodex a spin, I turned up the card with the saloon's address and telephone number. Grabbing his pen, I jotted the information on a small yellow notepad. Did the same for the Board of Realtors, too.

Masculine footsteps sounded just beyond the door. Faster, Angie! With trembling fingers I peeled off the top sheet and tucked it up my jacket sleeve. Turned the pages back to February 2, and did a brisk about-face. Deep, calming breath.

"You know, Jan . . ." Thumbing through the application forms, Matt flashed a smile of triumph. "I really appreciate your support."

Adrenaline had my heart pumping. "I just happen to think Gunnison Guaranty's going to benefit us all, Mr. Stockdale."

Especially the Rooleys!

Completing the savings account application took a good thirty minutes. Matt had one of the clerks come in and witness my signature. When we were through, he handed over my copy of the application, plus a brand-new bronze-colored Gunnison Guaranty passbook good at any branch office on the Western Slope.

With a sigh of satisfaction, Matt gave my phony check to the clerk. "Credit that to Miss Wanagi's account." Cast me a look of down-home invitation. "Sure I can't interest you in lunch, Jan?"

"Thanks, Matt," I replied, shouldering my purse. Fleeting glance at the wall clock. "But I'm meeting somebody at twelve o'clock."

Guiding me to the door, he asked, "Anyplace special I can drop you off?"

I thought of a way to save on taxi fare. "Well, I could use a lift back to the inn."

"No problem." He lifted his Stetson off the coatrack. "Let's go."


"You lost me," Chief complained.

My grandfather and I occupied a small corner table at the Paradise Cafe. The lunchtime clamor effectively muffled our conversation. Seasoning my hamburger with a touch of ketchup, I said, "It's very simple, Chief. A variation of the old Drop game."

"Okay, I'll bite." Frowning, he reached for his coffee mug. "How do you play the old Drop game?"

I swallowed my mouthful. "A con artist takes a wallet and stuffs it with counterfeit cash. Fifty- or hundred-dollar bills, usually. He selects a likely mark, passes him on the sidewalk, and tosses the wallet a few steps ahead. Just as the mark notices the wallet, our grifter pretends to find it. He gives the mark a glimpse of all those big bills."

"And then what?"

"Usually, the mark suggests they check to see if there's an address. If he doesn't, the grifter does. The grifter also mentions that they might get a reward for returning the wallet," I explained. "And then he goes into his act."

"Act?" Chief echoed.

"Right! The grifter says he can't return the wallet. He tells the mark he has a police record, and he's afraid the owner might think he stole it. He offers to sell the wallet to the mark for fifty dollars."

Sardonic grunt. " 'Course, now that the mark's seen all that cash, he has no intention of ever returning it."

"Exactly! The con man pockets the mark's fifty and strolls away." I lifted my hamburger. "When the mark tries to spend his, he gets busted for counterfeiting."

Chief nodded in understanding. "*Now* I get it. You sold Stockdale a worthless wallet."

"For a hundred thousand dollars," I added. "Gunnison Guaranty is in the red. He desperately needs a new line of credit to restore his cash balance."

"And he's willing to cut a deal with a woman he's never even met before?"

"Like I said, Chief, he's *desperate.*" Raising my porcelain mug, I smiled at him over the rim. "He's seen the *People* article. He *wants* to believe in Janet Wanagi and Prairie Investors, Inc. It's very comforting to know there's a group out there willing to lend him a few million."

Chief shook his head ruefully. "You know, when I was a kid, I used to look up to bankers."

"Don't judge all bankers by Matt Stockdale, Chief. The honest ones don't offer to pay bribes." Cleaning my lips with the napkin, I added, "He's a crook. Always was. Quick Start was a scam from start to finish."

Nod of agreement. "Did you get a chance to make those calls?"

"Uh-huh. Right after I changed clothes at the motel." Gone was the bouclé jacket and dress skirt. I was Rural Angie once more. Jeans, denim jacket, and moccasin boots. "Stockdale was at the Board of Realtors, all right. The receptionist told me the meeting broke up around four P.M."

"Did that give him enough time to get to your hotel?"

"Plenty! He could have been skulking around the Brown Palace from five o'clock on."

"So what time did he get to that saloon for dinner?"

"I don't know." Mild, frustrated scowl. "Nobody picked up when I called. Probably too early in the day."

At that moment a familiar masculine voice cut through the cafe's conversational undertone. "Angie!"

Turning, I spied Troy Rooley weaving his way through the lunchtime throng. Chief gestured at an empty chair. With a weary exhalation Troy unzipped his parka and sat down. "Any luck?"

"Some." Chief put down his mug. "Got talking to Mrs. Winslow over at the hotel. She says Karen was there yesterday about six o'clock. Wanted to buy a bus ticket to Denver but didn't have the money."

Grateful Angie smile. Thanks for covering for me, Chief.

"Well, that fits with what I've heard," Troy remarked. "I was just over in Butte Plaza, talkin' to a few kids from the high school. One of 'em saw Karen about seven last night."

"Where?" asked Chief.

"Teocalli Avenue," Troy replied. "She was ridin' in the front seat of an old black pickup."

The name sounded vaguely familiar. And then I remembered. "Near the hotel?"

Troy nodded.

"Anybody get a look at the driver?" Chief asked.

"Nope! Last they saw of Karen, she was headed east."

Fragments of memory exploded on the big screen of my mind. My first glimpse of the tumbledown Teocalli Hotel. Plus an image from Madge's funeral. A bewhiskered mourner sauntering away from the church, then climbing behind the wheel of a black 1956 Ford pickup. An old friend of Madge Rooley's. The man who had visited her from time to time at Turquoise Lake.

*Pop Hannan!*

# FOURTEEN

In its day, the Teocalli Hotel had been one of the most stylish in Crested Butte. Unfortunately, its day had ended a scant ten years after Colonel Looseslipper's suicide. Carved initials marred the quarter-sawed oak paneling in the foyer. Grime smothered the cracks between the floor tiles. I shook my head in disbelief. From Grand Hotel to flophouse in one hectic century.

As I entered the dingy lobby, the stiff scent of Lysol washed over me. A formidable odor, to be sure, but not quite strong enough to mask the faint traces of urine. Sitting on what looked like an old railroad bench was a balding, elderly man in a wrinkled gray coat. Arms folded tightly, he huddled at one end, carrying on a mumbling conversation with himself. An empty wine bottle sat by his side.

Facing the clerk's desk, I noticed a Tiffany stained-glass window set high on the south wall. The Teocalli's sole surviving fragment of elegance. The circular window admitted a shaft of daylight, giving the owner a chance to save on the electric bill.

The clerk was a heavyset guy in his late thirties. Short

sable-colored hair, porcine eyes, Nixonian jowls, and a dimpled chin. His white shirt swaddled a belly that looked like a slab of beef. "Yeah?" Sudden abrasive scowl. "What do *you* want?"

I reached the counter in four bold strides. "Pop Hannan around?"

"Who's askin'?"

Dipping into my shoulder bag, I retrieved my bogus federal ID. "My name's Janice Kanoshe. I'm with the Department of Labor."

Swinish eyes blinked in astonishment. "You that gal Pop was talkin' to at Kochevar's?"

"That's right." Showing a bureaucratic smile, I let him have a long look at the ID.

Snort of laughter. "No shit! Yeah, he told me about you the other day." His grin showed yellowing teeth. "I didn't believe a word of it."

"Believe it. Pop was a very big help to the department." After putting the ID away, I retrieved a computerized check. "As a matter of fact, that's the reason I'm here." Flash the item. "The voucher just went through. I've got Pop's paycheck right here. Is he in?"

Staring in amazement, he mumbled, "Four hundred?"

"Standard consultant's fee." I feigned a businesslike expression. "Would you page him for me, please?"

His expression filled with regret. "No can do, honey. He ain't here."

Returning the check to my purse, I said, "That's too bad. I know he needs the money." Public servant's smile. "Any idea where he went?"

Flabby shoulders twitched. " 'Fraid not. That Pop—he comes and goes. Know what I mean?"

I should've won the Academy Award for this next line.

"I don't mind waiting around for him."

He looked at me askance. "I wouldn't advise that, honey. Pop could be gone for days."

"Why do you say that?"

His dimpled chin jutted toward the front door. "I saw him loading the truck last night. He had his winter gear with him. Mountain backpack, heavy-duty sleeping bag, you know."

"What time was this?"

"I dunno. Seven o'clock, maybe."

Or a good forty-five minutes after I saw Karen at the bus stop, I reflected.

"Anybody leave with him?"

"Not that I noticed." Suspicion flared in his gimlet eyes. "Why are you so interested?"

Squaring my shoulders, I turned into Angela the Bureaucrat, relentless dotter of I's and crosser of T's. "Sir, I'm trying to find someone who knows where he is. I *would* like to ensure that Pop receives his renumeration."

Scratching his thick neck, the clerk grumbled. "Eh, you could try the Dry Gulch."

"I'll do that." I fielded one more question. "Did you see Pop talking to anybody before he left?"

Another shrug. "Just some kid."

A primordial shiver touched my spine. "Kid?"

"Yeah. Blond girl. Fifteen or sixteen, maybe. Saw her helping him load the pickup."

Somehow I managed to veil my anxiety. "Relative?"

"Naw. Pop don't have any relatives. Leastways not around here." He fondled his dimpled chin. "I dunno who she is. Looks kinda familiar. Maybe I seen her around town."

"Thanks."

Serenaded by the aged derelict's muttering, I danced down the hotel's front steps. My lips set in a frown of puzzlement. I couldn't figure it out. Why would Karen go off with Pop Hannan?

And, more important, where could they have gone?

My grandfather showed me a pensive frown. "You say they were headed east?"

"That's what the clerk told me," I replied, buckling my shoulder strap. "Those two could be anywhere by now."

Gnarled brown fingers turned the ignition key. "Not necessarily, Angie. What did Pop take with him?"

"Winter gear, mostly. Heavy-duty sleeping bag. Like that." Curious sidelong glance. "What are you thinking?"

"A man headed for Denver has no use for winter gear," he said, easing the Sierra away from the curb. "Could be he's headed for the high country."

Wry grimace. "Terrific! That narrows it down to seven hundred square miles!"

Ignoring my outburst, he added, "One thing's for sure—he ain't sleeping outdoors. Not in mid-winter. So he must have someplace to go to." Thoughtful hum. "You spoke to Hannan. Didn't he mention a mining claim?"

"You're absolutely right." Excitement set my nerves tingling. "Pop has a line shack up on Grizzly Peak."

"Somebody in town must know where it is. Want me to drop you off at Kochevar's?"

"Somebody does!" I thought instantly of the man who'd arrested Pop on many occasions. "Forget the bar, Chief. Stay on Elk Avenue."

"Where are we going?"

"To see Chet Hurtig!"

Two minutes later, our truck pulled up in front of the Old Muleskinner. I darted up the steps to the the wooden-railed porch. My hand closed around the ornate brass doorknob. It refused to budge. *Locked!*

Sidestepping to the right, I peered through the window. A small yellow light burned above the alarm box. Throughout the darkened store, display stands and clothing racks raised fearsome shadows in the gloom.

My gaze flitted to the plastic sticker in the bottom corner of the door's window. Scowl of confusion. Hurtig's supposed to be open until six-thirty today. What gives?

Chief glanced at the darkened interior. "So much for that idea."

"Maybe he's just stepped out for a minute."

To the left of Hurtig's store, sharing the same long wooden porch, was an old-fashioned barbershop complete with a red-and-white-striped pole. Briskly I strolled over to the door. A large bell jingled as I pushed it open.

I found myself facing a dapper, middle-aged barber whose lean face bore an Errol Flynn mustache. Chestnut eyes blinked in surprise. I'm afraid he wasn't used to women coming through that doorway. Uncertain smile. "Ah . . . may I help you?"

"That place next door." I tilted my head to the right. "Any idea what time Mr. Hurtig's coming back?"

Dusting off the big swivel chair with a whisk broom, he replied, "I'm afraid Chet ain't been in all day, miss. You lookin' to buy somethin'?"

I nodded. "Snowshoes. I'm going hiking in the Collegiates this weekend." This next ploy was a real long shot, but I played it just the same. "Chet said he was going to put me in touch with a guide. Fella by the name of Pop Hannan."

Beaming, the barber said, "Good choice, gal. Pop'll do you all right." Knowledgeable chuckle. "Long as you keep him away from *liquid refreshment.*"

"Do you know him?"

"Hell, everybody in C.B. knows Pop."

I flashed a folksy smile. "I hear Pop works a claim up on Grizzly Peak."

"That's right." He put his whisk broom on the counter. Then his thumb swiveled eastward. "Got himself a line shack up on Pieplant Creek. South side of the mountain. No way to drive up there, not this time of year. But it ain't too far in. Little more'n a mile, by my reckonin'. It's right off the old Forest Service road."

I grinned. My long shot had paid off. You can always count on a small-town barber for explicit directions.

"Thanks again." I reached for the doorknob. "Nice talking to you."

"You have a good day, miss. Y'hear?"

An hour later, my grandfather and I were cruising north on Forest Road 742. My first glimpse of Grizzly Peak brought a gasp to my lips. A dense overcast, pregnant with impending snow, smothered the summit. The scene left me with an impression of a mountain of impossible height, of evergreen forests and snowbound slopes rising clear into the stratosphere.

For a long, long time, people had considered Grizzly Peak one of Colorado's celebrated fourteeners. Then the U.S. Geologic Survey determined its actual height—thirteen thousand, nine hundred and eighty-eight feet. Close enough!

The barber's directions were right on target. The road led straight to Pieplant Creek. We left the Sierra parked against a high snow mound on the shoulder, donned our snowshoes, and followed the zigzagging trail upslope.

As we shuffled along, Chief remarked, "I don't like the look of that sky, Angie."

Upward glance. Neither did I. Snow-laden clouds drifted down the mountainside. Spindrift powdered the icy spires of the Engelmann spruce. It looked as if it might start snowing at any minute.

Trying to sound confident, I replied, "He said it's only a mile up the trail, Chief."

"I sure hope so." My grandfather's snowshoes made a *chush-chush* sound as he hustled along. "If it starts snowing, we just might have to hole up in there."

The lodgepole forest began yielding to hardy subalpine firs. The steep slope leveled off, widening into a small mountain meadow. Black ice covered the creek, muting the sound of its downhill journey.

My grandfather froze, putting out a restraining hand. Nestled against the mountainside, veiled by a grove of youthful firs, stood a slant-roofed line shack. Weathered elk antlers perched above the door. A plume of pallid smoke wafted away from the fieldstone chimney.

"Looks deserted," I whispered.

"Don't count on it, girl."

Rueful grimace. "Chief, I know better than to go walking right up to the front door."

"Just be careful, okay?" He gave my shoulder an affectionate squeeze. "I'm going to have a look around." He chuckled. "I'll leave the breaking and entering to the expert."

I made a roundabout approach to the shack. I darted from fir to fir, pausing for two or three minutes at every tree. Held my breath and listened.

Muffled sounds touched my ears. Soft plop of loose snow falling from a fir bough. Gentle burble of fast-running water beneath the ice. Upbeat chirping of the mountain chickadee. But the shack itself was silent.

Emboldened, I sidled my way onto the porch. One by one, I removed my showshoes. Stuck them upright in the snow. My moccasin boots made no sound on the snow-covered cedar planks. Taking a deep breath, I eased closer to the window.

Thick drapes veiled the glass. I tried peering through the narrow gap between drapery and window jamb, but it was no go. Too dark inside. Sigh of resignation. Looked as if I was going to have to try the front door after all.

Just then the flurry of footprints at the doorstep drew my gaze. Squatting on my haunches, I gave them a closer look. Three sets of prints. The first went directly from the yard to the doorstep. Large, masculine—the sole of a snowboot. A familiar starburst marked the size-eleven print. Instant tingle of recognition. A footprint identical to the sniper's. Our friend from the Brown Palace Hotel!

The second set streamed catercorner off the porch. A man running. Size seven or eight, I figured.

The third set featured two people. Our friend the sniper and a most reluctant guest. Small footprint. Pointed toe, no arch, noticeable heel. A woman. Her footprints dug deeper on the right. A woman straining to get away.

My stomach tensed in alarm. *Karen?*

I cast a frantic glance at the yard. Damn! Windblown snow had erased their footprints.

That settles it! I thought. I've got to get inside.

My hand closed around the doorknob. *Click!* Astonished Angie glance. It was open.

Once inside, I lifted my parka's rear hem and slipped my knife out of its sheath. A stainless steel survival knife, trade name Commando. Its hollow handle featured a mini-survival kit containing a snare wire, nylon fishing line, sinkers, needles, tinder, lifeboat matches, a birthday candle, and a gauze pad.

Unscrewing the compass cap, I plucked out a lifeboat match and struck it against the door. Feeble firelight showed me a kerosene lamp sitting on a nearby night table. Gingerly holding the match, I hurried right over there and lit it. Warm white light flooded the cabin, offering much better visibility.

My gaze circled the room, taking note of the rumpled bed, the cedar-plank walls, the hand-built fireplace, and the cozy kitchenette. Believe me, Pop Hannan would never win the Good Housekeeping award. Lamp soot marred the ceiling above the night table. Dirty dishware rimmed the porcelain sink. Books and papers littered the dining table.

Just then a familar shade of maroon caught my eye. Forlorn and forgotten, Karen's woolen scarf lay draped across a chair's tall backrest. Sudden anxious frown. So that *was* Karen's footprint on the porch! Where could Pop have taken her?

Hastily I searched the premises. I found three of Pop's worn winter jackets hanging from aspen pegs. His mountain backpack huddled beneath the unmade bed.

On to the big oak table. My, what a surprising array of reading material. Ray Phillips's *The Colorado Fourteens.* William M. Bueler's *Roof of the Rockies.* Plus a whole lot of brochures from the Bureau of Land Management. Detailed maps of the Grizzly Peak area. A masculine hand had scribbled heavily on all of them.

A school notebook crammed with stray papers lay on the grease-spattered tablecloth. Turning it my way, I flipped open the front cover. A ten-year-old typewritten letter met my gaze.

> Office of Vital Records
> Elkhart, Indiana
> *Heart of Amish Country!*

Mr. Albert P. Hannan
General Delivery
Crested Butte, CO 81224

Dear Mr. Hannan:

Thank you for your recent letter of inquiry. According to our town records, Richard Bohle was born here in Elkhart on June 21, 1859, the son of Jabez and Eliza (Landis) Bohle.

A boy named "R. Bohle" is listed in School Department records as graduating from the eighth grade in June 1872. As there is no record of employment or county death certificate listed in his name, I can only assume that Richard left Elkhart sometime after 1872.

I hope this information has been helpful to you.

Sincerely,
Mrs. Catherine Yoder
Executive Secretary

There was more in the same vein. Photocopied pages from books dealing with the Wild Bunch. Clippings from the *Denver Post*. A 1947 article contained an interview with the aged Marshal Stewart Palmer, describing his gunfight with Dutch Bohle fifty years earlier.

Tinker was right, I mused. Pop is obsessed with finding that missing treasure.

The notebook provided ample confirmation. It was Pop's personal journal, a detailed account of his forty-year search. The most recent entries held a distinct tone of bitterness.

October 17: First snow. Noticed some claw marks high up on a lodgepole Tuesday. That griz is back from Maroon Bells. Better move the icebox inside. Got a letter all the way from Lancaster, Pennsylvania. Turns out Dutch Bohle's daddy was born there. He was an Old Order Mennonite, just like I said. That old fart professor can go fuck himself. What does he know?

October 31: Heading down to C.B. today. Madge been ducking me. Says she's waiting to hear from Frank. I got a right to know, dammit. It was my idea to use the old Pieplant mine. What's that gal up to?

November 22: Talked to Madge again. Told her I want my cut. Same old story. Wait for Frank! I think she's holding out on me. And I ain't the only one!

December 24: Merry Christmas, ho-ho-ho! Money's running kind of low. Reckon I ain't buying myself that congratulatory bottle of Jack Daniel's this year. Dammit, I *know* it's up there. Dutch must have cached it in one of those caves on the north face. But which one?

January 10: Madge and her *big scores!* What the hell good is the money if you can't spend it? Had it out with that gal today. To hell with Frank, I told her. He could be inside for ten more years. Gal's cheating me out of my share. Holding out on me! Just like always. Dutch *must* have gotten word to the RJ Bar somehow. If he wasn't holed up there, then he must've been hiding out in Gothic. Family named Landis there. Dutch's momma was a Landis.

It's up there! I know it! I can *feel* it! Dutch cached the gold that summer. Then he headed north, fixing to hook up with the Bunch again. He would have sent word to Rooley, or he would have had his kin do it. There's no other way.

MADGE MUST KNOW!!! I'm going to *make* her tell. I'll wait for my cut if I have to. But no damned way am I giving up that gold. I've walked every square foot of these damned mountains for better'n forty years! I deserve it! It's mine! And no one—not even a Rooley!—is gonna to stand in my way!

Pop's scribbled ravings left me with a queasy feeling in the pit of my stomach. Flipping the notebook shut, I wondered if I'd found Madge's murderer.

Take one embittered prospector and stick him up on Grizzly Peak for forty years. Have him come up empty after decades of searching. And then let him think Madge Rooley was withholding some vital piece of information.

A motive that strong might tempt him to sabotage Madge's truck. It might also explain why he put the grab on her granddaughter.

But I didn't quite buy it. Not all the way. For one thing, there were *three* sets of footprints on Pop's snowy porch.

Playing a hunch, I crossed the room, then picked up one of Pop's drying snowboots. Carried it to the front door. Snowflakes powdered my face as I pulled it open. A storm wind whistled its way through the meadow.

I dangled Pop's boot just above a size eleven footprint. Grim Angie smile. How about that? *Two sizes too small!*

Which means he didn't leave with Karen.

My gaze pounced on the other masculine prints—the tracks scooting catercorner off the porch. Kneeling, I placed the boot's sole in one. Perfect fit!

Just then a sharp sound split the wintry silence. The tremolo cry of the Lake Superior loon.

Tossing the boot indoors, I stood erect. Then closed the door, crossed the porch, and donned my snowshoes.

Another bittersweet tremolo. Well, I thought, either a loon took a wrong turn at the Enger Tower, or that's my grandfather.

Oblivious to the thickening snowfall, I shuffled into the woods. Chief stood about thirty yards upslope, dwarfed by a trio of Engelmann spruce. Never had I seen him so grim!

Impatient gesture. *"Noozis, maajiibatoon!"*

*"Nimishoo, wegonen—?"*

The question died in my throat. Pop Hannan lay facedown in the snow, his arms outflung at unnatural angles. A large bullet hole, shiny with clotted blood, split the fabric of his dark blue lumberman's shirt. Windblown snow partly blanketed his worn Levis and hiking socks. Long gray hair flickered lifelessly in the wind.

Hard swallow. "He's dead."

*"Eyan!"* Chief nodded, squatting beside the body. "Looks like he was shot with a hunting round."

"Six-point-five millimeter?"

Studying the wound, he grunted in affirmation.

"Our friend from the mountain." Fierce Angie scowl. "How long ago would you say it happened?"

Chief shrugged. "He's frozen stiff. Makes it hard to tell. Maybe this morning. Maybe an hour ago."

Fussbudget frown. If it happened that morning, I reflected,

then the sniper can't be Stockdale. He was with me. But if it happened an hour ago . . .

Gesturing at Pop's stocking feet, my grandfather brought me out of my reverie. "Pop was in an awful damned hurry to leave that shack. How come?"

Briefly I summed up my search. "He and Karen had a visitor, *Nimishoo*. The sniper. Pop must have sensed a double cross. He made a run for it." Quick glance downslope. "Our friend shot him from the porch. Then he took off with Karen."

Chief's features brightened in understanding. "So that explains those tracks—"

"What tracks?" I snapped.

He crooked his finger. *"Ambe, Noozis."*

My grandfather led me uphill. Spruce boughs swatted at my hair. *Chush-chush-chush!* Our snowshoes beat out a whisper in stereo. Thick snowflakes pelted my face as we stepped onto a narrow mountain trail. Identical tread marks split the snow, running up and down the mountainside.

"Snowmobile," I muttered.

"Coming and going." Chief pointed out the furrow on the left. "This one's a little deeper. He was carrying extra weight—Karen."

I glanced upslope. The trail corkscrewed to the left, vanishing behind a snowy saddleback. Taking a step in that direction, I said, "That settles it, then."

*"Beka!"* His gnarled hand gripped my parka sleeve. "Where do you think you're going?"

Gesturing at the ridge, I said, "Up there!"

"Don't be a fool, *Noozis*. He's headed for McNasser Pass." Chief's obsidian eyes glimmered in warning. "We'll never catch him on foot. Not in this weather."

*"Nimishoo!* He has Karen!"

"I know that." His face showed sympathy. "Listen to me. They're above the treeline. Up in the scree. When the storm hits, it's going to be like the Arctic up there. Wind chills of eighty below. They'll be able to make it on that snowmobile. But if we get caught up there, we're dead!"

"We-we can't leave Karen—"

"We have no choice, *Noozis*," he murmured. "Think! He wouldn't take Karen on a joyride. He must have a shelter on the other side of the pass."

Folding my arms in frustration, I sighed heavily. "All right, then, What do you suggest?"

"Try following my *original* suggestion!"

I blinked in puzzlement.

"Drop a quarter on the Colorado State Patrol!" he added, his voice rising. "If you'd done that back in Denver, we wouldn't be in this mess!"

"*Nimishoo*, I can't do that!"

"Why not?" he snapped.

"I'll get sent back to prison!"

Clenching his teeth, he glanced at the dead man. "Well, what are we going to do about *Pop?*"

Feeble intermittent smile. "I, uh, I guess we're going to have to make one of those, uhm, anonymous phone calls."

"*Noozis*, we can't just leave him there!"

"And we don't dare tamper with a crime scene," I replied. My arms waved frantically. "All right, all right! I'll call the stateys as soon as we hit the highway."

Chief followed me back into the woods. "What are you going to tell them?"

"Where to find Pop. And that's all!"

Chief made a sound of frustration. "*Noozis!* Isn't this withholding evidence?"

"I prefer to think of it as covering my ass!"

His angry mutter pursued me downhill. "I haven't seen a man shot to death since the Big One. Thought it was all behind me. And now my granddaughter—" Sudden shout. "*Tayaa!* Where are you off to now, *Noozis?*"

"The shack," I answered. "I just remembered something."

"We just keep getting in deeper, don't we?"

I reached Pop's shack a few minutes later. Leaving my snowshoes upright in a drift, I padded into the house. Took special care to step inside Pop's footprints.

Once inside, I returned the castaway snowboot to its place by the fire. Pulling out my handkerchief, I wiped those spots where my fingertips had made contact with the table. Then I snatched Karen's maroon scarf and ran for the door.

I left Pop's diary on the table. Let the state patrol find it. By this time tomorrow, the contents of his journal would be on the front page of every newspaper in Colorado. Meaning that Madge's role in the armored car holdup was about to go public.

Oh, well! If Madge's memory must suffer, so be it.

I glanced at the maroon scarf in my mittened hand. Maybe I couldn't spare Sarah and her siblings this further humiliation. But at least I could prevent Madge's granddaughter from becoming unjustly linked to a murder.

Reaching for my snowshoes, I aimed one last uneasy glance at the mountain's evergreen slopes.

With luck, maybe we could prevent Karen herself from becoming the next murder victim.

On our way back to the ranch, Chief and I made a quick stop in Gunnison. If we were going to tackle Grizzly Peak in February, we needed the proper gear.

So we spent a hectic half hour at Traders Rendezvous, a well-stocked sporting goods store on West Tomichi. I let my grandfather, the ex-Marine, choose the contents of my day-pack. Pair of surplus army canteens, a USMC poncho, a woolen blanket, a Polar Shield survival blanket, hooded sweatshirt, Ranger mess kit, tri-fold shovel and one army cold-weather mummy bag, complete with cover. Just the thing to keep a lady snug and warm on a frigid winter night.

When we got to the ranch, Becky informed us that Troy and Merry were still out searching. Sarah, she added, was waiting by the phone, eager for any news. While my grandfather gave Becky a hand with the goats, I headed for the kitchen.

I gave the cupboards a hasty scan. Now, what can I pop into my daypack? Grinning, I reached for a small cardboard box. Of course! Lipton's Cup-a-Soup. One of these ought to keep me well nourished while I'm up in the high country.

Then I made Chief a roast beef sandwich for tomorrow's lunch. Closing the refrigerator door, I spied the antique Meissen rolling pin. Lifting it out of its cradle, I turned it over and studied the cylinder's strange pattern.

All at once I heard Karen's voice in my memory, telling me about the manufacturer. *Farm family. They were . . . what do you call 'em? Those folks who ride around in buggies.*

"Amish," I murmured. The word triggered a second memory. Pop Hannan writing about the outlaw Dutch Bohle.

*. . . Then he must've been hiding out in Gothic. Family named Landis there. Dutch's momma was a Landis.*

My hands trembled with excitement. Madge had sworn up and down that Dutch Bohle had never gotten in touch with her great-grandfather. But what if she were wrong?

Playing a hunch, I rummaged in my purse for a Gunnison County map. Spreading it open on the table, I rotated the rolling pin so that the rectangular bas-relief faced me. My gaze flitted back and forth between the ceramic and the map.

Nope, nope . . . that's not it. Try it sideways, Angie. Ah, here we go. Little bit more . . . *yes!*

Broad grin of triumph. The rolling pin's line of upraised pyramids was a perfect match for the Collegiate range.

Grabbing a pencil from the cupboard shelf, I leaned over and pinpointed the single flawed pyramid—the one marked with a slash. Then my gaze zipped to the topographic map. *Bingo!* I might have known. *Grizzly Peak!*

Standing upright, I thought, Looks like you picked the right mountain, Pop.

Lips puckered as I gave the map a careful scrutiny. Hmmm,

five miles northwest of Lake Ann. Limestone bluffs. Very steep. Must be a few caves up there.

I marked my USGS map, put it back into my purse, and replaced the Amish rolling pin in its cradle. And gave a moment's thought to that notorious member of the Wild Bunch, Richard "Dutch" Bohle, the outlaw who'd refused to draw on a Mennonite elder.

At last I understood the truth behind the legend. Plus the origin of his nickname! Bohle had grown up in a community of Old Order Mennonites. Pop Hannan had come closest to the truth when he backtracked the outlaw to Elkhart, Indiana. But he never quite made the connection.

Dutch Bohle . . . I mused. That's *Dutch* as in *Pennsylvania Dutch*, which is another name for the Old Order Mennonites— better known as the Amish.

Zipping my purse shut, I cast a final glance at the century-old rolling pin. Very clever, Dutch. As soon as you were able to ride, you left the RJ Bar, promising to send word to your partner. But you didn't ride far. Only up to Grizzly Peak, where you buried the stolen gold. Then you lit out for your relatives' farm in Gothic.

Wrapping Chief's sandwich, I wondered why Dutch hadn't confided in his relatives. Probably afraid they'd turn him in to the Pinkertons. Or perhaps help themselves to the gold.

Dutch had played it close to the vest, all right. He'd asked his Amish kin to cast the rolling pin for him. Then, while the clay was still moist, he drew his treasure map. And asked his kinfolks to ship it down to the RJ Bar.

That, of course, is where his clever plan came apart. A newcomer to the Bunch, Byron Lee Rooley knew nothing of Dutch's background. The Landis family gave him the Meissen rolling pin, no doubt complying with Dutch's last request. An unsuspecting Byron had accepted the gift, doubtless shrugging off the rectangle as some sort of unusual Amish design.

Excitement quickened my heartbeat. For a hundred years

Dutch Bohle's map had been lying around this kitchen. I thought of Madge and Sarah and Becky using it to roll out dough. Chuckle of irony.

Your *inheritance* was here all along, Madge. You just never realized it, that's all.

Putting the wrapped sandwiches in the refrigerator, I wondered if my grandfather would consent to a future weekend camping trip up on Grizzly Peak.

Whoa, princess! You've got more important work to do. Karen's rescue tops the list. After that you can relieve Mr. Stockdale of his ill-gotten hundred grand. Then we'll see about Dutch Bohle's treasure.

There's no guarantee it's still up there, you know. A hundred years is a long, long time. Some hippies could have stumbled over it a quarter-century ago and used it to finance their week at Woodstock.

As I strolled into the dining room, a familiar contralto voice rang out. "Angela."

Halting, I glanced at the study's doorway. There stood Sarah, her features drawn. Moment of shock. Karen's disappearance had taken its toll. The boss lady looked about ten years older.

Her blond head tilted decisively. "Could I see you for a moment, please?"

"Sure." Flashing a pleasant smile, I sauntered past Karen's mom. Sarah was back to Ranch Casual again. Light blue ruffled blouse and pepperwashed jeans.

She gestured at the swivel chair. "Have a seat."

Masking my wariness behind a bland expression, I sat down. Uh-oh! I thought. La Sutton sounds pissed. Probably wondering where I've been the past couple of days.

Cook up a story, Angie—*fast!*

Tearing a sheet from the printer, Sarah turned to face me. "I was downloading a few files this morning, and I came across something that should interest you." Her slender hand extended the sheet of paper. "See for yourself."

Obsidian eyes blossomed in horror. There, in glorious black and white, was a printout of my *Janice Kanoshe* driver's license!

Folding her arms, Sarah added dryly, "In a court of law, that's what's known as Exhibit A."

Oh, shit! I thought. I forgot all about that file. Sarah found it! Ohhhh, why didn't I erase it when I had the chance?

Sarah cocked an eyebrow. "*Who* is Janice Kanoshe? And what is your face doing on that driver's license?"

My mouth fell open. Shock paralyzed my voice box. A single desperate question kept bouncing around my brain. *Whom has she told?*

"I'd like an explanation, Angela!"

The paper crumpled in my quaking grasp. I had no idea what to say. This was the one possibility I hadn't foreseen—Sarah accidentally blowing my cover!

"While you're at it . . ." Taking three brisk steps forward, she loomed over me. "You can explain what you were doing at the Water Wheel Inn this morning."

Gaping in disbelief, I blurted out, "How did you—?"

"I saw you, dear. On my way back from the sheriff's office." Green eyes glittered in anger. "What were you doing all dressed up? And how did you get to be so chummy with Matt Stockdale?" Sudden contralto shout. "I want *answers*, young lady! Just what are you trying to pull?"

# FIFTEEN

"I'm waiting, miss!"

Swallowing hard, I tried to revive my stunned imagination. I had to tell Sarah *something*. But what? If I admitted to conning Stockdale, she'd send me straight to jail!

"Not talking, eh?" Scowling, Sarah reached for the telephone receiver. "Well, perhaps you'd rather explain yourself to Paul!"

"*No!*" I grabbed her wrist. A horrible vision sizzled through my mind. Angie back in the prison laundry, stuffing dirty clothes into a heavy wicker basket!

The receiver clattered in its cradle. Sarah pulled free of my grip. "One more chance, Angela! Either you tell me what you've been up to—*right this minute*—or I'm calling the sheriff!"

I pushed the phone out of her immediate reach. "Dammit, Sarah, I'm trying to *help* you!"

Skeptical glare. "Help me? How?"

I groped for a reasonable explanation. One that wouldn't convict me of obstructing justice. Before I could answer, my grandfather's gravelly voice said, "You'd better tell her, Angie."

Glancing to my left, I spied Chief and Becky in the hallway. Then Troy and Merry arrived, their youthful faces showing puzzlement.

Sarah picked right up on it. "Tell me what?"

Choosing my words with care, I began, "Your mother—"

"What about my mother?" she interrupted.

Deep breath. "The crash was no accident." My somber gaze found Sarah's. "Someone sabotaged your mother's truck. She was murdered."

"*What?*" Sarah's face trembled in disbelief. The news rocked her, but somehow she held on to that courtroom poise. "What are you talking about?"

Chief spoke up. "We had a look at the truck, Sarah. When you talk to the sheriff, have him inspect the master cylinder—"

Her hands waggled haplessly. "Wait a minute! Wait a minute! How do you *know* Mother was murdered?"

"Well, after what happened in Denver, Angie thought—"

She pounced on me. "*What* happened in Denver?"

"Somebody tried to kill you." Apprehension turned me into a chatterbox. "Well . . . actually they tried to kill me. They only thought I was you. I mean, they thought I was you because I was wearing your coat. It's, uhm, kind of complicated, Sarah."

"Then perhaps you'd better start at the beginning, dear!"

Conscious of all those grim Rooley faces, I began my narrative. "Remember the conference in Denver? You went out to dinner at the Wellshire that evening. Just before you called, this guy phoned our room. Later on, I found out it was Frank Blodgett. You know, the bruiser we ran into at the Dry Gulch—"

The memory brought a flush of crimson to Sarah's cheeks. "I know who he is. Continue."

So I did. I told how Chief had joined me in Crested Butte, how we'd checked out Madge's truck at the gas station, how we'd traced Sarah's mother all the way to Leadville. Mention of Madge's role in the armored car robbery brought gasps from all her children. Still, Sarah insisted upon hearing it all.

I deleted only one incident. Our discovery of Pop Hannan's body up on Grizzly Peak. I didn't *dare* mention that. If I did, Sarah would want to know why I didn't call the police. And I couldn't answer that. Not without revealing my Pocahontas identity.

Sarah gave me no respite. The minute I finished my tale, she began her cross-examination. "So Mother took that job at Trautmann's?"

I nodded slowly.

"She told us she was working at CVS," Becky added.

Arms folded, Sarah asked, "What was that name she used?"

"Marjorie Dexter," I replied.

"And they were all in on the hijacking," Sarah said. "Mother, Frank Blodgett, Jack Sunawavi, and Pop Hannan. How much was taken?"

"Four hundred thousand." My mouth felt as dry as Death Valley. "There may have been a fifth man involved—Matt Stockdale."

Abrasive look from Sarah. "Don't be ridiculous!"

"Wait a minute, Sally." Merry took a step forward. "You heard what Angie said. He stole all that money from the ranchers. Could be he doublecrossed Momma."

"I *told* you he was a goddamned crook!" Troy chimed in.

Sarah's index finger poked upward. "One topic at a time, people!" Her suspicious gaze zeroed in on me. "Why didn't you go to the police?"

I winced. Oooooh, I *knew* that question was coming. And there was no way could I successfully answer!

Fortunately, Chief came to my rescue. "Angie was worried,

Sarah. She was afraid the Department of Corrections would revoke her parole."

"That's one explanation," Sarah conceded. "On the other hand, she could have been after the robbery money *herself!*"

Outraged holler. "Hey! Just a minute, Slinky-dink!"

"*What* did you call me?"

Okay, so it slipped out. But I couldn't help it. I was livid. After all I'd done for that woman!

"You have one hell of a sense of gratitude, lady! I put my ass on the line for you!"

Sarah's warpath scowl easily outdid mine. "Young lady, I have no recollection of asking you to go out and commit *crimes!*"

"That could've been *you* in front of the hotel, Sutton! If not for me, you'd be dead right now!"

Sarah's forefinger stabbed at my nose. "*Shut up!*"

She had the exact same tone as Aunt Della—stern, hard, and loud. My mouth snapped shut.

Putting her hands on her denim-clad hips, she added, "I—I can hardly believe what I've been hearing. You know, I used to wonder how a girl with your brains could make such an absolute mess of her life. Now I know!" Exasperated shout. "Angela, have you any idea what you've done to your parole?"

"Okay, so maybe I did put a few dings in it, but—"

"*A few!*" Sarah counted off with her fingers. "Obstructing justice! Misprision of a felony! Failure to report a capital crime!" Shaking her head briskly, she added, "I'm afraid you need to spend a little more time in a structured environment, dear."

"*Sa*-rah!"

"I'm sorry about this, Angela. I truly am. But you have to face the consequences of your actions."

Technically speaking, I was guilty of *two* counts of failure to report a murder. But this definitely wasn't the moment to point that out. As she reached for the phone, I blurted out, "Wh-What are you doing?"

"Calling the sheriff," Sarah said, lifting the receiver. "I'm afraid I won't be able to represent you this time around. Don't worry. I'll fix you up with a good Colorado lawyer. We'll try to get the state of South Dakota to waive jurisdiction. With any luck, you won't be in Canon City for more than two or three years."

Touching my shoulders, Chief murmured, "Sarah, she only wanted to help."

"I'm sorry, Charlie." She aimed a somber glance at my grandfather. "But I don't have any other choice. I'm a lawyer—an officer of the court. I—I have to report this."

Sarah's forefinger landed on a touch tab.

The prospect of long-term residence at Canon City spurred me into action. "Sarah, wait!"

Pausing, she gave me a scathing look. "I'd advise you to do all your talking to your new counsel."

She was reacting to my seeming betrayal, of course, and I really couldn't blame her for that. I figured I had one last card on the table. I hated to play it, but I had no choice. I couldn't let her make that phone call!

"Sarah, you don't know what's at stake."

Emerald eyes flashing, she tapped out three more numbers.

"If you call the sheriff, it'll all go public," I warned. "The robbery. Your mother's role in it. Everything!"

Features grim, Sarah let out a quiet sigh. "I can live with it. Lord knows I've had to deal with worse."

"You can," I replied. "But what about *Karen?*"

Dead silence. Sarah's finger hovered above the phone tabs. Her castigating glance zipped my way. "What about Karen?"

"Pop Hannan gave her a ride out of town yesterday," I said. Incomplete truth. My specialty. "I—I'm pretty sure she's with him now."

"So that's who was drivin'," Troy remarked. "She's tellin' it straight, Sally. I talked to Karen's friends this morning. They saw her ride off in an old black pickup."

An irascible grunt sounded behind me. My grandfather. He doesn't always approve of my forays into deceit. But at least he understood the necessity.

Sarah hung up. "Why would Pop Hannan kidnap Karen?"

"Frank Blodgett told me your mother moved the loot," I theorized. "Karen used to live with your mother. Maybe Pop thinks she knows where it is."

True enough, I thought. That could be the reason Pop offered Karen the ride. But it didn't explain why Madge's killer had gone gunning for him after all this time.

Chief added his two cents. "We talked to the clerk at the Teocalli Hotel. He says Pop has a shack up on Grizzly Peak."

Sarah and Becky flashed identical expressions of surprise. Eyeing her sister, Becky murmured, "The cabin?"

"Charlie, did he mention a lake nearby?" Sarah asked.

Chief shook his head.

With a sigh, Sarah murmured, "I think it's time we called the state patrol."

"Wait a minute, Sally!" Troy touched his sister's arm. "What about Stockdale?"

"What about him?"

"You gonna let that son of a bitch get away with it?"

"Troy, that really isn't the issue here. He's—"

"You heard Angie!" Troy snapped, gesturing at me. "That Quick Start deal was a scam from start to finish. He defrauded us on purpose!"

"All right." Sarah emitted a weary sigh. "I'll have a talk with the district attorney. Right after we find Karen."

"What the hell good is *that* gonna do?" Her brother's face tensed in frustration. "Sally, that damned bank wants a hundred grand from us. If we can't pay it, the RJ Bar's finished!"

"Troy's right," Merry added. "The law's not going to do anything about it. You know that, Sally, and so do I. No way are they going to toss a loop around Mrs. Longworth's nephew!"

Daintily touching her collarbone, Sarah frowned. "What would you have me do?"

Troy's gaze shifted toward me. "Let Angie go on with it."

Amazement flooded her lovely face. "You have got to be joking!"

"Listen, Sally, there's no way we can settle that debt. Why should we lose our ranch because of that bastard Stockdale?" Expression of determination. "You know what I say? If Angie can pull it off, go for it!"

Sarah opened her mouth to reply, but Merry beat her to it. "Stockdale cheated Momma of her money. I'm not shedding any tears for him." Supportive nod. "Go ahead and take him, Angie."

Irritated by the siblings' revolt, Sarah glared at me. "You seem to have picked up a couple of allies—"

"Make that three," Becky added with a naughty smile. "Sorry, Sally. You're outvoted. Stockdale got us into this mess. It's only fair his money should get us out." Turning to me, she added, "Besides, what Angie says makes a whole lot of sense."

"Not to me!" Sarah dissented.

Unfazed, Becky went on. "You weren't here, Sally, so you didn't see it."

"See what?"

Quiet sigh. "I had a feeling something wasn't right. Momma changed during the past couple of years. She was restless—edgy—not very talkative. It was like when we were kids, and she was fixin' to go out on a job."

Oooooh, was that a sore point with Sarah! She didn't appreciate having the family laundry aired in front of me. Fists tightened until her knuckles showed white. "What you people are proposing is against the law!"

"So's fraud!" Troy snapped.

"And killing Momma," added Becky quietly.

Sarah's face reddened. "There's no proof that Stockdale had anything to do with Mother's death."

"He could be the fifth man," Chief pointed out.

I cut in before my grandfather accidentally mentioned Pop Hannan's diary.

"It's possible there was another man involved in the robbery, Sarah. Somebody who helped Hannan and Blodgett hide the money up in the Collegiates," I explained, my tone humble. "Check the scorecard, dear. Your mother's dead. Sunawavi's dead. Somebody dropped a quarter on Frank Blodgett. That could have been Pop, but I don't think so. Pop hasn't got the nerve to cross Frank."

Her face turned thoughtful. "So the *fifth man* told the FBI where to find him."

I nodded. "I think he's working with Pop." All at once I saw a possible exit from my dilemma. "And we know Pop has Karen."

Chief picked up on the timbre of excitement in my voice. "What have you got in mind, Angie?"

"Let's find out if Matt Stockdale really was involved in the armored car robbery."

Sarah shot me a leery glance. "How?"

"Stockdale's expecting me at three-thirty. Maybe I can stall him. Have him recount the money or something. Meanwhile, Chief and Troy can check out his house. If he's hiding Karen there, they can spring her. We'll keep her name out of it."

Chief's eyes narrowed. "What if she ain't there?"

Sickish Angie look. "Then you'd better call the state patrol."

Merry gasped. "You'll go to jail."

The J-word sent a nasty tremor up my spine. "True enough. But at least this way you'll get Stockdale's hundred grand. You won't lose your ranch."

"That's assuming *you* don't run off with the money!" Sarah snapped.

Fuming, I replied, "I won't even dignify that with a response, Mrs. Sutton!"

"It's a valid point." Sarah sported an identical scowl. "You have shown yourself to be completely untrustworthy."

"Maybe so." I struggled to keep the anger out of my voice. "But we have only two options, Sarah. Yours and mine." Quick, calming breath. "My way—we rescue Karen from the bad guys. After she's safe, we roll over Blodgett and company. Your way . . . well, let's look at the outcomes. I go back to prison. Your family loses the ranch. And Karen—*if* the state patrol can find her in time—becomes embroiled in yet another headline-grabbing Rooley felony. A robbery she had absolutely nothing to do with!" Pausing, I let the words sink in. "Do you really want to do that to your own daughter?"

Resentment gleamed in Sarah's eyes. I was forcing her choose between her daughter and her integrity. I hated to do that to her, but I had no other choice. I had to get back to town. Not to grab the money, you understand, although that in itself was certainly important. No, I had to see Stockdale one more time. If he was the fifth man, then he'd killed Pop Hannan, and he had Sarah's daughter stashed away somewhere. I had to stall him long enough for Chief to rescue Karen.

Misery engulfed Sarah's expression, banishing all traces of resentment. Integrity meant quite a lot to her. But not as much as her daughter.

Fists trembling, she muttered, "Your way."

Chief nudged me gently. "Better get moving, Angie."

Troy spoke up. "I'm coming with you."

"If you've got a rifle, son, we could sure use it."

"No problem, Mr. Blackbear."

The others cleared out, leaving me and Sarah alone in the study. Head bowed, she stood facing the window. My heart began to tighten. For weeks I'd wanted to see that proud woman humbled. Now that it had finally happened, I took no pleasure in it. Instead, I experienced the sting of a terrible dismay, plus an overwhelming urge to make amends.

"Sarah . . ."

"You know, I'll probably be disbarred for this." She lifted her head suddenly, addressing our reflections in the window-pane. "There really is no excuse." She turned slowly. "I don't care! I—I want her back, th-that's all. Find her for me, Angela."

Before I could answer, she gave way to a muffled sob. "I—I thought I was putting it all behind me. I thought—when I w-went to Pierre—I w-was closing the door on the past. I knew what Mother was. I—I thought I could shield Karen from it. And now it's struck at her."

"It's not your fault. You had no idea what your mother was up to."

"I *should've* known! Don't you see? Mother was never going to change. But—but I—I convinced myself she had. I—I should have known better!"

Gently touching her shoulder, I said, "The only thing you're guilty of is believing your mother's lies. That gives you something in common with everybody else."

I wanted very much to give her a hug, but I kept my distance. I knew there was no way Sarah would ever accept my friendship. Not after today. This incident would always stand between us.

This incident . . . and Paul Holbrook!

Quietly I retreated from the room, leaving Sarah to shed her tears, and promptly bumped into Becky. She put a finger to her lips. Then, taking my wrist, she hauled me into the parlor.

"I've been doin' some thinkin'," Becky whispered, her lips set in a knowledgeable smile. "Seems to me a law-abidin' gal would've called the state patrol *right after* she had that look at

Momma's truck. You're dead set against talkin' to them. How come?"

Panic triggered a response. "I—I—I wanted to be certain before starting all kinds of—"

"Bullshit!" Becky's smile widened. "There's a warrant out on you, isn't there?"

My mouth shut instantly.

"Don't worry. I ain't going to turn you in. I did a year's worth of laundry in Canon City. We ex-cons got to stick together." Curious gaze. "You on the dodge, Angie?"

Sometimes you just have to go with your instincts. Mine told me to trust Becky.

"Uhm . . . you might say that."

"Sally know about it?"

I shook my head vigorously.

"I thought as much." Rueful grin. "Don't you worry about that big sister o' mine. I'll handle her. You just concentrate on bringin' Karen home. Hear?"

"I'll find her, Becky. Girl Scout's promise."

Shortly after three-thirty I sauntered into the Gunnison Guaranty office. Stockdale's brunette secretary tap-tapped away on the computer keyboard. My heart thudded against my ribcage as I approached the counter.

Show time! I thought, firing a quick glance at the office clock. Troy said Stockdale owns a hobby ranch on Antelope Creek. He and Chief ought to be there by now. If only I can keep Stockdale busy for the next thirty minutes . . .

The secretary looked up. Brunette pixie hairstyle and heart-shaped face. Expression of mild curiosity. "May I help you?"

Displaying my best smile, I replied, "Hi! I'm Janet Wanagi. Mr. Stockdale's expecting me."

"Of course. Just a moment, please." Turning in her swivel chair, she scooped up her telephone receiver.

While she alerted the boss to my presence, I thought of a way to trace Stockdale's whereabouts.

Hanging up, she remarked, "He'll be out in a moment, Miss Wanagi."

"Great!" Lounging against the counter, I added, "You know, for a while there, I didn't think he was going to make it back."

Her expression registered confusion. "Make it back?"

Brisk Angie nod. "I phoned an hour ago. He wasn't here."

"Miss Wanagi . . ." Pert and pretty frown. "Mr. Stockdale's been in all day."

"He didn't leave after our meeting this morning?"

"No." Her lips puckered in a bewildered moue. "Who did you talk to?"

"Nobody," I replied. "The phone rang and rang."

"What number did you dial?"

I altered one digit in their office number. "Three-four-nine-nine-nine-two-seven."

"That explains it." Relief filled her delicate face. "Our number is three-four-nine-nine-nine-two-*six*."

Feigning an embarrassed expression, I chuckled. "I really have to do something about my handwriting. This isn't the first time I've gotten it wrong."

She had a fine soprano laugh. "I know what you mean, dear. I have the same problem with my grocery list."

Disturbing thoughts contributed to my chagrined look. If Stockdale had been here all day, then who had ridden that snowmobile to Pop's shack?

Stockdale left me no time to ponder the matter. Striding into the outer office, he smiled in welcome. "Janet!"

On with the sting, princess. "Hi, Matt."

We shook hands, and then he led me into his private office. "Glad you could make it," he said, placing a comradely arm across my shoulders. "How went your day?"

"Productive." As we strolled inside, I spied the sturdy Cordura satchel on his desk. "And yours?"

"A little hectic, thanks to you." With a wry chuckle, he rounded the desk. "But it's all here. My facilitation fee." Slowly he unzipped the bag. Curiosity lowered his eyebrows. "Going casual on us, Jan?"

"Beg pardon?"

One by one he withdrew stacks of bound currency. "You're not wearing your suit."

Self-consciously I smoothed my parka. "I'm on my way up to Horseshoe Springs."

"Doing a little night skiing, eh?"

I nodded. "Thought I'd give Keystone a try before I head back to Denver."

He finished emptying the satchel. "Need a partner?"

"Thanks, Matt." Coy smile. "But I already have a date."

"I'm jealous." He stepped away from the desk. "Is he anybody I know?"

"You've probably seen him around town," I replied. Especially when you look in the mirror!

"There you go." Removing the satchel, Matt left clusters of cash scattered across the blotter. "You're welcome to count it."

So I did. Crisp bills slithered through my busy fingers. A thousand images of Ulysses S. Grant. Five hundred of old Ben Franklin. One thing about Matt Stockdale. He did know how to follow directions.

The clean, hard scent of new money filled my nostrils. I tapped a stack on the blotter. *Thwap-thwap!* Mmmm-lovely sound! Slipping on its wrapping band, I thought, Stockdale probably had the Federal Reserve deliver it by courier.

And that gave me pause. If this were the case, Matt must've spent *hours* on the phone, arranging for a special delivery.

Could he have done all that and *still* been to Grizzly Peak?

I cast a surreptitious glance at Mrs. Longworth's nephew.

He stood beside the desk, idly looking over a computer read-out. No agitation in the hands. No restless urge to move about. Definite lack of eye twitches and perspiration beads on the forehead.

I pursed my lips suddenly. For someone who had supposedly shot a man to death, Matt Stockdale was very much calm and composed.

"It's all there," I announced, sliding my chair back. A hundred thousand dollars in cash. Salvation for the Rooley ranch. He handed me the open satchel, and swiftly I shoveled it all in.

"Be sure to call Prairie Investors a week from Monday," I advised, snapping the latch shut.

"Will do." Matt reached for a notepad. "What's the number?"

I selected a telephone number dear to my heart. "Area code six-oh-five-three-three-six-one-six-two-zero."

That's the telephone number of the Empire, South Dakota's largest mall. My favorite destination in Sioux Falls!

Matt's smile dimmed. Zipping the satchel shut, I remarked, "Anything wrong?"

"Hmmm?" His eyebrows rose quickly. "No, not really. I'm just wondering. How soon do you intend to acquire the RJ Bar?"

"In a month or two. Why do you ask?"

"I think someone else is interested in the property," he replied, pacing me to the door.

Curious upward gaze. "Really? Who?"

"That bastard Hurtig."

I halted in mid-step, holding the weighty satchel like an oversize purse. *Hurtig?* Now, that was news. Concealing my surprise behind a bland expression, I asked, "Have you talked to him about the ranch?"

He shook his head. "Hurtig and I aren't on speaking terms, Jan. I'm the one who convinced Aunt Dee to withdraw her support. She thought the world of that guy." Hostile expression. "He never fooled me though. I knew he was a damned crook."

Boy, talk about the pot and the kettle! "What makes you think he's interested?"

"I've been seeing a lot of him down at the courthouse," Matt explained. "Hanging around the Registry of Deeds. I talked to Mrs. Davies, the head clerk. She says Hurtig's been poring over county maps. Topographic maps."

*Topographic* . . . the word set off an alarm bell in the back of my mind. Heart pounding in excitement, I asked, "When did this start?"

He shrugged. "September. At least that's what Mrs. Davies says."

September, I mused. Right about the time the FBI put the grab on Frank Blodgett.

"Thanks for the tip, Matt." Lugging the bag one-handed, I gave him a jaunty wave. "I think I'll look into it."

He paused at the counter, lifting his hand in farewell. "Be seeing you up in Denver!"

Briskly I strolled into the hallway. Yielded to a triumphant-Angie smile. The hefty satchel bumped my hip as I bustled along.

Don't bet your pension on *that*, Mr. Stockdale!

"Reckon that'll be $15.95, miss." Peering over his bifocals, the postal clerk studied my package. He was a gaunt, stoop-shouldered fellow on the low side of fifty. Blunt nose, pointed chin, and red-rimmed eyes that reminded me of a forlorn basset hound. "Bein' Express Mail and all—the Rooleys oughta have it by noon tomorrow."

"That'll be fine. Thanks!" I replied, opening my purse.

I'd purchased the cardboard postal carton fifteen minutes earlier. Afterward, it was straight to the ladies' room. A stall provided the necessary privacy. Sitting on a commode, I balanced the open carton on my knees, lifted each currency stack out of the satchel, and carefully tucked it into the box. Two quick sealings with masking tape, and it was all ready.

I handed the clerk a twenty. Got back $4.05 and a receipt. Tingling with excitement, I watched as he pasted my mailing label to the box and stamped the upper corner. *Success!*

Into the canvas cart tumbled my tightly packed one hundred thousand dollars. He never even gave it a second look. Tucking the empty satchel under my arm, I grinned and walked away.

Leaving the counter, I went straight to the ice-rimmed window. Snowflakes trickled down from the leaden sky. Zipping up the street, my gaze zeroed in on the Ore Bucket Building. Stockdale's dark blue Buick Century hadn't budged. His office windows still showed light.

Mild fussbudget face. He's not in any hurry to leave the office, is he?

Twenty minutes passed. The brunette secretary left the building, but Stockdale's office lights remained lit. Doubts began to multiply. Frowning, I slipped into the nearby telephone booth. Its sliding glass door offered an unimpeded view of Stockdale's window.

Putting through a quick call to directory assistance, I retrieved the number I needed. Then I sent another three quarters tumbling down the coin gullet.

Three sharp rings, and a mellow baritone came on the line. "Howdy! This here's the Buck Snort Saloon. What can we do for you?"

Good imitation of Becky's Western Slope accent. "Howdy! My name's Toni Beauchamp, and I work for Gunnison Guaranty here in C.B. Got a minute?"

"Sure, Toni. What's up?" He sounded like a very neighborly cashier.

"Matt Stockdale—he's my boss—he had dinner there at the saloon 'bout a week or so ago. He's claiming it as a business expense, and he forgot to give me his receipt. I have to list it in our general ledger." Secretarial Angie. "Could you look up the exact date in your reservation book?"

"Don't see why not. Hold on a minute, gal."

I heard a hefty book being dragged across a podium, followed by the rustle of turning pages. Then the baritone returned. "What was that name again?"

"Stockdale. Matthew Stockdale."

"Hmmm—I don't know, Toni. I don't see it listed . . . whoa! Here it is. He's listed under guests. January twenty-second. Party of twelve. The Board of Realtors made the reservation."

So he was there, I mused. My frown deepened. I should have done this *before* returning to Gunnison Guaranty!

"What time did the party arrive?" I asked.

"Ohhhh, about five-fifteen, I reckon. They came straight out from Denver."

"What time did the dinner break up?"

"Eight-thirty or so." The cashier cleared his throat. "Do you want me to send you a replacement receipt?"

Playing along, I replied, "That'd be great, thanks." I couldn't hold him much longer, so I had to make my questions count. "Uh, what's that address again?"

"That's 15921 Elk Creek Road, Pine, Colorado."

Last question, princess. "How far is that from Denver?"

"Ohhhh, 'bout thirty miles, I reckon."

I gave him Gunnison Guaranty's address, offered a sincere thank-you, and hung up the receiver. *Thirty miles!*

Looked as if I was dead wrong about Stockdale. He'd gone directly to the saloon after the realtors' meeting, arriving around five-fifteen. Even if he made some excuse and ducked out again, it would have been at least an hour's drive to Denver on those snowy mountain roads.

Meaning Matt Stockdale couldn't possibly have been behind the wheel of that blue Mazda!

Putting up my fur-trimmed hood, I hurried into the parking

lot. An inch of fresh snow covered my grandfather's Sierra. I clambered behind the wheel, slammed the door, and opened the glove compartment. Laminated paper crackled as I unfolded my county road map.

If the killer isn't Stockdale, then who is he? I wondered. Frank Blodgett? And where could he have taken Karen?

My gaze darted about the Grizzly Peak area, seeking a possible hideaway. Pop's line shack occupied a meadow on the south face. The killer's snowmobile had been heading north. The old Pieplant mine? Nope! Too far to the west.

And then I noticed the small teardrop-shaped body of water on the mountain's north face. Bandolier Lake.

Becky's voice echoed in my mind. *". . . all those times Pop brought us up to the lake."*

And Sarah questioning my grandfather. *"Charlie, did he mention a lake nearby?"*

Giving the ignition key a turn, I did some thinking. Sarah and Becky had both mentioned those weekend trips to the lake with their mother and Pop Hannan. Fussbudget frown. *Somebody else* had made mention of that, too. And I *knew* it wasn't Frank Blodgett!

Pulling away from the curb, I put my memory to work. One by one, I reviewed the interviews of the past few days. Clacking windshield wipers serenaded me as I drove down Elk Avenue.

All at once, my memory conjured up the gravelly voice of Chet Hurtig. *"Yeah, Madge knew Pop pretty well. He used to take her and the kids up to the lake."*

I did a quick turnaround in the municipal parking lot. Sent the Sierra cruising back up the avenue. Let's see if Mr. Hurtig came to work today.

My boot settled gently on the brake pedal. The Sierra slowed to a crawl. Falling snow veiled the darkened windows of Hurtig's store.

Closed again! I thought. And judging from all the snow on his porch, he hasn't been in for a couple of days.

Minutes later, I put the Sierra in an empty space in front of the C.B. Drug Store. Once inside, I made a beeline to the phone booth. A slim, black Gunnison County directory dangled on a chain. I lifted the phone book and frantically turned the pages.

Ahhhh, here we are. *Hurtig, Chester B. 4421 Butte Avenue.*

Grim expression. Let's make sure, princess.

Butte Avenue was on the north side of town, one block up from Teocalli. I found Hurtig's house a quarter-mile past the corner minimall. A cozy bungalow with dark green shutters, much the same as its neighbors.

There were some differences, however. Hurtig's front walk and driveway remained unshovelled. Newspapers and envelopes crammed his sidewalk mailbox.

Stepping down on the accelerator, I thought, So you haven't been home, either. And you left in a mighty big hurry, Chet. You didn't even put a stop to mail delivery.

Why all the haste, Mr. Hurtig?

I had a strong hunch I'd find my answer up there at Bandolier Lake.


There's a trick to hiking comfortably in snowshoes. A trick Daddy taught me when I was three years old. You build a rhythym into your stride. Lift the toe and glide forward. No need to raise your knees. Just up and thrust—up and thrust—with your hips rocking slightly from side to side. After the first hundred steps or so, you forget you have snowshoes on.

Well, most people do. Once I tried to teach that technique to my college roommate. Lisa told me it was like trying to dance in high heels after putting down several shots of tequila.

Still, Daddy's technique worked just as well on Grizzly Peak as it did at Tettegouche. Dusk found me on the north side of McNasser Pass, shuffling downslope with a loose-kneed stride. Anishinabe princess in her hooded parka, choppers, and fur-lined moccasin boots. The weight of my daypack rested comfortably on my hips. Ululating winds showered me with crystalline snow.

Pausing in the hushed spruce forest, I patted my pack, making certain my Commando knife was still in place, then loosened the ties of my *mindjikawan*. I took out my folded map. Gave it a quick scan in the fading daylight.

Ought to be hitting that jeep trail anytime now . . .

I tucked the map back inside my chopper, tied the big gauntlet's strings, and then raised my khaki woolen scarf over my nose. Right now the wind was my main enemy, carrying with it the ever-present danger of frostbite.

With the scarf serving as a makeshift ski mask, I continued my trek, moving downhill through the silent forest. The pack's straps chafed against my shoulders. Each rhythymic step kicked up a fine spray of snow.

As I shuffled along, I remembered what Pop Hannan had written in his diary.

*Talked to Madge again. Told her I want my cut. Same old story. Wait for Frank! I think she's holding out on me. And I ain't the only one!*

Pop was getting antsy, I reflected. He talked it over with somebody else. The holdup's fifth man. I know it wasn't Matt Stockdale. The question endures—who was it?

Back in September, ex-sheriff Chet Hurtig had shown a sudden and uncommon interest in topographic maps. Stockdale simply assumed he wanted to buy the RJ Bar. But what if Hurtig had been looking for *something else?*

Such as the loot from the armored car job!

And why was he looking? Because Madge Rooley had removed the money from its original stash at the Pieplant mine.

At first I'd thought Madge had tipped off the FBI. Looking back on it, though, that really didn't make much sense. If be-

trayal was her intention, then why did she hang around
Crested Butte all winter? Why didn't she take off the minute
she laid her hands on the money?

On the other hand, if it was *Hurtig* who sold out Frank, then
Madge's actions make perfect sense. As soon as she heard
about Frank's arrest, she moved the money to a new locale.
She probably feared that Hurtig might try to grab it.

I remembered what Matt Stockdale had told me at the Paradise Cafe. How the state patrol had set up roadblocks all
through the county. Obviously, they'd been trying to nail
Frank's gang. Ex-sheriff Chet Hurtig had offered his assistance. But Stockdale had it all wrong. Hurtig hadn't been
throwing his weight around. He'd been memorizing the troopers' search pattern. Later on he had used a radio of his own to
guide Jack Sunawavi safely past the roadblocks. Which is
probably why Frank Blodgett had recruited the former lawman in the first place!

Looking back, I thought of another instance that should
have tipped me off. After all, it was *Hurtig* who had sicced me
on Stockdale. He'd told me that Madge and Stockdale had
hated each other. Yet, no one else had mentioned that. Indeed,
Sarah, Becky, and Troy had told me just the opposite.

I didn't think anything of it at the time. I mean, why should
Chet Hurtig lie to a woman he'd never seen before?

A sudden chill rippled down my back. A chill that had nothing to do with the snowstorm.

*Tayaa!* What am I thinking? Of course Hurtig had seen me
before! He'd seen me on Cement Mountain the previous day
. . . *in his rifle scope.*

Up ahead, the evergreens thinned out, revealing a large
mound of snow. Taking care not to skyline myself, I took off
my snowshoes, crawled to the summit, and peered over the
rim.

Fragments of snow clouds billowed through the treetops.
Drifting snow zigzagged down a well-plowed trail. The road

angled off to the left, disappearing into a thick stand of Engelmann spruce.

Just then, the mutter of a pickup's engine reverberated
through the trees, growing louder with each passing second.
Swiftly I dug a deep notch in the snow. Then, ducking beneath
the snowy horizon, I peered through my makeshift peephole.

A black Ranger XLT came rumbling down the trail. Snow
caked its upraised front plow. Even in the rapidly fading daylight, there was no mistaking Chet Hurtig's hard-chiseled features.

I ducked down as the Ranger whizzed past. Waited till it
was out of earshot. Then, strapping on my snowshoes again, I
skittered down to the trail's hard-packed snow.

Squatting on my bearpaws, I glanced at the Ranger's tire
mark. Grim Angie smile. The tread pattern was identical to
the markings I'd seen on Cement Mountain.

No doubt about it. Hurtig had killed them both—Madge
Rooley *and* Pop Hannan. I tried my best to blot it out, but the
awful question mushroomed, anyway, twisting my heart.

What has he done with Karen?

Anxious strides carried me quickly up the road. A plume of
white smoke wafted upward from the trees. Rounding a bend,
I glimpsed four holiday cabins strung out along the shore of an
icebound mountain lake. Smoke drifted from the fieldstone
chimney of the nearest one.

My first instinct was to head straight for the cabin. To see if
Karen was still alive. Then I halted myself. Caution tri-
umphed over instinct. Hurtig was probably working alone.
But, on the odd chance that he wasn't, I decided not give any
of his accomplices a target.

Keeping to the trees, I circled the clearing. Approached the
cabin from a roundabout direction. I listened like a bobcat,
seeking a discordant sound. Low-pitched murmur of the wind.
The soft *ker-plump* of snow dropping from an evergreen
bough.

Satisfied I was alone, I moved in closer.

I found Hurtig's snowmobile parked beside the clapboard cabin. Slipping my Commando knife out of its sheath, I grabbed the distributor wire and began sawing.

Memo to soldiers—whenever you disable enemy vehicles— do not, repeat, *do not* cut the wire in just one place. They can always tape it back together. Take the time to cut out a two- or three-inch segment.

Pocketing my fragment, I flashed a mischievous smile. If you come after us now, Chester, you'll have to do it on foot.

Pausing at the steps, I removed my snowshoes. Then my left hand tickled the doorknob.

*Unlocked!* Uh-oh! Not good, Angie. If Hurtig left it un- locked, he won't be away for long. Better move fast!

I swung the door wide open. Karen Rooley glanced my way, her green eyes wide with terror. A cloth gag muffled her cry of alarm. She sat in an upright chair beside the small dining table, wrists and ankles securely lashed.

Chair legs scraped the floor as Karen fought to loosen her bonds. Coming up behind her, I slipped off the gag. "Hold still. I'll cut you loose."

"A-Angie!" Her face wan and haggard, Karen peered over her shoulder. "H-he's crazy! He shot Pop Hannan!"

"I know." Secure half-hitches bound Karen's wrists to the chair's rear. Kneeling, I put my blade to the knot.

"Shot him in the back!" Her voice teetered on the brink of hysteria. "He-he used to be the *sheriff!* I—I don't understand any of it."

"What did Pop want with you?"

"H-he saw me thumbing a ride. W-we did some talking." Licking chapped lips, she gasped. "Mr. Hannan's a good friend of Nana's. I—I—I told him I was on my way to Denver. He said maybe I ought to think things over. Told me I could stay at his shack out here. So we stopped at the Teocalli to pick up some stuff—"

Swiftly I unraveled the ropes. "He left you at the shack overnight?"

Rubbing her chafed wrists, Karen nodded. "H-he came back this morning. We had some breakfast. Then he started asking me all these questions."

"About what?"

"About Nana." Brushing the tangled hair away from her face, she added, "He showed me this book. Asked me questions about somebody named Dutch."

"Dutch Bohle?"

"That's it!" Karen's features tensed in pain as she rose from the chair. She'd been in that cramped position for hours. "Pop wanted to know if Nana had ever talked about him. Then Hurtig showed up. He had a rifle. Pop didn't look too happy to see him." She looked past me suddenly, as if seeing that nightmarish scene all over again. "He whispered something. I—I didn't quite catch it. Hurtig laughed and said, 'Wrong again, Pop. I've got it.' That's when he made a run for it. And Hurtig . . . h-he stood in the doorway and lifted that hunting rifle to his shoulder and—" Shuddering, she squeezed her eyes shut.

"Karen . . ." Keeping my voice low, I held the girl's shoulders. "Did he . . . ?"

Lowering her gaze, Karen shook her head. "He dropped little hints though." Her teeth gritted. "S-said he was saving me for later. Going to use me as bait for Mother." Anxiety added a shrill note. "W-what does he want with Mother?"

Same thing he wanted when he stole that blue Mazda back in Denver. But I didn't tell Karen that. Instead, I helped her over to the quilt-laden bed.

"Lie down for a sec. Get your circulation back," I murmured. "Then grab your jacket and any of Pop's shirts you can. We're getting out of here."

Her eyes blossomed in alarm. "But Hurtig—"

"We're going back over the pass. He won't be able to follow."

"Angie! We'll need snowshoes."

I gestured at my bearpaws. "You can wear mine."

"What about *you?*"

"Don't worry! I'll make some!"

Easier said than done, princess. Hefting my knife, I glanced around the room. Red coals glimmered in the fieldstone fireplace. Beside it stood a woodbox with a hatchet at rest on the lid. Corner kitchenette with old-fashioned cupboards. A window above the counter, flanked by short nylon curtains. Cedar table and four chairs. Beyond, a pair of straw brooms leaned against the knotty pine wall.

Start with the curtains. I ripped them from the brass rod. As they spiraled to the floor, I moved on to the brooms. Grabbed one, held it upright, and stamped with my foot. My snap kick severed it cleanly at the base. Then I did the same with its mate.

Mild Angie scowl. For a proper pair of snowshoes, you need poles at least six feet long. The broomsticks didn't exactly measure up. Well, they'd simply have to do.

Next stop—the wood box! Taking the hatchet, I carefully split each broomstick down the middle. Then, holding one stick under my left arm, I shaped the ends with the hatchet.

Having spent many a winter weekend at my grandparents' cabin at Tettegouche, I was an old hand at snowshoe construction. It's one of those skills you must have if you really intend to winter in the Northland. Building a pair as a Girl Scout won me my first merit badge.

Reaching into the wood box, I pulled out some kindling and cut them into rectangular blocks ten inches long. Raw material for the heel plate and the pivot board.

*Whonk!* I sank the ax into the lid. Off came the cap of my survival knife. Eager fingers withdrew the spool of fishing line, then unwound a length of Mylex thread. Anxiety had me breathing in shallow gasps.

Faster, Angie! Perspiration dampened my forehead as I

lashed the broomstick tips together. My thoughts began to wander. I knew why Hurtig wanted to kill Madge. But why was he so intent upon killing Sarah?

That's a question better left to the county prosecutor, I told myself. Right now you concentrate on those bindings. Can't afford to have them unravel on the trail.

Dabbing at my moist brow, I surveyed the finished framework. Grin of satisfaction. Maybe it wouldn't win any merit badges, but it was sturdy enough to carry me all the way to Montana. Then I smoothed the curtains on the floor, placed my wooden frames on top, and then cut out two oval patterns.

"How are you doing?" Karen asked.

"Getting there." I plucked a sewing needle from the hollow handle of my survival knife. Ran one end of the Mylex line through its narrow eye. "Karen, check the cupboards. See if there's any food we can carry with us."

"Sure, Angie."

Quickly I sewed the curtain cloth to the frame. Faster! I told myself. Hurtig isn't out joyriding. Not in this weather. He *has* to be on his way back by now.

Karen hurried across the room. One of Pop's mackinaw shirts covered her parka. She flashed an apologetic grimace. "Sorry, Angie, there's isn't anything on the—" She went rigid all at once, her mouth gaping in horror. "Listen!"

I did. And my stomach abruptly turned over. A harsh mechanical murmur traveled on the wind—the sound of a laboring truck engine!

# ▼▼▼▼▼ SIXTEEN ▼▼▼▼▼

The thrumming of Hurtig's engine reverberated among the cliffs. Judging from the sound, he was just under a mile away . . . and closing fast!

My quaking fingers nearly dropped the needle.

"Karen!" I yelped. "The bed!"

She blinked in confusion.

"Pull it apart!" I shouted. "Grab the sheets and the pillowcases! Hurry!"

Looking at me as if I'd lost my mind, Karen hurried to the bed. I resumed sewing, fastening the cloth to the snowshoe's frame. Gasp of desperation. One down—one to go!

The engine noise grew louder.

I kept at it, trying to ignore the rapidly approaching truck. Dip the needle. Pull the thread. Angie the lunatic seamstress.

*Tayaa!* If only I could sew like Mother Shavano! She'd be all done by now!

Suddenly, the engine noise dropped an octave. Hurtig had just shifted gears on the upgrade.

Reaching the heel plate, I cross-stitched the Mylex thread,

tied it, and clipped it with my blade. Finished! Hopping to my feet, I helped Karen yank the bottom sheet off the bed.

"Hold it open," I said, hefting my knife.

Spreading her arms, she offered a wide expanse of white percale. Puzzled glance. "What are you doing?"

I cut a slit in the sheet. "Making us some snow camouflage."

I tossed the sheet over Karen. Her blond head popped through the opening.

"Wear it like a poncho," I told her. "Cover your hat with the pillowcase, and get those snowshoes on!"

"Angie!"

"I'll be right behind you. Go!"

Hurtig's truck began a bass crescendo.

Heart pounding, I slashed an opening in the top sheet, bundled it up, grabbed my makeshift Michigan bearpaw snowshoes, and ran to the door. An icy wind stung my face as I stepped onto the porch. Whirling, I set the lock, then slammed the door.

Karen held my pack for me. I slid my parka sleeves through the strap. The mummy bag gave me a gentle spank. Genuflecting before the cabin, I hurriedly laced my snowshoes.

Looking anxiously downslope, Karen whispered, "Hurry!"

I snapped a quick glance at the road. A high-beam glare moved steadily uphill, casting spruce branches into sharp relief.

Rising, I nodded at the forest. "Let's go!"

*Chush-chush-chush!* Our snowshoes kicked up a crystalline spray. Percale rippled in the wind. Grabbing Karen's hand, I shot an anxious glance to the rear. If only Hurtig would stay away a few minutes more! Given enough distance, our snow ponchos would blend right in with the landscape.

Just then Hurtig's Ranger ground to a halt beside the cabin. Twin headlights winked out. Hearing the metal door slam, I grabbed Karen and dropped into a squat.

"Angie," she whispered. "Can he see—?"

I shushed her. Together we huddled on our snowshoes, heads bowed, oblivious to the falling snow. I heard the crunch of footsteps on the driveway, punctuated by the muted creak of a porch step.

Turning my head ever so slightly, I saw Karen's captor facing the door. A high-powered rifle nestled in Hurtig's hand. Oooooh, what a liar you are, Chester! That sure looks like a Remington M700 to me! And I'd seen enough Tasco scopes on the Gunflint Trail to recognize one even at this distance.

The doorknob rattled in his grip. Frustrated mutter. "Ahhhh—shit!" Then he began rummaging in a side pocket.

Nudging Karen, I motioned toward the trees. We had to get moving. That door would stall him only a few minutes. The minute he found Karen missing . . .

*Chush-chush-chush!* Karen and I ran for the woods. A row of tall, dark spruces offered sanctuary. No sooner had we reached the trees than I heard an explosive slam, followed by a livid cry of *"Dammit!"*

*KAAAAAROWWWWW!* A gunshot split the night, reverberating along the ridge. I flattened against the nearest tree trunk and aimed a frantic glance at the cabin. Hurtig stood on the porch, working the Remington's bolt. Then, shouldering the stock, he moved the barrel from left to right. *KAAAAA-ROWWWWW!*

Karen trembled. "He's shooting!"

"Keep still," I whispered. "He can't see us. He's just trying to flush us out." Feeble reassuring smile. "So long as we stay in the shadows, we'll be okay."

Hurtig soon realized he was just wasting ammo. His furious mutter carried all the way across the yard. "Son of a bitch!"

Taking Karen's hand, I led her deeper into the forest.

Together we marched through the swirling snow. Far above our heads, a hurricane wind raked the peak's granite ridge. Mushroom-size snowflakes pelted my exposed face. My makeshift poncho started to freeze.

Hearing my partner's heavy breathing, I murmured, "Karen, you have to pace yourself." Pointed at her knees. "Don't lift your snowshoes so high. You'll wear yourself out long before we reach the pass."

"H-he'll come after us!" she rasped.

"I don't think so," I replied, sounding a whole lot more confident than I felt. "Snow's too deep. Even if he has a flashlight, it's going to take him a while to pick up our trail. Let's concentrate on putting some distance between us and that cabin. Okay?"

Swallowing hard, she nodded.

Gritty snow blasted us from on high. Lifting my scarf to shield my face, I leaned forward, balancing the pack on my spine, choosing each step with care.

At last we reached the ridge. My chattering teeth nearly drowned out the howl of the wind. Loose snow cascaded from my hood as I turned to Karen. "H-how are you d-doing?"

"Okay," she mumbled, shivering. "My—my face is getting kind of numb."

"Let me see."

I turned Karen's chin to the left. A pallid spot glistened beneath her cheekbone—the first telltale sign of frostbite. Swiftly I unwound my own scarf, took out my knife, and sliced it in half.

"Cover your face," I said, handing her a length of ragged wool. "We've got to get out of this wind."

Hustling over to the brink, I peered over the snowy balcony. Far below, a light gleamed among the spruces, weaving and bobbing along our back trail.

"Oh, shit!" I muttered, dropping into a crouch.

Hurtig's bulky shape emerged from the trees. His flashlight cast a feeble glow on the Remington's long barrel. He paused every few steps, letting the beam sweep the snow ahead of him. Each time he moved, his snowshoes kicked up a powdery plume.

Damn! I thought, easing away from the brink. He must have had an extra pair in the truck.

I dropped one final glance downslope. Rifle butt at rest on his hip, Hurtig began his ascent.

Well, you certainly didn't waste any time, did you, Chet? I thought, rejoining my companion. You got right on our trail. And if you've been following our tracks, then you know Karen's not alone. You'll be ready for trouble.

Alarm quickened my stride. Right now Hurtig had the advantage. I could move only as fast as my inexperienced partner. Judging from his movements, Hurtig was an old hand at mountaineering. With his longer stride, he'd catch up with us in no time.

My desperate gaze scouted the terrain ahead. The trail zigzagged upslope for sixty yards, then ran along the base of some lofty, ice-laden granite cliffs. Off to our left, the land leveled out a bit, leading into a cirque brimming with stands of snow-covered spruce. There were far fewer trees to the right. Looking up, I saw the reason why. Mammoth snowdrifts perched on the ridge, overhanging the slope. Tons and tons of snowpack reared above the avalanche slide, awaiting the catalyst that would send them careening into the valley below.

Teeth clenched, I turned to the right. Storm winds gusted through the trees, pushing along curtains of pristine snow.

And that gave me an idea!

Karen read my troubled expression. "What's wrong?"

"He's right behind us—" Eyes wide, she began to bolt. Gripping her shoulders, I added, "Karen! Listen to me. We can lose him."

"How?"

"Follow me," I replied, tugging at her wrist.

Together we plunged into the teeth of the wind. Stinging snow hammered my poncho and scarf. Karen locked my hand in a death grip. The gale threatened to peel us both right off the mountainside. Onward we struggled, swaying in the relentless wind, buffeted by blasts of swirling snow.

Shielding my face with my arm, I spied a lofty spruce just ahead. Drifting snow smothered its lower limbs. Sidestepping Karen, I glanced at our back trail.

Gleeful Angie smile. Snow showers swept across the trail, obliterating our tracks. *Perfect!*

Hope sent an adrenaline surge streaming through my veins. Standing beside the spruce, Karen watched in astonishment as I loosened my bindings, knelt on my snowshoes, and frantically began scooping away snow.

"W-what are you d-doing?"

"There's a pit under here," I explained. My choppers burrowed a small tunnel into the pine-scented darkness. "Falling snow never reaches a spruce's trunk. The branches are too thick. Get in here, Karen. Feet first—hurry!"

Like the fabled Alice, she obeyed, sliding down the burrow. One by one, I tossed in my snowshoes, then followed suit. I tried very hard not to disturb the snow-laden boughs above my head. Dark green boughs would be sure to draw Hurtig's attention.

My fanny bounced on a carpet of cold evergreen needles. Slipping out of my pack straps, I used my choppers to reseal the entrance. Karen pitched in as well, grunting and gasping.

Once finished, we sat with our backs to the trunk. I took my army canteen off the pack. Gave Karen the first sip.

"Lord, that tastes good!" With a sigh of satisfaction, she handed me the canteen. "Think he'll find us?"

"Let's hope not!"

"If he find us . . ." Her voice diminished into a dreadful silence. For the first time in her young life, Karen Lynn Rooley faced the possibility of her own death, and she couldn't quite put her feelings into words.

Hushed sob "I . . . I wish I'd told her . . ."

"Who?" I challenged. "The rich city lawyer lady?"

"Shut up, Angie!"

Suppressing a smile, I hugged both knees and waited for Karen to make the next move. Funny thing—I seemed to be having better luck with the daughter.

Morose teenage sigh. "Guess I had that coming, didn't I?"

"No argument from me, dear."

"She makes me so mad sometimes! Like yesterday, you know? I was only trying to help."

"By running away from home?"

Long silence. Another sigh. "All right, I wasn't trying to help. I—I didn't like it when she snapped at me. I—I—I guess I just wanted to hurt her back, that's all."

"Believe me, you succeeded," I replied, facing her. In the darkness Karen resembled an opaque silhouette. "She was up all night, worrying about you." Pausing, I squelched the tone of anger. Lengthy sigh. "Now that the score's been evened . . . where do you go from here?"

The question seemed to frighten her. "I—I don't know."

"An apology's a good place to start," I suggested. "You know . . . 'Mother, I'm sorry.' That's what you want to tell her, isn't it?"

"More than you'll ever know, Angie."

"You'll get your chance," I promised. "Just as soon as we get off this mountain—"

I cut myself short. Somewhere beyond the branches, I heard the *chush* of tossed-up snow.

"Down!" I hissed.

Karen flattened out on the pine needles. Heart pounding, I did the same, facedown beside the snowdrift, listening in breathless anticipation.

*Chush-chush-chush.* Hurtig's heavy footfalls drew closer. He sounded as if he were heading straight for our tree.

My skin prickled. Any second I expected Hurtig's rifle barrel to poke through the snow, spitting sudden death. Paranoid thoughts bounced through my mind. Why isn't he moving?

What is he up to? Shuddering, I clenched my teeth. *Move, damn you!*

All at once I heard a wheezy exhalation, punctuated by Hurtig's frustrated whisper. "Son of a bitch!"

I held my breath, not daring to move. Hurtig was less than three feet away, just beyond my ceiling of spruce boughs. My own frantic heartbeat kept rhythm with his labored breathing.

Then the snowshoe whisper resumed, becoming softer and fainter with every step. Rising to all fours, I poked a peephole through the snow. Hurtig was a silhouette in the flashlight's feeble backglow. Beefy man-shape lumbering through the blizzard. Each step kindled a muffled grunt of fatigue.

The climb took a lot out of him, I thought, giving way to a grin. Too much time in the easy chair, Chet!

Blowing snow veiled Hurtig from view. I waited until I could no longer see the flashlight's glow, and then we cleared the snow from our tunnel.

Emerging from the tree pit, I glanced at the sky. The snowstorm was getting worse. Much worse! Karen and I had to find some shelter—and fast! We couldn't last much longer out here.

I struck off on a path perpendicular to Hurtig's, hiking straight for the lofty cliffs of the north face. Huddled in her poncho, Karen tramped along at my heels.

My mind's eye conjured up Dutch Bohle's map. Somewhere on that cliffside trail lurked the cave where he'd hidden his loot. And where there was one cave, there were bound to be others.

Snow-laden gales howled down from the scree, tearing at my poncho. Rime ice clung to my woolen face mask. Step by step I struggled upward, gasping aloud as the pitiless wind blasted us with fusillades of snow.

Trailside spruces became smaller, interspersed with stands of warped krummholz. Once I tumbled, sinking to my knees in champagne powder. With Karen's help, I boosted myself upright again, shivering at the cold. My desperate gaze traveled along the cliff's face, seeking a crack or rock chimney that might lead to a cave. Smooth and seamless stone edged upward, silently mocking us both.

Intense shivering gradually gave way to a bone-chilling numbness. Halting momentarily, I looked at Karen. She swayed on her feet like a punch-drunk fighter. I took a step in her direction and nearly toppled. We'd been out in the storm too long. Despite our clothing, the sub-zero windchill was draining away our warmth. Unless we found shelter, we'd both die of exposure.

Slumping against me, Karen mumbled, "L-let's stop a minute, o-okay? G-gotta rest . . ."

"No!" My voice was a feeble whisper. "C-can't stop, Karen. W-we'll be too w-weak to st-stand . . . keep moving . . . only way . . ."

Snowflakes frosted my eyebrows. I could feel the chill eating its way into my forehead. Getting my arm around her, I walked her along. One baby step at a time. The wind's fearful howl smothered all other sound.

Suddenly, my numbed fingers lost their grip. Karen landed in the snow with a gentle plop. Dazed, I found myself on my knees, swaying tipsily from side to side. Before me stretched a drift of unbroken snow as soft and inviting as a newly made bed.

Darkness rimmed my field of vision. The snowdrift exerted a hypnotic pull, luring me into its icy embrace. Soft, ragged sigh. Just for a minute, I thought. I'll close my eyes just for a minute . . .

Then a strange, warm breeze caressed my face. Instinctively I turned in that direction, soaking up every smidgen of heat. Small murmur of satisfaction. *Ohhhhh, heaven!*

The breeze tugged me back from the brink of oblivion, banishing the frozen torpor from my mind. Bathing in that luxurious warmth, I began wondering where it was coming from.

Slowly my eyelids lifted. A teardrop-shaped hole spoiled the cliffside's white surface. Leaning closer, I felt that steady warm breeze on my cheeks. Grimace of confusion. Don't tell me somebody has a furnace in there?

All at once, I was back in the North Cascades, listening to a lecture by the Park Service geologist.

*The temperature in a cave usually hovers at about fifty degrees Fahrenheit. In the summer you get a nice cool breeze blowing out. But if any of you kids returned to the same cave in winter, it'd feel like you're standing in front of a stove.*

Crawling forward, I tore at the snow like a demented badger. My choppers scooped away handfuls of snow, widening the hole, exposing its limestone threshold.

Seeing that cavern sent a jolt of fresh energy through my half-frozen body. Seizing Karen by the wrists, I dragged her into the cave. Once inside, I slapped the snow off her clothing. Then, unsheathing my Commando knife, I plunged back into the snowstorm.

Minutes later, I returned with a handful of spruce branches. Spruce is the best wood for a winter campfire, you know. Once it catches, it burns with a hot, sizzling, crackling intensity. And best of all, dead, dry limbs are always found on the tree's bottom tier.

I decided to go with a Lakota pit fire. Off the pack with my tri-fold shovel. Straighten the blade and turn the grips. The shovel bit hard into the floor's loose sand. *Chuff-sigh, chuff-sigh.* I excavated a pair of pail-size pits about six inches deep, and then, using my knife, I dug a small ventilation tunnel between them.

Unscrewing the Commando's compass cap, I withdrew a tiny block of cotton tinder, a waterproof match and one of those novelty birthday candles. You know, the kind that relight two seconds after you blow them out. Striking the match,

I lit the candle and stuck it in the sand. It would burn for minutes, giving me plenty of opportunities to spark a fire.

Soon the spruce sticks were ablaze. Lifting my canteen, I filled my surplus Ranger cooking pot with water. Let it sit on the flames. That's the great thing about a Lakota pit fire. The surrounding earth channels the heat upward, cooking the food in mere minutes.

In no time at all, I had the water boiling. I soaked my handkerchief and carried it over to Karen. Her skin felt like a roast from the refrigerator. Tenderly I mopped her chilled face, holding the compress in place for several seconds.

Emerald eyes fluttered open. "An-Angie?"

"Right here." Smiling, I draped the warm compress across her brow. "How do you feel?"

"C-c-cold!" She licked her chapped lips. "W-where are we?"

"In a cave," I replied, lifting the handkerchief. "Can you sit up?"

Swallowing hard, she nodded.

"Come and sit by the fire," I murmured.

Karen gave me no argument. Drenching the hankie once more, I gave myself the same treatment. Another trick I'd learned as a rangerette. Warm water is the best remedy for frostbite. Oooooooh! My forehead felt like a pinchusion. Returning circulation packed quite a sting.

As soon as I finished treating our cold injuries, I pulled out the Lipton Cup-a-Soup envelope, pinched off the corner, and poured in the chicken-vegetable mix. Angie the Wilderness Chef. I let Karen use my mess kit, content to dine out of the canteen cup.

Judging from the way Karen wolfed down that soup, Hurtig hadn't bothered to feed her. Putting her pan aside, she flashed me a questioning look. "Where did you learn all this?"

"Tettegouche." Lifting the canteen cup, I sipped my soup. "My family does a lot of winter camping."

Worried teenage eyes glanced toward the entrance. "Do you think he'll find us?"

"Not tonight." Another hasty sip. "Hurtig won't risk a case of frostbite. He'll have to withdraw." Anishinabe smile. "Now that we've found shelter, the cold is our friend. His enemy! It'll keep him away from us."

"He'll be back," she warned.

"He's welcome to look." I shrugged. "It's a big mountain." Swirled a bit of soup around the bottom of my cup. "And we're getting off it the first thing tomorrow, Karen, so you'd best get some sleep."

Seeing me stand, she asked, "Where are you going?"

"Outside. I'll be back in a minute."

Actually, it took me ten minutes to break off an armload of spruce boughs. When I returned to the cave, Karen helped me shake off the snow and dry them before the fire.

"Don't let them burn," I advised, holding the last one just above the fire pit. "You don't want to smell charred needles all night."

Karen chuckled. "I'm just glad to be here." She pointed suddenly at the cave's mouth. "Angie, look!"

Turning, I saw innumerable stars gleaming in the frigid night sky. The wind dusted the entryway with icy splinters.

"It's stopped snowing," she said, glancing at me.

Uh-oh! Not good, I thought, facing the cave's entrance. Now that the storm's passed, the outside temperature is *really* going to drop!

"So I see." Somehow I managed a confident smile. "You'd better get in that sleeping bag. It's about to get pretty chilly."

The cavern floor canted upward several inches, meeting a layer-cake limestone wall. That became our bedroom. Together we built Karen's bed. Fold our snow ponchos lengthwise. Lay them down one on top of the other. Strew the white percale with springy spruce boughs. Lay the mummy bag on top of that.

Once Karen was nicely bundled up, I went to gather some more firewood. When I got back, the sound of teenage snoring smothered the crackle of my pit fire. Fond Angie smile. Try not to make any noise, princess.

Lifting my tri-fold shovel, I set to work. *Chuff-sigh! Chuff-sigh!* I excavated a narrow trench five feet six inches long. Then I scooped out depressions for my shoulders and hips. *Ka-chunk! Ka-chunk!* The shovel's keen edge split the spruce into burnable logs. One by one, I built a series of twig tepees down the length of the trench. Each tepee ten inches apart. Then, candle in hand, I knelt beside the first one and put the tiny flame to the kindling.

Disaster—the twigs failed to catch!

*Oh, shit!* I thought. The wood's too cold—too damp. It won't ignite!

Sudden panic gnawed at my consciousness. I had visions of turning into a Popsicle before morning. The memory of our hike to the cave was still quite vivid. Fingers trembling, I stuck my candle in the sand.

Standing, I broke off another spruce limb. My fingernails peeled off a long strip of bark. Carefully I wound it around the stick's blunt end, then thrust it into my pit fire.

To start those tepee fires, I'm going to need tinder, I thought, lifting my makeshift torch aloft. Maybe I can find some farther back in the cave.

Yellow flames blossomed from the bark. Holding my torch, I moved deeper into the gloom. At some time in the past, the Awishi or the Nuche must have used this place for shelter. Perhaps they'd left something behind—a broken basket—dessicated herbs—scraps of cloth—something flammable I could use for tinder.

My gaze moved from side to side, bouncing off the limestone walls, bypassing thick stalactites, sliding over low boulders. The dipping rock ceiling repeatedly tagged my spine. Scowling, I put my head down and shuffled along like a chimpanzee. Quasimodo Angela.

Just then, something caught my instep and sent me hurtling forward. Hands outflung, I landed facedown on the stony floor. I gasped as a small rock scraped my chin. My torch lay just out of reach, blazing away brightly.

I shot a quick, angry glance at the obstruction, then let out a surprised gasp. Beneath my left foot lay four bulging leather pouches. *Saddlebags!*

I jammed my torch between two ham-sized rocks. It wobbled but remained upright, casting its flickering glow over the worn leather saddlebags. A dank scent touched my nose. Kneeling, I ran my palm over the flap. Fingertips plowed shallow paths through a thin film of cave grime.

Excitement had my pulse racing. Frantically, I undid the bristly rawhide strings, then pushed the flap open. Soft cry of amazement. The contents reflected the torch's gleam, creating a hundred sparkles of golden light.

Extracting a single coin, I held it up to the firelight. *Tayaa!* Look at it! An uncirculated ten-dollar gold piece straight from the Denver mint!

And there were over *two hundred* of them in the saddlebag!

Flipping it in my palm, I did some hasty mental arithmetic. Over two hundred coins in each saddlebag. Four saddlebags in all. Hmmmmm—no doubt about it, princess. You just tripped over Dutch Bohle's long-lost loot!

Lifting a handful of coins, I let them tinkle through my grasp. A thousand gold eagles, I thought, yielding to a burst of ironic laughter. With a little artful trading in Denver, Minneapolis, and Sioux Falls, I could turn them into three hundred and seventy-five thousand dollars.

No sooner had the thought crossed my mind than I began rummaging through Dutch's saddlebag. With any luck, Mr. Bohle might have grabbed a handful of stock certificates when they hit the Mountain Zephyr. Gold wouldn't burn, and neither would that century-old leather. But I could use the paper as tinder.

My joy was short-lived. Crestfallen, I sat back on my heels. *No paper!*

Woeful grimace. Terrific! I thought. Three hundred and seventy-five thousand dollars' worth of gold, and right now I'd gladly swap it all for a single can of charcoal lighter fluid!

Just then, I noticed a badly frayed corner on the saddlebag's bottom. My fingertip poked the leather. Frown of confusion. Teeth marks?

Grabbing my torch, I gave the pouch a closer look. Sure enough, something had been chewing it over the years.

I lay prone on the cave's floor, my chin resting on sand, carefully scrutinizing the ground around the saddlebag. I spied a flurry of tiny five-digit tracks. Blink of immediate recognition. *Field mice!*

Hands trembling, I raised the saddlebag's flap. Hope sent a burst of fresh energy through my weary muscles. Heart thumping in desperation, I pawed through the gold. *Ohhh, where is it?*

And then my straining fingers made contact with a bristly swirl of dry grass.

Chuckling in triumph, I withdrew the crumbling remains of a mouse nest. A dusty melange of yellowish-brown grasses, dry flower stalks, and windblown twigs. Dutch's saddlebag leather had kept it dry all these years. Which is why the mice had nested there in the first place.

I tossed a broad Angie smile into the darkness. *Thank you, little friends!*

Leaving the gold behind, I carried my precious tinder back to our campsite. A distinct chill nibbled at my face. It was twenty below outside. I had to get those fires going.

Shivering, I knelt beside each tepee, tucking a bit of mouse nest beneath the kindling. Then I reached for my sputtering candle. Put the flame to the grassy tinder. Success!

In no time at all I had five small fires blazing. Stick by stick, I added fresh wood, taking care not to smother the flame. While the fires crackled, I took care of a few housekeeping chores. Broke out my blankets. Dried the boughs I'd set aside for my mattress. Melted some snow to refill my canteen.

Two hours later, my fires had become mounds of glowing red-hot coals. Using my shovel, I carefully spread the coals around the bottom of the trench, then covered them with three inches of sand. My palm passed over the loosened dirt. Welcome waves of warmth massaged my fingers.

Then I built my bed. First the spruce boughs, then my camouflage rain poncho, then my army blanket. Topping it all off was my Polar Shield survival blanket. Those buried coals would radiate heat, and my Polar Shield would reflect it right back at me, keeping me snug and warm all night.

After dousing my candle, I slithered beneath my blankets and cast a smiling glance at Karen. My companion had just become a well-heeled young lady. Maybe not in the same class as Mrs. Longworth, but there was plenty of money back there. Half of it belonged to Byron Lee Rooley—his share of that long-ago train robbery. Money enough to put Karen, Luke, and Laura through college and to send Merry to veterinary school. The Rooleys would never have to sweat a mortgage again.

With those pleasant thoughts in mind, I pulled the blankets under my chin, rolled over, and went to sleep.

Dreaming, as always, of Tettegouche.

"Angie?"

Karen's hushed voice lured me out of slumber.

"Angie, are you awake?"

My eyelids winked open. Peeping over the blankets' edge, I saw limestone walls and blunt stalactites. Bright sunshine had transformed the snow at the entrance into an eye-searing incandescence. A few feet away, an olive-drab mummy lay on its side. Karen's face poked through the mummy's hood. "Hey! Are you awake yet?"

Mammoth yawn. "I am now."

"What time is it?"

Rolling onto my side, I glanced at my wristwatch. "Quarter of seven." Cavern cold stung my face, jolting me into full consciousness. "Feel like some breakfast?"

She gave me a look. "We're out of food."

"That's what you think." I tossed my blankets aside. "Get your snowshoes on."

And so, while Karen gathered more firewood, I reached for my canteen cup and did some early morning grocery shopping. Fifty yards downslope, I found a snowy balcony offering a panoramic view of the spruce forest.

Huddled in my parka, I rubbed my arms briskly and watched the snowbound woods for a while. Sure enough, a bright red cardinal swooped into the trees. Within minutes, another pair followed suit. Broad Anishinabe grin. Ah, so there's the restaurant!

When I reached the spot, half a dozen cardinals took wing, chattering at me for disturbing their breakfast. They had quite the little larder in there. I made the rounds of the bushes, picking purplish-black serviceberries and dull scarlet squashberries and freeze-dried mountain cranberries.

On my way back, I spied a cluster of dessicated yellowbell growing on a rock ledge. I snowshoed right over there, stood on tiptoe, and uprooted a handful. Attached to each stalk were four peanut-size bulbs—an Awishi delicacy. You can eat them raw, but they taste much better cooked. Sort of like puffed rice.

Returning to the cave, I dismantled my bed. Reflected heat had pretty much dried out the spruce boughs. I plucked a handful of needles and dropped them in our now-cold firepit. Then, taking my shovel, I dug up a corner of my sleep trench. A cool breeze gusted across the coals, turning them as red as rubies. Gingerly I slid them into the firepit. Spruce needles burst into flame.

While Karen tended the fire, I molded the berries into twin cakes, added a sprinkling of canteen water, and slapped them down on the fry pan. Then I washed the bulbs in my canteen cup and added them to the meal.

Following a piping-hot breakfast of berrycake and yellow-bell bulbs, we broke camp. Karen shook out our white snow ponchos. Unsheathing my knife, I began whittling a rectangle of spruce bark.

Karen's brow tensed in curiosity. "What's that?"

"Snow goggles," I replied, carving a narrow slit in each eye-piece. "We're both going to need them. We've got a long hike ahead of us, and we can't afford to go snow-blind." I put it across the bridge of my nose. "How do I look?"

Adolescent giggle. "Like Robin the Boy Wonder."

"Thanks a lot!"

As soon as I finished Karen's domino mask, we made ready to leave. With my trusty tri-fold shovel, I refilled my sleeping trench, burying those live coals beneath inches of sand. After that, I dumped a few scoops of snow into the firepit, folded my shovel down to pouch size, rolled up the mummy bag, and re-packed my kit. On with the ponchos and makeshift snow goggles. And then the Mountain Avengers were on their way.

Chill winds buffeted us as we descended the steep trail. A single horsetail cloud scudded across the broad vault of ceru-lean sky. Morning sunshine gleamed on newly fallen snow.

As we reached the timberline, Karen lowered her scarf. "Which way, Angie?"

"Not that way." I gestured at the main trail.

"That'll take us straight back to the lake. If Hurtig spent last night at the cabin, he'll be on his way back up here."

Anxious look. "Could be he gave up."

Tugging at my choppers, I shook my head. "I don't think so. You saw him shoot Pop Hannan. He has to assume you've been talking to me." Sigh of resignation. "He can't let us leave this mountain alive."

"What do you have in mind?"

"Let's go straight down the south face," I said, tilting my head. "One of those gulches will take us down to Pieplant Creek. With any luck, we might run into Chief or Troy."

"Angie . . ." She bit the corner of her lower lip. "If I remember right, there's a cabin about two miles down from the pass. Nana took me there one time."

Hopeful glance. "With a telephone?"

"I-I'm not sure." She shrugged. "I don't rightly remember. It was ten years ago."

"Let's risk it."

Karen took the lead. Once we reached McNasser Pass, the journey was all downhill. Shifting the pack on my shoulders, I cast a nervous glance at the summit. Last night's storm had doubled the height of Grizzly Peak's snowy crest. The ridge resembled a breaking wave transformed into snow.

Ohhhhhh, not good, Angie! The sunshine's starting to melt the snow. If the temperature goes up after midday, there's danger of an avalanche!

Behind my grim expression, I did some hasty calculating. Let's see now . . . a mile to the cabin, then another mile or two to the creek. We descend each mile in, say, forty minutes. Okay, that's two hours' hiking time to get off this slope . . .

I sneaked a glance at my watch. Nine-twenty. Hushed exhalation of relief. By noontime, we should be well down Pieplant Creek . . . out of the danger zone!

Just then, Karen glanced back at me. "Angie, can I ask you a question?"

"Go ahead."

"Why'd you get mixed up in all this?"

I smiled. "You were in trouble, remember?"

Her mittened hand made a gesture of correction. "No! I mean, how'd you find out about Nana?"

So I told her, explaining how I'd chatted with Madge on the telephone, how Hurtig had mistaken me for Sarah that day in Denver, how I'd learned about the armored car robbery. I covered everything—right up to my confrontation with Sarah at the ranch. And that's when Karen interrupted.

"I don't understand. She had you dead to rights, Angie. Why didn't she turn you in?"

"Because you were in trouble," I said, following in her bear-paw prints. "You know what she told me, Karen? She said she'd probably be disbarred for doing this, but she wanted you back. Wanted you back more than anything in this world."

Incredulous tone. "My *mother* said that?"

"Newsflash, Karen! There's a lot about your mother that you don't know."

Snort of disbelief. "I know a lot more about Mother than you do, Angie."

Well, I could think of one thing Sarah wouldn't have told her offspring. "Did you know Mrs. Longworth had your mother booted out of school?"

"*What?*"

And so, as we headed down the mountain, I talked a bit about Sarah's early life. I tried to give Karen a feeling for what her mother had gone through, painting a vivid picture of the little girl who'd been shunted off to live with relatives.

I think I was a little bit successful. When Karen spoke again, her tone was quiet, pensive. "Guess she and Aunt Becky never did have much have a home."

"Not with your grandmother in and out of jail."

"Yeah." Karen uttered a weary sigh. "Reckon I know how she felt." Quick look at me. "I had to put up with Nana, too, you know."

"Maybe you and your mother have something in common, eh?"

She looked at me suddenly, her lips set in a thoughtful frown. She had much to think about.

The trail led through an evergreen forest, zigzagging its way downslope into a vast cirque. The alpine basin reminded me of a classic Greek amphitheater, with spruce and lodgepole taking the place of spectators. By my guess, the meadow at the bottom was a hundred yards wide. Through the middle spattered a fast-running creek, capped by windowpane ice.

Farther on stood a pair of weatherworn buildings—a deserted one-story ranch bungalow and a gambrel-roofed barn dating from the heyday of the Wild Bunch.

My spirits lifted instantly. Nailed to the bungalow's side was a crude telephone pole. A heavy-duty cable darted away from the house, streaming down the meadow toward Crested Butte.

Grinning, Karen made a flourish. "What did I tell you?"

"The taxicab ride is on me," I replied, quickening my stride. "Let's go."

Hurriedly we snowshoed across the meadow. Girlish giggles of relief and excitement. All I wanted was to reach that phone and call the state patrol. I could always cook up a good story while waiting for them to arrive.

All at once, I heard the groaning squeak of barn door hinges. Gust of wind, I thought. And then an unnerving bass voice carried across the yard.

"What's the rush, kiddies?"

Halting instantly, I snapped a glance to my left. Frank Blodgett's broad physique filled the doorway. Wrapped within his hand was a .40-caliber Browning pistol. In Frank's big mitt, it looked like a toy.

My hand flashed upward, reaching for my Commando knife.

The gun muzzle swiveled my way. "Unh-unh-unh! None of that, dolly!" Taking a step forward, he waggled the Browning's barrel. "Put your hands by your side. Away from the pack. Do it!"

I obeyed. Stepping forward, Frank took my knife away.

"What else you got?"

"Nothing!" Frustration clotted my voice. We'd come so close! So close to successfully escaping. And now they had us!

He tapped the rubberized pouch of my tri-fold shovel. "What you got in here?"

Blinking away frightened tears, I snapped, "Shovel!"

Rumble of low-pitched laughter. "Well, wasn't that thoughtful of you." Frank's merciless grin showed the stumps of yellow teeth. "Now I won't have any trouble at all *digging your grave!*"

# SEVENTEEN

"This is as far as you're goin', sweetie." Frank's gun made another jabbing motion. "Hands up—now!"

Heartbeat racing, I did as I was told. And did some frantic thinking, too. Key question—was Frank Blodgett there at Hurtig's request? If yes, Karen and I were sunk. But if Frank had merely stumbled across us—if he had no idea Hurtig was out there—we just might have a chance.

Hard swallow. "I'm a little surprised to see you here, Blodgett."

He chuckled. "Not half as surprised as me, gal. I was expecting somebody else."

I took a guess. "Your buddy Hurtig?"

The pistol muzzle lifted menacingly. "Maybe you'd better explain yourself, eh?"

"Beg pardon?"

"How did you know *that?*" he snapped.

Very much alarmed, I watched Frank's knuckles turn white. How could I tell him it was just a lucky guess?

Karen shouted, "Frank, no!"

"Stay outta this, kid."

"No!" She put herself between me and Blodgett. "You mustn't hurt Angie. She saved me!"

Echo of disbelief. *"Saved* you?"

Karen nodded briskly. "I was at Pop Hannan's when he got shot. Hurtig shot him. I saw it! He took me away with him— took me up to the lake. Angie helped me escape!"

Frank let out a pensive grunt. A strange look of comprehension crossed his blunt face.

"Wait a minute! Wait a minute!" I said, facing Karen. "You *know* him?"

"Sure!" she replied. "He's an old friend of Nana's. He came to see us in C.B. three years back."

Rich bass chuckle. Frank seemed to be enjoying a private joke. "Looks like Chet Hurtig got the story wrong, don't it?"

"What did he tell you?" I asked.

"That *you* shot Hannan."

Flashing a tart smile, I replied, "By all means, let's have the gory details. When did you talk to him?"

"Late last night," Frank replied. "I was at a bar in Gunnison. Happened to glance at the TV. Saw all'a them deputies cartin' Pop out of the woods. So I went out to my car and switched on the scanner. I heard the county dispatcher takin' my name in vain. Somebody rolled me over." The muzzle selected a target point just above my collarbone. "Was that you?"

Probably Sarah, I thought. She must've contacted Sheriff Quinn when we failed to return. *Tayaa!* You'll be the death of me yet, Slinky-dink!

"Wasn't me!" Innocuous Angela. "I've been on the trail since yesterday afternoon."

"Yeah!" Karen stood at my side. "We spent last night in a cave."

Hardcase scowl. "She tell you to say that, Karen?"

I let out an exasperated sigh. "Frank, you just saw us come

down the mountain. Could we have hiked all the way up and down Grizzly Peak in just a couple of hours?"

Credence flickered in his hard brown eyes. Now that we had some rapport, I worked up enough nerve to ask another question. "How did you get in touch with Hurtig?"

"Car phone. He's got one in the Ranger."

"Is that how you two coordinated the getaway?"

Feral masculine grin. "You know an awful lot about that robbery, Angie."

"I know Hurtig ran interference for you with the state patrol."

"That could be a dangerous thing to know, dolly!"

My shivering had absolutely nothing to do with the cold. I couldn't stop staring at the Browning's large muzzle.

"Will you put that down?" I willed my knees to stop shaking. "I'm not a cop. I don't care who knocked over that armored car." Hapless gesture. "I'm in enough deep shit as it is. I can't afford to turn you in. If I do, I'll be putting myself behind bars."

Deep thought put a noticeable curl in Frank's lower lip. "Y'know, I've been wonderin' about you. About your stake in all this. Maybe you'd better tell me."

"I didn't lie to you at the Dry Gulch, Frank. Madge was murdered."

"You sound pretty sure of yourself."

"I am. Hurtig sabotaged the truck's master cylinder."

Understanding softened his grim expression. "So that's what you were doing at the gas station."

My heart began to slow its staccato beat. "Hurtig double-crossed you all, Frank. I think that was his intention all along. As soon as he heard about Jack Sunawavi, he ratted you out to the Bureau. My guess is, he was going to grab the money, then sell out Madge and Pop, too."

Nod of agreement. "But Madge grabbed it first."

"Right! She knew one of them had to have sold you out, but

she wasn't quite sure which one. So she moved the money and used it as leverage to hold them both at bay."

His voice held a trace of pride. "I knew I could count on her."

"Question, Frank. Who recruited Hurtig—you or Madge?"

"Madge." Genuine sorrow filled his rugged face. "She said we oughta plant a man on the inside. Find out exactly where the state patrol'd be settin' up them roadblocks. Told me she knew this bent badge in C.B. He'd just been kicked out, and he was pretty sore about it. I figured we could keep him in line. Ex-cop ain't likely to sell you out. You know what happens to them shits on the inside."

"You figured wrong, Frank."

"Tell me about it." Rueful grunt. "I thought it was Pop. Man, that old fucker had the worst case of the shakes I ever saw. He was no help unloadin' the cash." Features tightening in puzzlement, he glanced at Karen. "Why did Hurtig put the grab on you?"

Slender shoulders lifted. "I—I'm not sure. He said something about 'payback time.'" Without thinking, Karen rubbed her sleeves, as if wiping away the ugly memories. "He said he wanted us both—me and Mother!"

Frank went rigid, his craggy face flooding with rage. He snap-fired a furious glance at the mountain. "That son of a bitch!"

His reaction intrigued me. Why should Frank be so upset? But there was no time for idle questions.

"What time did Hurtig say he was stopping by?" I asked.

"Two o'clock this afternoon," Frank replied, his tone terse with anger. "I figured to get here first. Y'know, have a look around."

"Good thing you did." I jabbed my thumb at the snow-clad ridge. "Listen, Frank, we lost him up there last night. My guess is, he's been hunting us all morning."

"Wrappin' up all the loose ends, eh?" Frank scowled. "Has he got the money?"

Karen nodded. "That's what he told Mr. Hannan."

Frank's chin rose. The expression in his eyes changed, shifting from residual anger to a merciless graveyard glance. "Makes sense. Once he had the money, he could go after Madge." Sepulchral tone. "Reckon it's high time me and Chet had a little talk."

"There's no need for that," I said, gesturing at the barn. "You could hide in the barn—get the drop on him . . ."

Frank's baleful glare swiveled my way.

Skittish Angie smile. "Well . . . it was an idea."

His left hand fished a key ring out of his coat pocket. Tossing it to me, he muttered, "I'm parked just down the gulch. Take Karen and get the hell out of here."

Keys jingled as I made the catch. "You could come with us."

"No way, dolly. I got business to attend to—"

Suddenly, he lunged backward, both knees rising high, as if he'd slipped on a patch of ice. Coat fabric exploded in a spray of wet crimson. Arms twirling haplessly, he tumbled into the snow.

*KAAAAAROWWWWW!* The rifle's roar came rolling down the meadow. The sound seemed to go on and on, reverberating among the mountain's snow-massed ridges. It shattered my horrified reverie, diverting my attention away from Frank's falling body and focusing it upon my own personal survival.

My reaction time would have put a jackrabbit to shame. Before the roar had even dimmed, I spun to my left and hurled myself at an equally stunned Karen. Flawless NFL tackle. Down we went!

Just in time, too. An invisible missile punctured the airspace we had most recently occupied, letting out a faint supersonic shriek. The bullet spanged off the barn's rusty drainpipe.

*KAAAAAROWWWWW!*

I visualized Hurtig sliding the bolt. We had maybe two or three seconds before he lined up the crosshairs again. Rising to my knees, I shouted, "Karen—the barn—*run!*"

Tottering upright, she made a break for it. Her snowshoes kicked up a miniature blizzard as she lunged toward the open door.

I started the count. *One thousand—two thousand—* Every fiber of my body urged me to flee, but I kept still, flattening in the snow, making myself as small a target as possible.

Uttering a terrified scream, Karen plunged headfirst through the doorway. A bullet splintered the wooden cross-piece. *KAAAAAROWWWWW!*

Go, Angie! I jumped up and ran. Head down, shoulders hunched, and snowshoes skimming the crust of the snow. Up-down . . . up-down . . . I was moving like a speed skater, leaning forward, swinging both arms in short, tight arcs. An icy spot took shape right between my shoulder blades. I could feel Hurtig's crosshairs coming to rest on my spine.

At that second I was moving faster than I ever had in my life. Yet, I felt as if I were drifting along in slow motion. The doorway lay tantalizingly beyond my reach. The fateful count ticked away in the back of my mind. The two seconds Chet Hurtig needed to squeeze the rifle's trigger.

*One thousand—two thousand—*

You're not going to make it, princess!

"Oh, shit!" I threw myself headlong, sailing over the threshold. Something tugged twice at my fluttering white poncho, and I felt a sizzling breeze on my right buttock. Friction heat from the bullet's passage. The Remington provided an in-flight serenade. *KAAAAAROWWWWW!*

Hard landing! Facedown, I skidded across the barn's dusty wooden floor. My shoulder careened off an antique milk can. Karen's horrified voice rang out. "Frank!"

Rolling onto my back, I glanced through the doorway. Soft

yelp of amazement. Frank Blodgett was clawing his way through the snow, features contorted in agony. Crimson stained his wake. The Browning pistol stayed clutched in his white-knuckled grip.

A snowflake geyser erupted in the snow at his side. *KAAAAAROWWWWW!* It wouldn't take Hurtig long to adjust to a prone target. Kicking off my snowshoes, I sprinted to the doorway, grabbed Frank's wrists, and pulled him over the threshold.

Karen took hold of his left arm. Together we dragged him away from the door. Set him upright against a cobwebbed bench.

Frank's face was the color of stale dough. Beneath his chin, neck muscles stood out like telephone cables. Each breath was a ragged gurgle, moist and drawn out. Falling back on my rangerette training, I yanked open his ski parka and hastily unbuttoned his shirt.

A suppurating bullet crater sundered Frank's chest just above the left nipple. Torn flesh rimmed it like a hideous rosette. I felt dizzy—faint. A fountain of nausea tickled my throat.

Hard to believe he was still alive. Frank had taken a direct hit from a 140-grain bullet traveling at 2,560 feet per second. Enough force to kill a full-grown caribou! Air leaking from the lung created tiny blood bubbles in the wound.

With Karen's help, I put him on his back. My shaking hands fumbled for my pocket first aid kit. The bullet had collapsed Frank's lung. I had to get some gauze on that wound before he began drowning in his own blood.

"Frank . . ." I murmured, opening the dressing's adhesive strips. "I'm going to need your help to do this. I want you to breathe out—all the way—then hold your breath. Ready?"

He nodded feebly.

The exhalation sounded like a death rattle. I planted the

gauze pad squarely on the wound, then taped the edges to his chest. "Try to lie still."

"Hey!" Chet Hurtig's hearty voice reverberated across the meadow. "Hey, Karen! Come on out!"

Hugging her knees, Karen sat with her back to the wood-box. Questioning eyes sought mine. *What do we do now, Angie?*

"Come on, Karen." Impatience flavored the baritone. "How long are you gonna sit in there, eh? There's no way out, and you know it. Who's gonna protect you—*Frank?*" Bark of laughter. "He won't last the hour, kid. And I know I hit that Indian broad."

"Yeah?" I hollered. "Better get your scope fixed, asshole!"

*"Heather!"* Harsh laughter traversed the clearing. "Still kickin', eh?" Snarling shout. "Not for damned long, bitch!"

*Heather?* I thought, grimacing. Head down, I crept toward the door. Ooops, I forgot! Hurtig knows me as *Heather Nahni,* would-be author.

Sidling up behind the doorjamb, I stuck my forefinger through the bullet hole in my poncho. Brisk overall Angie shiver.

"Hey, Hurtig!" I yelled.

"Yeah, gal?"

Distance softened his shout. He sounded about a hundred yards away. I peered beyond the doorjamb, scanning the wintry panorama of towering ridges and spruce-covered slopes and blowing snowdrifts. Anxiety lines creased my forehead. *Where is he?*

"You told me you didn't place orders for 6.5-millimeter Swedish."

Deep baritone laughter. "I don't! I load my own. It's my favorite round."

I winced. *Should've thought of that, Angie!* No doubt there's a fully equipped gunsmith shop in the rear of Hurtig's store. A man skilled in firearms would have had no trouble customizing his Remington M700 to fire that round.

Keep him talking! "Is that your favorite gun, too?"

"Bet your ass, sweetie. In the Army, we called it the M40. I won a marksman's medal with one of these." Tone of nostalgic pleasure. "That got me my first job as a cop. SWAT sniper in Phoenix. Too much shit going down in the big city, though. I preferred the quiet life."

"More opportunities to dip your hand in the till," I needled.

His tone soured. "How'd you hear about that, Heather?"

"Matt Stockdale."

"That sleazy little pissant!" The venom in his voice startled me. "I'd still be the sheriff if he hadn't turned his aunt against me! Him and all them crooked bastards on the county board! I gave thirty years to this fuckin' county! And what do I got to show for it, eh? *Nothing!*"

"What did they do, Hurtig? Lift your pension when you resigned?"

"Right on the nose, gal!"

The snow glare made my eyes itch. I scanned the first line of trees, alert for any sudden movement. "So when Madge asked your help, you were delighted to volunteer."

I noticed an odd lascivious lilt to his laughter. "Madge always did have a mighty persuasive way about her."

Behind me, Frank let out a sudden furious snarl.

Shading my eyes, I kept up the search. "So tell me, Hurtig, when did you decide to sell them out?"

"Funny thing, Heather. The thought never crossed my mind. At least, not at first." Jovial chuckle. "Seemed like a pretty good deal. Twenty grand for sippin' coffee with the troopers on stakeout. Then Jack Sunawavi got hisself killed, and all at once I had me a bigger share."

"That's when you decided to grab it all," I shouted.

"Thieves are always fallin' out, Heather. Didn't you know that?" Knowledgeable chuckle. "Some punk gets cheated on the split, and he rats out his buddies to the law. You wouldn't believe how many times I've seen that happen."

Ahhhh, now the light dawns! "So that's why you sold Frank to the Bureau."

"Couldn't take the chance of him 'n' Madge leaving with their share." Hurtig's voice seemed to be coming from the line of snowdrifts beyond the cabin. "I knew Frank wouldn't be sent up for long. He'd be back in a few months. Real pissed off, too! I figured to kill all three of 'em. Make it look like they'd been arguing about the split. The state patrol would've bought it."

"Don't be too sure of that, Hurtig."

"Oh, they'd have been convinced. Madge pulled the same job some years back. As for Frank . . . well, why don't you ask your new asshole buddy to recite his rap sheet?"

Mention of Madge tickled my curiosity. "What about the Rooleys? Why drag them into it?"

"I couldn't be sure how much Madge had told her kin." Shouting hoarsened his voice. "I've been keepin' tabs on that bunch. I noticed Madge'd been makin' a lot of calls to Sally. Knew I had to do somethin' about that."

"So you sabotaged her brakes." I knew the answer to the next question, but asked anyway. "Did you trail her to Denver?"

"Damned right, gal. I saw Madge losin' it up on Monarch Pass. So I slid by on the right and gave her a nudge toward the edge. One problem disposed of!" Sudden angry snarl. "Must've used up all my luck at the pass, though. I tried to get Sally in Denver. Tried to run her down in front of her hotel. Damn, she's a quick one! Never seen a woman move that fast!"

I didn't bother to tell him it was me. "You killed Madge *first*, Chester. Why?"

Wrathful bellow. "She owed me!"

"That's what you said before."

Just then I spotted a bright glimmer in the snow. A gleam identical to the one I'd seen on Cement Mountain days before. Sunshine flashing on Hurtig's rifle. *Bingo!*

"You think I risked hard time in Canon City for a lousy twenty grand!" he bellowed. "She promised to make it worth my while. But when it came time to collect, she backed down. She told me to leave her alone. She threatened to tell Frank! Two-bit, lyin', connivin' bitch!"

Suddenly I understood Hurtig's dig about Madge's *persuasive* ways. I realized, too, just how she had recruited him into the robbery team.

Hurtig was still ranting. "I might've known! She played me for a sap. Just like *Marlene!* Battin' her eyelashes, then walkin' out the first chance she gets." He seemed to be confusing Madge with his ex-wife. "Nobody does that to me! Do you hear? Nobody!" All at once he made an odd sound, a kind of whining laugh. "Madge was always like that, you know. Even when she was Karen's age. I'd slap on the handcuffs, and she'd give me that look. Toss that long blond hair o' hers and glance over her shoulder. 'Here it is, Chester. Are you man enough?' She had no idea how many times I wanted to—" Sudden sob. "Couldn't she see how I felt about her? We could've gone away—just the two of us. I—I told her how it would be, b-but she said no. She wouldn't leave Frank." High-pitched tone of despair. "She shouldn't have done it! She shouldn't have *double-crossed me!*"

Crouched behind the doorjamb, I wondered if Sarah's mother had ever realized what she'd started. To the teenage Madge, it had been little more than a game—a testing of her feminine charms on the older married man. Perhaps she'd been attracted to Hurtig because he seemed so "dangerous."

Of course, Madge had no idea of how dangerous Hurtig truly was.

"How long are you folks gonna squat in there?"

Hurtig's query caught me off guard, but only for a moment.

"Just till you go away, Chester."

"Y'know, I just might join you."

"I wouldn't advise it. Frank still has the pistol."

"That son of a bitch won't live till nightfall. You know that." Teasing laughter. "How good a shot are you, gal?"

"Fifteen bullets in the magazine, Chester. I'm bound to improve with practice."

"That's assumin' you can see your target."

"What are you trying to tell me, guy?"

"I came prepared this time, Heather." Triumph added a ringing note to his voice. "Got me a Litton night scope. It'll be dark in another few hours. First time one o' you sticks their head above the windowsill . . . *blammo!* It's all over."

No idle threat, that. Two hundred yards out, Hurtig was well beyond pistol range. He could sit out there all night long, tossing 6.5-millimeter bullets our way. Even worse, he could change his position after dark, move in closer, and try for a better shot.

"Your choice, Heather. You can end it now . . . or you can end up a Popsicle. What'll it be?"

"You're hilarious, Chester."

"How come you ain't laughin'?"

Puckish grin. "Because I can't see your face!"

The varnished wood above my head exploded. *KAAAAA-ROWWWWW!* Splinters dusted my parka as I took cover beside Karen. Three more shots rang out. A bullet slammed into an antique horse collar mounted on the clapboard wall.

I slammed the barn door. Bullets thunked into the aged wood. Trembling, I glanced at Karen. "Touchy, isn't he?"

"Angie, what are we going to do?"

The fusillade continued. Wagging my fingers, I motioned for her to follow. "Come on! Let's get you out of here."

Dim daylight revealed an array of rusting farm tools. Beside the bullet-marked horse collar dangled an old-fashioned steel rake. Taking it off the wall, I whispered, "While he's busy working out his frustrations, let's open another door." I jammed the steel prongs between a pair of clapboards. "When you leave, Karen, head in *this* direction." I made a chopping motion with my right hand. "That'll keep you out of his line of sight."

"What about you, Angie?"

"Don't worry! I'll be along shortly."

"Angie!"

"Go on," I urged, gripping the rake's wooden handle. "I have to stick around. If Hurtig doesn't hear my voice, he'll know we're up to something. Head straight for the woods. With any luck, he won't even know you're gone."

Emerald eyes misted with concern. "But what about you and Frank?"

Uttering a rasping cough, Frank boosted himself into a sitting position. The pistol gleamed in his grasp. "Do as she says, Karen. I—I'll w-watch out for her."

Wood groaned as the prongs bit deeply. Breathless with apprehension, Karen grabbed the long handle, as well. I motioned for her to wait. Didn't want him to hear us pulling nails. *KAAAAAROWWWWW! KAAAAAROWWWWW!* Hurtig began firing again. High-caliber gunfire reverberated along the ridges. For a moment I thought I heard another sound—a distant ominous rumble, like thunder on the horizon.

Fussbudget face. What was *that?*

Karen left me no time to wonder. Nodding at me, she whispered, "On the count of three, okay? One—two—"

*Screeeeeunch!* Hand-cast nails tore out of the wood. The tall clapboard bounced free. Karen tightened the lashings on her snowshoes. My hands caught the wobbly board and worked it back and forth. Within seconds, I had an opening large enough.

Karen gave me a fleeting hug, then lowered her head and slipped through our makeshift escape hatch.

The sound of gunfire faded. Turning to Frank, I asked, "How are you doing?"

"Jesus! Chest feels like it's fillin' up." Grimace of agony. "Can't seem to c-catch my b-breath—"

Kneeling, I put out my hand. "Give me the gun."

"Fuck it! I c-can hold up m-my end."

"Frank!"

He aimed the muzzle at me. "Unh-unh! No arguments." Brown eyes began to glaze. "Don't bother with that asshole out front. I'll take care of him." He nodded at the rear wall. "Go on, Angie. Get outta here."

"You don't have to do this, Frank," I said, my tone non-threatening. "Karen will bring help. All we have to do is hold him off. There's been enough killing already."

"H-he's right, y'know." The pistol wavered in his grip. "I ain't gonna make it."

I lifted my palm. "Listen to yourself, Frank. You sound delirious. You'd better give me the gun."

"No fuckin' way! I ain't lettin' you p-pull some wild-ass stunt." Despite the pain, he managed a grin. "You con me only *once*, dolly. Get the hell outta here."

"Frank—"

He cut me off. "One other thing . . . you g-gotta p-promise me. S-Sally . . . you tell Sally how I—I cashed in." I opened my mouth to agree, and he flashed me a stern look. "J-just Sally, you understand?"

At first the request puzzled me. Then I remembered Frank's still-unexplained phone call to Sarah's hotel room. The tenderness with which he'd carried her out of the Dry Gulch.

Our eyes met. Shrugging, Frank showed me a brittle smile. "So you've figured it out."

"Sarah's your *daughter*," I said, rising to my feet.

Stiff nod. "Like that asshole says . . . Madge always was kind of hard to resist."

A spasm doubled him over, turning his mirth into a pain-racked gurgle. I rushed forward to help him. The pistol zeroed in on my face. "Unh-unh-unh! We're playin' this *my* way, dolly." He tilted his head toward the back wall. "G'wan! Get outta here!"

"If you insist—"

The snow glare dazzled me as I emerged from the barn. I slid down my homemade snow visor. Instant eye relief. Peering through the twin slits, I saw Karen sixty yards ahead of me, tramping through the snow. Beyond lay the cirque slope and its evergreen rim.

Just then I noticed the hip-high snowdrift just beyond the barn. Mountain winds traversing the meadow had scoured the snow away from the foundation, leaving a narrow trench between the drift and the building. And that gave me an idea.

From Hurtig's viewpoint, I told myself, it'll look as if the snow comes right up to the building.

A satisfying scenario played itself out in my mind. Angie scurries down the windswept trench, huddles against the snowdrift, listens for the sound of Hurtig's snowshoes. As he passes my position, I pop up and . . . *gotcha!*

I was certain it would work. Wary of Frank's gun, Hurtig's full attention would be focused on the barn. I'd sneak up behind him and grab his rifle. Nobody would be hurt.

Bending at the waist, I shuffled down the trench. Blowing snow dusted my white poncho. Reaching the corner, I shot a quick glance over the rim. Postcard imagery. Weather-beaten rural cabin surrounded by pristine snow, with a cloudless blue sky overhead. Fifty yards beyond, the terrain sloped upward, easing into the evergreen forest. High above the trees loomed that curling ridge of snow.

Heart in my mouth, I squatted beside the drift. Cold tickled my entire left side. Ohhhhh, Angie, this had better work!

Alert as a bobcat, I let my sense of hearing fan out into the meadow, seeking a snowshoe's whisper. Minutes passed.

The only sound was the triphammer beating of my heart. Then, all at once a rifle shot rang out. *KAAAAA-ROWWWWW!*

Flinching, I let out a startled gasp. *KAAAAA-ROWWWWW!* Mild frown. He's still shooting?

As the gunfire died away, I heard that odd sound again. That freight-train rumble dancing along the ridge. It sounded a little bit louder this time.

*KAAAAAROWWWWW!* The gunshot slapped my ears. My frown deepened. Waaaait a minute, princess! That shot was definitely louder than the other two. And that's impossible! Unless, of course, he's moving in . . .

Slowly I raised my head. The view above the snowdrift sent a cascade of ice water shooting through my veins. Chet Hurtig was on the march. Beefy ex-lawman in his parka and watch cap and snow goggles, working the rifle's bolt. *Click-chock!* He closed in rapidly, his head low, stern gaze fixed on the barn, the Remington rifle at his hip, ready to fire.

Desperate Angie gasp. Hurtig had no intention of waiting till dark. He'd circled the cabin, approaching the barn from an oblique angle. His strategy was simple, workable, and deadly. Random shots to keep Angie and friends pinned down. Then close in, kick open the door, and kill everyone inside.

Coming from that direction, he'd reach the barn in less than three minutes. And if he looked straight ahead, the first thing he'd see would be the anxious Anishinabe princess hunkered down beside the snowdrift.

Swiftly I ran through my list of options.

*Warn Frank?* Forget it! He's in no shape to come to my rescue.

*Make a break for the door?* Unh-unh! If Frank's still conscious, he'll be shooting at anything that moves.

*Duck behind the barn?* Biting my lower lip, I considered it. How far to the corner? Ten feet? Eight, at least. Could I make it safely to cover? Hushed sigh. Probably not. Hurtig would fire at the first sudden motion. At this range he couldn't possibly miss.

Even if he *did* miss, he'd realize that Angie was now outside the barn, and he'd come hunting me.

I had no desire to play ring-around-the-barn with a one-time SWAT sniper!

That left me with only one other option. Plus one factor in my favor! Hurtig thought I was still *inside* the barn!

Thrusting both hands into the drift, I withdrew a half-pound of fluffy snow. As I shuffled along, my chopper-clad hands molded the snow into a loosely packed ball. I glided past the door, careful to make no sound. Didn't want to draw Frank's fire.

I kept my gaze fixed on the snowdrift's rim. My heart thundered as I waited for Hurtig to move into view. My right arm reached backward, cocked and ready.

Just then the peak of Hurtig's watch cap intruded into the blue sky. His follow-up stride offered a full view of his head and shoulders. Another step, and his upper torso came into view. Sunshine gleamed on his snow goggles.

Suddenly, he halted. His grim face swiveled my way, the mouth spilling open in shock. The rifle began to swing.

I let him have it—an overhand fastball right in the face. The snowball exploded upon impact, caking both goggles in white. His trigger finger flexed instinctively. *KAAAAA-ROWWWWW!*

By then I was already in motion, diving headfirst into the snow. Knocked off balance by the recoil, Hurtig stumbled. Without thinking, he swept his gloved hand across his goggles, trying to clear them, but that only made it worse.

"Aaaargh! Goddamn Indian!"

As he rose to all fours, I saw Hurtig groping blindly for the Remington's bolt and realized he was trying to reload. *Move it, Angie!*

Launching myself like an Olympic sprinter, I burst out of

the snow. Imminent peril triggered a fresh surge of energy. Churning like pistons, my legs stirred up a powdery cloud. Still blinded, Hurtig raised the rifle. A hellish sound stung my ears. *Click-chock!* With a shriek of alarm, I threw my hundred and five pounds against his outstretched arms.

The impact knocked us sprawling. Turning in mid-fall, I landed spread-eagle on the snow. The rifle twirled like a majorette's baton. *Plop!* A skinny crevasse marked its landing place in the snow. Turning at the waist, Hurtig made a clawing grab for it. But one snowshoe tripped over the other. Down he came like a Ponderosa pine.

Hurtig flexed his knees. Perhaps he thought the crust would support his weight. If so, he was wrong. The snow was too fluffy, too loose. What my people call *nokaygonaga*. And the ex-sheriff tipped the scales at well over two hundred pounds. His knees plunged deep, leaving him buried to the hips.

Seeing my chance, I rolled to the left, straining to reach the rifle. As I did so, I suddenly became aware of that sound again. That peculiar freight-train rumble. I looked up instantly. And, as my gaze traveled from meadow to evergreen forest to blue sky, I felt that something was dreadfully wrong. Glancing once more at the treetops, I realized what it was.

*The snow ridge was gone!*

This time the rumble grew ominously louder. Its low-pitched mutter became a crescendo roar, the volume rising with each passing second. A billowing cloud of snow appeared behind the trees. A sight familiar to this Anishinabe princess. I'd seen it before—in a Park Service training film. A single horrifying word flashed through my mind. *Avalanche!*

"Now I gotcha!"

Hurtig's goggles were up, exposing a pair of murderous eyes. Teeth clenched, keeping a firm grip, he waded through the deep snow. I felt myself sliding toward him. Knuckly fingers balled into a fist. "Good-bye, Heather!"

Shuddering, I glanced at the mountainside. The oncoming wall of snow began to swallow the uppermost trees.

I blocked Hurtig's punch with an upraised leg. "Idiot! Let go of me or we're *both* going to die!"

He struck again, and I swerved to the right. His hammer blow sank into the snow beside my face.

"You're the one who's dyin'!" he bellowed, lashing out once more. "You've messed me up for the last time, bitch!"

At the last second, I averted my face. Hurtig's punch skimmed my jaw, slamming into my right shoulder. "Owww!"

Murderous rage ushered him forward. His free hand reached for my throat. "I'm gonna wring that scrawny neck!"

Had he been a trifle faster, he could have strangled me one-handed. But his little speech gave me the split second I needed to twist in the snow, rolling onto my front side. My choppers lashed out, catching Hurtig's wrist in a death grip.

Instant Mexican standoff! He couldn't hit me, and, if he let go of my leg to free his other hand, I'd roll safely away. The impasse shattered what little patience he had left. That bull-dog face turned the shade of cooked lobster. Spittle sprayed from a corner of his mouth.

"Bitch!" His shout momentarily eclipsed the avalanche rumble. "Sneaky little Indian bitch!"

Grim Angie smile. "I asked you nicely the first time, ass-hole." Drew my free leg to my chest. "Let go!"

*Whomp!* I drove the bottom of my snowshoe against his face. Hurtig let out an enraged roar. The goggles hung askew on his forehead. Blood dribbled from one nostril. A fishnet pattern marked his ruddy face. I cocked my leg again.

*Whomp!* As I drew my foot away, Hurtig's head wobbled. Through mashed lips, he snarled, "K-kill you!"

The avalanche rumble filled the air. I felt the snow sliding beneath my spine. Gasp of despair. One more chance was all I had!

This time I swung my leg back, then pitched it forward,

kicking from the hip. My snowshoe struck with a meaty thump. Hurtig's grip sprung free. He tottered backward through the snow, groaning in agony.

Rising shakily to my feet, I cast a horrified glance at the mountain. Tons of ice and snow tumbled downslope, cascading into the cirque. A Niagara of rampaging snow spilled over the rim. Spruce trees toppled like matchsticks. Clouds of snow billowed skyward, hurled aloft with unimaginable force.

"Oh, shit!" I hollered, turning to run.

Peeling off my white poncho, I raced toward the distant wooded slope. Since I was doing the hundred-yard dash on snowshoes, I really had to cut down on the wind resistance. Long strides—knees high. *Chush-chush-chush!*

Fleeting backward glance. The avalanche followed the cirque wall downslope, clinging to the existing slide. Nothing to crow about, of course. Karen and I had taken three hours to descend that slope. At the speed the avalanche was moving, it would reach the meadow in minutes!

Knees churning, I tossed my gaze at the wooded slope just ahead. If I could reach the high ground in time, I'd be safe!

The avalanche's dreadful roar drowned out all other sound. Ahead hovered the tree-lined hillside, wobbling in my field of vision like some crazy Arctic mirage. I saw Karen halfway up the slope, her mouth open in a soundless shout, waving her arms. A warning?

One last glance toward the barn. Hip-deep in snow, Hurtig staggered toward his fallen rifle. He fished it out of the snow, brushed off the white stuff, and brought it to his shoulder. Swinging the muzzle my way, he put his right eye to the scope.

Suddenly, Hurtig found himself cloaked in shadow. As he looked upward, his expression changed, shifting from feral glee to wide-eyed terror. Ice blocks the size of dump trucks came tumbling across the meadow, backed by a surging wall of snow four stories high.

I watched as the avalanche swallowed the old ranch cabin. Hurtig vanished in a cascade of white.

Letting out a shrill yell, I kept right on running. My snowshoes ate up the yardage. *Chush-chush-chush!* To my rear, the relentless rumble grew ever louder.

It's got to stop! I thought desperately. It's got to! It's on flat terrain now. It *has* to run out of steam!

Displaced air, pushed along by the avalanche, provided a sudden unexpected tail wind. Gasping breathlessly, I sprinted toward the hillside.

*Tayaa!* Come on, princess! Faster!

Then the avalanche's leading edge overshadowed me. A blast of hail peppered my parka and moccasin boots. A gargantuan invisible hand scooped me up and hurled me into a chilly universe of speeding snow.

Over and over I cartwheeled, as helpless as a straw in a hurricane. Rag-doll Angie swept along by an irresistible wave of fast-moving snow. Rangerette training kicked in. Instinctively I began swimming perpendicular to the flow, hoping to reach air before I was buried too deeply.

My breaststroke had just begun carrying me upward, when a speeding iceberg—no doubt the one that had sunk the *Titanic*—collided with the back of my head. The avalanche roar dwindled to a whisper, and the icy white universe faded to black.

Numbing cold stung me back into semiconsciousness. A fearful chill raced through my bloodstream. Something icy and granular smothered my face. Gone was the comforting tug of gravity. I felt as if I were suspended in midair, my outstretched arms as limp as a marionette's.

Memories of the avalanche came rushing back, accompanied by a single hellish thought. *Buried alive!*

Rasping and gagging, I moved my head from side to side. Packed snow pressed my half-frozen features. Gasping, I hollowed out a small air pocket and took a deep breath. Obsidian eyes fluttered open.

I found myself suspended in an eerie grayish-white twilight zone. Despite my frantic mental urgings, my arms and my legs remained motionless. The snow had me trapped.

Just then I heard the shuffle of snowshoes overhead. The intervening snow muffled Karen's voice. "She went down here! Right around here!"

A male voice responded, "Spread out. We'll all start digging."

Hoping to catch their attention, I decided to shout. Big mistake! As I drew in a lungful, the supercooled air triggered a spasm of coughing. Gasping and hacking, I tried to form intelligible words. But it was no use.

Red mist encircled my field of vision. My temples throbbed with each and every cough. An overwhelming dizziness swept over me. Once more I plunged into oblivion.

For a long, long time I remained in darkness, and then a familiar sound reached my ears—the sizzling snap-crackle of a campfire. The scent of wood smoke tickled my nostrils. Something warm, weighty, and woven enveloped my body. Fabric brushed my chin. It felt like wool.

My eyes slitted open. Two olive-green army blankets had been wrapped around me, forming a crude but effective sleeping bag. A spruce lean-to hovered overhead. Rolling onto my side, I spied the campfire with a three-log heat reflector behind it.

Luxuriating in the warmth, I stirred in bed and let out a small sound of contentment. *Rescued!* Thank goodness!

I heard the snow crunching underfoot. My grandfather peered under the lean-to, blocking out the afternoon daylight. *"Anamikage, Noozis. Taneki kinawa?"*

*"Nin ganayndawis.* Just fine, *Nimishoo."* Pushing unruly

raven locks away from my forehead, I flashed a feeble smile. "How'd you find me?"

"You can thank Karen for that." Crouching, Chief rested his choppers on his knees. "She saw the exact spot where you went down. She led us straight there."

"I know. I think I heard you."

He grinned. "Same here. I told Troy that wasn't a vole coughing away under the snow."

Giving his forearm a squeeze, I murmured, "Thanks for digging me out, *Nimishoo*."

"You're welcome." Chief's features turned somber. "Who was that asshole doing all the shooting?"

"Chet Hurtig. He trailed us over the pass."

"Now, that wasn't the smartest thing in the world to do." He shook his head disapprovingly. "Blasting away with a high-powered rifle right beneath a huge snow overhang."

Curious blink. "Is that what caused the avalanche?"

"*Eyan!*" He nodded. "The gunfire vibration weakened the snow. Whole damned ridge collapsed of its own weight."

"When did you and Troy get here?"

"Right after the slide." He jutted his chin southward. "We were up on Caliber Ridge when we heard all the shooting. Had me a feeling my granddaughter was in trouble again."

"You're so perceptive." All at once I remembered the avalanche hitting the cabin. "*Nimishoo!* Frank Blodgett—he was in the barn. Did he—?"

Chief's expression turned grim. Standing erect, he offered me a view of the alpine meadow. "See for yourself."

I let out a gasp. Where once the barn had stood, a handful of broken timbers poked out of the windswept snow. Chief's hand patted my shoulder. "I'm sorry, *Noozis*."

Suddenly Karen's voice cried, "Hey! She's awake!"

Through the evergreens they came, a smiling pair of Rooleys. Karen and her youthful uncle. A hefty backpack rested on Troy's brawny shoulders.

"Still with us, I see," Troy said, setting down his Winchester rifle. "How are you feeling, Angie?"

"Little better," I replied, switching to English. "What time is it?"

"Oh, about three-thirty."

We sat together under the lean-to. I thanked them all for the rescue, praising Karen for her presence of mind. Troy told me how he and Chief had been tracking us since the previous day. We talked in turn and in unison, sometimes grim, sometimes jovial, touching and holding, reassuring each other that we'd come safely through.

In the end, as the fire burned low, talk turned to the future. Troy glanced toward the low-hanging sun. "It's gettin' late. We'd best be headin' back."

"I'll second that!" Karen added, her face drawn and weary. "I'm looking forward to a good, hot bath." Teenage giggle. "But I'll let you go first, Angie. You probably need to thaw out."

Shaking my head, I replied, "It's all yours, Karen. You two go on without us."

"Angie! It'll be dark in another couple of hours. You've got to—"

Chief cleared his throat. "It's better this way, child. If Angie and I return with you, there'll be questions."

"And I can't afford a chat with the state patrol," I added, my expressing tinged with regret. "This is the way it has to be, Karen. Sorry."

Troy looked up thoughtfully. "What do we tell Sheriff Quinn?"

Before I could reply, Chief said, "Tell him the truth. You found your sister . . . but you didn't find her *here*. She was holed up in a canyon near the ranch."

"Don't you fret none," Troy said. "Me 'n' Karen will make it sound real convincing."

Troubled, Karen glanced toward the wrecked barn. "What about Frank?"

"We'll take care of it," I promised, giving her a hug. "Get going. You want to reach that Forest Service road before sundown."

Karen's arms looped around my neck. "Bye, Angie!"

"Hey! With any luck, we'll be seeing each other in Pierre." Grinning, I held her at arm's length. "Take good care of that mother of yours, okay?"

"I will, Angie . . . and thanks!"

We watched them go, Chief and I, waving farewell when they reached the ridge. Huddled in blankets, I sat upright and tossed another spruce branch on the fire. Chief doffed his daypack and, using it as a cushion, sat down beside me. His sigh held a trace of exasperation.

Sidelong Angie smile. "Okay . . . what's on your mind?"

"Have you given any thought to where we're supposed to spend the night, missy?" His gaze swept across Colorado's snowcapped peaks. "I don't see too many motels out here."

"Don't worry, Chief. I've got it covered." My forefinger swiveled in the direction of McNasser Pass. "There's a cave up yonder. That's where Karen and I spent last night. If we leave in the next ten minutes . . ."

"Cave?" he echoed, flashing a warpath scowl. "Angie! I've already spent one night outdoors! I'm getting too damned old for this winter-camping shit."

I laughed. "Says the man who spends most of January icefishing on Lake Superior!"

"It's an uphill hike, missy."

"But definitely worth it. This is the Hyatt Regency of caves, Chief. Twenty-four-karat accommodations. Take my word for it."

I wondered how he'd react to the sight of all that gold.

His expression turned skeptical.

"It's a historical site, too," I added, lobbing a spruce twig into the fire. "The Wild Bunch sometimes used it as a hide-out."

"How do you know that?"

Glorious Angie smile. "You'll see!"

Tuesday morning found me at the UPS counter at Stapleton International Airport, scribbling on a shipment form. Smiling princess in her black leather coat, gray cashmere turtleneck sweater, and black suede slim skirt. Sitting on the counter was a large cardboard box.

Once finished, I took a small notebook out of my purse, ripped off a clean page, and wrote a very brief letter of explanation.

Dear Rooleys:
This belonged to your great-granddaddy. Enjoy!

Folding the note, I slipped it beneath the cardboard lid. Then, grimacing at the weight, I lugged it over to the main counter and asked the clerk to seal it. Skilled hands plucked lengths of heavy-duty masking tape from the dispenser.

Grunting, the clerk remarked, "Kinda heavy. What've you got in here?"

"Family heirlooms," I replied, tongue in cheek.

"Would you like to insure them?"

"Sure!" I watched him reach for a pen.

"How much are they worth?"

"Five thousand dollars," I replied. That's the face value of Mr. Rooley's five hundred gold coins. Of course, they'd bring a whole lot more at auction.

He jotted down that amount. "Okay, you're all set. We guarantee next-day delivery to Crested Butte."

"That'll be fine. Thank you."

Yielding to an impish smile, I strolled into the airport lobby.

Too bad I had to get back to Pierre. I would've loved to have seen the look on Becky's face when she opened that box.

Chief occupied a lounge chair beside the newsstand. Seeing me approach, he lifted his copy of the *Denver Post* and showed me the front page.

The headline read: TWO MEN SLAIN AS AVALANCHE ENDS SHOOTOUT. Just beneath were photos showing the demolished barn and four state troopers standing beside a helicopter. Apparently the state patrol had taken my anonymous phone call seriously.

Down the page and to the right was a string of portrait photos—Frank Blodgett, Pop Hannan, and their killer, Chet Hurtig. Beneath them was another headline reading: DEAD MEN LINKED TO ARMORED CAR HOLDUP.

"You'll find another interesting story on page ten," Chief advised.

As I opened the paper, a photo captured my gaze. Sarah and Karen, both on the verge of joyful tears, with their arms around each other. A grinning Troy stood in the background.

## MISSING GIRL FOUND BY UNCLE

*CRESTED BUTTE* (AP)—Karen L. Rooley, missing since last Friday, has been found.

Miss Rooley was found on the east side of Point Lookout Sunday afternoon by her uncle, Troy Rooley, 20, co-owner of the RJ Bar ranch.

Rooley told the sheriff he "had a hunch" that Karen might have "gotten close to home" before being overtaken by last weekend's snowstorm.

"When we were little, Karen and me used to play horse tag up by Double Top Springs," Rooley explained. "I figured Karen took shelter in the old line shack and then got snowed in."

Rooley's hunch proved correct. The girl had taken refuge there Friday night, burning firewood to keep warm.

My grandfather cleared his throat. "They won't stay buffaloed for long."

"Who?" I asked, refolding the newspaper.

"The law. They've got Pop's diary. Pretty soon they'll figure out Madge's role in the robbery."

"Let them." I dropped the paper on an empty chair. "By that time, you and I will be safely out of Colorado."

"They'll come at Sarah and the others."

"True enough. Don't worry, though. Sarah can handle them." Smiling, I took the seat at his side. "In fact, she's going to have them examine her mother's truck."

"So Hurtig gets nailed for all three killings, eh?"

I nodded. "I think the law will be satisfied, Chief. The bullets taken from the bodies match Hurtig's rifle. Pop's diary implicates Madge. They'll think he had the same motive for all three murders—double-crossing his partners."

Chief glanced at me. "But that wasn't his motive, was it?"

I shook my head. "Not with Madge."

He sighed. "Will you ever tell Sarah the truth?"

"Tell her what, Chief?" I replied, keeping my voice at a whisper. "That her mother was a self-centered and foolish woman? She already knows that." I gestured at the newspaper. "Should I tell her how her mother came on to a sociopath? That Madge really didn't care about her daughter *or* her granddaughter? That all she lived for was the excitement of that last big score? Is Sarah *really* better off knowing all that?"

"What about Blodgett? He was her father, Angie."

Languid smile. "Sarah's been trying to get out from under her mother's shadow for a long, long time. I'm not shackling her to Frank Blodgett, too."

"Is that your decision to make, missy?"

"No . . . but I'm making it, anyway." Lounging in the chair, I brought my fingertips together. "Sarah has more important things to think about these days—her daughter—their future together." Gamine grin. "If you ask me, it's high time that woman put the past behind her."

Shaking his head, Chief uttered a chuckle. "I wonder if she realizes what a friend she has in you."

"I doubt it! I do tend to go unappreciated."

With a deep-throated chuckle, he rose from his chair. "The penalties of playing Pocahontas!" Slipping on his winter jacket, he added, "What time's your flight to Rapid City?"

"Ten-thirty," I replied. "Uhm . . . by the way, did our package get off to the Northland all right?"

"You bet." Chief tilted his head toward the Air Express office. "I sent it second-day air. I'll be waiting at Tettegouche when it arrives."

My smile broadened. I had a satisfying vision of the future. A warm spring day in the Superior National Forest. Angie and Chief sweeping away the brown pine needles, digging those shallow holes, lowering the birchbark *makuks* filled with outlaw gold.

As we strolled down the airport corridor, Chief shot me a quizzical look. "What do you plan on doing with all that gold, Angie?"

"You know the old saying, Chief. Save for a rainy day."

"Your next *nandobani?*"

"Hey! Who says there's going to be another *nandobani?*" I replied, gingerly touching my breastbone.

"I do!" Simmering look. "You don't fool anyone, young lady. You really enjoy this Lone Ranger business."

Impish smile. "Well, I am rather good at it."

Chief let out a bark of laughter. "I bet Nero Wolfe would've figured it out sooner."

"*Nero Wolfe?*" Disdainful glance. "Are you kidding? That

old couch potato wouldn't have lasted five minutes up on Grizzly Peak!" Smoothing my hair, I added, "Besides, I'm not making this my life's work, you know. I did it only to help Sarah."

Low-toned chuckle. "I can't wait to hear the excuse next time."

"I tell you, there isn't going to be a *next time.*"

"Sure of that?"

"Quite sure, Grandfather of mine."

"Positive?"

"Absolutely!"

His elbow gave me a gentle nudge. "How much of that gold are you willing to bet?"

Laughing, I gave him a one-armed hug. "Forget it, Chief! You know I never play sucker's odds."